HELD IN THE GRIP OF THE CHINA SHADOW

FLORA BAIN was raised in innocence as daughter of a vicar. Her initiation into the harsh ways of underworld London came at nineteen—and her tumultuous life at Armitage House soon followed. There, she learned to love...and to fear.

HENRY ARMITAGE, scion of a wealthy merchant family, controlled the vast fleet that brought back the treasures of the Orient—one of them a wife. But would she live in the atmosphere of tension at Armitage House...or die there, as the others had?

JESSICA ARMITAGE, Henry's sister, had a venomous tongue and a naked hate for any woman who cast eyes at her brother—like the last governess at Armitage House, who soon drowned in a pond. Were Jessica's words her only weapon...or was murder one, as well?

CLARISSA ROSS
CHINA SHADOW

 AVON
PUBLISHERS OF BARD, CAMELOT, DISCUS, EQUINOX AND FLARE BOOKS

CHINA SHADOW is an original publication of Avon Books. This work has never before appeared in any form.

AVON BOOKS
A division of
The Hearst Corporation
959 Eighth Avenue
New York, New York 10019

Copyright © 1974 by W. E. D. Ross.
Published by arrangement with the author.

ISBN: 0-380-00189-6

First Avon Printing, December, 1974.
Third Printing

AVON TRADEMARK REG. U.S. PAT. OFF. AND
FOREIGN COUNTRIES, REGISTERED TRADEMARK—
MARCA REGISTRADA, HECHO EN CHICAGO, U.S.A.

Printed in the U.S.A.

To my editors Nancy and Ruth who conceived the idea for this novel; to my agent Don and his girl friday, Maureen, for whipping the good idea into a firm contract; and to the faithful Marilyn who worked with me on every line of it; I dedicate this book.

Contents

Book One

London

Chapter One

FLORA BAIN's first glimpse of London was late on a May night in 1861 during a bad thunderstorm. She was a passenger in a stagecoach that had left from Sussex early that morning and as she was sitting next to one of the windows, she so was able to peer out into the murky, rain-swept night illuminated occasionally by flashes of blue lightning.

The rest of the passengers, including her new friend, Herbert Sweet, were asleep as the coach rattled over the wet cobblestones. She saw the blurred outlines of buildings and occasionally the glow from a street-corner gas lamp. Her excitement grew despite the bad weather, for she would soon be meeting her Uncle George. She had told the driver she wished to be let out at Barker Square where her uncle lived. According to the driver they would pass it on the way into the city.

Suddenly the carriage came to a halt. The burly assistant to the driver appeared at the door and called out,

"Here you are, miss! Step lively! We have no time to waste!"

"Thank you," she said. As she got up to leave the crowded stage she saw that Herbert Sweet was still asleep.

"A wicked night, miss," the driver said as he helped her down onto the wet cobblestones into the drenching rain.

She clutched her cloak and hood. "Where would Twenty-four Barker Square be?"

"Just bear to the right," he shouted against the thunder. "And don't lag! The streets of London can be dangerous, miss!" With this parting warning he jumped up on the front seat of the coach again. The vehicle rumbled off in the rain, its lantern bright and swaying. In a moment she was left alone and desolate in the storm.

As she stood there clutching her valise she wished that she had wakened Herbert Sweet and asked him to see her safely to her uncle's house. She was certain he would have done so. The grave, white-haired man had introduced himself to her almost as soon as she'd gotten into the stagecoach.

"My name is Herbert Sweet," he'd said. "And I'm going to London to join the cause of William Booth of whom I'm sure you must have heard."

"I'm afraid not," she'd apologized. "I've lived all my life in a country village and this is my first trip to London. My name is Flora Bain and my recently deceased father was the Reverend William Bain, the vicar of our village."

The tall grave-faced man was friendly. "Then your late father was also in the business of saving souls for Christ. I'm only a lay person like yourself but I'm interested in becoming an evangelist and London is a city of sin!"

"I'm going to London to join my Uncle George who resides in Barker Square. I have not heard from him in some time but I'm looking forward to meeting him and to seeing London! Nelson's Column and the Strand! And St. Paul's Cathedral!"

"That is one side of London," Herbert Sweet said soberly. "But there is another. Dreadful slums, some of them acres wide, make up a good part of the city. Barker Square is a rich, fashionable area but generally close to such areas there are slums filled with disease and crime. There are many passages and courts where it is dangerous for strangers to stray."

Flora had listened to the serious words of the middle-aged man as he went on telling about the dangers and despair of London. She had not been eager to come to the city but her father's accidental death had left her without any choice. There had been little money left her and her only living relative was her uncle in London.

On his deathbed her father had gasped, "My brother George is a widower. He has no children. He is boastful and a bully but he will surely take you in. You must try to get along with him. He has made a fortune in speculations and has a fine racing stable. I do not approve of his way of life, but that is not of any importance at this time!"

Now she was standing in the rainy midnight just a short distance from his door. She picked up her valise and began walking towards an impressive row of houses. Just as she reached the first of them a strange thing happened. From a house further down the storm-swept street, a figure came running towards her. Lightning flashed and she saw the man's emaciated face, pinched nostrils and wild eyes. He wore no hat and his long hair was matted with wet and clung to his forehead. He gave her a brief frightened look and raced past her to vanish into the darkness.

Somewhat shaken, she continued on to Number Twenty-four and saw it was the house from which the scarecrow individual had emerged. Hoping this wasn't a signal of trouble, she mounted the steps of the stately townhouse. When she reached its door she was further concerned to find it partly open. After a moment's hesitation she entered the large vestibule and noted that the inner door with its fancy glass panels was also ajar. She saw the pull knob for the doorbell and gave it several sharp tugs.

No one came, although she saw a lamp burning on a table inside. Worried by this strange atmosphere, she made her way inside and found that the entire lower floor of the house appeared to be in darkness except for that one

13

lamp. She began to feel distinctly uneasy, especially from the memory of the ominous figure racing out of the house as if the Devil had been at his heels! She moved back into the foyer and stared up the curving stairway with frightened eyes.

There was a night lamp in a bracket on the wall near the head of the stairs. This encouraged her to slowly make her way up to the second level. All the while she had a growing fear of the house and what she might find in it. All the pleasant anticipations she'd felt about meeting her Uncle George had vanished. Reaching the landing, she halted and stood there uneasily.

Noting an open door slightly down the hall on her right, she walked toward it. It opened on a bedroom, and she stepped forward and peered in. Just as she did there was a rumble of thunder and flash of lightning from the outside. The lightning illuminated a scene she would never forget!

From a beam in the ceiling of the room there hung the body of a man. His feet swayed gently a distance above the floor. In the flash of lightning she caught a glimpse of the rope around his neck and the distorted, purple face with its distended tongue and bulging eyes.

She screamed and turned from the ghastly sight in horror. Then she moved along the hall and frantically started making her way down the stairs. She had never met her Uncle George, but she was somehow certain that the body she'd glimpsed hanging from the rope was his.

What to do? She debated going out into the stormy night again to seek aid. She could not stay long in this deserted house with the body of a suicide. Then from the dark behind her she heard a sneeze!

Turning, she saw an old woman with a shawl over her head and a bulging pillowcase in her hands. "What are you doing here?" she asked.

"I've worked here for George Bain for twenty years," the woman said.

"You worked for my uncle?"

The elderly servant showed interest. "Him upstairs is your uncle?"

14

"If the man hanging from the rafter is George Bain, he is my uncle."

"It's George Bain all right!" the old woman said with contempt. "May the Devil forgive him, for the Lord won't! For months he paid none of us servants. They all left him but me. He kept promising to pay me but he went on gambling and going into debt. Now once the money-lenders find out what has happened they'll take everything!"

Flora eyed the white sack. "What is in that pillowcase?"

The old woman crouched like an animal at bay. She whined, "Just a few things to take to the pawnbroker. Barely enough for me wages. I don't want to die in the workhouse!"

"You shouldn't be stealing," she said sternly. "And who was that man who ran out of here?"

The old woman looked wary. "Me son, miss. He's half-witted and the sight of the dead man fair upset him!"

"I suspect he was running off with money or valuables!"

"You're wrong, miss. It's just that poor Percy is daft! You're tired and over-wrought, miss, and soaked from the rain. Let me get you a cup of hot soup to make you feel better. There's some on the stove now that Percy and me was having before we discovered the master hanging from the rafter up there."

Flora hesitated. "I must get word to the police," she said. But she suddenly realized how weary and how hungry she was. "Perhaps I could take time for some soup."

"I'll fetch it at once," the crone said. And she did. Then she suggested that Flora enter a small bedroom nearby and sit in a comfortable chair near the hearth while she supped the soup. At the same time the old woman lit a fire in the fireplace. "Might as well be comfortable," she told her.

Flora finished the soup and suddenly felt not only tired but dizzy. The room was floating around her. She vaguely knew she'd been drugged, but somehow didn't care. She staggered over to the bed and lay down just as unconsciousness overtook her.

Chapter Two

FLORA OPENED her eyes to find the bedroom still in darkness. It took her a moment to realize where she was. It was only yesterday morning that she'd left the quiet of the country vicarage in Sussex and here she was in a fine London mansion with the dead body of her uncle hanging from a beam in one of the upstairs bedrooms! The memory of it made her sit up with a shudder.

Memory returned to her rapidly now and she recalled the old servant, Annie, being so kind to her. There had been the warm supper and then the waiting bed. Only in the last few seconds before sleep overtook her had she guessed that the kindness had been part of the housekeeper's devious scheme to escape with the pillowcase filled with silver. She had no doubts that the old woman had long since gone, and as she began to realize the grimness of her position, her fears came crowding back.

The candles on the dresser had burned out. She halted before the mirror and considered herself. There were dark circles under her eyes and she looked pale. Not much wonder! She knew she had to proceed carefully. Do all the right things. It was obvious she had to begin by washing and dressing. Then she might find some food still left in the kitchen. After that she must contact the police.

As she busied herself with her toilette she realized that she'd counted too much on her Uncle George. The fact that her father had not liked him should have warned her. It was only in desperation that he had directed her to seek out her dissipated uncle. She had reached him too late. He had become a victim of his own excesses. Now he hung grotesquely from a noose of his own making in that upper room, surely a warning to all who would take his path in life.

Old Annie had made one statement that Flora felt to be true. The old woman had warned that once word of her uncle's suicide was out, the house would be beset with the many moneylenders and other creditors to whom he was obligated. By the time they had recovered a small part of what was due them there would be nothing for her. Not even a roof over her head.

She must face it. She was in London on her own and without any resources. After she had dressed; she found her way to the kitchen, which was in a chaotic state. She managed to find tea, bread, and cheese and made herself breakfast. She was amazed that she was actually hungry.

Flora was now faced with the problem of how to contact the proper authorities. Perhaps she could contact a neighbor who would send a servant for the police. She was standing by the foot of the stairs deciding this when she saw shadows through the frosted-glass panes of the front door. The bell rang.

Frozen with fear, she debated what to do. Could these be creditors already aware of her uncle's suicide? After a moment of indecision, she decided to open the door to whoever it was and find out what they wanted. Two men, one much older than the other, stood in the vestibule.

Both men wore fashionable black top hats. The young one had on a blue coat and fawn trousers with a flashy red cravat and a mustard-colored vest. He also carried a thin bamboo cane. The older man, who was quite stout, was dressed far more conservatively in a black coat and gray trousers, but his blue cravet was fastened with a gleaming diamond stickpin and his vest was a dark blue plaid. He carried a cane as well, but it was a stout Malacca.

The young man was blond, with a small goatee and mustache. His eyes were blue and he had a pleasant, even-featured face. He smiled at Flora and exclaimed, "Well, I declare! I didn't know that George Bain was hiding anything as pretty as you in this house!"

The older man removed his hat and bowed to her. "Your servant, miss. You will forgive my young friend. We have come to call on Mr. Bain."

She stood there, hesitant about allowing them in. "Who are you?" she asked.

The young man laughed. "Friends of George's, of course. May I return the question, who are you?"

The older man intervened. "You are not exhibiting proper manners, Nelson," he reproved his younger friend. He turned to Flora with an apologetic look on his friendly face. "My name is Horace Wright and this young fellow is Nelson Reed. We are good friends of Mr. Bain. We belong to the same gaming club where he was to meet us last night. He did not keep the appointment, so we have come here to see him."

Flora did not move. She said quietly, "Mr. Bain was my uncle. I am his niece Flora. I came from Sussex yesterday to live with him."

"So that's why he didn't keep the appointment," Nelson Reed said boisterously. "I can't say that I blame him. It's not too often that old George has the company of a beauty like you!"

She gave the young man a stern look. "You did not hear me correctly, Mr. Reed. I said that George Bain *was* my uncle. I fear that he is no longer alive."

This announcement had a strong impact on the two. They glanced at each other in consternation and then at her. Their faces wore looks of disbelief.

Nelson Reed spoke up first, "Are you telling us that George is dead?"

"Yes."

"You are certain?" the older man enquired heavily.

"Yes. I am certain. I have seen his body. When I entered the house on my arrival I discovered him hanging from a beam in his bedroom—a suicide!"

"Damme!" Nelson Reed's pleasant face showed shock. "What a welcoming for you!"

"It wasn't what I'd expected," she was ready to admit.

The older man's face had gone a deep red and he looked as if he might have a fit of apoplexy right there in the vestibule. He gasped, "You say he took his own life?"

"He hung himself," she replied.

"Is he up there now?" Horace Wright wanted to know.

"Yes."

The young Nelson Reed gave his older companion a grim look. "I'm not surprised. You know the way the cards and the horses have been going against old George. Everyone knows his losses have been tremendous."

The portly Horace Wright nodded solemnly. "May I say that George had borrowed heavily from me."

"And from me," the younger man said. He turned to her and with his top hat in hand, bowed and said, "You must forgive me, Miss Bain, for my earlier lack of delicacy. I was not aware of the situation. You have my deep sympathy and that of my friend, here."

"You must surely do," Horace Wright breathed an affirmation as he clasped his top hat to his chest. "Is there anything we can do?"

She stood back. "Thank you, gentlemen. As my uncle's friends I feel that I may impose on you for aid. I have not yet informed the police or anyone else."

"Where are the servants?" Nelson Reed asked.

"They've run off," she said. "All but one were gone when I came here. And she drugged me and then ran away with a bag of stolen silver. I'm quite alone in the house."

The two men had come into the shadowed foyer and Nelson Reed nodded to indicate upstairs as he said, "Except for him."

"Yes."

Nelson Reed turned to the older man with a look of uncertainty. "I suppose we must go up there and see for ourselves," he said grimly.

The big florid man sighed. "Quite! Nothing else for it! Most unpleasant. Are you ready?"

"As ready as I will be," Nelson Reed said with distaste. He turned to her again. "You will excuse us for a few minutes, Miss Bain?"

The two men rather hesitantly began to mount the curving stairway, arguing in low voices between themselves. Flora felt their arrival had been a great piece of luck. They were close friends of her late Uncle George and they would know how best to handle the tragic business.

Of the two she much preferred the older man. Horace Wright had a bluff kindness about him which had been immediately apparent. The young Nelson Reed was pleasant enough but he had not impressed her as being of strong character. She had heard her father refer to several wild young men as rakes. She had an idea this term might well fit Nelson Reed.

She sat in a high-backed chair in the living room waiting for them to come back downstairs. All at once she felt very lonely. Her eyes brimmed with tears as she thought about the happy, if quiet, days she'd known at the vicarage. As the daughter of a country parson she had the respect of the villagers. Her father had savored the finer things of life and implanted an appreciation of literature, art, and music in her. Even though their financial means were small and her life in the village was limited, she had been able to enjoy some of these things first hand. Her father supervised her reading and liked to read aloud to her from the works of Milton, Shakespeare, Scott, and the popular new novelist, Charles Dickens. He also gained permission to take her to several of the homes of titled gentlemen near the village and had given her a tour of their art collections. As for music, an aged organist at the church had played the works of great composers for her and had given her lessons on the piano.

Looking back, she saw it as an enviable life. More healthy than any this great city could offer her. And if she had been cut off from the companionship of young men because of her attendance on her father that would likely have only been a temporary thing. Sooner or later a desirable young man would have appeared—perhaps a schoolmaster or a son of one of the wealthy and titled parishioners who attended her father's church. It would surely all have worked out well.

Her life was a shambles now. All the delights of the peaceful Sussex village were lost. Her first taste of London had been a bitter one. She was caught up in this tragedy of her Uncle George's suicide without knowing much about what had led to it. However, she knew enough to be sure that she was going to have to brave this new life without help from anyone.

There were footsteps on the stairs and the sound of low voices approaching. The two had taken in the hideous scene above and now were coming back to make their pronouncements. She prayed that they would not try to escape their responsibilities in the matter since she so desperately needed their help. She rose from her chair as the two men appeared in the doorway of the living room. Horace Wright was the first to approach her.

"Well, miss, we have seen him and a sorry sight it was. Poor old George is done for and that's the truth."

"You will inform the authorities for me," she said.

"Yes," he said with a frown. "I shall do that at once. But after that it will be mostly up to young Nelson."

"Oh?" she said, not understanding.

"I do not wish to disclaim any responsibility," Horace Wright said at once. "I want to discharge my duties as a friend, but I have a business appointment that will take me to Liverpool for at least a week. I have to leave this afternoon. So I will not be here to do much more. However, I can promise you that Nelson Reed will act on my part as well as for himself. You may depend on him."

"Thank you," she said.

The young man now came up to her. "You mustn't worry about anything. Leave it all to me. I shall arrange everything."

"That is very good of you," Flora said, meaning it.

The young dandy made a deprecating gesture. "Not at

all. Hoarce has some good friends at police headquarters. He will take care of things there and I will supervise the balance of the arrangements while he is away."

She said, "I would like to get away from here before the police come."

Horace Wright's double-chinned face showed sympathy. "I can understand your feelings in that respect. But this is now your home. You must remember that."

She said, "Surely you can't have missed the desperation of my uncle's plight. Everything, including the house, has evidently been mortgaged to the hilt. The moment word of his death gets out the vultures will gather."

Nelson Reed nodded agreement. "She's right. The place will be besieged by creditors. It would be wise for her to get out of here."

"You really think so?" Horace Wright queried him.

"I do," Nelson said.

The stout man looked unhappy. "You think there'll be nothing left of any of this?"

"I know it," the younger man said. "George Bain was heavily in debt when I first knew him. After his last year's losings his estate must be completely devoured."

"What about Miss Bain?" Horace Wright worried. "Where will she go?"

"Why not the Plough and Sickle?" Nelson asked, naming an inn which seemed to be known to the older man.

"Excellent idea!" he agreed at once. "Take her there. They know me well. Tell them it is my wish that she have the best."

"I'll do that," the young man said.

"And I shall go on to the police," Horace Wright promised.

"I don't know how to thank either of you sufficiently," she lamented.

The stout man smiled sadly. "I could only wish that you'd come along before your uncle did this dreadful thing. I'm sure you might have been the means of saving him."

"I wish I had been," she agreed.

"Well, little in life is as we hope it to be," the stout man sighed. He reached for his gold watch chain and drew a large watch from his vest pocket. "I just have time to do everything neatly and catch my railway train to Liverpool. I must be on my way," he said, bowing over her hand. "You have my deepest sympathy in this moment of your bereavement."

"Thank you, Mr. Wright," she said.

The stout man then took Nelson Reed by the arm and they went to the door together. He gave him some instructions and last minute advice and then left.

The young dandy came back to her. "Well, I think we have everything under way," he said. "What are your plans following the funeral? Horace was just asking me now. You can remain at the Plough and Sickle until then. Would you like me to arrange the booking of your railway passage back to Sussex?"

It was a difficult moment for her. She fought to contain her tears. "I cannot return to Sussex," she said. "There is nothing to return to. My father died recently and I came here at his wish."

"You mean you have no one else in the world except that dead man up there."

"No one."

"I'm most awfully sorry," he said awkwardly. "I'd assumed you'd just come here for a visit or to spend a few months at the most."

"I was coming to live with Uncle George."

"Do you have any private means?"

She looked down in embarrassment. "Only the few pounds I had left over after paying my father's debts."

"I see. Well, that is too bad. But I'm sure we can do something about it."

She gave him an urgent look. "I don't want any kind of charity. I'm willing to work. All I ask is a position of some kind, so that I may earn my own living."

The young man nodded. "I understand. You need have no misgivings about accepting immediate board and lodging from Horace and myself. We will try and find you a suitable position and you can then pay us back."

"I shall be forever grateful to you," she told him.

"It's not all that important," he said. "We are happy to do it. In other circumstances I'm sure your Uncle George would have been glad to help any niece of ours. Friends are meant to help one another."

"Sometimes that is forgotten."

"Horace and I are not that sort," the young dandy said in his lofty way. He was studying her with a good deal of interest at the same time. She had the feeling that he was carefully appraising her for future work possibilities.

She asked, "How long will we remain here?"

"Until the police arrive. Are you packed?"

"Everything is in my valise," pointing to where it sat at the foot of the stairway.

"Excellent," he said. "Then as soon as the police get here we can be on our way." He glanced around the room. "Are there any small personal things you might like as mementos? Things which would be of no value to your uncle's creditors in any case."

She blushed. "I don't want to take anything to which I'm not entitled."

Nelson Reed stood there imposingly in his vivid blue coat and the red cravat. "I would not suggest that since I am one of the creditors. But there may be items of no value to anyone else which would have great meaning for you. I urge that you take a look around."

"Very well," she said. And she began a tour of the luxurious living room. There was a grand piano, which she would have liked to try, and on one panel of the wall a giant oil painting of a battle scene. But she knew these would be turned into cash to pay her uncle's debts. So she continued to examine even the smallest things.

At last she came to a framed tintype on one of the many tables. It was beginning to fade but she could clearly identify her father and mother and Uncle George. They were all standing together in a garden somewhere looking so young and happy it made her throat tighten with sorrow. She carefully picked up the tintype and put it in her valise.

It was at this point that the police made their appearance. There were four burly officers in blue uniforms and helmets who were led by an older man in plain clothes. Nelson Reed greeted them and everyone went upstairs but Flora. Later the man in plain clothes and Nelson Reed joined her in the living room.

Nelson Reed introduced her, "Miss Flora Bain, the late lamented's niece, Inspector John Dickson of the London police."

The inspector bowed to her. He was a big man with large black whiskers. "This is a sorry business, Miss Bain."

"Yes, it is," she agreed.

"Did you have any hint that your uncle planned to kill himself?" the inspector asked.

"None. I never met him when he was alive. By the time I reached here last night he'd already hung himself."

The inspector raised his heavy eyebrows. "How distressing! Who else was here in the house with him when you arrived?"

She was reluctant to drag the unfortunate Annie into it. Even though the old woman had drugged her and stolen the silver she had done it in a desperate effort to collect the wages that should have been paid to her. Under the circumstances the best thing would be to mention the old woman and pretend not to know her name.

She said, "There was a woman. She claimed to be the housekeeper. I don't know whether that was true or not."

The inspector was listening and writing the information down in a small black-covered book. "Please go on," he said.

"She gave me food and found me a bed. I believe she drugged me. She left while I was asleep and took a pillow-case of silver with her."

Inspector Dickson made a face. "You can count on never seeing the silver again."

"I suppose not."

"London is full of fences who buy such things for a fraction of their worth," he told her. "There is a constant trade in stolen valuables."

"The woman claimed that wages were owed her."

"She'd be bound to say that. What was her name?"

"I don't know."

He eyed her sharply. "You don't know?"

"I arrived here in the middle of the night and I only saw her for a short time," she went on, hoping that she was making it sound likely. "I didn't think to ask her name. I was too shocked by the discovery of my uncle's body for one thing."

"Ah, yes," the inspector said, this last seeming to satisfy him. "I can inquire of the servants in the neighboring houses. No doubt they will identify her."

"No doubt," she said.

"You saw no one else?"

"No."

The inspector snapped his book closed. "Well, that is all we can do for the moment. Do you plan to remain in the house?"

Nelson Reed came forward and said, "No. I and another friend of her uncle's are providing room and board for her at the Plough and Sickle. She will remain there until after the funeral."

"A very sound plan," Inspector Dickson said. "This house would be much too gloomy to remain here alone. Well, then, when my men remove the body we can lock the place up. It's the best thing until the death is fully investigated. Not that I suspect anything queer but it is necessary to hold a complete inquiry."

Nelson Reed said, "We would like you to deliver the body to the Grantmoor Undertakers when you are finished with it. We shall hold the funeral at some nearby chapel."

Inspector Dickson nodded. "I will see to that. You can let the undertaker know the arrangements you wish made."

"I shall," Nelson Reed, promised. "I'll go there directly after I have taken Miss Bain to the inn."

She and Nelson Reed left the house just as the police were coming back in with a stretcher to carry out her uncle's body. It gave her a strange, sinking sensation to think about it. Nelson was at her side carrying her valise. He kept up a running conversation to take her mind off this unpleasant moment.

He had a hansom cab waiting. The moment the driver

saw them he jumped down from the high rear seat to take the valise from Nelson.

Nelson told him, "We're going to the Plough and Sickle first. It's just off the Strand."

"Yes, sir," the man said, opening the door of the cab for them.

She stepped inside and sat on the narrow seat. The interior of the vehicle smelled of horse sweat and straw. Nelson Reed came in and seated himself at her side. He smiled at her in the semi-darkness of the cab.

"I hire this fellow by the day," he said. "Saves me the expense of my own coachman. The cab is not as grand as a private coach but it does."

"I think you're very fortunate to have it," Flora said.

This seemed to please him. He laughed. "You surely aren't spoiled, little country girl. I can think of a half-dozen ladies of the town not possessing a fraction of your beauty who have complained bitterly about this accomodation."

She felt embarrassed. "I hope you're not making fun of me."

"Quite the contrary," he said, pressing a gloved hand on hers. "I think you are refreshing and charming."

She glanced out the side window of the cab as it started on its way over the cobblestone street. "Do we have far to go?"

"No. Just a short journey through the fashionable part of town."

She kept staring out the window, enthralled by the spectacle of a great city alive in the busy daylight hours. There was a throng of traffic, drays, carts, bright-lettered omnibuses, four-wheel and hansom cabs, saddle horses, broughams and chaises. And every so often a splendid vehicle with a liveried coachman and footmen passed by. At the crossings where pedestrians crossed the roadway, sweepers of all ages swept up the manure. They reached the area of fine shops and she saw women magnificent in heavily flounced crinoline skirts, pagoda sleeves, and elaborate mantles. The colors of the women's dresses were bright and eye-catching. There appeared to be more men

27

in the streets than women and they nearly all wore dull-surfaced black or gray top hats.

"What an exciting place London is!" she exclaimed, turning a glance at her companion with delight.

"Something for everyone's fancy so they say," Nelson Reed drawled. "This is your first taste of London?"

"I have never been here before."

"Well, you shall see it properly, I promise you. I can think of no better guide than Nelson Reed, Esquire!"

She smiled gratefully. "I can't take up your time, Mr. Reed, you must have work to do."

"Call me Nelson," he told her. "I was a close friend of your uncle's and I should like to be a good friend to you."

"Do you really have so much time to spare?"

"Yes," the young dandy said with self-satisfaction. "I happen to be a gentleman-about-town. I do not work for a living. I live by my wits. I belong to several of the best clubs and I have had a long run of luck at the gaming tables."

She stared at him worriedly. "Like my uncle?"

"No," he said. "I'm much wiser than old George. I know when to plunge and when to hold back. It takes talent to be a gambler, have you ever thought of that?"

"I haven't," she confessed. Indeed, she had never known that there were men who made their living solely by gambling until she'd heard about her Uncle George.

"It takes a deal of talent," Nelson went on confidentially. "And if I say so myself, I have it. Lucky Nelson Reed they call me."

She studied him with concern. "I hope your good luck continues."

His smile was lazy. "I'm sure that it will. Meeting you convinces me of it."

Flora was not quite certain that she understood the full meaning of his words. There had been a mocking quality in his tone which she did not like. She'd heard him use it before and it had made her a trifle uneasy about him.

Chapter Three

THE PLOUGH and Sickle, a pub with rooms upstairs, was a pleasant enough place and well operated. Nelson Reed saw Flora safely installed in one of the rooms with a view of the street below. She was thrilled with the comfortable room and duly grateful to the young man who had befriended her.

As he was ready to leave she saw him out to the corridor. "I don't know how to thank you," she said.

"You mustn't worry about it. I shall now look after the details of the funeral and come back to take you out to dinner."

"Don't let me be a nuisance!"

He smiled. "You're far from a nuisance. I shall enjoy showing you off before the town. Wear your best dress."

She hesitated. "I haven't anything all that grand. And do you think we should go out to dinner when I'm in mourning?"

"Who will know you are in mourning?" the young man

wanted to know. "And how can you seriously mourn for someone you never knew and who let you down very badly?"

"I suppose that is true," she said.

"Of course it's true," he replied emphatically. He had the habit of sounding emphatic about many things. "Wear your best and I'll be back at six o'clock to pick you up."

She didn't try to argue with him further because she felt that once he'd made up his mind it would be almost impossible to change it. She felt a little guilty about going out so soon after her uncle's death, and she worried that she had no dress stylish enough.

Going back into her room, she opened her valise and took out her things. The only dress which in any way would fit a smart occasion was a rose crepe de chine the village seamstress had made for her to attend a summer lawn party. She felt that it was awfully plain for sophisticated London. But since it was the only party dress she owned it would have to do.

She spent a good part of the afternoon looking out her window at the fascinating street drama offered. It amazed her that so many people lived in London. And the traffic was unbelievable! There was a brisk business in the pub below with people coming and going regularly. She wondered if her room would be noisy at night.

As evening drew near she changed and dressed for her meeting with Nelson Reed. The dress looked better on her than she expected but she had difficulty getting her hair right. And she was ashamed of her only cloak and hood, for although the garment was crimson it was of a rough material and hardly suited to dining out in a fine restaurant.

Nelson Reed arrived at six. He had changed to a black coat and a white tie and looked quite handsome. He surveyed her from the doorway of her room.

"You look very well," he said. "I'm going to enjoy having you on my arm."

The same hansom cab was waiting. She sat very straight and prim on the seat, ill at ease in her modest finery and not at all certain that she should have agreed to the excursion. At her side sat Nelson Reed, more mocking in manner than ever.

"You're distractingly lovely tonight," he said, "but you seem so ill at ease."

"I'm nervous," she told him. "And I'm still upset about Uncle George. What have you done about his funeral?"

Nelson Reed sighed. "Ah, yes, the funeral! I have arranged with the undertakers to have the body on display in the nave of St. Bridget's Church. The vicar has agreed to this in exchange for a donation I have made to his missionary fund."

"What time is the funeral?" she asked.

"Two-thirty tomorrow afternoon," the young man replied. "I have sent out notices to his friends and his host of creditors. I cannot guarantee they'll all be there but if they should turn up they'll fill the church."

"I hope it's a nice funeral," she worried.

"Let me take care of it," Nelson Reed told her. "I shall hire a few mourners just to make sure. All will go well. But must we spend the entire evening discussing the funeral?"

She gave him a reproving glance. "It's just that I wanted to know what you'd done."

"Well, now you know. Shall we drop the subject?"

"If you prefer to," she said, turning away from him to gaze out the side window of the cab.

Nelson Reed said disconsolately, "It's not that I am all that unfeeling, it's just that I want you to enjoy your evening."

"Thank you," she said quietly.

"I feel responsible for you," he went on. "And don't think Horace Wright won't question and criticize me when he returns. He wants nothing but the best for you."

Flora said, "He's a wonderful man!"

"What about me?" Nelson Reed asked.

She looked at him in the near darkness of the cab and smiled. "You're very nice as well."

His face brightened. "I'm glad to hear you say that. Do you know where I'm taking you tonight?"

"No."

"The Holborn Restaurant. It is a favorite of mine. Not the most dressy dining room in the city but it offers lively company and there is always a fine selection of good food at modest prices."

She was relieved by his mention that it was not too stylish a place. "It sounds very nice."

"I hope you still think so after we've been there."

The restaurant proved huge, much larger than she had imagined. He escorted her in with an air of triumph and saw that her cloak was taken by a lady attendant. Then he led her in to show her the Grand Salon. It was immense with many rows of long tables.

"We won't be eating in there but in the smaller grill room," he told her.

"I'm glad. It seems more like a great exhibition hall than a dining room," she said.

Nelson laughed good-naturedly. "A very apt comment! I declare you may become a wit! An exhibition place it is for many to show off in. You were very close to the truth."

Now he guided her to the smaller grill room where the tables were for two, four, or six. It was pleasant without being too elegant and she at once relaxed. Nelson ordered for them, insisting she try the turtle soup and the half duckling. He also ordered a bottle of wine, making a grand ritual of this. The dining room was only partly filled so they sat in a corner by themselves. She was also thankful for this and able to relax.

As they waited for dinner, she asked him, "What sort of work do you think you'll be able to find for me?"

"Who knows?" he asked with a twinkle in his blue eyes. "Maybe I'll ask you to marry me and take you out of the work force altogether."

She felt her cheeks blaze at this and she protested, "Please, I'm serious!"

"So am I," he said. "Does the prospect of marriage with me seem so undesirable?"

"I'm not ready for marriage," she said. "And we don't know each other. I think one should only marry for love."

Nelson Reed raised his eyebrows. "My, what high principles we have!"

"You're making fun of me again!"

"Not at all," he said. "The truth is that even if I wanted to marry you it would not be practical. My sort of existence does not lend itself to a wife and family. I was only jesting."

"I was sure of that."

He raised a manicured hand in protest. "Don't misunderstand me! The prospect of marriage with you is delightful to me. It's just that I'm in no position to establish a home or become a husband."

"You are too dedicated to your gambling," she said.

"That's it. I'm a thoroughly selfish creature. I live this odd life by choice and have come to place much stock in my freedom."

"I wish you happiness if that is the sort of life you desire," she said.

"That is most generous of you," he said with a return of his wryly humorous manner.

The waiter came with their first course and ended the talk without her ever having gained any satisfaction from him. She discovered that she was hungry and that the food was excellent. When the duckling and the wine came she welcomed it.

She told Nelson Reed, "You couldn't have brought me to a better place."

"Thank you, my dear," he said. "The desserts are generous and excellent as well. I don't think you'll be disappointed."

She wasn't. But when she sat back from her plate she felt that she'd eaten far too much.

Nelson poured the balance of the wine into their glasses. He urged her, "Drink up! It will help your digestion!"

"So much red wine," she gasped. "I've never had so much."

"Not a lot really," he said. "And now I'll pay our check and go out and find the cabby."

"I'll sleep when I get back to the inn," she promised him. "Such a meal."

"But we're not going directly to the inn," he told her. "I'm stopping by at one of my clubs along the way. I want you to see the excitement, and maybe we'll meet a few of my friends. Even people who knew your uncle."

She put down her wine glass. "I don't think it wise. I should go directly home."

"Nonsense!" he objected as he waved for the waiter. "The night is young!"

Flora felt a small panic rising up in her. He had ordered a second bottle of wine at dinner and had drunk it all himself, as well as a large share of the original bottle. Now she could see that he was more than a little intoxicated and belligerent. Her experience with drunken men had been strictly limited as a vicar's daughter. Never before had she to deal with one directly.

Nelson finally settled the bill after a good deal of loud argument and difficulty in making the proper change. Then he led her out to get her cloak. The sad-faced woman attendant gave her a sympathetic glance as Nelson mumbled drunkenly at her side.

They went out into the night and she was surprised to find a heavy fog had descended on the city. The glow from storefronts, windows, and gas lamps took on a fuzzy kind of magic. As she stood admiring the weird beauty the fog brought to the ordinary night, Nelson was at the curb signaling for the waiting cabby. She felt her escort was making far too much of a scene.

The driver seemed resigned to abuse. He drove up his ancient hansom cab and alighted to let them in.

"Where were you hiding?" Nelson demanded of him in a loud, offensive voice.

"Just over there," the coachman said meekly.

She stepped into the cab quickly wanting to avoid a scene. She heard Nelson give the man the name of some club and then he got in and sat beside her. "Stupid oaf!" he complained.

"I think you were far too hard on him," she said accusingly.

He glared at her. "Don't tell me how to behave, country girl!"

"I'm sorry. I had no intention of offending you. Please take me back to my hotel."

Nelson chuckled drunkenly. "Now we're all hurt feelings. I swear you are a true female! Impossible to please!"

"I'm tired," she said. "After the ordeal of yesterday and last night. I need rest for the funeral tomorrow."

This seemed to strike him as a humorous remark and he laughed heartily at it. "We're stopping at one of my favorite clubs. But we won't stay long, I promise you!"

She knew there was nothing she could do. It would be impossible to find her way about London on her own. And even if she got away from him and found a cab, she wouldn't be able to pay for it as she'd left her small reserve of money locked in her valise at the hotel. She could only resign herself to allowing him to extend the evening as he pleased. At the same time she hoped that he would begin to weary.

At last the cab came to a halt before a fine mansion with marble steps leading up to its entrance and gas lamps flanking the steps at street level. Nelson made a great show of helping her out of the cab and guiding her up the stairs. He was more sober by now. He pulled the bell knob and waited for the door to be opened. It was drawn back only after they'd been carefully scrutinized through a peephole in its center.

The doorman, a huge ex-prizefighter type with a battered face, gave Nelson a welcoming smile. "Evenin', Mr. Reed," he said in a hoarse voice. "Good to see you."

"Good to be here," Nelson said. "Is it a lively night?"

"The tables are all busy," the doorman said.

Nelson guided her in through a large room with subdued lighting where well-dressed men and young women sat at tables located around the walls drinking and talking. Some of them stared at her with open curiosity as she passed through the room. It was clear that they were aware of a new face.

They went through double doors to a huge room filled with cigar smoke and loud talk. Its whole length was apportioned to various tables where a different gambling game was being played at each. There was always an operator conducting the game for the house. Most of the tables were crowded with men and women in fashionable evening dress.

Nelson turned to her with a smile. "Is this your first visit to a gaming house?"

"My father was bitterly opposed to gambling," she replied.

"Too bad your Uncle George hadn't the same convictions or he would still be alive," he said with brutal disregard for her feelings.

"You forced me to come here."

"I'm sorry," he said contritely. "I've been rude to you. Forgive me. I want you to see the place because it is part of my way of life. Seeing it you'll better understand me."

She said, "Very well. At least you've given me a good reason for coming here."

He said, "Let me explain it to you. That game they are playing over there is called Hazard. It's played mostly with dice and very popular."

"Why?"

"Chiefly because it is easy to get rid of the equipment in case of a raid," he said. "These places are all outside the law and always have been. That doesn't stop the best people from coming to them as you can see."

She gazed at the people standing by the tables and said, "Most of them do seem of the upper classes but I have never seen faces so strained and tense."

He looked grim. "Some of them are wagering large amounts. That's always a strain. The Duke of Wellington and Talleyrand were members of Crockford's in the old days and they had a chef named Monsieur Ude who was reckoned the best in the world."

"People will always gamble, it seems."

"And why not?" he demanded. "The Queen has a prudish view of it and they brought in the new gaming act a few years ago. It makes raids on places like this easier but gambling still goes on. There's a different game at every table here such as baccarat, roulette, and trente-et-quarante."

"What game do you play?"

"It varies," he said. "At the moment I favor roulette. We'll indulge in some play after I have a drink. Do you want anything from the bar?"

"No," she said. "I want nothing more."

"Then you'll excuse me for a moment," he said. He bowed and left her standing close by the roulette table. She heard the croupier call out for bets, saw the wheel spinning and the tiny ball whirling around to finally come to rest on the winning number.

There were groans from around the table as the winning number was announced. Mixed with the groans were the ecstatic cries of several winners. One balding, red-bearded man wearing a monocle walked away from the table with an ashen face. He passed close by her in a kind of dazed despair. Watching him leave the gambling room she thought that her Uncle George must have left the tables on the night before his suicide in much the same condition. Despite the glamour of the place she began to understand her father's hatred of gambling.

"Good evening, my dear! You are new here!" Flora was addressed by a jaded, throaty woman's voice.

She turned in surprise to find a remarkable-looking female. The woman was clearly in her late forties and grotesquely made up with carmined lips, painted cheeks, and heavily-powdered skin. Her auburn hair was braided and puffed in the latest style. There was a false black beauty spot on her cheek near the left corner of her mouth. Her low-cut dress revealed nearly all her bosom. Most remarkable of all, she was smoking a large black cigar.

Flora, at first rather taken back, finally found her voice. "Yes. I am new. I have never been here before. Who are you?"

The woman smiled with a creasing of her rather puffy face. In the same sophisticated, throaty voice she purred, "My name is Madame Irene DuBois. I am British but my dear late husband was of French extraction. A diplomat. Nowadays I live in London."

"My name is Flora Bain."

The woman stared at her. "Not any relation to George Bain?"

"He was my uncle."

The woman at once clasped a pudgy hand on Flora's arm, as she held the cigar in the other. Sympathetically, she said, "I have heard the news! Poor George! I shall make a point of attending his funeral tomorrow! St. Bridget's, isn't it?"

"Yes," she said, slightly uncomfortable. There was something about the woman's familiarity that made her uneasy.

Her hand still on Flora's arm, the older woman went on, "George was here almost every night. I can tell you he is missed by us regulars. How unfortunate that he had that losing streak!"

"It was," she said. "But I'm sure many people have the same experience."

Madame Irene DuBois sighed. "Ah, that is so true! My late husband died of overexcitement at the tables. I still come to play but only with very modest amounts. I do not care whether I win or lose. It is a place to come and meet my friends."

"That seems the wise attitude."

"But what are you doing here?"

She blushed. "I didn't want to come here tonight with my uncle in his coffin, but my escort insisted that I should. I was helpless to do anything about it as I do not know London well enough to have gone home on my own."

"Poor dear!" the older woman purred. "And may I ask who your escort is?"

"A friend of my uncle's, Nelson Reed."

"Nelson!"

Flora stared at the woman with her diamond necklace and her fingers loaded with the sparkling, bright stones.

She said, "Do you know Nelson as well?"

"But of course, I do," the older woman said with a wise smile. "He is one of the most talked-about young men in London."

"So he says."

"Where is Nelson just now?"

"At the bar."

"I might have guessed," Madame said with a knowing

wink. "You are lucky to have him escort you. He is not usually available." She leaned her head close to Flora's to say, "He has an arrangement with a very good friend of mine, an older lady like myself whose name is Mrs. Fraser. He is rarely seen without her. They are a devoted pair."

"Indeed," she said. She had felt from the start that Nelson Reed behaved more like a married man than a single one. Now this explained it all. She realized he'd been very careful not to mention the name of this Mrs. Fraser with whom he apparently was deeply involved. In view of the fact he'd made her a mocking offer of marriage she was glad to know about the affair.

There was a wicked look in Irene DuBois' eyes. "I trust I have not let a cat out of the bag," she said, placatingly touching Flora's hand.

Flora drew herself up. "Not at all. I've only known him for the one day I've been in the city. He has been kind to me because of his friendship for my uncle."

"Of course," the woman said in her purring way. "And do you plan to remain in the city?"

"Yes."

"You are not returning to the country and your family?"

"My parents are dead," she said, not liking all this pointed questioning. "I have no one there now."

Madame DuBois was all sympathy. "Ah, my dear! But I'm sure you'll do very well in London." She gave her dress an appraising glance. "I know that Nelson can find you a suitable dressmaker, and with a few introductions around you could become a toast of the town."

Flora said, "I intend to find a suitable position."

The older woman stared at her blankly. "But of course! That was what I was only just saying! You must depend on Nelson. He knows London!"

"I will," she said uneasily. She was not at all sure that the colorful Madame DuBois knew the sort of work she had in mind. She certainly didn't want to be like those young women she'd seen seated with men in the dimly lighted outer room.

At that moment Nelson returned with a glass in his hand, surprised to see Madame and her talking together. "Well, I didn't know you two had met!"

Madame DuBois gave him her sharklike smile. "But we have! Only just now! Such a delightful child! So naive! What taste you show in your female companions."

Nelson Reed's weakly handsome face showed a sickly expression of amusement. "You are your usual attractive self, Madame!"

She touched him playfully. "How nice a compliment coming from you! But then we are long time good friends as I was just telling Flora."

"True," he said grudgingly. "Have you enjoyed watching the play, Flora? I fear I left you too long alone. I met some friends at the bar. You must forgive me!"

Flora said, "But I have been having a most interesting talk with this lady. The time passed without my noticing it."

Nelson nodded and turned to Madame DuBois. "Once again I am indebted to you," he said. "You have come to my aid so frequently!"

"Delighted to be of some use, dear boy," the woman said mockingly. "I know you do not want me intruding on your evening with this lovely child so I shall move on."

Flora said, "Must you go?" She'd decided she'd just as soon have the woman near her as to deal with Nelson alone, especially if he did more drinking.

Madame DuBois turned to her. "I really must move about the room," she said. "But we shall meet again. I promise. I shall attend the funeral tomorrow."

"That is so kind of you," she said sincerely.

Irene DuBois nodded and moved on majestically. Nelson stood there looking rather shaken. "I trust she did not annoy you?"

"Annoy me?"

He crimsoned. "I mean she is rather a character. You must have noticed that!"

"Unusual, but obviously a lady," Flora said with all the worldly wisdom of a girl brought up in a Sussex vicarage.

"I can forgive her ways since she lived in France so long. Her late husband was a diplomat, she told me."

"Did she?" Nelson said, looking astounded.

"Did you ever meet him?"

"No, I never had that pleasure. But I'm sure it would have been a most rewarding experience."

"She seems to know everyone," Flora said.

"That she does," Nelson agreed. "At least I'm glad that your impressions of her are favorable."

"Very favorable," she said. "She is eccentric, of course. But after all that might be expected of the widow of a prominent French diplomat. Don't you agree?"

Still looking confused, Nelson Reed nodded solemnly. "You are surely right. I do agree. Shall I take a turn at the wheel?" He seemed anxious to have her move on. They went to the table, where he explained the game to her in more detail. While they were there she saw him lose and win large sums. However, it turned out to be one of his lucky nights, and he made a substantial winning.

As they moved away, she asked him, "Did you come out ahead finally?"

"To the tune of about twenty-five pounds," he said happily. "I do not demand large earnings but I try to make them regularly."

She said nothing more to him about his gambling. It was with some relief that she stepped out into the foggy London night once again. This time the cabby was waiting close by the entrance and within a few minutes they were rattling over the cobblestoned streets on their way to the Plough and Sickle. Nelson seemed well pleased with his winnings and less drunk than in the early evening. She was tempted to ask him about his friend Mrs. Fraser but she thought better of it. In any case, his affairs were none of her business.

When they reached the hotel he saw her upstairs to her room and she found it rather difficult to get him to leave. She finally tried by making a reference to the funeral, asking him, "What time will you be coming to take me to the funeral?"

Nelson Reed, looking somewhat abashed, said, "I shall

come by shortly after one. You will want to be there early."

"Thank you and good night," she said, with intended abruptness.

"Is that all you have to say?" he asked.

"What more is there?"

"After my working so hard to make your evening a pleasurable one," he lamented.

"I do appreciate all you've done and also Mr. Wright's part in it," she told him, pointedly reminding him that Horace Wright was the one underwriting this benevolence.

"Horace Wright is not here," he said. "I am." And then without warning he suddenly took her in his arms and kissed her with great ardor. Caught by surprise it took her a moment to push him away.

"That was not at all gentlemanly," she said angrily and went into her room and slammed the door. She heard his laughter from the corridor before he walked away.

She listened by the door for a little to make sure that he had gone. Then she began preparing for bed. She felt that it was unfortuante Nelson Reed had such a weak character, not a person to really be depended upon. This especially worried her as she had no one else to turn to in her search for employment.

A heartening thought was that Horace Wright might return from Liverpool earlier than he had expected. She had full confidence in the older man and knew that he would be much more helpful in finding her the right sort of work.

She extinguished the candle on her night table and got into bed. From below she could faintly hear lusty singing in the pub. Within a short time she drifted into a deep, exhausted sleep, filled with nightmares.

Twice she woke up in a perspiring fright only to realize she was in the hotel room. Below the singing had ended and there was only silence. She went back to sleep, this time dreaming that she was at her uncle's funeral. She saw Madame DuBois standing by the coffin with one of her sharklike smiles and waving to Flora to join her by the casket. Reluctantly Flora crept up beside her, looking down with frightened eyes to see her uncle's body. Instead of a body there was a roulette wheel with the tiny ball spinning around!

She glanced at Madame DuBois who now hooted with laughter. Flora could stand it no longer. Screaming, she backed away from the bizarre woman. And she was screaming when she woke up to see a dwarf standing at her bedside. The ugliest dwarf she'd ever seen in all her life!

Chapter Four

FLORA SCREAMED once again. The dwarf had a flat, wrinkled face with small eyes and his hair was black and unruly. It stood out from his head in all directions like a spread mop. He was wearing a green apron and he stood there glaring at her.

"No need to make such a fuss!" he rasped.

She held the bedclothes to her as she sat up. "Who are you and what are you doing here?"

"I'm Sam. I'm from the pub below," he said.

Her eyes still showed her terror. "How did you get in here?"

The dwarf looked disgusted. "We have keys for all the rooms!"

"How dare you come in on me like this?" she demanded.

"I've come to find out what you want for breakfast and later I'll fetch it," the dwarf replied.

"You're a waiter!"

"If you want to call me that," he said impatiently. "What would you like?"

Feeling somewhat foolish she told him, adding, "Would you please knock before you ever come in here?"

"If that's what you wish," the little man said sullenly, turning to leave on incredibly bowed legs.

She waited until he'd gone out; then she rose from the bed and started to wash and dress. She'd feel better if she were properly dressed when the dwarf returned. Pulling up the blind she saw that it was still foggy.

She continued to stand by the window looking down into the street where a drayman was cruelly whipping his horse. The sight sickened her. Just as the drayman drove on there was a knock on her door. She went over and opened it to find the dwarf standing there holding a big tray.

"Thank you. You can put it on the table near the window."

"Yes, miss," the dwarf said in a sullen voice. He crossed the room and set down the tray.

"What about the dirty dishes?" she asked.

"You can put the tray outside your door when you're finished."

"Do you supply meals at any time of the day?"

"Any time," the dwarf said. "Just come down and ask for Sam. I'll be around for your breakfast every morning in any case."

"But you will knock first," she pleaded. "I'm very nervous and I was having a bad dream when you woke me up this morning."

Sam showed a smile on his ugly face. "Reckon I wasn't a very pretty sight to wake up to. I'll knock, miss." And he went on out.

With a sigh she sat down to the excellent breakfast. London was a strange place. Some of the ugliest people she met turned out to be the most pleasant, while some of the supposedly attractive were proving to have sinister sides to them. It was much different from the simple Sussex village in which she'd been raised and where everyone could be taken at face value.

She spent much of the morning getting her black dress, bonnet, and cape ready for the funeral. By one o'clock she was ready and waiting for Nelson Reed. When he did not arrive as promptly as she'd expected she began to worry. She feared that he might have become annoyed and would not bother coming to take her to the funeral.

She sat watching at the window. About one-thirty the familiar hansom cab stopped outside the pub. She at once went out to the corridor locking her room door after her. She met Nelson on the stairs.

"How did you know I'd arrived?" he asked in surprise.

"I was watching from the window," she said.

"Oh! I see. Sorry to be late. Had a few problems along the way."

"Just so long as we get to the church in time."

He escorted her down the stairway. "You mustn't worry about that. It's only a short drive from here."

And so it was. St. Bridget's was an ancient church located in a somewhat down-at-the-heel district. Its red brick façade was dark with soot from the nearby factories and its spire was lost in the gray fog as they drove up to it.

"There don't seem to be any others here yet," he speculated as he led her across the sidewalk to the entrance of the church.

"And we're not all that early," she worried.

"Well, we shall see," he said.

The church was damp and melancholy. She saw the casket on a stand midway down the nave. A bent, gaunt figure came shuffling towards them and on reaching them gave a deep bow.

"I'm Gandy, the undertaker from Grantmoor's," he announced. "I'm in charge of the funeral."

"Very good," Nelson said. "Are we the first here?"

"The very first," the shabby Gandy said with an unctuous smile of sympathy on his gaunt face. He was mostly bald and he held large bony hands clasped before him almost in a manner of supplication.

"Where is my uncle to be buried?" she asked.

Gandy showed surprise. "Didn't they tell you? There is

46

an unused section out here behind the church. We've had the gravediggers find a spot there."

Flora smelled the heavy odor of liquor on his breath, which made her even more annoyed. "No one discussed it with me."

Gandy looked uneasy. "Those were the instructions given us. Put him in the nearest lot, was what they told us."

Nelson Reed showed embarrassment. "If there is any blame it must be placed squarely on me. I'm afraid I gave the undertaker rather sketchy directions."

"It doesn't matter," she said quietly.

"We have a closed casket," the undertaker said with a meaningful look, his hands still raised in the odd clasped position.

"My uncle did look rather bad in death," she was willing to admit. She turned to Nelson. "I'd like to go stand by the casket for a moment."

He accompanied her down and stood a respectful distance with his top hat held at waist level. She bowed over the extremely plain casket, trying to summon some feeling of understanding for the dead man within it. This was a difficult task. Calling on her childhood training she repeated a simple prayer and then returned to Nelson's side.

"Surely there will be someone else," she said in a low voice.

"I should hope so," Nelson Reed sighed.

"That Madame DuBois said she would attend."

He looked upset. "You mustn't put too much stock in what she says."

"No?"

"No. She drinks a great deal and has a bad memory," he said hastily as they moved on back to the vestibule of the church once again.

She had the feeling that if Nelson had searched out the most dismal church in all London this one would at least be its match.

The undertaker appeared from some hidden corner. With him was a thin boy in ragged clothes. "This is the sexton! His name is Ralph and he's a remarkable lad!"

Flora was startled. In Sussex the sextons were always old, reliable men, well versed in the traditions and ways of the church. This lad couldn't be more than twelve!

"Isn't he young for the job?"

"Young in years but old in experience, miss."

The boy looked up at her with a questioning expression on his thin face. "Shall I ring the bells now, miss?"

"The bells?" she said.

"Yes, miss," the youth said. "The rector lives across the street. He's rare deaf and he won't come over until I ring the bells."

Nelson Reed opened his waistcoat and consulted his watch with a frown. "It is almost twenty-five after two," he said. "I should say it is high time the bells were rung and we began this business."

The undertaker waited, saying, "Whatever you wish?"

The whole spectacle was so dismal to her that she could only wish it over with quickly. "Ring the bells and get him here! I very much doubt that anyone else is coming."

"Right away, miss," the boy said happily, skipping off towards the belfry at a most undignified speed.

The undertaker glanced after him mildly. "The boy is full of spirit," he said.

Flora could not resist murmuring, "And he is not the only one!"

The undertaker didn't seem to hear her but Nelson Reed did and he smiled thinly and said, "It is the curse of the profession. I declare there are more drunken undertakers in London than sober ones."

While Nelson was telling her this the undertaker went to the door of the old church to greet four remarkable-looking figures who had suddenly appeared. The three men all wore black crepe tied around their top hats and trailing down their backs, while the woman wore a heavy black veil. Mr. Gandy made a great show of shaking hands with them.

She turned to Nelson in surprise. "Who can they be?"

"Professional mourners," he said, with a twinkle in his blue eyes. "They were included in the funeral price. I thought it a precaution against us being the sole attendants at the service. It would seem that my precaution was an excellent one."

"I find it extremely distasteful," she declared. "I have never heard of such a thing!"

"It is common here in the city," he assured her. "I have known funerals to cost as much as fifteen hundred pounds and include just such a group as we have here. And even that enormous sum was not enough to guarantee the undertaker being sober."

Now Mr. Gandy showed the professional mourners to a pew near the body. They behaved in a most solemn manner, which suggested they were attending the funeral of someone near and dear to them. While this charade was under way the bells began to sound. Flora thought that the young sexton's enthusiasm made them sound more fitted to a wedding than a funeral. They had a positively joyous note.

Flora was now more in a mood of exasperation than mourning. Then the entrance door suddenly opened again and in marched Madame DuBois looking as unique as ever in a black mourning outfit complete with veil. She had turned the veil back over her bonnet so that her painted face was visible.

She came up to Flora, and with what was meant to be a sympathetic smile said, "My dear child, you have my most sincere compassion on this sad day."

"Thank you for coming," she said in a small voice.

Madame DuBois now turned to Nelson Reed. "How good of you to remember your old friend and be here," she said. "It only makes me admire you more."

"Your own presence is a tribute to your character," he said with familiar gallantry.

"I would not have missed this. I want to see dear George properly buried."

"Of course," Nelson said. And he nodded to Mr. Gandy who had just returned to join them. "Mr. Gandy will see you safely to a pew."

"Delighted!" the undertaker said, offering his arm to the Madame and showing her down the aisle to a pew directly behind the professional mourners.

Flora then saw a strange apparition in flowing white surplice over a black cassock come toddling down towards her. No doubt this was the ancient and deaf rector. He was a thin man, quite bald except for a ridge of long white hair that streamed out wildly. He had a lantern-jawed face and his eyes were doleful and sunken. His mouth gaped open and he carried a prayer book in a trembling hand.

Halting before Flora, he asked her, "Are we ready to begin?"

"Yes," she managed faintly.

As the rector held up the prayer book, she saw that he was suffering from advanced palsy. His head nodded in time with his trembling hands. In a high-pitched voice, he informed her, "We have no choir! There can be no hymns! But I shall read the service here and at the graveside for your departed aunt!"

Flora was shocked that the old man had not even managed to get the gender of the dead person right. She was going to correct him, but realizing his deafness and generally debilitated state she felt it wasn't worth the effort. Besides, he was now lurching down to the altar to begin the service.

She gave Nelson Reed a concerned look. "You heard him!"

"It will make no difference to George," Nelson whispered. "He's beyond it and so is the rector. The others probably won't notice."

"You're right," she said weakly.

They took their places in the pew opposite the one occupied by the professional mourners and had to sit with bowed heads while the palsied rector read the funeral service with feeling references to the dear departed sister. The service took only a short time, then Nelson Reed and the three professional male mourners bore the casket of Uncle George out of the church and around the side path to the cemetery.

The rector stumbled along behind the casket, followed by the ragged young sexton who appeared to be enjoying the whole affair more than anyone else.

The female professional mourner trailed the rector, now and then touching a hankie to her mouth and uttering a low wailing sound. It was a most effective touch.

Madame Irene DuBois marched beside Flora with dignity. But as they entered the cemetery she whispered to her, "Did you hear that old man during the service? 'Our dear departed sister.' Are you quite sure we're attending the proper service?"

"Yes," Flora whispered back. "The rector seems very confused and Nelson felt we'd better let it just proceed."

They weaved their way through ancient tombstones until they came to the freshly dug grave where Uncle George was to be buried. The grave diggers were standing by, or rather leaning on their shovels in the background with red faces and glazed eyes. It took Flora only a minute to realize that they were even more drunk than Mr. Gandy!

The casket was set down on ropes beside the grave and the rector took his place at the head of it. He opened his prayer book, tottering slightly. Only a frantic Mr. Gandy rushing forward and grasping him by the cassock saved the old minister from tumbling down into the grave head first.

This crisis over with, they took their places at the graveside where the ancient rector recited a second service with references to the female gender of the dear departed. Then Mr. Gandy supervised the lowering of the coffin into the grave. Even before it had touched bottom the rector and his alter ego, the ragged little sexton, had vanished. Almost at once the professional mourners turned and walked briskly out of the cemetery. This left only Flora, Nelson, Madame DuBois and Mr. Gandy. The two gravediggers had come forward and were arguing loudly with the undertaker. He argued back with them in a constantly rising voice and then turned and came over to Nelson Reed with an expression of dismay on his gaunt face.

"This is a most embarrassing situation, Mr. Reed, but these two seem to think they haven't been fairly paid."

Nelson frowned. "Grave digging was included in the fee I paid your firm."

"Yes," the undertaker said unhappily, "and I have paid them the usual fee, but they claim it wasn't enough. That there was a great deal of rock and gravel. And they refuse to fill in the grave unless they get five shillings more for each of them."

Madame DuBois arched her heavy black eyebrows. "They refuse to finish the burial of my dear friend, George Bain."

"That is about the sum of it," Mr. Gandy said.

Nelson glared at the two who now stood by the grave with their shovels in hand. "They're drunk. Can't you see that?"

"They always are," Mr. Gandy sighed.

Flora spoke up, "And you are not sober either, sir."

The gaunt man gasped with dismay. "Miss, how can you make such an accusation!"

Madame Irene DuBois looked at the undertaker with a bored air. "It is not an accusation but an observation. Your breath gives you away, my man!"

Nelson impatiently took some money from his pocket and gave it to the undertaker. "Give them their extra five bob and let them get on with it."

Mr. Gandy's melancholy features showed gratitude. "Thank you, sir. You are a gentleman. And if you again suffer bereavement remember Grantmoor the Undertaker."

Madame DuBois drew her pudgy figure up to its full height and said, "We would all much rather be lost at sea!"

With that comment the three of them turned and walked out of the cemetery in dignified silence. Flora had heard ugly rumors about how badly city burial services were conducted when she'd lived in Sussex, but she could never have imagined anything like the one she'd just witnessed.

The hansom cab was waiting and Nelson ordered the cabby to drive them back to the Plough and Sickle.

Nelson Reed said, "Well at least your Uncle George is now buried."

"Yes," she said quietly.

"Only barely," was Madame DuBois' comment. "He

lived a most intemperate life, but he deserved more dignity in death."

"The less we think about it the better," was Nelson Reed's offered opinion.

On reaching the Plough and Sickle, he took them into the Ladies' Bar where they were served by Sam, the dwarf. Flora had her usual sherry but she noticed that both Nelson and Madame DuBois ordered double whiskies.

It was not until the second round of drinks that there was any air of easiness at the table. Then Irene Dubois gave her attention to Flora. "The next thing, of course, is to plan this lovely creature's future."

Nelson glanced across the table at the woman with an uneasy expression. "All in good time," he said.

"One must plan," Madame DuBois said.

"I will need to work as soon as I can," Flora said, feeling much more warm and comfortable after her second sherry.

"Work!" the older woman echoed in disgust. "Have you no ambition, child?"

"I hope I have. That is why I want to find a suitable job," she said.

"We who are blessed in having feminine beauty do not think of work. Work is a sacrilege to the lovely! One thinks of finding a companion, or even a suitable marriage!"

Nelson gave her a warning look. "Madame, I do not think you properly understand. Flora would like to find a post as some ailing lady's companion or even as a governess."

"Though in truth I'm not very good with children," Flora confessed.

Madame DuBois regarded her with curiosity. "Where was it you were brought up, my child?"

"In rural Sussex," she said.

"I must remember that," Irene DuBois said grimly.

Nelson was becoming increasingly nervous. "Madame, I know that you must be anxious to return home. Otherwise you will be too weary to make your usual rounds of the gaming houses tonight. I'm going to place my cabby at your disposal so you can leave at once."

Madame DuBois looked pleased. "That is most kind of you. I am a bit tired. I shall need a nap before dressing for dinner. I will avail myself of your offer."

"Fine," Nelson said, his face showing obvious relief.

Madame rose and went over and kissed Flora on the cheek. "You are filled with strange ideas," she said, "but I still find you charming. And I do wish you good luck in locating a post."

"Thank you," she said with a smile. "And maybe some day I will have the good fortune to marry some wonderful person. Maybe a French diplomat as you did!"

Madame DuBois looked startled but she quickly regained her composure. "That is a very good goal for you to have, my dear," she said patting her on the shoulder.

Nelson saw them out to the street and left Flora for a moment to help Madame DuBois into the waiting cab. He put on his top hat and came back to Flora. "I fear that good lady was becoming a little tipsy."

"But she is so amusing. I'm glad she came to the funeral."

They were standing by the door opening onto the stairway to the hotel. Nelson Reed nodded. "So am I. I'm sure she cared for your uncle."

"I think so," she agreed.

He frowned. "I fear the funeral arrangements were not quite what they should be. But I paid well for them. You never can tell in these strange times. The workers are getting out of hand."

"You did your best. You need have no regrets," she said. "I think we should put it out of our minds."

"That is very sensible," the young man said.

"My main problem now is to find a position," Flora said worriedly.

"Yes," he said frowning. "You are sure you want to be a companion or governess?"

"What else is there?"

He shrugged. "Madame DuBois was not so wrong, you

know. If you could make the right marriage it would be the best solution."

She gave him a bitter smile. "Is that what you are planning with your Mrs. Fraser?"

Nelson Reed looked shocked. "Who told you anything about Mrs. Fraser?"

"Someone."

"It had to be Madame DuBois," he said with annoyance. "What did she tell you about her?"

Now she began to regret that she'd brought the woman's name up. "Nothing much. But she did say you were old friends and that because of that you'd be interested in no other female."

"Indeed!"

"I'm sorry," she apologized. "I didn't know it would make you so upset."

"I am not upset," he snapped. But his entire manner betrayed that he was. "Madame DuBois has no right to gossip like that."

"She meant no harm."

"But harm has been done," he insisted. "She has managed to give you a low opinion of me."

"No one could do that," she protested. "You and Mr. Wright have been so generous to me."

Nelson Reed paid no heed to her words. "Mrs. Fraser is my dear friend. I will not have a word said against her. She has suffered with a husband who is a drunken sot and I have tried to console her. The woman is a martyr!"

"I'm sorry."

"Her name should never be sullied by the likes of the Madame. I hope this makes the situation clear to you."

"It does," she said.

He stood there in silence for a moment. Then he said, "I regret that I will not be able to take you to dinner tonight."

"I did not expect it," she said.

"You can manage here at the pub?"

"Yes. I have only to call on Sam and he will bring my meal up to me," she said. "There is no need to worry."

"Very good," he said, still in an annoyed tone. "I shall be in touch with you some time tomorrow."

"Don't cause yourself any inconvenience," she said.

"But we must find you employment."

"Perhaps you could give me the address of some employment agency," she said. "Or of some person who might need to hire a governess. I could then go see about it myself."

"I can do better than that," the young man said absently. "Give me overnight to consider it."

"Whatever you think," she said. "It's just that I don't want to run up a large bill here. I shall expect to pay you and Mr. Wright back for whatever the total is."

"We needn't be concerned about that," he said. "Just be patient and I will come and see you tomorrow. Probably in the afternoon."

"Thank you for everything," she said sincerely. "I really do appreciate what you've done."

"Nothing," he said brusquely. And then he tipped his top hat to her and strode off to hail a passing cab.

As she watched him go, she could tell by the way he held himself that he was still angry. She blamed herself for being so indiscreet as to annoy him. But at the same time she couldn't imagine why he should be so touchy on the subject. If he were in love with this Mrs. Fraser why be so upset that people knew it. She supposed it was because the woman still had a husband who she was perhaps still living with. Then such an affair would be bound to make tongues wag.

Flora turned and went upstairs to her room. When she was safely inside it she felt better. It was already beginning to seem a little like home to her.

Later she went down to tell Sam that she would be having dinner in her room. When he brought it up to her she was pleased to note that he knocked on the door before attempting to enter. After he had crossed the room on his wildly bowed legs the ugly little man hesitated by the door.

He said, "A pretty girl like you shouldn't be eating

alone. You should be having dinner at one of the fine places with some gentleman."

She smiled. "I did that last night."

"You should be doing it every night. That's what the stage actresses do. I've heard them tell about it. And you're every bit as pretty as any of them."

"Thank you," she said.

He smiled. "I'm going to a ratting show tonight."

"A ratting show?"

"Surely you've heard of them," the dwarf said. "It's all the vogue in London. The public house down the street has a ratpit. They bring in good country rats, not the sewer ones that can infect a dog's mouth!"

"What do they do with these rats?"

The dwarf stared at her. "You never saw a ratpit? Why, miss, they have dogs to kill them. Gentlemen bet on how many rats the dog will kill! Any man touching the dogs or rats disqualifies his dog! It's a rare sport! There's usually a half-dozen dogs entered in the contest and maybe fifty or more rats killed in the run of an evening!"

She was shocked by what she heard. "It sounds a very bloody sport!"

"There are hundreds of such ratpits in London," the dwarf told her. "It's one of the chief entertainments."

"I think London must be a very cruel city," Flora said.

The dwarf nodded. "I won't deny it, miss. It is." And he went on out.

Chapter Five

THOUGH SHE did not realize it Flora was about to discover how cruel London could really be. That evening she spent quietly in her room. The singing and raucous laughter from the pub below provided welcome company. When she finally slept it was a peaceful sleep without any nightmares, which she took to be a good omen.

When Sam brought her breakfast the next morning, he informed her, "It's raining fearful hard, miss! Not the sort of day to venture out into the streets."

She looked out to see that the rain was truly pouring down. The few people on the sidewalks were hurrying along with bent heads and dripping umbrellas. Occasionally a cab or dray went by splashing muddy water.

As the dwarf placed her breakfast tray on the table she said to him, "I have no reading matter, Sam. Can you get me something? It looks as if I might be trapped here all the day and night."

"I have the first copy of Charles Dickens' magazine

Household Words," he said proudly. " 'Twas left in the pub by a gentleman called Forster who is a friend of Mr. Dickens. I've been saving it but you can have it."

"Thank you," she said gratefully. "I shall only want to read it. You can have it back."

"No, miss. I want it to be my present to you," he said. "I'll fetch it when I come for the tray." And he waddled out happily on his twisted little legs.

She lingered over breakfast since she had no plans for the day. Glancing out at the rain again she decided it was unlikely Nelson Reed would visit her on this stormy day to help her seek employment. She did want to find work as soon as possible, and it troubled her that she was running up a bill at the pub. Perhaps tomorrow would be fine and Nelson would locate work for her.

There was a knock on her door. She opened it to find Sam there, carrying a paper in his hand. "That's the *Household Words* I promised you," he said. Then he went over to get the tray.

Flora saw that it ran twenty-four pages and each page had two columns of reading matter. At the top of every page was the line, "Conducted by Charles Dickens."

She said, "It looks interesting."

"Yes, miss," Sam said. "I hope you like it." And he went on out with the tray.

As soon as she was alone she curled up on her bed, which she'd made up immediately after breakfast, and with a hand supporting her head began reading the magazine. She read on until she felt sleepy and put the magazine aside to have a nap. When she awoke the rain was still coming down. And as she'd anticipated there had been no word from Nelson Reed. So she resumed reading again.

When Sam brought up her evening meal he inquired how she liked the magazine. "Have you enjoyed it?"

"Very much. I've almost read it through."

The dwarf walked over to the door, ready to leave. "The rain is letting up a little. But then I suppose the fog will settle in."

"Do you think so?"

"Usually does at this time of year, miss."

"It was foggy the other day," she recalled. "And at night as well."

"You don't call that fog! Why I've seen it so thick that police with flares have had to guide the buses in the streets. That's a true fog!"

"I believe such fogs are peculiar to London," she said. "We never had anything like that in the country."

" 'Tis the factory smoke, miss. It mixes with the fog and makes a pea-souper. When you experience one you'll be bound to remember it."

After he left she had dinner. Then she spent some time watching the street where traffic was a little heavier now that the rain was ending.

She was reading again when Sam came for the tray. When she finished the magazine she occupied her time pacing up and down listening to the revelry from the pub downstairs. She tried to reassure herself that tomorrow everything would be different. Tomorrow Nelson Reed would come to take her to some employer.

The next day it was bright and sunny again. She could not stand being in the small room any longer so she did go out to stroll along the street for a while. The fast pace and noise of the city was a little frightening to her but she felt better than if she had stayed up in her tiny bedroom. She studied the windows of a draper's shop and found herself tempted to go in and ask for work.

She also paused to stare at the wares of a millinery establishment, but it seemed to be doing so little business that she doubted if they would have any work to offer. She continued on back to the pub with a feeling of deep depression. Nelson Reed had shown his true character, a character that she'd always doubted, by cruelly deserting her. There was nothing left for her to do but contact the police in her desperation.

Just as she reached the doorway leading upstairs she saw a cab stop at the curb. Her heart gave a leap of hope, hoping Nelson Reed would emerge from it. But when the cabby opened the door it was not him but the painted, bedecked Irene DuBois who stepped out. On seeing Flora she came hurrying across the sidewalk to take her hands and kiss her on the cheek.

"My dear child!" the older woman exclaimed as she stood back to admire her. "How well you look! I was afraid you might not be here!"

Flora told her, "I'm not feeling at all well. I'm very worried. I've been waiting for Nelson Reed and he has not come."

Madame DuBois frowned. "Are you saying that he has deserted you?"

"I suppose it amounts to that. I think I made him angry the other night."

"Indeed?"

"Yes," Flora said unhappily. "I had no idea he would react as he did or I would not have mentioned the name of Mrs. Fraser."

"You mentioned that woman to him?"

"Yes. It was a mistake."

"I should think so!" Madame DuBois declared. "Well, you'll learn to be discreet one day, my girl."

"I didn't mean any harm," Flora protested.

"I can imagine," Madame DuBois said wryly. "The cab is going to wait for me. Shall we go in and have a drink at the pub?"

"If you wish," she said, not sure how she should act. Madame DuBois was generous but there was something about her that made Flora uneasy.

Once again they sat together in the ladies' lounge of the Plough and Sickle. Flora had her usual sherry while Irene DuBois drank whiskey. After their drinks were served the older woman eyed her speculatively.

"Nelson is very touchy about his liaison with Mrs. Fraser. I should have warned you."

"Why? He seems to have little enough conscience about anything he does."

The Madame smiled. "That is true! But you see, Mrs. Fraser is a wealthy woman whose husband is still alive and liable to cause trouble if there is too much talk."

"He said that Mr. Fraser was a drunken sot."

"He drinks," the older woman admitted, "but I'd hardly call that a fair description of him."

"It may be I'm doing Nelson an injustice. He may be ill and not able to come to me. The trouble is I don't know his address so I can't send a message to him."

"He is not ill," the woman across the table from her said. "I saw him last night at the gaming house where you and I first met. I asked him about you and he behaved strangely. He said you had returned to the country."

"An untruth!" she said indignantly.

"I suspected it," Madame DuBois agreed. "And so I made up my mind to come by here today and see if his story were true. And of course it wasn't."

"Why would he tell you that?"

"He clearly didn't want me to see you because he feared I might try to help you."

Flora asked despairingly, "Why does he want to punish me so?"

Madame DuBois shrugged. "You must know him well enough now to realize he has a cruel streak."

"True."

The older woman studied her closely. "Did that young man ever try to force his attentions on you?"

She blushed. "Yes. Once. But I reminded him that it was his friend, Horace Wright, who had promised to pay my bills. I threatened to tell Mr. Wright if he tried to take advantage of me."

"That must have gone down well with him," she said dryly.

"He became quite angry and upset, but he didn't misbehave any more. He once suggested that he might consider marrying me but when I mentioned that I knew about Mrs. Fraser he became enraged."

Madame DuBois sighed. "I can tell you, my girl, that you know very little about handling men."

"I'm not used to men of Nelson Reed's type."

"All men are his type," the older woman warned her. "Well, now the fat is in the fire and you are stranded."

"If you can give me his address or better still the address of Mr. Horace Wright I might be able to get some aid," Flora said.

"I don't know Horace Wright and even if I gave you Nelson's address I fear he will ignore your pleas for assistance."

"Then I must approach the police," Flora said desperately.

"You know where that could lead. You might wind up in a workhouse!"

"Workhouse!" she exclaimed. It was a word that terrorized most people.

"And what about your bill here?" the older woman asked.

"I don't know!" she said unhappily.

"But you are so naive! You fail to see that you have at least one stalwart friend to whom you can turn!"

"Who?"

"Me!"

Flora was amazed and embarrassed. "I can't ask charity from you!"

"It need not be charity," the older woman told her. "I'm willing to help you and I can find you a suitable post that will enable you to pay me back."

"You really mean that?"

"Of course. I did not want to interfere while Nelson was looking after you, but from the start I felt I could do much better for you."

"It never occurred to me!" she said gratefully.

"I shall pay your bill here and we'll pack your things. Then I'll take you to meet a dear friend of mine, Mrs. Fernald, who specializes in finding the proper sort of lady companions for her clients."

Flora was ecstatic. All her worries cast aside. "But that is exactly what I'm looking for!"

"One must never lose faith," Madame DuBois said piously. "I shall look upon myself as your guardian angel."

Had Flora not been so grateful and enthusiastic she would have noticed that any similarity between Madame DuBois and an angel would be detrimental to the accepted picture of angels. She said, "I promise I shall see you paid back every penny!"

Madame DuBois said, "I have no doubt about that. Not the least!"

"I was getting so depressed," Flora said, finishing her sherry.

Madame DuBois stood up. "You hurry upstairs and pack while I settle your bill with the owner of the pub. I don't want to be too late calling on Mrs. Fernald, as she usually takes a nap late in the afternoon."

Flora got to her feet. "It won't take me long at all."

On the way out of the pub she met Sam. He nodded to her. "You're taking a look at the city now the rain is over?"

"Yes," she told him. "I'm leaving today. I'm going to take a job. And I do want to thank you for your kindness to me."

The little man looked pleased. " 'Twas my pleasure," he said. "What sort of job are you taking?"

"I'm going to be a companion," she said. "Madame DuBois has been kind enough to refer me to a friend."

"You mean that one who just ordered the whiskies?"

"Yes. Why?"

"You know her well?"

"Yes," she said. "She is a friend of another friend of mine."

"I see," the little man said, looking relieved.

"Why did you ask?"

He hesitated. "To be truthful, miss, she's not exactly your type. She's a woman of the world if you know what I mean."

Flora smiled. "How right you are. Would you believe that she is the widow of a prominent French diplomat? And that surely makes her a woman of the world, doesn't it?"

"I suppose so, miss," he said looking uneasy. "Good luck to you!"

"Thank you. And if I'm ever in need of lodgings again I shall surely think of this place."

She went upstairs to pack her meagre belongings, including the tintype of her father, mother, and Uncle

George. There was a gentle rap on the door and when she opened it the Madame was there waiting for her.

"Are you ready?" the older woman inquired impatiently.

"Yes. I have my valise packed," she said. She put on her cloak, gave the room a farewell look, and went out.

Within a few minutes they were on their way to Mrs. Fernald's. Flora was beginning to be a little nervous again.

"I do hope Mrs. Fernald approves of me," she worried.

"Never fear," Madame DuBois said.

"What sort of lady is she?"

"She is a woman I have known for years."

"Then she has social position."

"She is of that opinion."

They were traveling through a section of London that was strange to Flora. She thought it a little more run down than where she had been. But then she was no judge of the city since she'd seen so little of it.

"Does Mrs. Fernald have a fine house?"

"She has a house. It does her very well. She is a woman of more modest ambitions than me, but we have had a long understanding."

"It is all so fortunate for me," she said. "When I'm well established in my new work I shall think of you."

Madame nodded. "Think kindly of me, my child."

The Madame purred and patted her hand. "You are such a sweet, wholesome creature."

"But please don't think of me as a stupid country girl. I'm sick of being looked upon as a country girl. I'm sure that is how Nelson saw me!"

"We shall create a new image of you," Madame assured her.

"I want to be more a city person!"

"And so you shall be," the older woman promised.

They drove on a little farther until they turned into a street of old houses, all seeming exactly alike. The cab went midway down the street and then halted before one of them.

"Here we are," Madame said with a jaunty air. "We shall soon have it all arranged."

"I can hardly believe it!" Flora said.

The cabby opened the door for them and they got out. Madame ordered him to carry Flora's valise up to the door and gave him instructions to wait for her. They mounted a tall set of stone steps and knocked on the plain black door at the top of them.

There was rather a long pause before the door was cautiously opened and an old crone peered out. Seeing Madame DuBois she appeared less cautious and wheezed, "Oh, it's you! The missus is expecting you!"

"I know that!" Madame DuBois said haughtily. And in a whispered aside she told Flora, "The maid is one of Mrs. Fernald's old retainers. She should have been dismissed long ago but my friend keeps her on. It is one of her failings, she is too kind-hearted."

"She must be like you then," Flora said.

They were marching along a narrow, dark hall that smelled of cigar smoke and stale perfume. Flora decided they must be going to the very rear of the big house. Then they suddenly came out into what was an ordinary enough parlor cluttered with rather cheap furniture. It was dominated by a large plaster figure of cupid with his arrow mounted on a wooden pedestal and a circular table with a rose-shaded lamp in the middle of it.

"So homey here!" the Madame said.

Flora was about to reply when from behind a curtained doorway the figure of a middle-aged woman appeared. She was wearing some kind of flowered kimono and her black hair was in curlers. But it was her face that astounded Flora. The woman had the grumpy features of a bad-tempered parrot.

"My dear!" Madame DuBois said with exaggeration and went over and pecked the woman on the sallow cheek.

The beak-nosed one had small, beady, suspicious eyes. She had them fixed on Flora at the moment. "Is this the girl?"

Madame had linked her arm in that of her friend's and

was now smiling at Flora. "But of course! Isn't she pretty? A true darling!"

Her friend continued to eye Flora grimly. "You don't know much about make-up, do you?"

Flora blushed. "I hardly ever use anything but a bit of face powder. Will my work require it?"

Madame spoke up. "Anything you need to know Mrs. Fernald can teach you!" She turned to her friend, "Maggie, this is Flora Bain."

Mrs. Fernald took a few steps over to her. "So you are George Bain's niece?"

"Yes."

"I knew him. He often used to come here."

She privately wondered what her uncle would be doing in such a place and with such a friend as Mrs. Fernald, but she felt it was necessary to be polite. She said, "You knew him much better than I, then. I didn't arrive until after his death."

"I would have been luckier if I could have said the same. Took a good bit of cash from me, George did."

She was alarmed to hear this. "I'm very sorry."

Madame came forward quickly. "That is of no concern to us now. Flora has come to you for employment. I'm sure you can find her something of the right sort."

Mrs. Fernald nodded gloomily. In a grudging tone she said, "She's pretty enough."

"There, you see!" Madame said with what was surely forced enthusiasm. "I knew she'd like you, Flora."

Flora said, "I'm willing to take any work offered. I'm willing to learn."

"Well, that's fair enough."

Madame asked, "Why don't we all have some cakes and some of your fine Chinese tea?"

Mrs. Fernald nodded somewhat irritably. "Yes. I guess it is time for afternoon tea."

"Don't let us put you to any trouble," Flora begged her.

"I always have tea and cakes at four. I'll go have Sally Ann prepare things for us." And she turned and left the room.

Madame came up to Flora and in a conspiratorial whisper said, "You have won her over! I can tell!"

"She doesn't seem all that enthusiastic."

"It is her way," the Madame warned her. "You have to learn to understand her. Don't judge her by her manner or her looks. She is quite an amazing woman. And her success in placing young girls in the proper positions can't be equaled in all London."

"I am impressed," Flora said. "But she is a very strange looking person, isn't she?"

"I know," the Madame whispered. "Looks exactly like a parrot. Don't let it bother you."

Their conversation was ended by Mrs. Fernald's return with the crone wheezing along behind her carrying a tray of tea and cakes.

"How nice this is," Madame DuBois gushed in what Flora felt was exaggerated praise. "It reminds me of the days when I used to entertain the diplomatic corps."

The two older women began to discuss friends of whom Flora had no knowledge. She sipped her tea, which had a rather bitter flavor. She assumed it was because it was a special kind of Chinese tea, and she knew that she didn't care for it. But to be polite she forced herself to drink it and eat a little of one cake.

Madame DuBois turned to her and said brightly, "Now we must discuss you."

"Thank you," she said, realizing the room was very warm and that because of her nerves she felt a little dizzy.

Madame turned to Mrs. Fernald. "Do you think you can place her, Maggie?"

Mrs. Fernald's parrot fact was solemn. "Oh, yes, I can place her. I can always find a place for a new girl," she said.

Flora tried to follow her words but didn't quite manage it. She felt the room swirling around her and with great dismay realized that she was going to drop her cup and plate, that everything would be spilled. She tried to tell Madame DuBois this but her mouth froze in an open position as everything went dark and she tumbled forward.

Chapter Six

FLORA OPENED her eyes and groaned. It took her several seconds to focus her gaze on the cracked and dirty ceiling. She stared at it stupidly, not yet fully awake to her surroundings. There was a dreadful throb in her head and her mouth was dry and parched. All at once her memory returned.

The weird tea party with Madame DuBois and her friend Mrs. Fernald! She recalled her apprehensions and then the moment when her head had begun to reel and she'd collapsed. Either she'd taken ill or she'd been drugged.

Drugged!

The frightening thought made her sit up too quickly and her head began to swirl again. She pressed her hands down hard on the cot on which she'd awakened and fought the nauseating giddiness. Gradually the room stopped moving about and she was able to make out the details of it.

She was in a small room furnished with two cots separated by a washstand. There was a single window high up and it was barred! The one door was a heavy wooden one with a kind of slot in it. Now the slot, which apparently opened on the outside, was closed; it was like a prison cell. The blankets on the bed were gray with dirt and there was no covering on the rough plank floor. She rose to her feet unsteadily and went over and tried the door. It was locked! As she stared at the window with its heavy bars across it, she realized she was a prisoner.

She began to pound on the door, crying out for someone to come and open it. But she knew as she kept on shouting that no one could hear her. The room was clearly far removed from the rest of the house and no one would be bothered by the disturbance she was creating.

After keeping up her clamor for a little while she felt weak again. Sitting on the edge of the cot, she quickly considered her situation.

Though she'd been brought up in a quiet country vicarage, she'd heard enough lurid tales about the city and its dangers to realize she was most likely the victim of professional white slavers. She could not imagine why she'd not been more alert about Madame DuBois and her offer of help. The dwarf, Sam, at the pub had hinted that he was suspicious of the painted Madame. Even then she'd not caught on.

As a result she'd walked straight into a trap. The more she thought about it the surer she was that Mrs. Fernald was running a house of ill-fame. All the signs had been present and she'd ignored them. In retrospect she couldn't imagine how she could have been so stupid. Tears of anger and fear welled in her lovely gray eyes.

Flora sat there limp with self-pity, but she knew that feeling sorry for herself was not going to solve anything. She would have to plan some practical means of defending herself against these predators. But how? She'd walked so far into their trap that it would not be easy. There could be no denying that she was faced with the most desperate kind of situation.

Whether Madame DuBois had worked in association with Nelson Reed or not, she couldn't guess. In any event the wily Madame DuBois had certainly been the main agent in the plot.

Nelson Reed had been openly startled when he'd first found her in conversation with the Madame. Probably he, along with all the others in the gambling house, knew what her profession was. The title of Madame was singularly apt, though it was very doubtful that she had ever been married to any Frenchman in the diplomatic service.

It was all like a hideous joke except for the fact she was now in dreadful danger. She had a feeling that the weird Mrs. Fernald was capable of almost anything.

She had heard of instances where innocent and pretty young women were forced into prostitution and reduced to debauched, gin-sodden, prematurely-aged wrecks. And now she might be threatened with the same fate. Mere resistance would not be enough to save her, as she could certainly be physically crushed by the forces of Mrs. Fernald. Whether her mind or spirit would be broken by such pressure was difficult to know. But very soon they would begin their moves against her and she would have to deal with them.

Her head began to feel a little better and she started to pace restlessly to relieve her nervous tension. It was at least an hour later when she heard footsteps outside the door of the room. The slide in the door was pulled back to reveal malevolent eyes studying her through the opening.

She stood before the door angrily and said, "I demand that you let me out of here at once!"

The eyes vanished from the slot a moment to be replaced by another set, which had a dull look. Marching close to the door she cried, "What kind of games do you think you're playing with me?"

The second set of eyes vanished and the first set appeared again. Then she heard Mrs. Fernald say in her harsh voice, "I have someone here with me for protection. If I open the door do you promise to behave yourself?"

"I don't think any promises are required on my part! You are the one who has betrayed me!"

The cold eyes in the slot stared at her unblinkingly as Mrs. Fernald warned her, "I can do what I like with you.

If you prefer to remain in there without food or drink we can try that for awhile. If you wish to be reasonable we can open the door for a nice little chat."

She thought rapidly. If she allowed herself to be subjected to starvation and thirst she would become weak and helpless, which would surely not place her in a more favorable position.

So she said, "You can open the door."

"You'll behave?"

"Yes," she said quietly and tautly.

The eyes vanished from the slot. "Open the door, Rufus. But watch out! She could be trying some game on us!"

A moment later the door was thrust open to reveal a big, burly man with a battered nose and face of an ex-prizefighter. His hair was matted on his forehead and he looked more like a sullen animal than a human being. He stood in the doorway so that she could not get past him.

Mrs. Fernald, still in her shabby kimono, stepped from behind him. She stood there with a grim expression. "I've made a sizable investment in you," she informed Flora. "It will be better for both of us if you do what I say."

Flora said, "How dare you lock me in here?"

"You came here seeking employment with me," the older woman told her.

"I didn't expect to be made a prisoner!"

"We have to be careful," Mrs. Fernald said.

"Careful?" she demanded. "What do you mean?"

"We must be sure we have the right type of girls!"

Flora pretended ignorance of what the other woman was saying. She asked scornfully, "What do you mean by that?"

"Our work is special."

"It must be!"

"You knew what it was when you came here," Mrs. Fernald accused her.

"I did not. Madame DuBois said you'd find me a position as a companion or governess!"

The woman smiled gruesomely. "You didn't really believe that?"

"I did!"

72

"Come now," Mrs. Fernald said. "Everyone knows the sort of house I run."

"I didn't."

"But you do now?"

"I think so."

"Then why not behave sensibly? You can do well with me if you use your head. If not, you can have a miserable time indeed."

She stared at the thin figure of the woman and the strong-arm man standing behind her. There was an implied threat in their glances.

Mrs. Fernald said viciously, "I paid Madame DuBois well for bringing you here to me. Now you must not disappoint me!"

It was too incredulous to believe. Wearily, she asked, "What do you want with me?"

Mrs. Fernald looked more like a parrot than ever. "I want you to be reasonable."

"What is reasonable?"

"You will do as I say."

Flora said impulsively, "Look, I'm not a vengeful person. I'll admit I was stupid in coming here as I did. But you were also wrong in not presenting things truthfully. We both have made a mistake. Let me go and I'll say nothing to anyone!"

Mrs. Fernald smiled maliciously. "I'd like to believe that story!"

"I mean it!" she insisted.

"You'll say nothing to anyone because you're not going to leave here."

"But you can't want to keep me cooped up in this room forever," she argued. "It doesn't make sense!"

"You're going to make a trip soon," the older woman informed her.

"A trip?" There was something in the mention of this which frightened her. Something implied!

"Yes," Mrs. Fernald went on coldly. "The likes of you are too intelligent to work in this country. You'd be bound to get us all in trouble. We make out best by sending your sort to France. They know how to deal with you there. And maybe after that they'll move you on to Italy."

"France! Italy!" she exclaimed. "I don't want to leave England."

"You've cost me plenty. I will send you where you'll be the most valuable. They'll like you across the channel!"

"No!" Her panic was increasing.

Mrs. Fernald nodded. "In the meanwhile you'll do best to rest quietly and make no trouble. I'll have your dinner sent up to you shortly."

The thin woman backed away from the door so that it could be slammed closed. Flora cried out for her to wait but she paid no attention. The door was locked and bolted again within seconds. There were the sound of footsteps retreating and Flora was left to lean against the door and weep alone.

Perhaps a half-hour later a bowl of soup and some bread were thrust in through the door. A jug of water was also included on the tray. Because she was now becoming really hungry, she decided to try the soup. She ate nearly all of it and wolfed down the bread. The water tasted good and was most welcome.

Rufus came back later for the empty tray. She tried to talk to him but he merely made motions for the tray and then slammed the door on her again. She had an idea he might be a mute but she couldn't be sure.

She sat on the edge of her cot debating whether there was any plan of action possible to gain her freedom. She had a small wooden spoon, a battered tin cup, the water jug and an ancient pail, along with two or three mean candles and a couple of matches. These were the only necessities with which the kindly Mrs. Fernald had provided her. None of them suggested usefulness alternately as a weapon.

She rose from the cot and went over to the one at the opposite side of the room. By standing on it she was barely able to peer out the bottom of the window. All she could see were rooftops and chimneys, which let her know that this house was higher than the majority of others and she was at the very top of it.

Darkness came and with it new tensions. Several times she heard eerie squeakings and rustlings. She finally fell asleep in a sitting position, frequently awaking with a start, and each time the room seemed a little colder. Her broken periods of sleep were tormented by nightmares.

When she awoke again it was morning. She heard heavy footsteps in the corridor outside, the door was opened and Rufus thrust in another tray with her breakfast of a dubious porridge, skim milk, and two stale buns. She knew she had to eat it to keep up her strength no matter what.

When he returned for the tray later again she tried to talk to him. And again he ignored her.

Her utter naiveté in allowing herself to be trapped like this continually tormented her. She blamed herself as much as she did the self-centered and cold Nelson Reed or the utterly devious Madame DuBois. She hoped that one day she might manage to confront her and turn her over to the police.

The day passed and she knew that soon Rufus would be coming again with her evening meal. She was seated on the cot in a mood of deep depression when she heard the footsteps outside again. But this time there was something new added. From the corridor she could hear a young girl's voice crying out angrily.

A moment later the door was thrown open and a short, brown-haired girl was literally thrown into the room. She let out a howl of rage as she stumbled forward and almost struck Flora. Then she turned towards Mrs. Fernald, who was standing in the doorway with Rufus, and directed a stream of angry words at her.

"You got no right to treat me like this!"

Mrs. Fernald told her, "You can consider yourself lucky. There are other ways to deal with your sort and you may yet find out about them if you're not careful."

"You don't scare me!" the girl howled back at her.

"Because you haven't the intelligence to recognize your danger," was Mrs. Fernald's reply.

"You promised me a proper job and this is how it turns out!" the girl cried, rage flooding her pretty freckled face.

Her hair was in two pigtails and she wore a very plain gray dress. She wouldn't be more than eighteen.

Mrs. Fernald turned to Flora, "You might try and calm down your new companion since you'll be making the journey to France together in a few days."

Having made this announcement she signaled for Rufus to close the door on her two prisoners. The girl hurled a string of foul epithets at the two as he did so. Flora quietly told her, "I don't think all that fuss is going to help you any." The girl stared at her with raised eyebrows. "All I can say is that you're taking it mighty cool. Do you want to join the life?"

"I don't want to join anything," she said calmly. "Nor do I intend to be shipped to France like a piece of merchandise!"

The girl was calming down a little. She kept staring at her. "You talk like a lady," she said. "Where do you come from?"

"I was brought up in rural Sussex," she told the other girl. "My father was a vicar there."

"Ow! A parson's daughter! Well, what do you know? I end up in fancy company! As well as in a bloody awful mess!"

"I'm sorry," she said.

The other girl threw herself down on the sofa and sat on its edge still gazing up at Flora. "Sorry, are you? Now that's going to do us a lot of good."

"Probably just about as much as your screaming."

The other girl sighed. "I guess you're right."

"Since we're in this together I think we should be friends," Flora suggested.

The other girl eyed her doubtfully. "You're not working for her? Pretending to be friendly with me to soften me up for what she wants of me?"

"No!" She shook her head. "Nothing like that. You must believe me! I was drugged and brought up here as a prisoner."

"I don't bloody well know who to believe these days," the younger girl complained. "I gave up me steady job as kitchen maid on the promise of a parlor maid's job with that old harridan you saw bring me in here just now!"

"Mrs. Fernald."

"Mrs. Humbug!" the girl said disgustedly. "I come here and she proposes that I become a very special kind of parlor maid. I told her I wanted no part of that. I'm a decent girl and I never heard such talk from an older woman's lips in all my life!"

"She's vicious!" Flora agreed.

"When I found out what my big opportunity was to be I told her she could keep it. I started to go out and that big plug-ugly came and blocked my way. Next thing I knew I was being dragged up here!"

"I heard you before the door was opened," she agreed. "You put up a good battle."

"Much good it has done me! Here I am locked up in a garret!"

"I'm sorry it happened to you," Flora said. "But I'm glad to have company."

The girl looked around her. "I should expect so," she said with a grimace. "It's not exactly the Buckingham Palace, is it?"

Flora gazed at the walls with their ripped, faded wallpaper and the miserable cots. "No," she said with a sigh. "It isn't."

The girl stared at her again. "You know, I think you are all right. I mean, you're telling me the truth."

"I should hope so."

The girl stood up. She extended a small, work-worn hand. "My name is Dolly Wales, late kitchen maid at Mrs. Wallis-Coldam's. Not much of a job I can tell you that. Still a good deal better than finding myself here!"

"I'm glad to know you, Dolly," she said. "I'm Flora Bain. I came to the city to live with my uncle, but he killed himself, and so I was left on my own."

Dolly's eyes widened. "Killed hisself! Lor! Sorry," she said. "I met this girl in a bar in the Strand and she tells me that I can improve my position in life. I asks her how and she says see Mrs. Fernald. She kept on going over that until it fair rattled through my head. See Mrs. Fernald, she said, and you'll find your life changed so you won't know it." Dolly grimaced again. "I have to say she was right. Look at me now."

"She must have been an agent for the woman," Flora suggested.

Dolly nodded. "The housekeeper at Mrs. Wallis-Coldam's used to always keep saying to us girls, watch out for the underworld women of the streets. They'll be looking for the likes of you, trying to enlist you in the Devil's band. And we'd laugh and make faces at her behind her back. I wish I could see her now and thank her. Not that it did me any good!"

"I was just as stupid."

"But I was raised in the city!" Dolly pointed out as if that made all the difference. "I should have known better. And I didn't! This girl was just about my own age and dressed in real finery. She paid for all the drinks until my head was dizzy. She said she had gotten her job through Mrs. Fernald and she would never know how to thank her enough. Her way was to get other young women on the same good road!"

Flora smiled. "It was really pretty obvious when you think about it."

"Now it is," Dolly said unhappily. "Then I thought it was my chance to get a parlor maid's job in a really fine household. She said Mrs. Fernald knew all the best people and I believed her. So here I am on the underground ready to be shipped to France!"

"Is that common?"

"You read about it all the time in the penny horror papers," Dolly confided. "Girls who are too stubborn to give in to them here are shipped to France where no one speaks their language and they can't escape to make any complaint. We'll both be goners once they ship us over there and the Frenchies get their hands on us."

"We mustn't let it happen!"

"With a barred window and the only door bolted I don't see us going far on our own!"

Flora sighed. "I know it does seem pretty hopeless."

"It is hopeless," Dolly lamented.

"I won't accept that," she said. "Not now that I have you here to help me."

"Don't expect much from me. After all, I got myself in here too," was the younger girl's reply.

"We'll think of something," she said. "We must!"

"How did you wind up in this place?" Dolly asked.

"It's a long story," she said. "It began with my uncle's suicide as I told you." They sat down on a cot together and she recited all the events that had led her to falling into Mrs. Fernald's trap. She ended with, "I think I was truly beginning to give up hope when you arrived. Now that I feel better, I must put all my effort in trying to escape rather than thinking about how I got here."

"Makes good sense," Dolly agreed.

"Mrs. Fernald only visits us about once a day. But Rufus comes three times with food."

"So he's the one we see most?"

"Yes. So we have to work it from there," she said.

The younger girl frowned. "If there was only some way we could get to the police."

"How?"

"I don't know. Bribe Rufus?"

"With what? And even if he'd do it on a promise of payment I don't know how you'd communicate with him. He's mute or acts as if he were. He may be deaf and mad as well."

"Bright prospect," Dolly said with disgust.

They kept on talking, trying to decide what to do until evening. Once again Mrs. Fernald arrived with Rufus, who now carried food for two on the tray.

Mrs. Fernald eyed them warily. "You've settled down very nicely," she observed sarcastically.

Dolly gave her a meek look. "Yes, ma'am," she said.

Mrs. Fernald sneered. "Hard to recognize you as the little wildcat who fought Rufus so!"

"I was fair upset," the brown-haired girl said, putting on a show of defeat.

"You are late coming around to good sense. You might have spared yourself a channel crossing if you'd behaved better."

"I see things in a better light now, ma'am."

"It will do no good," Mrs. Fernald said. "Your passage is arranged along with this other girl's. We'll see how the Frenchies take to you."

Flora took several steps towards the woman. "Isn't there anything we can do to make you change your mind?"

"You could have worked here! Much less trouble for me! But you wouldn't," Mrs. Fernald said vindictively. "Now it's on your own head!"

"I don't want to leave England," Flora protested.

"Nor do I," Dolly chimed in.

Mrs. Fernald smiled sourly. "Travel ought to be the very best thing for you!" And she went on out.

"Old biddy!" Dolly said, sticking her tongue out at the spot where Mrs. Fernald had stood. "You know what it is! She's had double the money from the Frenchies for what she paid for us. She will ship us over there and turn a fine profit."

Dolly glanced gloomily at the tray with their evening meal. "Let's eat this lot of leftovers," she said. "To think that I complained about the food at Mrs. Wallis-Coldam's. I wish I was back there in her scullery now. Live and die there I would to escape having this happen to me!"

After they'd eaten as much as they could manage they began to talk again. It was only natural that their conversation should mostly deal with escape.

"He'll be back shortly," Flora said. "Do you think I might try to communicate with him once again? Maybe he'll listen to me this time."

"No," Dolly said. "Don't count on it. He's wrong in the head. He looks like a pug who took too many beatings. He's not all there."

"Who else, then? We've appealed to her and it has done no good."

"No chance of that."

"What then?" Flora asked.

Dolly's small round face was wrinkled in thought. "We have to do it ourselves."

"Easy to say. But how?"

Dolly said, "Maybe if we sleep on it."

"With the rats bothering us all the time we can hardly get more than a half-hour's sleep at a stretch."

"Still, it needs sleeping upon," Dolly insisted. "That was what cook always did at Mrs. Wallis-Coldam's when she had a problem. She'd say, 'I'll sleep on it, girls.' And it nearly always worked out."

"I hope it does for us," Flora said bleakly, though she had small hope that it would.

Chapter Seven

THE NEXT morning Flora and Dolly were paid a surprise visit by Mrs. Fernald. Standing in the doorway of the tiny room, she told them, "Girls, you will be traveling tonight. I will be coming for you shortly before midnight, so I strongly suggest that you get some sleep during the day."

Flora gave her a pleading look. "Must we go?"

"It is all arranged," Mrs. Fernald said firmly. "In any case you may be better off over there. Some of the brothels in France are very well managed."

"The likes of you are bound to suffer," Dolly Wales cried angrily.

"I'll bring you cloaks when the courier arrives for you," she told them, ignoring Dolly completely.

The old woman went out and the door was bolted as usual. Dolly stood there the picture of dismay and Flora felt for the younger girl. Dolly had not even known the good years that she'd experienced at the vicarage. The younger girl had been a slavey all her life, and because she'd tried to better herself she'd been exploited by Mrs. Fernald's agent.

"We must do something!" Dolly sobbed.

She gazed around the room, having studied it so many times before without coming up with any solution. Suddenly she went motionless and her eyes fixed on the remaining candle in its holder on the commode.

"I have it!" she exclaimed.

Flora was at once alert. "What?"

"We'll set the place on fire! Burn down that vulture's sweet little nest of vice! And it won't be that easy for her to start over again!"

Flora was shocked. "Burn the place down?"

"Why not? We have the candle and matches, the blankets and the mattresses. That will get it started. I wonder I didn't think of it before. And once we get it started this old building will burn like tinder. It's just waiting for a match!"

"But if we start the fire in here we'll either be burned to death or smothered," Flora protested.

"Better that than be shipped to France for a brothel!"

"We don't have any choice," Flora agreed.

"And we needn't die in the fire. It's a matter of timing."

"Go on!"

"We'll wait until late at night. Just as soon as we hear any sounds outside we'll be ready with the fire. She spoke about bringing us up cloaks. It is my guess she'll check on us before the courier arrives. That's when we can get the blankets smoking good, and while she and Rufus are trying to put the fire out we'll skip by them!"

"It sounds wonderful!" Flora enthused. "Do you think you can really manage it?"

"I know how to raise a lot of smoke in just a few minutes," Dolly bragged. "I played a trick on the housekeeper once. She thought the whole place was ablaze and there was only a little smoke."

"We can touch a match to both cots," Flora said.

"The worst that can happen is that we destroy ourselves," Dolly said, "and that old vixen is out to destroy us in any case!"

"That's true!" Flora agreed. "You see, sleeping on the idea did bring results."

Dolly laughed merrily. "And you thought it wouldn't!"

In their desperation it didn't matter to them that the odds were as high as they could be. They were going to risk their lives for this tiny chance of freedom. For the balance of the day they worked out details. It was important that each understood the other's moves. They could not afford to fumble in this great gamble.

Rufus brought them their evening meal. They both knew that the next time anyone arrive to open the door it would be the signal for their plan to be put into action. Their tension grew as the evening went on. It was now dark outside and it wouldn't be long before Mrs. Fernald came to prepare them for their journey.

Dolly whispered to her, "Are you nervous?"

They were standing together in the center of the candle-lit room. Flora nodded. "Yes."

"Don't let your nerves spoil everything. We have to work together. Remember everything we planned."

"Yes."

"When the smoke gets thick be sure and hold onto my hand," Dolly said. "We mustn't get parted in the smoke or we'll not both get out."

"Yes," Flora said. "The main thing is that we don't get parted in the confusion."

Dolly went over to the candle and held up the two remaining matches. "We have these for a reserve. But we ought to be able to touch everything off with the candle."

"I wish she'd come," Flora said dolefully.

"I know," Dolly agreed, her pert little freckled face highlighted by the glow of the candle.

Their vigil went on for almost an hour longer. Then the moment they'd been waiting for came. The footsteps of Rufus and the old woman could be heard a distance away.

Dolly gave Flora a nod and then they both went to work. The blankets had been gathered up so that a bonfire could be made of each of them. Dolly touched off one and then the other. Then she applied the candle to the old mattresses. The mattresses had years of accumulated dirt and grease in them and went into flame at once. The tiny room filled with thick smoke. Dolly and Flora stood with hands clasped and wet cloths pressed to their mouths and noses to give them some scant protection.

Flora felt the intense heat and saw the flames billowing up from the cots. Unless the door was opened in a moment they would surely perish right there in the room. Vaguely she heard shrill screams from outside!

"Fire! Fire!" Mrs. Fernald was crying out in dismay. "Get the door open! I see smoke from in there! What have those two done?"

The smoke was so thick Flora could no longer see Dolly, although they were still holding hands tightly. The door burst open and old Mrs. Fernald stood there screaming.

"The fire! Put out the fire!" She was tugging at the arm of the ugly giant. But a strange frightened expression had come over his face and he turned and ran off. She screamed after him. "Come back! The place will burn down!"

But there was no question of his coming back and she must have known it. She plunged into the burning room and tried to pound out the flames on the far cot with the burning blanket.

Flora tugged on Dolly's hand and they both quickly slid out the door leaving the screaming old woman amid the flames. As they raced down the smoke-filled hall they knew from her frenzied cries that she'd been caught in the inferno and would die there before the old house collapsed from the raging blaze.

They reached a narrow, steep flight of stairs and stumbled down them. On the next landing there were loud feminine voices inquiring what had happened.

Flora and Dolly took refuge for a moment in a dark closet off the landing. As they braced against the wall with fear, they saw a half-dozen of Mrs. Fernald's girls in various states of undress racing up the stairs.

As soon as they vanished Flora and Dolly came out of their hiding place and hurried down the next flight of stairs. The smoke had now penetrated to the lower floors. They raced down the long, dark corridor which ran from the rear of the house to the front door. Flora was leading the way and when they reached the door she undid the bolts and threw it open. She and Dolly ran out into the street just as the clang of the arriving fire engines could be heard.

They fled across the street and found an alley from which they could watch without being seen. A number of men of all ages came running out the front door, taking off in all directions. Several of them were carrying their jackets and vests on their arms as if they'd dressed hurriedly.

The upper story of the tall old house was now wreathed in flames and the fire was gradually working downward.

Dolly squeezed Flora around the waist and laughed with delight. "Blimey, I wouldn't have missed this!"

The firemen in their gold helmets and red uniforms were a dashing sight. They quickly went to work to fight the fire. But it must have been evident that the best they could manage would be to contain the fire in the old structure.

The firemen were assisting the girls out of the house, the girls then huddling in a group on the side watching the blaze.

Suddenly Dolly said, "Look! Up there to the left!"

She did and in one of the windows she saw the head and shoulders of a giant man. "It's Rufus! He's caught up there!"

"The flames terrified him!" Dolly said.

Then there was a roaring as a floor collapsed and the giant vanished from the window as flames billowed out of it.

Flora said, "That's the end of Rufus!"

"And the old biddy died up there as well," Dolly exulted. "For once they took on more than they reckoned. We fixed them."

"Yes, we surely did," Flora said faintly. "I think we should get away from here now. Some of Mrs. Fernald's agents might spot us and try to get us trapped again."

86

"I doubt it," Dolly said. "But just the same we ought to get away from the area before the excitement dies down."

They left the alley and hurried down the street into the darkness. It was only when they were a distance away in a dark and deserted street that Flora realized their situation was still desperate.

"What can we do? Where can we go?" she asked.

"I don't know this part of the city," Dolly confessed.

"Are you cold?" She asked since neither of them had cloaks.

"Some," Dolly said, her teeth chattering.

"We must find some shelter," she said.

They began walking towards the river. Now a faint fog gave the night a ghostly air. Flora and Dolly clung close together for warmth and also because they were terrified that any moment some new threat might appear from the shadows. At last they reached the river bank and under the arch of a brick bridge they saw a tiny fire in the fog.

As they drew close enough to make out the details of the scene it proved to be a familiar one in the poor districts of London. Huddled under the arch on either side of the fire were perhaps twenty men. Most of them were asleep and stretched out on the ground though a few sat dozing dejectedly by the fire.

"Nothing but men!" Flora whispered.

"At least there's a fire," Dolly whispered back.

"But we can't go there!"

"We must!"

So they crept in quietly beneath the shelter of the arch and sat just behind a group of males by the fire. No one seemed to notice them and they spent the remaining hours of the night there clinging to each other.

Flora was relieved when dawn came. But now they were faced with new problems.

Flora watched as the men who'd spent the night by the fire got up and moved on. They were mostly derelicts in desperate physical condition, either through alcoholism or starvation. One of the older men came over to speak to them.

"You'll be wanting breakfast," he said with a trace of a Scot's accent. "There's a new mission down the street a distance that will take care of ye."

Flora got to her feet. "Thank you so much," she said.

The old man tipped his battered hat.

The girls left the shelter of the bridge and walked down the mean street the man had indicated. It didn't take them long to find the mission. Already there was a line at its entrance. Despite the fact this was a charity line there was a kind of jaunty air about the people standing there. They knew they were about to be received inside and given food and any other aid they might need. Flora felt they had the same joyous anticipation she'd sometimes noticed in crowds waiting outside a theatre to get in.

Dolly shivered. "I may have caught cold," she said.

"It was chilly," Flora agreed.

"Well, maybe we can get our bearings now," the younger girl said. "I may be able to get back to my kitchen maid's job if the mistress will believe my story. She'll be thinking I left without a notice!"

Flora smiled bleakly. "I'm sure I don't know what I'm going to do. My best hope would be Mr. Horace Wright, but I'm not sure where he lives."

"Then you're going to have a time finding him," Dolly predicted. "Probably there are two or three Horace Wrights in London. Maybe even more!"

"It's almost hopeless," she agreed.

The line began to move and they entered the mission. At the door a big man with a full gray beard greeted them. He had sad, haunted eyes and a kind manner.

"Food first," he chanted over and over again. "You'll find ample breakfast food on the table ahead."

They moved on and at the left ahead several young women behind a huge plank table were doling out gruel and bread and hot tea. They remained in line and received their helping, after which they moved to a table at the other side of the big room.

The hot gruel and tea made Flora feel much better. She noticed the dignified man who'd been at the door strolling over to them. With a friendly smile, he said, "We don't get too many young ladies of your age. I am glad to have you here."

"Thank you," Flora said. "The food is good."

"We try," the kind man said. "After breakfast we are having a short prayer service. You don't have to attend but we would be happy to have you."

Dolly spoke up. "Thank you, sir," she said. "We need to wash and clean up our clothes if we can."

He nodded gravely. "Yes. You can do that here. I'll put you in touch with one of our workers after the service."

Flora smiled at the man. He seemed like a very strong individual and she felt he had surely found his right calling in mission work. They finished their breakfasts and then joined most of the others in the rear of the big room while the man they'd talked with offered some prayers.

When the service was over most of the poor unfortunates shuffled out into the street. Flora and Dolly waited for the man to direct them to where they could wash up.

While they were waiting a tall, white-haired man with a kindly face passed by Flora. He halted and quickly turned around.

"My word!" he gasped. "It surely can't be Miss Bain! Miss Bain of Sussex!"

"It is," she said with a feeling of delight. "And you are Mr. Herbert Sweet, the man I met on the coach."

"That is correct," he agreed, looking astonished. "But what are you doing here? Why aren't you at your uncle's place?"

"It's a long story. If you care to hear it I'll be happy to tell you."

"Give me the highlights," he urged her.

And she did. She went over the whole story hurriedly and when she came to the part involving Madame DuBois and Mrs. Fernald she saw a shadow of anger cross his lined face. "We both barely escaped with our lives last night!"

He stared at her. "What experiences you've had since last I saw you!"

"That is so true," she agreed. "I have met people I

didn't think existed and had a taste of a world I had never been told about."

"Better that you shouldn't know about it," Herbert Sweet said grimly. "We know too well the Mrs. Fernalds of this old city. We have so often to deal with the human wreckage they create. Young women old before their time, their lives blighted with vice, disease, and shame."

Dolly said, "At least Mrs. Fernald and her house are gone!"

Flora said, "The gentleman who was at the door, the man with the gray beard, said we could remain here to wash up."

"But of course you must," her friend from the stage-coach said. "And I'm sure he'll want to help you both to the fullest extent after I've told him your story."

As he finished speaking the man they'd been discussing joined them. "Ah, yes, the two young ladies!"

Herbert Sweet said, "Sir, I know one of these girls well. She is a vicar's daughter from Sussex. She came to the city to live with her uncle only to find him a suicide. And from there on she has had a most remarkable set of experiences."

"Indeed," the tall, distinguished man said.

"Let me introduce William Booth," Herbert Sweet told the girls. "He is a man under whom I am glad to serve."

William Booth proved to be a man of great magnetism. He asked the girls their names and took them to an upstairs room where they met his wife. She supplied them with a tub, water, and soap to wash themselves and their clothes. She also arranged a change of clothing for them while their own things were drying.

When they returned downstairs in their borrowed clothes they were summoned to the private office of William Booth. He sat at a rolltop desk which was strewn with papers and motioned them to plain chairs.

Flora said, "I don't know how to thank you."

William Booth raised a hand to wave this aside. "No thanks are required. We are doing the Lord's work and that is no more or no less than any of us should be doing."

Dolly said, "Lor luv you, sir, you are a proper gent. We've been at the mercy of a she-Devil!"

He nodded, his sad eyes fixed on her. "So I've heard. I listened to your story with the greatest interest. The way in which you escaped convinces me you were never as much alone as you felt yourselves to be. Now you must justify your good fortune by leading good Christian lives."

Flora said, "I'm sure that is our aim. Though I'm not so certain how we'll go about it."

William Booth sat back in his chair. "Let me help you get a fresh start."

"That is too kind of you," Flora said.

Dolly gave her a reproving glance and in her outgoing way said, "Anything you can do we'll be grateful for, sir."

"I could use an extra young woman here. You might be ideal for the post, Miss Bain. You would be dealing with young women who have unfortunately fallen for the wiles of the Mrs. Fernalds of our city."

"Thank you," she said. "But I don't think I'm fitted for mission work. I assisted my father but I lacked his dedication."

William Booth listened to her gravely. "Well, you are honest and I give you great credit for that. And you should not engage in evangelistic work unless you have truly felt the call. So perhaps it would be better to have you take a post somewhere else as a governess or companion."

"I would like that very much," she said.

"And I'm a very good kitchen maid," Dolly intervened. "It would be first class if you could place me in the same household where Miss Flora is employed."

"That might be possible," he said. "I shall certainly try. I want you to remain at the mission overnight. We have a large dormitory for women upstairs and one for men down here. I have a gentleman coming by tonight who may be able to help you much more than I."

"You are extremely kind," Flora said. "When I met Herbert Sweet he told me he was joining you and that you hoped one day to form a united army to fight poverty, vice, and crime."

His sad eyes brightened. "I was originally a Methodist, Miss Bain, so I consider myself a very practical man. My evangelism is not rooted in Biblical analysis but in the practical application of Christ's teachings."

"And that is why you want to build a Christian army?"

"Yes," he said. "I think we need to organize strongly against evil. I have found that the evil organize very cleverly for themselves. I propose to create a series of colonies where the needy and destitute can be given useful work. This will reduce pauperism and vice."

"It sounds like an excellent idea," Flora agreed.

"Then we'd give attention to discharged prisoners and the reclamation of fallen women, not to mention the drunkards and all their problems. I say we need such an army and God willing I am going to work until I have founded it."

Dolly seemed enthralled by what he said. She spoke up, "Will you have a drum, sir? Every soldier needs a drum to march by!"

William Booth chuckled. "You are right, young woman. My army when it is formed deserves a drum to march by, and why not a band as well? A full band to lead our Christian soldiers!"

"A lot would follow just to keep in step and hear the music," Dolly predicted.

The man gave Flora an amused glance. "It seems to me your young friend has an inventive and lively mind which should one day raise her higher than her present station of life."

"I'm certain of it," Flora agreed.

"Well, I won't keep you here while I lecture any longer. Rest yourselves and be ready to meet my guest tonight. He is one of those who earnestly tries to make London a better place in which to live."

With this they left the small private office and went out into the main body of the mission.

Suddenly Dolly caught Flora by the arm and said urgently, "Over there! Look!"

"Who?" she asked, sensing her friend's upset.

"Standing by that table looking around. She's the one!

She's the one who took me to that Mrs. Fernald! She's here looking for us. She wants to pay us off for what we done!" There was fear in Dolly's voice as she clung to Flora.

Flora studied the hard-looking young woman with the painted face who Dolly had indicated. But the mission was full of this type of female seeking aid. She felt Dolly was being melodramatic.

She said, "I wouldn't worry."

"I can't help it," Dolly said. "Look, she's staring this way!"

Flora now saw the girl was right. The woman was staring at them malevolently. And suddenly she started across the room. "She's coming towards us!" Flora whispered.

"I want to run," Dolly lamented.

"We can't run," Flora said.

The woman was near them now and all at once Flora saw her reach in her handbag and whip out a short, gleaming knife. She bore down on Dolly, but Flora sprang between them to save her friend.

Chapter Eight

THE WOMAN cried out vengefully as she drove the knife into Flora. Dolly was shrieking with fear and heads were turning to see what was happening! Flora felt the hot, burning pain of the knife as it sank in the flesh of her shoulder. The woman turned and started running out of the mission. But by this time the watchers had sprung into action and she was blocked and grasped by several of the men who happened to be standing in the area.

The woman was screaming epithets at everyone as they led her away to the side room where William Booth had his office. Meanwhile Herbert Sweet and Dolly were bending over Flora, who had collapsed to the wooden floor.

Herbert Sweet had a cloth pressed tight against her wound to staunch the loss of blood. He promised her, "We'll have a doctor here in a few minutes."

Dolly was tearful. "She took the knifing I should have got! She did it to save me!"

Herbert Sweet said, "No matter! She'll be all right. And that vixen will be turned over to the police."

Flora, seeing how badly upset Dolly was, told her, "Don't worry about me. I'm going to be all right." Her voice was weak but she knew that she was mostly suffering from shock and a loss of blood. The wound had been a minor one.

Dolly said, "That was the one who worked for Mrs. Fernald. She meant to finish me, she did!"

Herbert Sweet agreed, "It's only a miracle that she didn't fatally wound Miss Bain."

William Booth came pushing his way angrily through the ring of onlookers. "Is she all right?" he asked.

"She will be," Herbert Sweet promised.

"Is there a doctor on the way?"

"Yes. I've sent somebody for the doctor," Herbert Sweet said. "What about the woman?"

"In the office crying now," William Booth said with disgust. "But I have sent for the police. Tears will not save her." He bent down over Flora. "I'm sorry this happened here!"

"Not your fault," she replied weakly.

"I always feel responsibility for anything that goes on here. We ought to have been organized so that an incident such as this could not happen. There must be a more complete check made of those coming in here!"

Dolly said, "I think she should be moved where it is more comfortable."

"You are right. Carry her up to the dormitory," William Booth instructed Herbert Sweet. "Place a screen around her bed so she may have some privacy. There are several screens against the wall near the door."

"Very good," Herbert Sweet said. And he told Flora, "I'll try and carry you gently."

He carried her up the stairs to a room that had at least twenty-four beds in it, set out in two rows. He placed her on one near the entrance, and while Dolly stood by to watch over her he found the screens and placed one around the bed.

He said, "I'm going down to wait for the doctor. But I'll return soon!"

When he left Dolly became loudly remorseful again. "It was my fault! I shouldn't have let you get between us."

Flora looked up with a wan smile. "I wanted to save you if I could. I was sure I could shove her aside and prevent anyone getting hurt."

"You oughtn't to have taken the risk!" Dolly said.

"I'm not badly hurt."

"No thanks to that one," Dolly replied angrily. "She'll be getting her pay in the prison."

Flora said, "At least we can be sure we broke up the vice ring to send her into such a rage. So we can be thankful for that and for being here in good hands."

Dolly wondered, "How did she know we were here?"

She said, "This is the only mission in this part of London. She'd think of it first."

Dolly nodded. "That's so."

"And we lingered a while watching the fire. Possibly someone followed us to the river. And when we left the bridge this morning they may have trailed us here."

"Or questioned one of that crowd that hangs out under the bridge," Dolly said. "I guess it was easy enough."

"Of course," Flora said. Her arm was paining and she wished that the doctor would come.

It was some time later that he did arrive. He turned out to be a brisk young man who went about his medical tasks with swiftness and dexterity.

After the doctor left, Dolly came back to stay with her. "The doctor says you must remain in bed until the morning at least. You are as white as a sheet and the floor was covered with your blood."

"I do feel weak," she admitted.

"I was down there when they took Mrs. Fernald's agent away. You should have heard her screaming! The police officer said he was coming back later to get a statement from you. He didn't want to interrupt while the doctor was here."

"I wonder how long she'll be in prison?"

"She tried to murder you," Dolly said. "I reckon she ought to be kept there until she knows better."

Just then William Booth came up to see how Flora was doing. "I'm sending one of my kitchen men up with dinner for both of you on a tray. You have special permission to eat up here."

"Thank you," Flora said.

"Not at all. And later on this evening my good friend and patron will be here. He has promised to come up and see you and discuss finding you a position."

Dolly said, "When will the police be back?"

"I would expect in the morning. They took that woman with them. I gave them most of the information they required and they took testimony from onlookers. They'll merely want Miss Bain's statement."

The head of the mission went back downstairs again and within a very short while a tall, gangling young man with a gaunt face and high-cheek bones came with a tray of food. His heavy head of brown hair flopped as he walked and there was a twinkle in his brown eyes.

He placed the tray on a table beside the bed and with a jolly smile asked Flora, "You feeling better?"

"Yes," she said.

"Me name is Shanks," he said. "I'm at your service. I used to be a dipper before I came here!"

Dolly, who was standing at the other side of the bed stared at him. "A dipper?"

The young man wobbled his skinny hands in the air making circles with them. "I was a pickpocket! That's what a dipper is! Then I saw the light and came here."

Flora stared up at him as he stood there beaming and waiting, she felt, to be complimented. She said, "I haven't heard the term dipper before either. It must be London street slang."

"Bloody talk of the town," the youth said airily. "I was well on my way to being a fine wirer when I gave it all up. More's the pity! But I'm doing a better work now!"

"What in the world is a fine wirer?" Flora asked.

The young man held back his head and laughed. "You two don't know nothing! A fine wirer is a pickpocket wot knows how to do it just right. And most of the time he steals from the ladies!"

Dolly eyed him with disgust. "And was that your ambition? To become a fine wirer?"

"I didn't know no better then. But I listened to that William Booth and I saw that there was a more useful way of life!"

Flora sat up and smiled at the young man. He was likeable but a very unusual type. The clothes he wore were shabby and didn't seem to fit him. He had a loose-jointed frame which made him look more like a floppy puppet than an ordinary human being.

She asked, "How long have you been here?"

"Almost six months now," he said happily. "And when William Booth forms his army I'm going to be an officer in it!"

"You an officer!" Dolly said scornfully.

"And why not?" he asked indignantly.

"There's no reason why not," Flora said quickly, not wanting his feelings to be hurt by Dolly. "I think it's a wonderful ambition."

He smiled broadly. "Thanks. Guess I'd better get along. There's always plenty to do here."

Dolly seemed unable to stop herself from picking on him. She asked him, "Where did you get that suit?"

"It's a bit of all right, ain't it?" Shanks said, apparently thinking she was going to compliment him. "I got it for a song in a jerryshop!"

"A jerryshop?" Dolly said.

"A pawnbroker's! You don't know much of anything!"

"I'd know better than to buy that suit. It looks as if the rats had chewed it!"

Hurt feelings and indignation showed on Shanks' face. "You're the flip sort of judy what causes trouble wherever you are. I know your sort. You ain't fit to associate with a proper lady like her!" And with a nod to indicate he meant Flora, he marched out of the dormitory and down the stairs.

"You shouldn't have talked like that to him," Flora told Dolly. "He's easily hurt."

"He thinks too highly of himself!"

"I don't think so," Flora said. "That's just his manner."

"Maybe."

"I'm sure of it."

Dolly smiled bleakly. "At least he thinks you're a proper lady," she said.

"I'm sure he'd approve of you too if you were half-way nice to him," she said. "I think he's a good type for evangelistic work and he may one day be an important helper of Mr. Booth's."

Dolly came around the end of the bed to set out their dinner plates. "Well, we have plenty of time to wait for that. Let's forget him and eat our dinner."

The food was plain but good. After they finished Dolly took the plates downstairs. When she came up again there was a smile on her face. She said, "I had a chat with Shanks. I think he's not so cross at me now. You were right. He's not half-bad!"

"I told you," Flora said, glad that the feud between the two was over.

Soon other women came upstairs to occupy the beds in the fairly large dormitory. Flora was glad for the protection of the screen which gave her some privacy.

Most of the women went to bed promptly, though some of them stood in a dark corner and gossiped for a little. Flora was tired. It had been many nights since she'd had a proper rest. Dolly also looked weary and excused herself to find one of the other beds.

Flora lay back and closed her eyes, but almost at once she heard male voices. She opened her eyes to discover William Booth standing at her bedside with a visitor. He was a stern-looking middle-aged man with prominent side-whiskers.

"Miss Bain, may I present a dear friend of mine, William Ewart Gladstone, the Chancellor of the Exchequer."

"How do you do," she said in a small voice. She had heard of William Gladstone. He was a leading politician in the Liberal Party.

"Charmed, I am sure," Gladstone said, extending his

hand to her. "May I sit with you a few minutes?" he asked after they had shaken hands.

"Please do," she said.

William Booth stood by with a pleased look on his face. "I have told Mr. Gladstone of your strange adventures which culminated in the attack made on you here today."

"A most remarkable story," Gladstone said.

"I feel lucky to merely be alive," she assured them.

"I can believe that," Gladstone said solemnly. "I know too much about the vice rampant in London and the fate of far too many poor girls. I have carried on a personal campaign against the Mrs. Fernalds and their agents for some years."

"Yes," William Booth said. "Mr. Gladstone often goes out alone at night and walks the streets seeking out women of ill-fame whom he attempts to reform."

Gladstone said in a sonorous voice, "Naturally my motives have been misunderstood. There have been a number of slanderous accusations made against me. But none of that bothers me if I can continue to save souls."

"Well said," the evangelist said. "I tell you that friend Gladstone has done more good in this city than you can imagine. He places these unfortunate women in institutions where they are taught an honest trade. Many of them go out into the world to good positions, and a majority of them make happy marriages."

"Which is precisely what I want," Gladstone said, compressing his lips until they were almost in a straight line.

"I never knew there was such a trade in vice," she said.

"There is much more than most respectable people are aware of," Gladstone said. "Every night I walk the streets I hear some shocking story."

"I came here quite naive and unprepared to be alone," she said.

"Mr. Booth has told me about your coming to join your uncle and of his suicide. Most unfortunate!"

She said, "For a short time I was helped by two of my uncle's friends. Would you know either a Nelson Reed or a Horace Wright?"

William Ewart Gladstone frowned. "Young Nelson Reed

100

is a thorough blackguard. You must have heard that his father threatens to completely disinherit him."

"No."

"It is true. The old man is a member of my political party and a fine, upstanding man. He is shamed by the behaviour of Nelson and he has not bothered to conceal the fact."

"What about Horace Wright?"

"The railway promoter?"

"He is an older man."

Gladstone nodded. "That is the one. I know that he has been very busy trying to raise money to set up railroads."

"He is a rather portly man but very nice," Flora said of Horace Wright.

"I would say a first-rate fellow," Gladstone said in his pleasant voice.

"Had he not been called to Liverpool on business I'm sure I would not have found myself in this state."

Gladstone agreed, "I'm sure he is a dependable person. The thing now is to find you a good post. I have a friend living on the outskirts of London who recently lost the governess to his ten-year-old daughter. He asked me to suggest anyone I might think of for the position. Until now I had not come on any name. But with your permission I should like to offer yours to him."

"It sounds exactly the sort of thing I'd been hoping for," she said eagerly.

"Then I shall talk to this man tomorrow," Gladstone promised her.

"There is my friend," she said hesitantly. "A girl I met along the route of my adventures. I would like it if I could find a post for her in the same house. She has had experience as a kitchen maid but I believe her capable of performing most household tasks."

Gladstone raised his eyebrows. "Well, I can speak to my friend. He does have a large household and a good-sized staff of servants. It is quite possible there may be another position vacant."

"Thank you," she said.

"But whether I can find a post for this other girl or not you are interested in becoming a governess?"

"Oh, yes!"

"Good!" Gladstone looked pleased. "You have no taste for evangelistic work?"

"I'm not certain I have the calling," she said.

"Your father was a clergyman."

"Yes. That makes me more aware of what the profession entails," she said.

He stared past her into the shadows. "There is many a night when the fog is thick and the frost heavy that I would prefer to retire to the comfort of my bed. But my urge to try and reach the lost women of London drives me into the streets."

She said, "Mr. Booth appears to think your work well worthwhile."

"I do what I can," Gladstone said. "Sometimes the women shy away from me in shame and I have to be the one to accost them. But always I offer a message of hope and the opportunity to reform. So far I have had a most gratifying response."

Flora said, "It is a terrible feeling to be trapped and locked up at the mercy of a Mrs. Fernald. She was shipping us overseas to a French brothel."

"Hundreds go that dreadful road," Gladstone said grimly. "A slaughter of the naive and stupid. These monsters even traffic in mere children! I would not want you to hear some of the stories I have been told!"

She could tell the politician was shaken by what he had learned about the vice markets. In a low voice, she said, "I shall never forget the ordeal that my friend and I went through."

Gladstone's manner changed, he lost his abstract mood and once again directed himself to her. "You will go on to a new and better life, I promise you."

"I hope so."

He smiled one of his rare smiles. "Perhaps you will never again enjoy the tranquility that you knew in that vicarage in Sussex. But I can promise you if I'm able to secure you the position at Armitage House it could be a happy new beginning."

"Armitage House," she said.

"Yes. Named after the family. The man whom you'd be employed by is Henry Armitage. He is a widower with an only child to whom he is much devoted."

"A little girl?"

"Yes. I believe her name is Enid. Her grandfather lives in the house. He is also a widower; his wife died long years ago. And there is also her aunt, Henry's sister. An interesting family group. The old gentleman has given up any active part in the business and Henry Armitage is thus the one responsible for the family's fortunes."

"What business are the Armitage family in?"

"The China trade," Gladstone said promptly. "Their firm probably does more business with the Chinese than any other in all England."

"It sounds fascinating."

"Their house, just outside London, where I have frequently been a guest, is full of priceless Chinese antiques," Gladstone went on. "Few people in this country appreciate the importance of China." Gladstone rose. "Well, I have talked enough. I shall do what I can for you about this post. And I shall let Mr. Booth know how I make out."

"Thank you so much," she said.

William Booth, who had left them for awhile, was now back. "I can see that you two have had an enjoyable talk."

"Most enjoyable," Flora said.

"And profitable too, I trust," Gladstone said with meaning.

The two men bade her good night and left. Flora lay back on her pillow filled with new hope. Armitage House sounded very grand and the people in it were undoubtedly very special. She pictured them as cultured and dedicated to their business interests. It could be a most stimulating place to work. If only Mr. Gladstone could interest them in her. And hopefully in Dolly as well. She went to sleep filled with these thoughts.

The next morning her shoulder was very stiff and sore

but generally she felt better. Dolly joined her early and once again the lanky Shanks brought up a meal for them. He was just as full of bounce at breakfast as he'd been at dinner time.

He said, "What a lot we have downstairs this morning! You should see them! We've palmers and patterers and skippers galore!"

Dolly raised her hands. "Wait! Wait! Just what are palmers and patterers and skippers?"

Shanks gave her an amused look. "I forgot you ain't acquainted with the Queen's English," he teased her. "Palmers is shoplifters, patterers do sales talks on the streets and sell fake goods, and skippers don't have nothing to do with the sea—they are tramps who sleeps in hedges and outhouses!"

"I don't know how anyone can tell what you're saying," Dolly said with amazement.

He wobbled his free-wheeling hands. "All the crowd downstairs talks the same lingo."

"Then it must be a regular Tower of Babel," was Dolly's wry comment.

Shanks turned his attention to Flora. "You going to get down below today?"

"I hope so," she said. "I'm sick of being an invalid. I'd like to do something to help."

"We've got a line all the way down the street for soup," he said. "They sleep on the embankment and then head for here first thing in the morning."

"Aren't there any lodgings for the very poor?" Flora asked him.

He shrugged. "There are packs and padingken's. But neither of them offer much you can't get outside. And in them you run the risk of being robbed as well. Robbed even for a ray, that's one and sixpence, or less!"

Flora said, "Living outside the law is really very hazardous then. Aren't you glad you've given up crime?"

The loose-jointed youth pondered this. "Yes, miss, I think so. But I would have liked to have gotten to the top of me line before I did. You always has regrets!"

"I wouldn't regret not being a pickpocket," Dolly told him.

He said, "Well you never were part of it. That's why you don't understand: But I'm happy here! I like what I'm doing and I wouldn't go back to picking pockets for any kind of money!"

Dolly said, "That's what I like to hear!" She sounded a little more enthusiastic.

After breakfast Flora made Dolly take down the tray. While her friend was gone she rose from the bed and dressed herself. Her own clothing had been returned after being washed and ironed. She had to dress slowly because of her stiff arm but she managed. She even somehow made her hair look halfway decent.

When Dolly returned she stared at her in shock. "The doctor didn't tell you that you could get out of bed!"

"I told myself."

"But you shouldn't have!"

"Why not? I'm much better and staying in bed is weakening."

"They'll all be angry and they'll blame me," her friend lamented.

"I won't allow that," Flora promised. "I'll let them know that it is my own doing."

After a short argument they went downstairs. As Shanks had told her it was a busy morning. The mission was filled with a new group of the destitute. She looked at the many ravaged faces and felt a great pity for these derelicts. She made her way to the table where volunteers were dishing out food to the latecomers.

Herbert Sweet was overseeing this effort, and when he saw Flora he came hurriedly over. "Were you given permission to get up?"

"No. But I felt better," she said with a smile.

Herbert Sweet looked worried. "I can't think what Mr. Booth will say."

"He won't mind as long as he knows I'm well enough to get about."

"I hope not."

"I'd like to do something to help."

"Not until you've asked Mr. Booth," was Herbert Sweet's firm reply.

"Where is he?" she asked.

"In his office."

"Then I'll ask him at once."

She made her way through the crowded room. The air was heavy with the smell of the many dirty bodies and cheap liquor. She felt for a moment that she might faint. Her head began to reel but she fought back the feeling.

The door to William Booth's office was only partly open. She rapped on it and in a moment his stern voice bid her enter. Somewhat hesitantly she went into the room and found that Mr. Booth had a visitor.

He showed mild surprise on seeing her. "I thought you were still in bed."

"I felt better and came down," she said. "I'd like to do some easy task which I can manage with my right hand."

He looked impressed. "I admire your spirit," he said.

"No one will let me do anything without your giving permission," she explained.

"I see," he said. "Well, I can do that later."

"I wish you would."

"Just now, I'm glad you're here. I was going to bring this gentleman up to talk to you."

"Oh?" She stared at the man and saw that he had an ordinary, red-blotched face.

"This is Inspector Craig of Scotland Yard. And this, Inspector, is Miss Flora Bain, the young woman who was stabbed by that streetwalker."

Inspector Craig was on his feet now and all business. "Happy to meet you, Miss Bain," he said. "I'd like a short statement from you and a description of your attacker."

"Anything I can do," she said.

Inspector Craig was writing laboriously in a little book. "You knew who this woman was?"

"My friend recognized her first," Flora said. "She knew she had been an employee of Mrs. Fernald's."

The inspector nodded solemnly. "Yes. The same Mrs. Fernald who kept the sporting house on Mavor Street which was burned to the ground. The lady also lost her life in the fire as did several others."

"I know," she said with a shudder. "It was awful."

"So in your opinion the young woman attacked you out of revenge?"

"Yes. I'd say so. She didn't really attack me. It was my friend Dolly Wales she tried to stab. I stepped in the way to stop her and she drove the knife into me."

"I have all that," the inspector said. "There is one other point."

"Yes," she said, suddenly feeling that the police inspector was about to make some startling revelation because of the tone in which he spoke.

Inspector Craig cleared his throat awkwardly. "There can be no question that this young woman criminally attacked you and should be punished for her crime. Unfortunately while on her way to jail she escaped with another prisoner and is now at large. I fear you may be in some danger."

Chapter Nine

"SHE IS free!"

"Unfortunately, yes," Inspector Craig said with a grim look. "Came about quite unexpected. We lose one or two of them every now and then."

William Booth showed concern. "What are the chances of her being picked up again?"

"Very good, sir. We usually find them before too long. But in the meanwhile Miss Bain and Miss Wales are in danger, not only from the girl herself but from any of her pals whom she might send here.

William Booth frowned and stroked his long gray beard. "What you say is true."

Inspector Craig suggested, "Would you have any other place to send the ladies?"

"Let me see," he said. "Yes, I think I can solve this. There is a good lady who has been a patron of the mission and who has offered additional help whenever we might need it. If I call on her I am almost sure she would give

Miss Bain and Miss Wales safe shelter until they can be placed in proper positions."

Flora gave him an apologetic glance. "I'm afraid I'm a terrible bother."

"Not at all," William Booth said as he came over to stand by her. "This woman escaping is no fault of yours. We must see you have protection and guard against any other incident of violence taking place here."

"Exactly, sir," Inspector Craig said. "It would be best for all concerned if this young lady could be removed quickly and kept somewhere these criminals wouldn't think of looking for her."

William Booth nodded. "You can consider it taken care of, Inspector. And I would like a report from you concerning the escaped prisoner. Let me know when she is captured."

"I'll keep you in touch, sir," Inspector Craig promised. "Well, I must be on my way now." He bowed to them and left.

As soon as the inspector left the room William Booth turned to Flora. "I'm going to write a note to the lady I mentioned and then see you and Miss Wales are taken to her. Mr. Sweet will accompany you to see that you are safe. While I write sit down here for a while. With that girl free I don't think you should expose yourself in the main room for any length of time. Better to stay out of sight."

"Very well," she said quietly, and seated herself on one of the plain chairs. She watched as he composed the letter to the lady he'd mentioned. When he finished he sealed it and stood up. "I'm going to summon Mr. Sweet now and have him take you to the home of Mrs. Weatherbarrow. You will find her a kindly lady, perhaps a trifle odd, but her heart is surely filled with Christian kindness."

"Thank you," she said, rising.

"Come with me," he said and led her back into the main room.

The room was not quite as filled now and they made their way over to Herbert Sweet without any great difficulty. William Booth at once explained to his assistant what he had in mind. "I think you should leave at once."

Herbert Sweet turned to Flora. "I shall be glad to see you in a proper home for a while."

"I'll get Dolly," she volunteered. "Then we can start on our way."

William Booth extended his hand to Flora. "I wish you all good fortune, my dear. I shall tell Mr. Gladstone where you are so his friend will know where to reach you."

"I don't know how to thank you, Mr. Booth. I can only promise I shall always be grateful to you."

He smiled. "No need. It is all part of our work."

She left the two men discussing the best route to take to Mrs. Weatherbarrow's. It took her a moment to locate Dolly. She saw her friend talking with a worn-faced woman at the far end of the mission.

Hurrying down to her, she told her excitedly. "We're leaving!"

Dolly turned from the woman to whom she'd been chatting and stared at her in surprise. "Leaving?"

"Yes," she nodded. "We have to. Mr. Booth has arranged for us to go to the home of some woman."

"Why?" Dolly wanted to know.

"It's a long story," she told her. "That girl who tried to kill you escaped from the police. They're afraid she might come back here for another try or send someone else after us. Mr. Booth and the police feel it best that we shouldn't be seen here."

"Lor! I should think not!" Dolly wailed, alert now to their danger. "Stupid it was of them to let her get away like that!"

"They expect to arrest her again but they don't know when," she said. "Meanwhile we're in danger. So Mr. Sweet is taking us somewhere."

"Right now?" Dolly asked.

"Right now," she said.

They started up the long room to join Mr. Sweet only

to be met along the way by Shanks, who came dancing up to block their path with a mischievous look on his face.

"Hear you two are going," he said.

Dolly's round face took on a smug expression. "Yes, and I'll venture you're glad to see the last of us!"

"No," the boy said, serious at once. "No. I'll miss you."

Flora smiled. "Thanks. We'll remember you and all your strange talk. You know a lot of wonderfully different words, Shanks."

Shanks laughed. "Maybe we'll meet again!"

Dolly teased him. "And you can teach us some more of the Queen's English!"

"You can bet on that! When I finish with you I can vouch you'd be able to tell the difference between a stock buzzer and star glazing!"

"Now that's really too much!" Dolly said. "You are showing off again!"

"We must be on our way," Flora told the youth. "I hope you go on working with William Booth and when he founds his army you do turn out to be an officer in it."

Shanks' eyes were bright. "That's my plan! And good luck to the both of you. And so you'll know, a stock buzzer is a handkerchief thief and star glazing is taking out a pane of glass to rob a house. I don't want you two leaving here in ignorance!" And he laughed again as they moved on.

Dolly's round, pretty face was crimson with annoyance. "Him and his talk!" she sputtered.

Flora gave her a sly glance, "No matter what you say, I think you really like Shanks!"

"Me like him? I should say not!" But there was a hollow note in her protest.

Herbert Sweet in black top hat stood waiting for them by the front door. He asked them, "Do you both have bonnets?"

"No," Flora said. "I'm afraid we've lost the ones we had."

"I can't walk you through the streets of London without bonnets. We'll see what they have here." And he went to ask the stout woman in charge of clothing. She at once opened a large wicker basket, rummaged in it for a few minutes, and produced two rather battered bonnets.

He came back to Flora and Dolly and held out the bonnets. "Take your pick," he said. "Not that I can see there is any."

"I'll take the plain blue one," Flora decided, selecting the tiny blue bonnet.

Dolly showed pleasure. "Am I to have the one decorated with the daisies?"

"So it seems," Herbert Sweet said with a grave smile.

She put it on and tied the strings under her chin. Turning to Flora she asked, "Now do I look like a proper toff?"

"Your bonnet suits you," Flora assured her. "You look ever so much better with it on."

Dolly touched a hand to it to adjust it delicately. Then with a swagger she said, "I'm ready for the street!"

Dolly's antics drew attention from those standing by and Flora was relieved when they went out to the street.

Herbert waited anxiously by the curb with them at his side. He kept his eyes fixed on the several omnibuses that went clattering by and finally he hailed one with great yellow letters on its sides. There were just two hard board seats running the length of the omnibus and facing each other. The passengers already seated pushed closer together to make room for them. Dolly and Flora sat side by side and Herbert found a place opposite them. They swayed with the motion of the vehicle and felt each bump of the cobblestoned streets. The driver kept the horses moving at a smart pace, halting only occasionally to let a passenger off or to pick one up.

Herbert Sweet finally motioned to them. "This is our stop, girls!"

They descended from the bus to find themselves in a much better neighborhood. It was a street of pleasant little brick houses, all vine-covered, with white-painted doors and yellow chimneys. Though the houses were identical on either side of the short street, they were all well-kept and there was an air of affluence about them.

"Where are we?" Dolly asked.

"Upper Trane Street," Herbert Sweet told her. "This is the street where Mrs. Weatherbarrow lives. She is a rich widow and you mustn't mind if she seems a trifle strange. She is a very good person who dispenses a great deal of charity."

Flora recalled that William Booth had made a similar assertion about the woman they were going to stay with and she was curious to know what it might mean. Mrs. Weatherbarrow was a little odd! But in what way?

In an effort to find out she asked, "Do you know her well, Mr. Sweet?"

He glanced down at her. "Not really. She comes to the mission occasionally but she spends most of her time with William Booth."

"Here we are!" he exclaimed, halting before one of the houses and preventing her from asking any further questions. He took the letter William Booth had written from the inner pocket of his jacket and mounted the several brick steps. Flora and Dolly hovered behind him.

Flora watched him lift the heavy brass knocker on the door to announce their arrival. They waited for several seconds and then the door was opened by a thin, sour-faced little woman in a maid's uniform.

"Yes?" she inquired in a querulous voice, eyeing them all in a suspicious manner.

"I have a letter for your mistress. It is from William Booth. Would you kindly take it to her?" He handed the woman the letter.

She took it with a hesitant air and asked, "Are you waiting for an answer?"

"Yes," he said. "These young ladies and I will wait."

"Very well," she replied and she withdrew, closing the door on them.

After a few minutes the door was flung open by a buxom woman in a black dress with black hair, obviously dyed, parted in the middle in the fashion of Queen Victoria. She also had the pouting face of the queen, though she was a good deal older and had double chins.

"How dreadful that you should have been kept waiting

out there!" she exclaimed. "Do come in, Mr. Sweet, and bring the young women along."

She showed them down a dark hallway to a large parlor with partly drawn drapes on the windows that kept it in shadow even on this bright morning.

When they were seated she said, "I have William Booth's letter and I shall be happy to have these young women remain with me for a few days. I have told William that I am always ready to help in any way that I can."

Mrs. Weatherbarrow addressed herself to Flora. "What a terrifying experience you have had, my dear."

"It was frightening," she agreed. Thus far she had not noticed anything too eccentric about the woman.

"And for you," Mrs. Weatherbarrow said, turning to Dolly.

"Yes, ma'am," Dolly agreed. "It was a fair horror, it was!"

"Well, you'll both be quite safe here. I have small rooms for you and you can remain until you are able to find employment. I think it most impressive that William Ewart Gladstone is interested in your case. He is a fine man and a rising politician."

"One of our firm supporters," Herbert Sweet informed the woman. "Though I must say we have no better one than yourself."

Mrs. Weatherbarrow smiled, "But then my contribution is not all that important. I'm not as eminent as dear Mr. Gladstone."

"All the same, William Booth is deeply appreciative of the many things you have done. Since all is settled here I must return to the mission. Every extra pair of hands is needed there."

Mrs. Weatherbarrow got to her feet. "Tell William Booth the girls are welcome. And I shall be visiting the mission again next week."

The tall man nodded. "Thank you." He turned to Flora. "It seems we are about to part again. This time I hope you have better luck."

She and Dolly had also risen. With genuine gratitude

she told him, "I can never thank you or William Booth enough."

Dolly said her thanks also, and then Mrs. Weatherbarrow accompanied him to the door. While the girls waited for her return they took in the details of the parlor. The most noteworthy thing about it was the portrait hanging over the fireplace of a thin, austere-looking man with a bald head. His face seemed to dominate the room. Flora saw that it was draped in black crepe to suggest mourning.

She whispered to Dolly, "That must be a portrait of her husband. Judging by the black crepe he surely has died recently."

Dolly's young face wore an awed expression as she studied the portrait. "He's a rum-looking cove," she observed. "Don't imagine he ever smiled in his life!"

"Careful!" Flora admonished the younger girl as she heard Mrs. Weatherbarrow's heavy footsteps advancing along the hall.

The widow came in to join them a moment later and seeing that they were standing under the portrait, she said, "My dear, late-lamented husband, Charles!"

Flora said, "We were just admiring the portrait."

"Exactly like him," the widow said staring at the painting and sighing.

"Did he die recently?" Flora questioned her.

"It seems recent to me," the buxom widow said. "Charles died ten years ago at Whitsuntide."

Flora was startled. She knew that mourning was carried on for some time but she'd never known a case like this. Charles Weatherbarrow might have died only a few days earlier from the air of sadness shown by his widow and the mourning tokens.

The next moment Mrs. Weatherbarrow said, "This evening we shall all sit here together and I'm sure that Charles will have a message for you."

Dolly's mouth gaped open and she glanced up at the portrait. "A message from him?"

"But of course," the widow said. "Surely you have had some experience with the spirit world?"

"No, ma'am," Dolly said nervously.

115

Trying to save a difficult situation Flora at once spoke up. "Neither Dolly nor myself are old enough to know much about such things."

The widow nodded gravely. "I can understand that. We think more of death as we grow older. I have constantly investigated the spirit world since Charles' death. And now I'm able to reach him. He sends me the most interesting messages."

"Really?" Flora said in a small voice realizing she had not up until now guessed the full extent of the widow's eccentricity. She did not dare look at Dolly to note her reaction.

"You shall find out for yourself tonight," the buxom woman said pleasantly. "I find myself close to Charles during the twilight hour. But enough of that. I will show you to your rooms."

The rooms were small, the beds narrow but clean, but Flora knew they would be safe from danger in the quiet house. As soon as Mrs. Weatherbarrow left them Dolly came to join her in her room with a frightened expression on her pretty face.

"Did you hear what she said?" the younger girl demanded.

"I did," Flora said. "Herbert Sweet warned me she was a little odd but it's nothing to be frightened about."

"You think not?" Dolly worried. "It fair gives me goosepimples to think about what she said."

"Don't show your fears," Flora advised her. "We need shelter here until Mr. Gladstone sends his friend to get us."

They spent a quiet day in the little house. When dinner was served they sat at the table with their benefactress in the oak panelled dining room. And as soon as the meal was over she again brought up the subject of talking with her dead husband.

Smiling at them from her place at the head of the table, she announced, "Soon we shall gather in the living room and learn what Charles has to tell us. Are you excited?"

"It sounds thrilling," Flora said politely while Dolly sat there looking stunned.

Mrs. Weatherbarrow sighed. "Now that the dear queen has been bereaved I'm certain that spiritualism will become more accepted in our land. I cannot conceive of Victoria not attempting to reach the spirit of her dear, departed Albert!"

"Do you think that possible?" Flora asked.

"If she believes as truly as I do," the widow said. "I have written her a letter of condolence of course, but more importantly I have described in my letter how I have kept in touch with my own Charles. I hope that she will take heart and follow my example."

They were then marched into the parlor which was now in almost complete darkness as the drapes had been fully drawn. The sour-faced maid came tip-toeing into the room and set out burning candles at various strategic places.

Mrs. Weatherbarrow, dominant in her black dress, brought out a small table and set it before her favorite chair. "Now do sit here with me," she bade them.

They sat in the plain chairs placed before the table and waited. The widow sat down and produced a three-cornered wooden object on tiny legs. "Do you know what this is?" she asked, placing the wooden object on the table top.

"No," Flora said truthfully.

"It's a ouija board," the widow said triumphantly. "An invention of the French, a most amazing race! You and I shall place our hands on the pointer, Flora, and then the spirits will move it to spell out a message. You see the letters marked on the table top."

Flora strained to study the rows of black letters in the indifferent light. "I do now," she said.

"You may join us later," the widow said to Dolly. "I want Flora to share this experience with me first."

Flora found herself trembling in the eerie atmosphere of the candlelit room. Looming above them in the shadows was the stern face of the man from whom they were supposed to get a message from the grave.

The widow said, "Place your hands on the pointer with mine."

She obeyed, not wanting to refuse the woman who was showing them such kindness. As her fingers interlaced with those of the older woman she found the widow's flesh cold and clammy. This made her shiver again.

Mrs. Weatherbarrow's pale face peered at her in the darkness. "You are frightened!" she said.

"I am nervous," she said.

"You mustn't be," the widow warned her in a low voice. "Just free your mind of every thought. Let it remain open."

Flora tried desperately to obey but found it difficult. She kept wondering how far this eerie experiment would go and what the outcome of it would be. She also worried about poor Dolly, who was so awed that she'd lapsed into a motionless silence in the chair at her side.

The widow intoned, "Charles, are you there?"

There was a deep quiet in the dark room. Flora was conscious of the beating of her own heart.

"Charles!" the widow called her husband's name, in almost a wail. "Charles, do you have a message for Flora?"

Again there was a period of waiting. And then a sharp chill shot through Flora as she realized the pointer that she and the widow were holding was in truth beginning to move. She knew she wasn't consciously causing the movement and could only think that the widow was. She glanced at her and saw a tense, excited look.

Then the widow began to spell out, "D-A-N-G-E-R-I-N-L-O-V-E." And when she came to the last letter she fell back in her chair in near collapse, releasing her hold on the pointer.

The woman looked so ill that Flora was alarmed. She leaned over the ouija board. "Are you all right?"

"Yes," the older woman said hoarsely.

"You seem suddenly ill."

"No," the widow said, regaining some of her composure. "No. But it is always a strain to receive a spirit message."

"That was a spirit message?" Flora queried.

"Yes. You surely felt the pointer moving across the board and indicating the various letters."

"I thought you must be moving it."

"Not at all," the widow said sharply. "The spirits caused the movement, not I. But Charles meant the message for you."

"For me?"

"Yes. It's quite clear. He warned you, 'Danger in love.' So you must be careful to avoid any immediate romantic entanglements, my dear."

Flora shook her head. "Romance is the least likely thing I expect to encounter."

"You never know," the older woman warned her. "You are about to begin a new life. Who knows to what it may lead?"

She sighed. "I hope it will be less trying than the ordeals I have so recently experienced."

"You must be wary. Charles hardly ever sends me a message that isn't of value. You should take his warning seriously. Those on the other side can see much further ahead than we do."

"I suppose so," she said with a tiny shudder. The widow was making such a strong case for the supposed spirit message that she was almost beginning to believe in it.

Then Mrs. Weatherbarrow turned to Dolly and said, "Now you can try with me."

Dolly's head and shoulders moved in the shadows as she gave a nervous cough. "Lor', ma'am, I'm afraid to try it," she said in a tense voice.

"Nonsense. Charles does not want to harm you. He only wishes to help you!"

Dolly gave Flora a plaintive glance. "What do you think?"

"It's a weird experience but it is something like having your fortune told," she said, knowing that Dolly had a weakness for fortune tellers.

"Like the gyspy who read me palm?" Dolly said.

The widow told her, "It's much more accurate than that. I'm sure your gypsy was just guessing about the future. But when Charles makes a prediction about the future he really knows. Just place your hands on the pointer with mine!"

Dolly sighed and obeyed. Now Flora sat back and watched as the other two went through the same eerie pattern. The widow wailed out her appeal to Charles and asked for information about Dolly's future.

Even though Flora was only an onlooker this time she felt the same ghostly chill seep through her. The widow was crooning softly now as she wailed for the pointer to move. Dolly had gone a deathly white as she crouched over the board.

Flora again looked up at the stern face in the portrait. She almost expected the lips in the dark painting to begin moving, spelling out the words of a message. Then her attention was turned back to the widow again as she heard her begin to spell out various letters in a thin voice.

The widow was saying, "A-C-C-I-D-E-N-T." As she finished she fell back weakly in the same way she had before.

Flora exchanged a troubled look with Dolly, who had just let go of the pointer. The younger girl's face was ashen. Flora said, "It seems we will both have to be cautious."

Dolly replied in a mere whisper. "It moved! Moved by itself!"

Before Flora could mention that it might just have seemed to move, the widow recovered and said, "I'm glad you admit that, my girl. And you must indeed be wary. Charles has clearly spelled out that you are in danger of having an accident of some sort!"

Book Two

Armitage House

Chapter Ten

EACH NIGHT that Flora and Dolly remained in the widow's house the weird performance at the ouija board was repeated. On the succeeding nights she did not ask for messages for Flora or Dolly but queried about her own problems. In almost every instance she received an answer.

Flora noted that the answers usually pleased the widow. She thought perhaps they came about through autosuggestion on the older woman's part. She may have forced the movement of the pointer without actually being aware of it. When the message was received she would separate it out into words and glance up at the portrait of Charles with a murmured thanks.

By the time the third evening had passed Flora began to wish that Henry Armitage, the young China export merchant, would come to interview her. Mr. Gladstone had promised that his friend would call and talk to both her and Dolly. But time was passing and nothing was happening.

The fourth morning of their stay at the house found London in another heavy fog. As she was gazing into the street, feeling rather depressed, a fine carriage pulled up in front of the house and a slender male figure emerged from it. He spoke to the driver of the cab, apparently asking him to wait, and then crossed the sidewalk to mount the steps of the widow's house. A moment later she heard the knocker and waited eagerly at the parlor window as the maid answered the door.

Flora was only able to hear part of the exchange between them but she did manage to catch the name Armitage and her heart gave a leap. Mr. Gladstone's friend had come at last. A moment later Mrs. Weatherbarrow's friendly voice joined with the others in the hallway. Then a moment or two later the widow came into the parlor where Flora was waiting. The young man trailed behind her.

The widow said expansively, "Flora, I'd like you to meet Mr. Henry Armitage, the friend whom Mr. Gladstone mentioned. Mr. Armitage this is Flora Bain. You can chat with her while I go fetch the other girl."

"Thank you," he said politely as the widow bustled out of the room. He now turned his full attention to Flora with a shy smile and she had her first opportunity to thoroughly appraise him.

He was slim, of medium height, and had an even-featured face. There was a serious cast to his deep-set blue eyes. His bronze-colored hair curled slightly. He was dressed neatly in brown tweeds and carried a soft tweed hat in his hand.

"How do you do, Miss Bain," he said in a pleasant voice. "Mr. Gladstone was as good as his word. He came to visit me personally about you. Unfortunately I was supervising the unloading of a vessel that had just arrived here from China. Please accept my apologies for the delay."

"There's no need to apologize," she said at once. "Dolly Wales and I have been most comfortable here."

"I'm glad of that," he said. "You know why I'm here."

"Yes. To secure a new governness for your ten-year-old daughter, Enid," she said with a smile.

The young man lifted his eyebrows. "You're very well informed."

"Mr. Gladstone mentioned the post and told me a few things about the family. I've forgotten most of it, but I did manage to retain your daughter's name."

Henry Armitage's expression became clouded. In a troubled voice, he said, "I may as well give you all the particulars. My wife died when Enid was born. It was a great tragedy for both me and the child. Enid has been raised by a series of nurses and governesses."

"I see," she said.

"My own mother has been dead for years," he went on. "I do have my sister, Jessica, two years older than I, who has been very good. But she has her own life to live and I cannot expect her to give my daughter all her time."

"Of course not."

"Happily Enid is old for her years. She has always been a most mature child and she's responded well to care by various strangers. Fortunately her first nurse was with us for five years at the most critical period of her growing up. But now we have need of another governness. And let me say that just talking to you has convinced me that you would be well suited to the post."

She smiled happily. "I would be most grateful for the chance," she said.

"Then you shall have it. The position will pay two pounds a month plus room and board. And if we are all happy with the arrangement I shall give you another pound raise at the conclusion of your first six months."

"That seems most generous."

"It appears to be the going rate."

"I wouldn't really know. I have never worked for anyone before."

He nodded. "Gladstone told me your story. I hope this marks the end of your bad luck."

"I'm sure that it will," she said.

"There is also the other girl who you encountered in your ordeals and befriended. Gladstone mentioned she was a kitchen maid and that you would also like to gain employment for her."

"Yes," she said. "I feel responsible for her in a way. I'd like to have her near so I could talk with her and perhaps be able to offer her advice when it might be needed."

The young man listened with an approving look. "I think that is kind of you. We have a large household. I'll be glad to hire this girl as well. Salary one pound a month and all found."

Just then Mrs. Weatherbarrow returned with Dolly at her side. She introduced the girl to the handsome Henry Armitage and when Dolly found out Flora was to join his household as governess, she gladly agreed to take a job as kitchen maid.

He smiled at both of them. "So it is all settled. Is there any reason why you can't come with me now to Armitage House? I have my carriage waiting and it is only a short distance outside London."

Flora said, "We can leave anytime. I'm afraid we have no possessions to pack."

"We lost them in the fire in that den of vice!" Dolly lamented.

Henry Armitage said, "You must have no concern about that. If you need things before you have a chance to buy them I'm sure our housekeeper, Mrs. Brant, will find them for you. She is a most capable person."

Mrs. Weatherbarrow beamed at Flora and Dolly. "I shall miss you both," she said. "We had such cozy little sessions at the ouija board, didn't we?"

"Yes, we did," Flora said from a sense of gratitude.

"I shall write to you if I have any more messages for you from Charles," the widow told her. "As soon as you get settled send me your proper address."

"I will," Flora promised. She turned to the young man. "We mustn't keep you waiting. We'll be ready in five minutes."

"Plenty of time," he assured her as he consulted a large watch that he took from his vest pocket. "In spite of the fog it won't take us long to get to our destination."

So it was that within ten minutes the two girls were seated in the carriage with Henry Armitage as it moved slowly along the London streets.

Flora was aware that this private carriage belonging to Henry Armitage was much more comfortable to ride in and better built than the ordinary commercial vehicles in which she'd been a passenger. It was also going at a slower pace than most of the carriages she'd ridden in. She and Dolly sat on the seat with their backs to the front of the vehicle while he sat facing them.

He smiled in the semi-darkness of the carriage and said, "You must forgive our slow passage. My driver informed me there are great risks because of the fog so we will have to move at a snail's pace. If you look out you'll notice that you can hardly see the sidewalk."

Flora leaned forward and saw that what he'd said was true. The fog was the worst she'd ever seen. "It's bound to be dangerous in the thick of the traffic."

The young man nodded. "Before you know it a heavy dray or an omnibus could come crashing at you. I'll warrant that as the day progresses the public vehicles will have guards carrying torches walking before them to guide the way and offer a warning."

Dolly spoke up, "I was lost in me own block once. Had to stay with a neighbor, I did. 'Course I was only six at the time."

Henry Armitage offered her a considerate smile. "As long as our journey is to be tedious I may as well fill in part of the time by telling you both something about Armitage House and its people. In that way you'll be prepared for things when we do arrive."

"That is very considerate of you," Flora said. She was much taken with the young man. He seemed one of the nicest persons she'd met since arriving in London.

"Our housekeeper, Mrs. Brant, is a woman of about sixty. Her husband is the gardener. I think I mentioned her earlier."

"You did," Flora agreed.

"Mrs. Brant is most trustworthy. She has been with the family since before my mother died. In fact she was in

China with my parents when Jessica and I were very young. After my mother's death when I was four, Mrs. Brant took over the duties of running the household and she has the family's full confidence."

"I should imagine so by this time," she said.

"I was raised by nurses and tutors," he went on. "I vowed that when I had children of my own they would have no such experience. But fate had more to say about it than I did and my beloved wife died in childbirth leaving me Enid to be brought up."

Flora said, "That is very sad."

"I have grown resigned to it," the young man said. "As I told you earlier, my sister, Jessica, lives in the house. She has grown into a lovely young woman. I find it difficult to understand why she hasn't married but she seems to prefer to stay with me and my father."

"Your father is still alive, then?"

"Yes. But retired from the business. He is a great mountain of a man. Some claim that is why he commanded such respect when he first went to China to establish trade between the Chinese and England. He is six foot, six inches and he is very heavy now, much overweight. Unfortunately he has suffered from a mild form of palsy for several years. His hands and head shake uncontrollably much of the time. Yet his mind is still sharp and clear."

Flora said, "But he is able to get around on his own?"

"Fortunately, yes," the young man said. "He walks with the aid of a heavy walking stick. These days he spends much of his time upstairs taking care of a growing collection of fine Chinese antiques and objets d'art. His collection is regarded as one of the finest in the country. When he dies the house will be stripped of those treasures and they'll be turned over to one of the great museums."

"He is lucky to have an interest to occupy him," she said.

"Yes. He has nothing to do with the business any longer. Oh, he may offer me advice when I need it or ask him for it. But for the most part he is content to spend his time at Armitage House. He has taken the attic and the floor below it for his collection and the storing of items that he hasn't yet had time to uncrate. Of course many of the treasures already catalogued and put in good shape are scattered through the lower floors."

"It sounds as if it must be an unusual house," she said.

"I'd say it was," he agreed. "Father never did get over the sudden tragic death of my mother. His friends have told me he changed a lot at that time. He aged almost over night and his hair turned white, though he was a comparatively young man when it happened."

"What did happen to your mother?"

The young man looked grim. "Her health had been failing and she had become melancholy about this. They were on a ship owned by my father's firm returning from China. She vanished one night. Disappeared into thin air. There was no doubt that she went over the side. It is painful for me to say it even now; she took her own life."

Flora felt sorry she'd asked him this question. She apologized, "I didn't mean to pry."

"Quite all right," he assured her. "These are things you would want to know anyway. Better to have them cleared up and out of the way. Now you will understand my father better and why he can be strange and remote at times. He lives with a tragic memory."

"Of course," she said. "But he must have been a fine business man to have established his firm so soundly that it has lasted for years."

"He built well," Henry Armitage agreed. "I'm proud that he scorned any traffic in opium, and this has been excellent for his reputation in China. Our firm handles mostly tea, silk, and porcelain in about that order. We have specialists working for us both in China and in this country. That is why I've been able to take over the running of the firm even though I'm fairly young in years. We have good men working for us."

She asked, "Have you visited China very often?"

"Several times since my adulthood," he said. "It is a fascinating country."

"Will you go again?"

"Undoubtedly. But it is a long journey and not one to

make unless it is completely necessary. Lately we've had no serious problems and I've been content to run things from here."

The carriage was moving a little faster now and as she looked out the window she saw that the fog in this area wasn't quite so thick. She said, "The fog doesn't seem too bad here."

"We are outside London now," he informed her. "In fact we are not too far from Armitage House itself and I have noticed that the fog is sometimes not so serious out this way."

"I feel that I know your family very well already," she told him. "Though you have neglected to tell me much about your own daughter. The girl who is to be my particular charge."

He smiled wanly. "It is hard for me to discuss Enid in an objective way. To me she is perfect. She is tall and slender for her age and has black hair and eyes like her mother. I fear she also may have inherited some of her mother's temperament. My late wife would quickly become violently angry even though she was a wonderful person in every other way."

"I see," she said.

"Enid also sometimes has fits of temper," her father confessed. "But they pass swiftly. So I do not think you should worry about them. She is a good scholar and all her other governesses have been much impressed with her progress."

"I wonder that they would leave such a pleasant position," she said.

He made a gesture with his left hand. "You know how it is with young women. They marry or they receive an offer to travel with some relative, or something of the sort. There are any number of reasons for their leaving."

Flora was suddenly aware that the carriage was turning off the main road and heading up a tree-lined private driveway, which soon gave way to open green lawns and a great stone mansion. Directly before it was a large pond.

She said, "So this is Armitage House!"

The young man nodded. "Yes. I do hope you will like it here."

"It's very impressive," she said. As the carriage rolled up before the front entrance of the house she glanced out again at the large pond, which was scattered with water lilies. A wooden bird house rose from its center and a pair of graceful swans were gliding over its surface.

Noticing her interest in the pond, he told her, "It's a natural pond and extremely deep in spots. We improved on nature and made it a beauty spot of the property."

"It is most unusual," she agreed. She continued to study it as the carriage came to a halt, and what she didn't tell him was that for no reason she could understand the pool had made a peculiar impression on her. It had a strange, appealing beauty, but she felt its smooth, dark surface might conceal some malevolent secret.

Dolly had wakened from her short nap and asked, "Have we arrived?"

"Yes," she told her friend. "We're at the end of our journey."

Dolly looked embarrassed. "I fell asleep."

"Nothing to be ashamed of," Henry Armitage told her. "You've gone through a lot in the past week or so."

The driver opened the carriage door for them and he jumped out first and then helped them down from the vehicle. Escorting them up to the door, he said, "The house has been owned by our family for more than a half-century, but we did not build it. It was constructed one hundred and fifty years ago by a strange old earl who died soon after he'd seen it completed."

Henry Armitage turned to Dolly and somewhat apologetically told her, "I'll be turning you over to the housekeeper, Mrs. Brant, I'm sure she'll do well by you."

"Thank you, sir," the younger girl said.

Dolly's pert little face bore almost a frightened look as she turned to Flora. "But I shall be seeing you?"

"Of course," Flora assured her. "At intervals we'll be able to meet and chat when we've finished our work."

"Most certainly," Henry Armitage agreed, joining in the

conversation. "This is not the workhouse, it is my home. I promise you may meet when you like."

The discussion was ended as the entrance door was opened to them by a tall, spare woman in a long dark dress and a tiny knitted white bonnet over her iron-gray hair. She had a narrow, severe face. Flora guessed at once she was Mrs. Brant.

Henry Armitage confirmed this by introducing Mrs. Brant to them. The severe-looking housekeeper at once took Dolly off with her. The two vanished along a dark passage that led to the kitchens in the rear of the house.

Flora offered Henry Armitage a rueful smile. "I have an idea Dolly is overwhelmed by your home."

"I wonder," he said. "She didn't seem too happy. I think it's the prospect of being parted from you a good deal of the time after being your constant companion."

"It will seem strange."

"You need have no hesitation in going to the kitchens to see her whenever you like," he said earnestly. "And you can meet upstairs in your room or out on the grounds."

"Thank you," she said.

Henry Armitage gazed down at her. "Let us see if we can find the others," he said. He escorted her into a great, high-ceilinged living room which was empty, so he continued on through the big room with its chandeliers, mirrors, paintings, and luxurious furniture to a smaller drawing room at its rear. Coming to the open double doors she heard voices.

They entered the room, and there before a marble fireplace stood an immense, white-haired old man leaning on a cane. She recognized at once from the description given her by Henry Armitage that this had to be his father, Bradford Armitage. Standing facing him was a slender, beautiful woman with auburn hair and green eyes who she felt must be Henry's older sister Jessica.

Flora felt conspicuous as the two appraised her. She saw that the looks on their faces were cold.

Henry broke the awkward silence. "This is Miss Flora Bain, the new governess."

Old Bradford Armitage bowed with a solemn air. "How do you do, Miss Bain."

It remained for Jessica, strikingly lovely in a gown of pale blue, to come slowly across to her and extend a languid hand in greeting. With a tiny smile that seemed almost scornful about her full red lips, she said, "So you are the remarkable young woman whom Mr. Gladstone so nobly rescued from the streets!"

Flora shook hands lightly and with flushed face said, "Those are not exactly the facts."

Jessica raised shapely eyebrows. "Then he didn't find you on the streets, how disappointing!"

Henry gave his sister a glance of rebuke. "Flora had a very bad time in the city after discovering her uncle a suicide. She finally arrived at William Booth's mission looking for help. It was there that Mr. Gladstone found her, not on the streets."

"So that is it!" Jessica said with a smirk on her almost perfect oval face. "I misunderstood poor Mr. Gladstone then. I thought Flora was a vicar's daughter who had fallen into disgrace."

"Well, now you know better," her brother said, almost curtly. "Where is Enid?"

"Your daughter misbehaved badly this morning and when I tried to reprimand her she was extremely rude to me," Jessica told him, her green eyes blazing with anger.

"Oh?" He looked upset.

"Enid was running through the living room after tripping one of the young parlor maids. She stumbled against a side table and knocked off one of your father's precious Chinese vases. When I ordered her up to her room because of it she called me a vicious old maid!"

Henry dismissed this with a wave of his hand. "You should know better than to let anything she says upset you."

"The remark was cruel and uncalled for," Jessica said sternly. "I had Mrs. Brant take the child up to her room and lock her in. That's where you'll find her now."

"You know I dislike her being locked up there. I wish

you'd waited until my return and allowed me to deal with her."

Jessica continued to show anger. "I had to discipline her in some way. She was rude to me and broke one of Father's treasured vases!"

Henry turned to ask the big white-haired man, "Was it truly a valuable piece, Father?"

"I have one upstairs to replace it," his father said. "Don't punish the child on my account."

"There! You see!" Henry said turning to his sister.

The lovely Jessica shrugged and told Flora, "I can only say that I'm glad you have arrived. I'm weary of trying to discipline that child and getting no thanks for it."

Henry Armitage looked repentant. "I'm sorry," he said. "I know you mean well. But Enid is young and full of mischief. She certainly didn't mean to break the vase."

"She had no business carrying on with the maids in the living room. Goodness knows, it is difficult enough to get them to do their work and keep them in their place without her spoiling them."

He frowned. "I'll speak to her about that."

"I know," Jessica said with a grim smile. "She'll twist you around her finger as always. She's only a child but you are no match for her wiles."

"Please, Jessica. If you go on this way you'll discourage Flora from taking the position before she even begins to work."

"I very much doubt it and I think it only fair she be prepared."

From the fireplace Bradford Armitage gave his son and daughter a reproving frown. "Let us have an end to your bickering," he told them. "The damage is done. Enid meant no harm. I suggest you forget the whole incident and let this young woman be responsible for her in the future. Then you'll have less to argue about."

Jessica shrugged. "Whatever you like, Father. I know I wasn't given such liberties when I was her age."

"Enid is a different type," Henry reminded his sister. "She is a very sensitive child. The last time she was locked in her room she became very depressed."

"I don't recall it," Jessica said in a bored tone.

"You must," Henry insisted. "She was really very upset. She cried in my arms for some time. I had all I could do to bring her out of it."

"Spoiled!" Jessica said.

"She has been without a mother from the moment of her birth," Henry reminded his sister. "That has not been easy for her."

"Our mother died when we were very young," Jessica reminded him.

"But we at least had each other," Henry protested. "That had to make a difference. We have grown up devoted to one another as a direct result."

Bradford Armitage rapped his walking stick on the stone front of the fireplace. "Enough of this," he said. "I want to hear no more of it!" His voice was deep and had a ring of authority to it.

Henry's face crimsoned. He looked like a small boy who had been reprimanded. "I'm sorry, Father," he apologized. "I'll take Flora up to meet Enid."

"High time!" the old man said.

Jessica smiled at Flora in her cold way. "I do hope we haven't made too bad an impression on you, Miss Bain. We are really a very happy family here despite an occasional disparity in our points of view. I'm very fond of Henry." As if to prove this she reached out and linked her arm in his and gave him a warm smile.

Henry patted her hand. "I'm certain Flora understands," he said.

"I do," Flora was quick to reassure them, but she had been amazed at the display offered by the two. She could see that Jessica was used to getting her own way and was terribly possessive of Henry. Perhaps even to the point where she resented his love for his motherless daughter. This might also make her more severe on the child than she would normally be.

Jessica seemed in an excellent mood now. Removing her arm from Henry's, she said, "Well, go along! See how your spoiled daughter has taken to her imprisonment. Listen to her stories against me! I don't mind."

135

Henry said, "I'll not encourage her to talk against you, I can promise you that. I will reprimand her. But I am worried about her being locked up there alone.

Having said this he took Flora by the arm and silently guided her out a side door of the rear parlor and along a hallway to the bottom of the stairs.

Then Henry confided, "Jessica is not good with children, as you may have guessed."

She said, "Some women aren't."

"Jessica is a prime example," Henry said as they hesitated at the bottom of the stairs. "She has always depended a great deal on me. When we first went out in society I escorted her everywhere. I naturally supposed that in time she'd find some suitable young man for herself. But she didn't. And when I married Enid's mother Jessica showed unreasonable jealousy of her. Just as she does of Enid now. She means no harm, but it is a curious flaw in her nature and I'm certain our father is aware of it."

"He didn't seem to encourage her," Flora agreed.

"He tries to protect Enid but it is difficult. He is an old man and not able to get about as he used to. That is why it is so important we have a proper governess here."

She smiled. "I've had little experience in the work but I'll surely do my best for your daughter."

"That is all anyone can ask. I tremble to think what Enid's mental state may be after having been locked up in her room this long. I'm sure she won't think she's done anything to justify such harsh treatment."

"It's too bad," Flora said.

He sighed. "Well, we may as well go up and face the music. Perhaps having you here will help. It will tend to put Enid on her best behavior." They started up the curving stairway.

When they reached the landing she was struck by a fine oil painting of a lovely young woman in a full dark velvet gown. "What a fine painting of your sister!"

Henry paused before the painting of the auburn-haired beauty and said, "You're wrong. That is not a painting of Jessica but a portrait of my mother when she was young. This was done before her illness."

She stared at the painting and saw the same haughty yet lovely face and the same dazzling green eyes. She said, "Jessica is remarkably like her mother in appearance."

"Yes," he agreed. "And this, of course, makes her my father's favorite."

She felt there was a note of bitterness in his voice as he said this.

They walked down a long hallway which led to a paneled door. The key was in the door. Hesitantly Henry turned the key and swung the door open. The room was large and furnished in excellent taste. It was dominated by a large four poster bed with a canopy over it.

Stretched out motionless on the bed was a slim, dark-haired girl, her eyes closed as if in death. And protruding up from her chest was the handle of a large knife!

Chapter Eleven

HENRY SOBBED out his daughter's name as he reached her bedside. "Enid!"

Suddenly the still form on the bed came to life and Enid sat up with a burst of laughter. She reached over and held up the knife, which had been artfully arranged to seem plunged in her as she held it pressed between her body and her arm.

"I knew you'd be terrified, Father!" she said, bubbling with laughter as she spoke.

"How could you play such a trick on me?"

"You locked me in my room again! Or at least Jessica did. I decided to teach you both a lesson!" The girl swung around and got down off the bed. She was unusually tall for her age. She was also thin and pretty in a childish way.

Her father was still stunned. "What made you think of such a diabolical thing?"

"I tried to think what might frighten you most," Enid

138

told him frankly. "I saw the knife and decided to pretend I'd killed myself."

"That was very wicked of you!" her father said, as Flora stood numbly by.

"Jessica was cruel to me!" the youngster retorted. And now she turned to Flora. "Is this the new one? My new governess?"

Henry nodded. In a tired fashion he said, "This is Miss Flora Bain and I hope she'll succeed in teaching you how to be a proper young lady and not the mad magpie you are now!"

The winsome, dark-haired girl laughed. "I'm not all that bad, Father. Only when I'm dealt with unfairly. And Jessica dotes on being unfair to me!"

"We'll discuss that at some more appropriate time," Henry Armitage said. "In the meanwhile I'm going to leave you in Miss Bain's care and hope that she will not be too discouraged by you."

Enid grimaced and there was a merry light in her black eyes. "You're not afraid of me, are you, Miss Bain?"

"No," she said as evenly as she could. "Though I do hope you'll refrain from any more charades like the one you've presented for us just now."

Enid looked delighted. She grasped her father's hand and said, "See, Father! Miss Bain understands! It was a charade! You first taught me how to play them."

He gave his daughter a resigned look. "At the time I did not anticipate your indulging in anything as macabre as that knife business."

"No harm done!" Enid laughed. "And thank you for finding Miss Bain, Father. I'm certain we're going to get along."

"I wish I could be as sure," her father said with a sigh. He turned to Flora and said, "I'll leave you with her for a little while and I'll see you downstairs at dinner. I wish you good luck."

As soon as he left the room and closed the door after him Flora confronted the girl with the black pigtails and plain yellow dress.

"That was a most shameful thing to do," she said. "Did

you hear that cry of pain from your father who loves you so?"

The youngster eyed her with disdain. "He deserved it!"

"You're wrong! He didn't!"

Enid looked uneasy. "We don't want to begin by quarreling, do we?"

"No. If only for your father's sake," she said. "I hope that from now on you'll remember you're a young lady and behave like one."

The keen black eyes searched her face. "Didn't Mr. Gladstone find you in a brothel?"

This jolted Flora. "He did not!" she retorted. "And where did you learn a word like brothel?"

"Jessica told me," the child said, delighted to implicate her aunt. "This morning she told me that Father was bringing a brothel hussy to tutor me because it was all I deserved!"

Flora's face was crimson. She knew that Enid had not made this up. The ten-year-old, precocious as she might be, had certainly heard this talk from the jealous Jessica. It angered her to think how lightly her name had been taken.

She faced the child sternly. "None of that is true," she told her. "My father was a vicar and we lived in Sussex. I was only in London for a short while."

"I was only repeating what Jessica said!"

"Don't repeat it anymore, it is sheer nonsense. I want to begin with you honestly and we'll do much better if we are friends."

"I don't mind being your friend," Enid decided.

"Let us begin there," Flora suggested. "You must tell me how far you've advanced in your various studies."

"I'm way behind. My last governess, Lily, was madly in love with Father. She paid no attention to me at all. She was out to marry him!"

"How can you say that?"

"Everyone said it. Even Grandfather, and he doesn't talk much to anyone. He's always upstairs in the attic with those Chinese treasures of his. Lily annoyed him with her mooning about after my father!"

"You are much too young to know about such things," Flora told her.

"No," Enid said with delight. "I know all about it. In the end it was why we lost Lily."

Flora knew she had to take a strong stand from the start with the difficult young miss or she might not be able to handle her at all. So she said, "I want to hear no more of that!"

Enid looked crestfallen. "Don't you enjoy gossip?"

"No!"

"I do!"

"That's obvious. But we're going to have to divert your interests to some more useful channel."

The child stared at her curiously. "You really mean that, don't you?"

"Yes!"

Enid stood up. "I won't be bullied! I'm almost as tall as you!"

"It doesn't make any difference how tall you are," Flora said. "You're still only a ten-year-old and I intend you shall behave like one. Not trip the maids when they're at work and run off to break your grandfather's valuable vases."

The girl looked chagrined. "Jessica told you about that."

"I've heard a good deal about you," she warned.

Enid surprisingly broke into a smile. "I like you, Flora," she said. "Maybe it will be fun having a governess again."

"And you will address me as Miss Bain," Flora informed her.

"Do you mean it?"

"I do. It is one thing you must do. Address your elders in a proper fashion. And I happen to be your elder."

"All right," Enid said in a small voice.

"Now let us get down to finding out about your studies," she said sternly.

That was how she began with Enid. The youngster responded slowly but she did yield to Flora's will. It did not take Flora long to learn that the girl was intelligent far beyond her ten years. Flora was pleased and certain that

141

if Enid's energies were directed properly there would be no major problems with her.

By the time they went down to join the others at dinner Flora had drilled two lessons into her charge. One was to be more respectful in addressing her elders and the other was to wait for her turn in any conversation. As a result Henry Armitage congratulated Flora after dinner for the marked improvement there had been in his daughter within only a few short hours.

"You are remarkable! A born governess!" he declared.

She smiled faintly. "I don't deserve compliments yet, but I hope to given time."

Jessica had been vaguely indifferent to it all. She had spent most of her time imposing herself on her brother in a shameless way. Flora noted that the elder Armitage sat there observing all this with a good deal of disgust. And when dinner ended in the high-ceilinged, paneled dining room the old man contrived to see her out to the living room and to be her partner in an after-dinner brandy.

When they were safely established in a quiet corner of the big room, with glasses in hand, the old man said in his booming voice, "Have you noticed the vast amount of art treasures I have brought back from the mainland of China with me?"

Flora said, "How could I miss them?" She indicated a tall screen in red, white, and gold enamel that stood against an opposite wall of the room. "That screen alone must be worth a fortune."

The big man chuckled with pleasure. "I must admit you have good taste. That is perhaps the single most valuable item in my collection. It bears fine scene studies of the mountains and lakes of China."

"I must make a tour of the house when I have time," she said.

"If you will warn me in advance I shall arrange to join you and give you a conducted tour of the place," he said. "I think you will do a vast amount of good here. Before you sent my granddaughter up to bed I was aware of an improvement in her behavior."

She smiled faintly. "That is only a start. Really helping the child will take time."

"Forgive my great delight in the child but I am a lonely man and she means a great deal to me."

"I understand."

"I'm not sure that you do. My children, Jessica and Henry, no longer look up to me. I'm now merely their rather childish old parent. They refuse to listen to me about most things. So I'm left with only that little girl to respect me and share my thoughts with."

Flora was touched by the old man's words. "I'm certain she's very fond of you. And she is no longer a little girl. I'd call her large for her age."

"She takes after me," the old man said happily. "Large people are the rule in my family. It is strange that Jessica and Henry don't have the trait, but it was passed on in Enid's case."

Suddenly the old man's mood changed. With a raised finger he cautioned, "You mustn't allow yourself to be scared away from here."

This sudden warning startled her. "Why should I be frightened of this house?"

The man took a sip of his brandy and then said, "You are right! Why should you be frightened of this house?"

"You haven't answered my question by merely repeating it," she pointed out, feeling slightly uneasy.

"Really I meant nothing," he assured her rather too hastily. "I'm so anxious that you should remain with us I have been overemphatic. You must forgive me!"

Her eyes fixed on his florid face. "I suppose this house like many others has some dark secrets in its past." It was a chance, but she saw at once it had registered.

Looking thoroughly upset the old man said, "Armitage House is no exception. But you need not be touched by its dark history. You are only here as an employee."

Just then Henry Armitage came up to join them. The slender young man looked amused.

"I'm sure Father is telling you about his rare Li Ti paintings or perhaps about his imperial Kuan porcelains.

143

You mustn't allow him to bore you with dry talk of his collection."

Bradford Armitage told his son, "You are quite wrong. Miss Bain and I were discussing Enid and her problems. I'm anxious to see my granddaughter off to a good start with her governess this time."

"I quite agree," Henry said with a smile for her. "I'm happy that you remained down here with us this evening. I feel it important that we get to know you well and that you feel yourself to be one of us."

"That is very kind of you," she said.

"Mind you," the elderly Armitage intervened, "I will not promise to refrain from giving you a tour of my Chinese collection one day soon. I do have some fine pieces, and the queen was pleased to accept a gift of a Chang Seng-yu painting which I sent her."

"Just glancing about is a treat to the eye," Flora told him. And it was true. The house featured every sort of Chinese art treasure, from the plates used for formal dining, to the lacquer paintings, the earthenware of centuries earlier, and the great metal Buddhas gazing down from their stands in various niches.

"We don't lack things Chinese," Henry said with a wry smile. "But then, because of our business connections with China, we are in an excellent position to pick up fine art pieces."

As he finished speaking two newcomers suddenly arrived. A stooped, gray-haired man with a straggly beard and a beautiful young blonde woman came into the living room and were at once greeted by Jessica.

"Please excuse me for a moment," he said. "I must greet Sir Thomas Waring and Madge."

Flora turned to Bradford Armitage and said, "Sir Thomas has a very beautiful daughter."

The big man chuckled as he leaned heavily on his cane. "Wife, Miss Bain! Madge is the wife of Sir Thomas!"

"Really?" She was shocked. "There must be a great age difference between them and he seems in such feeble health."

"He is not well, although they were married only recently," Henry's father said. "Perhaps a young wife will help restore him to full vigor again."

"It is to be hoped so," she said quietly, feeling she had been wrong in making any comment on the match.

However, Bradford Armitage seemed anxious to pursue the subject. "Madge was about to become engaged to Henry once but they had some lovers' misunderstanding and broke it off. I never did get the facts. Her family is not rich and I suspect she married Sir Thomas, who is older than her parents, in a bid to restore her family's fortunes."

She glanced up at the old man. "I would consider that a poor basis for a marriage."

"I quite agree," he said. "Sir Thomas is our neighbor; he has the estate to the right. Our grounds meet and we have no boundary fences. For years we have lived in great harmony with his family. Now he is the last of the line."

"So you are bound to remain friendly with him," she said, considering the older man's explanation.

"Exactly," he said. "And Madge shall always be welcome here. Though I do think that Henry's seeing her as the bride of Sir Thomas causes him some pain. But that cannot be helped. There have been marriages of convenience before and there are bound to be many of them in the future. One must be realistic. Let me take you over and introduce you to Sir Thomas."

She would have preferred to have gone up to bed but she saw no escape. She would have to remain to at least meet Sir Thomas and his bride. Bradford Armitage laboriously made his way across the room, puffing a little and leaning on his cane.

By the time they reached Sir Thomas his wife had moved away for a private conversation with Henry in another part of the room. Sir Thomas was standing with Jessica engaged in a rather strained exchange. Bradford Armitage at once introduced Flora to the old man.

Sir Thomas was kindly in his greeting of her. His sunken eyes fixed on her as he said, "You have a nice glow of health in your cheeks, young woman. You did not get that in our London fog."

"I made my home in Sussex until recently," she said.

"Ah!" he exclaimed. "That explains it then. In my younger days I was a country squire. I enjoyed the life!"

"I shall always remember Sussex with pleasure," she agreed.

Jessica spoke with a cool smile and raised chin as she said, "Miss Bain is our new governess."

"Indeed," the old man said absently. Her words had made no impression on him, though Flora suspected the statement had been made to keep her in her proper place.

The two men began to discuss politics and she found herself thrown into Jessica's company.

Jessica eyed her in an appraising manner. "We must soon fix you up with a proper wardrobe. That dress you're wearing is rather shabby for an occasion like this."

She blushed. "It is all I have at the moment. But I do plan to get other things."

"I should hope so," Jessica said. She turned her glance to the distant Henry and Madge. "If you had half the dresses of that greedy little creature you wouldn't know what to do with them."

"Really?" She didn't know what to say to this.

"Yes," Jessica went on in her acid way. "She has that doting old husband of hers buy her twice the amount of clothes she can use. Perhaps it's her idea of compensation." Jessica gave Flora a sour smile. "You see she's not happy in her marriage. She has always loved Henry. But Henry doesn't love her. He's sorry for her but it ends there."

"I see," she said awkwardly.

"Because Henry is an attractive man and a wealthy one as well there are all sorts of females setting their caps for him," Jessica went on. "But I don't think he's interested in any of them. I'm convinced he'll never marry again. His first marriage was a tragic mistake."

She stared at the lovely, but bitter, girl. "I had the impression they were ideally happy until her tragic death."

"She wasn't right for Henry," Jessica said emphatically. "There are times when I think that her death was fortunate. Not that I would ever say so to him. And she left him a difficult legacy in Enid. I often think that child is mad!"

Flora said, "Precocious, perhaps. But surely not mad!"

"Sometimes it is hard to draw a line between the two," Jessica suggested. "It also means the nuisance of having governesses here. Though I'm sure you will prove no problem."

"Thank you," she said quietly, aware that Jessica likely thought her one. This jealous sister of Henry's resented the presence of any other female.

Jessica gave her a meaningful look. "You must have heard about Lily?"

"The governess before me?"

"Yes. A silly little thing, though she was pretty enough. But not a brain in her head," Jessica went on viciously. "And of course she fell in love with Henry and hoped that he would marry her."

"Oh!" She was dismayed by the revelation and wondered if Jessica was offering it as a warning to her.

"It was terribly embarrassing," Jessica said, her eyes on Madge Waring again. "And now we have that one coming here with her ancient husband and pouring all her woes into Henry's ears. I'm certain he would prefer not to hear them but it gives her an excuse to be in his company."

Flora knew that in Jessica's opinion no girl was worthy of her beloved brother. It became clearer and clearer to her that one of the unpleasant things about living at Armitage House would be having to endure Jessica's mad obsession where her handsome brother was concerned.

Feeling ill at ease, she said, "I think it is time I should retire."

"Without meeting Lady Waring?" Jessica said maliciously. "I'm positive Madge would be disappointed and hurt. She knows you were discovered by Henry and she must be curious about you."

As if to offer proof of Jessica's comment Henry and Madge now came strolling towards them. Seeing Madge at closer range she was struck by her pale, almost frightened face. The young woman appeared to be under a serious strain, though even this did not detract from her loveliness. She had the typical peaches and cream British complexion and the fragile beauty which accompanied it.

Henry came up and introduced her. "Lady Madge Waring, I'd like you to meet Enid's new governess, Miss Flora Bain."

"How do you do," Madge said in a small voice that suited her looks.

"I understand you and Sir Thomas are neighbors," Flora said in an effort to relieve the general tension.

"Yes," the blonde woman said. "I often go for walks on the grounds. No doubt I'll encounter you and Enid."

"That would be very pleasant," she said.

Henry seemed anxious for them to be friends. He turned to Madge and said, "Miss Bain had a most harrowing series of adventures on her arrival in London. It is amazing that she has survived them so well. I hope that she will be happy here with us."

Madge Waring gave her an anxious look. "Yes. I hope you like it here."

"I think I will," she said. "I find the pond especially appealing."

The reaction to her words was puzzling. Henry crimsoned while Madge's lovely face took on an expression of dismay. It remained for Jessica to make a reply.

"You are not the first to notice its peculiar quality."

Not knowing what to say, she replied, "Really?"

Henry seemed to have recovered his poise for he now spoke up quickly, saying, "Such ponds are unusual and it does add to the beauty of the grounds."

Jessica smirked as she glanced over at Madge. "Still I doubt that you would want a similar one, would you, Madge?"

"No, I think not," Madge said in a small, frightened voice.

None of it made any sense to Flora. She felt a strong urge to get out of the room and away from these people. She was weary and uneasy in their company.

She said, "If you will excuse me. I have a slight headache. I think I will go upstairs."

"Of course," Henry said at once. "It was good of you to

remain down here so long. We shouldn't have insisted on it your first night here."

She managed a wan smile for him. "I didn't mind. And I have thoroughly enjoyed meeting everyone."

She said good night and left. She thought to herself, it had been an unusual night. Evidently something was not quite right about the gloomy old mansion and the people in it. The people of Armitage House were living under some sort of eerie tension that seemed to extend even to their neighbors. As yet she had no hint of what it might be. But she knew something was wrong and was being concealed from her.

She had sensed it in Bradford Armitage's manner and again when she'd talked to Madge and Henry. Even Jessica had mysteriously hinted at things which had not been explained. She felt that the wild, erratic behavior of the ten-year-old Enid also reflected the shadow under which everyone in the old house lived. And now she had become a member of the household and she might come to fall under that shadow.

What was it old Bradford Armitage had said in an effort to placate her? "You need not fear for yourself, since you are only an employee here."

Surely this meant something. And she very much doubted that it made any difference whether she was an employee or not. She had come to live at Armitage House and she would most likely share the same tensions as the others. But what were the secrets of the ancient mansion? How would she discover them?

These questions raced through her troubled mind as she made her way up the curving stairway to the upper landing. She paused here to study the portrait of Jessica's mother. A shaft of blue moonlight cut across the landing to illuminate the painting. Again she marveled at how the mother and daughter resembled each other. And she pondered on this woman who had died long ago and mysteriously at sea. This beauty who had become so surfeited with life that she had plunged over the side of the vessel returning to England to drown in the murky depths of a distant sea. And yet her likeness remained alive here in this strange old house of dark memories.

She was about to move on to the next stairway when she saw a movement in a distant corner of the landing. Then out of the shadows a thin hand emerged and reached out for her.

Chapter Twelve

FLORA FOUGHT the impulse to cry out in fear as the hand showed itself. Then very gradually a form took shape in the shadows.

"Flora!" A familiar voice said, and she knew it was Dolly who had been hiding there waiting for her.

"Dolly!" she gasped as they stood together in the darkness. "You terrified me. At first all I could see was your hand."

"Sorry," Dolly said. "But I wanted to see you and I didn't know how else I could manage it."

"I understand," she said. "Are you making out all right in the kitchen?"

"Good enough," the younger girl said. "It's the same sort of work I was doing before but at least it's better than what Mrs. Fernald had planned for me."

"We should both be grateful," Flora said.

"I suppose so," Dolly agreed reluctantly. "What about you? Are you satisfied?"

"The girl I'm to take care of will be a problem," she

said. "She's high-strung and given to playing practical jokes. Also, she dislikes discipline of any kind."

"Sounds like you'll have your hands full."

"I expect so. Yet she's very intelligent. I'm basing my hopes on that. With luck I may reach her and be able to do something for her."

Dolly sighed. "Like everything else this isn't just what we'd hoped for."

"Things seldom are," she said.

"There's something else."

"Oh?"

"There's whispers below stairs that there's a ghost in the house."

Flora said, "Are you sure?"

"Yes. I heard cook talking to the first parlor maid. And cook wanted to know if anyone had seen the ghost lately and the parlor maid said no, but that didn't mean anything. Sometimes it doesn't show itself for weeks and then people see it two or three nights in succession."

A chill ran through Flora. "Did they describe the ghost?"

"No. They stopped talking when I came near."

"And you weren't able to get any information from anyone else?"

"I tried to get some of the other kitchen girls to talk about it but they just looked scared and clammed up!" Dolly told her.

"Very strange."

"That's what I say. Why did we have to come to a house that is haunted."

"We can't be sure that it is yet," she replied. "Why not stop worrying until we learn more about this?"

"I'll try to find out all I can. Soon as I know anything I'll get the word to you somehow."

"Do," she urged the younger girl. "And if I learn of anything I feel important I will advise you."

"I wish we were together," Dolly lamented.

"So do I," she said.

"Where is your room?" Dolly asked.

"The next floor. It adjoins the child's."

"I'll remember," the younger girl said. "Now I must be back off to my own room before I'm missed."

"Take care," Flora told her. A close bond had grown between them in the short time they'd spent together.

Dolly scurried down the curving stairway and on up to the next floor. The news that the house was haunted did not come to Flora as a surprise. In fact it fitted in with her own feelings that there was a shadow over the house. She clung to the railing in the dark and finally reached the next landing. Then she made her way along the corridor to her room.

She let herself inside and lighted a candle. At least she was no longer in total blackness. Lifting up the candle-holder she went to the door connecting her room with Enid's and slowly opened it.

The child was in her bed fast asleep, breathing deeply. Satisfied that her charge was safe, she withdrew into her own room and prepared for bed.

She had been in bed for perhaps a half-hour and was almost asleep when a scream came from somewhere in the house. It was sharp and short-lived but it brought her fully awake and into a sitting position. What did it mean and where had it come from?

She remained awake and sitting up in bed for some time thinking that the scream might be repeated but it wasn't. There was no sound from the adjoining room so she assumed that Enid hadn't been awakened by it, and after a long while she lay back in bed and finally slept again.

But as she slept she was tormented by a strange dream. The door of her room opened and a ghostly figure entered the room. The figure of a woman wearing a hooded black garment. The face of the woman was lost in shadow. She sat up in bed as the intruder continued to advance on her.

"Who are you?" she cried out in her dream but there was no reply.

The figure came to her bedside and only then did she see the gleaming knife blade in the ghost's hand. She cried out and hunched back on the bed in fear. Now the ghost lifted the knife high and at the same time the hood fell back to reveal the head of Jessica! Her lovely face wore an expression of grim hatred as she swung the knife down at Flora.

Flora dodged back just in time to avoid the blade and at the same instant came awake. Her heart was pounding with fear and she expected to see the ghost above her but the room was empty. There was no one! It had merely been an ugly nightmare induced by all she had seen and heard. Yet she took it as an ill omen and perhaps a warning of dangers which lay in store for her.

The balance of the night she slept without interruption. When she awoke the morning sun was streaming into her room, and she got up to wash and dress. It was while she was thus engaged that a soft knock came at her door.

Still in her nightgown she went to the door and asked, "Who is it?"

"Mrs. Brant, the housekeeper," came the reply. "May I come in?"

"Of course," she said as she unbolted and opened the door.

The stern-looking woman entered carrying several dresses and other clothes in her arms, which she placed on the bed.

"I think you'll find that all these will fit you very well," the housekeeper said. "There's a pretty good supply of all you'll need."

"How can I thank you?" she said. "You must allow me to pay you back."

"That is unnecessary. The clothes happened to be here in storage so you may as well make use of them."

Flora examined some of the clothing and was impressed by the quality. "These are good dresses," she said. "To whom did they belong?"

The housekeeper eyed her coldly. "They were hers."

"Hers?" she asked blankly.

"Lily's," the housekeeper said in the same icy tone.

The name registered with her. "You mean the young woman who was governess here before I came."

"Yes."

"Won't she need them? Did she just leave them to pick up later?" Flora wondered.

"No," the housekeeper said. "You can keep them and not worry about them. She won't want them."

"I see," she said, though in truth she didn't.

Mrs. Brant went to the door and hesitated holding the knob. "No need to mention this to anyone. Just take the clothes and be grateful for them."

"Of course!" she replied.

But Mrs. Brant had already left and closed the door. Flora held up one of the dresses and saw that it would indeed fit her.

On impulse she decided to wear a pretty brown one with light brown facing, jabot, and sleeve ends. She barely finished dressing when the door joining her room with Enid's opened and the ten-year-old came bursting in.

"Good morning!" Enid cried with a smile.

Flora smiled back. "Yes, it is a good morning. But you startled me. Hasn't anyone told you to always knock on doors before you enter?"

The slender dark girl wore a black dress. She skipped to the window to casually glance out. "I don't know. Maybe."

"If they have you can't have paid much attention to them," she said accusingly.

Enid turned to her with a shrug. "Is it so important?"

"Yes, it is," she said firmly. "It's a lesson I want you to learn and always remember. Knock on doors before you enter a room!"

"All right," the youngster said sullenly. Then her face lit up and she exclaimed, "I know that dress. I've seen it before!"

Flora stood before her embarrassed. "Have you?"

"Yes. It belonged to Lily."

Flora felt she must face her squarely. She said, "Is that important? Mrs. Brant brought it to me and told me I could have it as I have no dresses. So why make so much fuss about it?"

Enid said, "I don't mind if you don't."

"Why should I mind? And why should it concern you?"

she asked. "If you were a polite little girl you would not have mentioned it!"

"Why not?"

"Out of consideration for me," she said. "You might have hurt my feelings."

"Oh!" Enid seemed to suddenly understand.

Primly, she said, "If we have that settled we can now go down to breakfast and then begin lining up your studies."

"Can we work at my studies outdoors if it is a warm day?" the little girl asked.

"I see no reason why not," she said.

"I like to study outdoors," Enid said. "It's more fun!"

A little later in the morning they set out for the garden, their arms laden with books. Flora had noticed a marble bench at one end of the pool, which she thought might make a good spot for their work. Enid had run on ahead of her and so she now called to her.

"Wait!"

Enid turned and came back across the grass. "What is it?"

"Why don't we work by the pond rather than go on to the gardens?" Flora asked.

A strange look came to her face. "No," Enid said. "I don't want to sit there."

"Why?"

"I don't like the pond," Enid told her, with a tremor in her voice. "It's ugly! Full of ugly secrets!"

"Enid!" she exclaimed in reproach. "That's very silly of you!"

"I don't care! I hate the pond and you can't make me sit by it!" she cried, and raced off in the direction of the garden.

Flora was nonplused. She watched the child vanish behind a tall green hedge of the garden and then turned to gaze at the pool. It was placid, its surface green from the reflection of the nearby trees. One of the swans was swimming about gracefully while the other sat on the wooden ledge of the bird house in the center. There was nothing here that spoke of anything but quiet beauty to her.

She walked on to join Enid in the garden, amazed at the child's reaction to studying by the pond. She wondered if it might have anything to do with a fear of water. There was so much about Enid that she did not know. But she knew she must proceed slowly or nothing could be accomplished. So she decided not to say anything further about the pond and proceeded with lining up a course of study.

Enid was seated on a bench near the rose bushes and she was deep in a book as Flora came up to sit on the bench with her.

"What are you reading?" Flora wanted to know.

"It is a child's history of the Crusades," Enid said, looking up at her. "I love to read about history."

Flora smiled at her. "Do you? Well, that's a good sign. We'll read a lot of it."

Enid closed the book and stared up at her with childish seriousness. "But then history is being made all the time, isn't it? Even today."

"That's so. History is a record of past events. Events that were once lived by someone just as we live in the present."

"Have you read about the Crimean War?" Enid wanted to know.

"I lived through it," Flora told her. "And so did you, although you must have been only about three years old when it began. But I can remember my father taking me to see the soldiers gathering to climb on a wagon and be trundled off to join their regiments in London. It was very sad."

"Did your father have to go to war?"

"No. He was older and the vicar of a church."

"Did you live near the church?"

"Always."

"What about your mother?"

"My mother died when I was young. I had only my father."

Enid's eyes widened in wonder. "You were just like me!"

"I suppose in a way, I was," she agreed, anxious for any link that would bring her closer to the child.

"My mother died when I was born and I have only my father. But then I had nurses and governesses. What about you?"

"I was brought up by a faithful housekeeper and my father acted as my teacher, so I needed no governess."

Enid looked forlorn. "My father rides off to London every day and works in his office. I would much prefer that he stay here and teach me like your father did."

She offered the youngster a sympathetic smile. "Your father has wide business interests. He is a man of affairs. He can't stay at home. The others in his firm wouldn't know what to do without someone to direct them. My father's duties were different, you see."

The dark girl nodded. "He had only to preach on Sundays?"

"He did more than that but it didn't require his leaving home for London," Flora told her.

"My father trades with China."

"I know."

"He says he's going to take me there one day."

"That would be exciting."

"He says if we do go there he'll hire a Chinese woman to look after me and she will be called an *amah!*"

"Indeed!"

"Would you like to go to China, Miss Bain?"

"I really have never thought about it," she admitted. "I suppose it might be interesting."

"You have been in London?"

"Yes."

"I've only been there once," Enid lamented.

"You really live on the outskirts of London," Flora told her.

"But I'm talking about right in the city. The streets were so exciting with great wagons and omnibuses. And in the parks there were fine ladies and gentlemen on riding horses. Once we saw a fire engine racing by and making a great noise and there were men in red uniforms and shiny helmets riding on it to the fire."

She smiled. "Yes. London can be a most exciting place."

"Father talked of sending me to Mrs. Hartley's School for Young Ladies as a boarder. But when he took me there he couldn't make his mind up to it. Jessica was in a rage."

"Why?"

"Because it had been her idea in the first place."

"I see," she said. This didn't surprise her. She wondered why Jessica hadn't hit on some such plan to rid herself of this child's presence at Armitage House since she hated her so much.

"It was a very strict school and my father thought the little girls there all looked very sad."

"Maybe they did."

"My father didn't like it at all so we left and spent the rest of the day shopping. I loved the stores."

"I can imagine."

"There were fine, thin gentlemen behind the counters to serve you and Father even bought some lovely velvet cloth for Jessica so she wouldn't be too angry at his bringing me home again. But she was angry just the same."

"Why should it make any difference to her?"

"Because she doesn't like me," the youngster said with wisdom beyond her years. "And that doesn't matter since I don't care for her either."

Flora warned. "You mustn't say such things."

"Then when we came home Jessica refused to accept the velvet from Father and so he gave it to Mrs. Brant. Jessica didn't speak to me for days and it was after that Father hired Lily. And now you are to be my governess."

"I was hired for that purpose," she said. "But so far we haven't made any beginnings."

"I disagree," Enid said. "I've learned a lot of things about you and you've heard how I almost was sent to a boarding school."

"Let us proceed with our lessons so there'll be no danger of that happening again," Flora said. "Let us begin with history since you enjoy it. I'll mark you out some reading assignments."

In that way the lessons began. Within a short time Flora had a week's work planned ahead. Enid was bright for her ten years, much more like an adult in her thought and conversation. She felt if she could just keep her interest there would be no problems in teaching her. When they finally had the work all lined out she told Enid she might have the rest of the morning off.

The little girl jumped up from the bench with bright eyes. "Do you really mean it?"

"Yes. You must have time for play as well as study."

"That's wonderful! I try to meet cook's little girl every morning out back by the stables. The groom lets us watch him take care of the horses and sometimes he puts us on their backs for a ride. And afterward we play hide-and-seek!"

"Exercise and the outdoors are good for you," Flora said with a smile of dismissal.

"Thank you, Miss Bain!" Enid exclaimed and ran out of the garden in the direction of the house.

Flora remained on the bench for a few minutes, straightening out the various books and the notes she'd jotted down. Then, with a feeling of a morning's work well done, she got up and also strolled across the lawn towards Armitage House.

When she entered the cool interior of the house she was greeted by a cold smile from Jessica, who had just come down the curving stairway.

"I saw you and your charge in the garden. Isn't it distracting, attempting to study in the open?"

"No," she said. "I don't think it makes any difference at all. And it's so much more pleasant."

Jessica's eyes were fixed on her. "More pleasant for you, you mean, of course."

She felt her cheeks crimson. "More pleasant for me and much healthier for Enid."

The girl at the bottom of the stairs laughed derisively. "I find that amusing."

"I can't see why."

"Let me tell you that Enid has had a long succession of would-be governesses like you when she should be in a boarding school. And I don't expect you to be any more successful with her than the others."

"I find her very bright."

"You will discover she is too brilliant for you," Jessica warned her. "Wait for some of her tricks! You'll find out!"

"I think she does very well considering she has no mother and the tensions which she must face in this house," Flora declared as she defended the girl.

Jessica raised her eyebrows. "How interesting! You have already formed an opinion about all of us!"

"Rather of the general atmosphere of the house."

"Much the same thing," Jessica said, dismissing her explanation. "I'm certain you aren't going to last long here."

"I'll leave only if I'm undermined in some way," Flora told her. "I want no quarrel with you, Miss Armitage, but you are making my position here difficult with your comments. If I have to suffer many more of them I shall feel impelled to complain to your brother."

"To Henry?" Jessica asked with a quiet maliciousness.

"Yes."

The red-haired girl threw back her head and laughed. "I don't think you have caught the atmosphere of this house as well as you think, Miss Bain. It is I not Henry who makes the final decisions here."

"We'll see," she said quietly.

Jessica descended the step and came across to inspect her. "My what fine feathers we are wearing this morning. No wonder you are in such a saucy mood. If I'm not mistaken you are wearing one of your predecessor's dresses. That brown dress you have on belonged to Lily."

"I'm only wearing it because Mrs. Brant brought it to me," she said.

"I have no complaint, Miss Bain," Jessica said suavely. "Not as long as you keep a civil tongue in your head!" And with that she turned and marched off into the living room.

Tears welled in Flora's eyes. She went to the library and placed the study books on an empty table. Then she turned and literally raced out of the house, down the steps, across the lawn. In her blind flight she almost ran straight into Bradford Armitage, who was out for a morning stroll.

He halted and stared at her. "What kind of a state are you in, Miss Bain? Didn't you see me?"

"I'm sorry," she said. "I'm afraid I didn't. I was very upset."

"So it appears," he said with some interest.

"Please forgive me."

"Easily," he said, leaning on his cane. "But I first must know what induced this unhappy mood in you? Has Enid been tormenting you?"

"No. I've had no trouble with the child."

"Ah," the big man said knowingly. "So it was Jessica?"

She gave him a troubled look. "I very badly need to make good in this post, Mr. Armitage. I don't dare risk losing it."

"You have not answered my question."

"I can't."

"You don't have to tell me anything," he said. "I know exactly what you have been up against. Jessica can be a bitter tongued vixen when she wishes."

"I'd prefer to forget all about it."

He nodded. "Believe me that might be the best thing to do. And don't allow her to make you so miserable in the first place. It is what she wants. I warned you not to allow yourself to be frightened away, and I meant it. I meant it in connection with several things, including Jessica. She is trying to make my son believe that Enid can only be educated in a boarding school. So part of her vicious plan is to frighten off every young lady who comes here as governess."

"I guessed that."

"So you've seen through her?"

"Yes."

The big man smiled sympathetically. "Then don't be a ninny! Don't allow her to put you in a state of tears and confusion! You might very well have knocked me down!"

She was forced to join him in a smile at the thought of her being able to knock him down. "I consider that very unlikely."

"Where is Enid?"

"I gave her permission to play for a little. She was a very good student this morning."

"Excellent," the old man said. "Let my son know that when he returns from London this evening."

"I will."

"I shall also talk to him and to Jessica. I won't mention our discussion but I'll let her know I'm watching her actions closely. Enjoy your walk, Miss Bain."

She moved on feeling much better. She felt she had at least one good friend in the house. Bradford Armitage was eccentric but she believed that in spite of his failing health he was clear-minded and would not tolerate any abuse of his granddaughter.

Now she strolled slowly towards the edge of the woods. She halted, seeing that there was a wide path through the tall evergreens and at the other end of the path open fields. And standing on a hill above the fields was a large Tudor mansion. She decided this must be the home of Sir Thomas Waring and his young bride, Madge. What a December and May match that was!

Flora turned from the woods' path and walked back to the pond. For no reason she could understand she felt herself drawn there on many occasions. She walked to its edge and stared down at its green surface. Once again she knew an easing of her tensions. She stood there for a few minutes lost in thought. Then she heard a footstep on the gravel behind her, followed by a gasp. She turned at once to find herself staring at Madge Waring.

The young bride from the adjoining estate was quickly apologetic. "I'm so sorry," she exclaimed. "Forgive me! For a moment I thought you were a ghost!"

Chapter Thirteen

FLORA STARED at the young woman in her fashionable blue gown and bonnet. "Why should you think me a ghost?"

Madge Waring looked embarrassed. "I couldn't see your face. But the way you were standing appeared familiar, and so did that brown dress you're wearing."

"You recognized it?"

"Yes. It belonged to Lily, didn't it?"

Flora nodded. "Yes. I believe it did."

"It never occurred to me that you would be wearing it. You are not only just about Lily's size but have the same coloring. You can understand that with your back to me the mistake was an easy one to make."

Flora listened to the other girl with growing curiosity. "But surely you knew Lily had left Armitage House?"

"Yes," she said quietly.

Flora was beginning to realize that this girl knew something that she didn't. "Did you know Lily very well?"

164

"I often met her here near the pond," Madge said, seeming extremely nervous now.

"Indeed," Flora said. "She surely came here with Enid."

"Yes, of course."

She stared at Madge, whose lovely features showed great uneasiness. "Did you see her before she left?"

Madge Waring shook her head. "No."

Flora's eyes were fixed on her sharply. "I find it strange that you thought I was a ghost. That would have to mean that Lily is dead."

Madge looked as if she wanted to turn and run away. After a moment's pause, she said, "But surely you know that she is?"

Flora was shocked. No one had told her what had happened to Lily. There had been snide comments that the girl had become infatuated with Henry Armitage and so had to be let go for that reason.

Trying to collect her thoughts, she asked in a taut voice, "How?"

Madge made a gesture towards the pond. "She drowned herself!"

It was all so clear to her now that she didn't know why she hadn't guessed before. The girl's clothes having been left at Armitage House and being so readily available to her. Enid's fear of the pond and her aversion to going near it.

Flora said, "How long ago did this happen?"

"A month or so. It was terribly sad," Madge said. "I assumed you must have been told."

"No," she said. "This is the first time I've heard the truth."

"I'm sorry," Madge said uneasily. "I didn't mean to cause trouble."

"I would have been bound to learn about it sooner or later. Better that I have heard it now."

Madge looked frightened. "It was such a grisly happening and the Armitages are so sensitive about it! You won't let on I told you, will you?"

"Not if you would prefer that I didn't," she said. Her

eyes met those of the other young woman. "Were you and Lily good friends?"

She hesitated. "I don't know what to say. We met a number of times and talked a lot about various things. She was very friendly."

"I've heard her criticized as having been too friendly," Flora pointed out.

Madge continued to look uneasy. "I don't know what you mean."

"I've heard that she fell in love with Henry Armitage and made a nuisance of herself."

She made no answer right away. Flora could tell that her words had badly upset Madge, who was rumored to be in love with Henry herself. Her behavior the previous night had surely suggested this as did her obvious confusion now.

Flora again asked, "Do you think that Lily was in love with Henry Armitage?"

Madge raised her eyes. "I don't know," she said unhappily. "I'm not good at reading other people's minds. Certainly she had never mentioned any such thing to me!"

"Did Lily really take her own life?"

"Of course. She threw herself into the pond! It is very deep in spots!"

"Couldn't someone else have pushed her into it?"

"I don't know," Madge said fearfully. "I suppose so! The idea never struck me!"

"Then you must have thought Lily was unhappy and you must have expected her to be a suicide?"

"I didn't expect anything! I talked to her one day and she seemed the same as always. The next morning I heard she'd drowned herself here in the pond!"

"Madge, you can think of no reason for this?"

"I can only think that the rumors you've referred to were true. That she must have been in love with Henry!"

Flora eyed her sharply. "And what about him? Do you suppose he reciprocated her feelings?"

"He couldn't have!" Madge exclaimed in a tone of certainty, which she exhibited for the first time.

"Why? She was young and attractive and in love with him."

"He wouldn't fall in love with a servant!" Madge cried out. "I'm sorry. I didn't mean it to sound that way. I meant to say that he wouldn't allow himself to become involved with someone in his employ. Henry is scrupulous about not taking advantage of people."

Flora said quietly, "I understand you. You are probably right. Henry would be unlikely to allow his feelings to take control knowing the girl was in his employ."

"She was really very nice," Madge said, trying to ease the situation.

Flora gazed at the green surface of the pond with its lovely waterlilies.

"I'm sorry. I've been very stupid."

"Why do you say that?"

"Henry and the others couldn't have wanted you to know and I have given the secret away. I assume they feared you might decide to leave at once if you learned the truth."

"I might very well have," she agreed.

"And now?"

"I don't know."

"But you promised not to involve me in it," Madge reminded her.

"Yes. I did. And I won't go back on my word."

"Thank you," she said gratefully. "The Armitage family are our closest neighbors. Sir Thomas is unwell and these days depends on them greatly for company. You understand."

"I think I do," she said evenly. She was thinking that the panic-stricken Madge was not as worried about her husband as she was for herself. She did not want her close friendship with Henry to be impaired.

"I must go," Madge said. "I hope my telling you about Lily won't make you change your mind about remaining here. Enid needs someone so badly and Jessica is not fond of the poor child."

"I've discovered that for myself," Flora said. "I'll not be frightened away without considering my position here."

"Good," Madge Waring said. And she turned and hurried off across the lawn at the rear of the pool, continuing until she'd taken the path and was out of sight in the woods.

Left alone to ponder on what she'd just heard, Flora felt she must have been extremely stupid not to have realized before that something was wrong. She was standing here in the dead girl's clothes, not even aware of what had gone on until she'd been mistaken for Lily's ghost.

What did it all mean? Lily had been found drowned in the pond and assumed to be a suicide. But Madge Waring had seen no sign of depression in the girl. There had been no hint that she was on the verge of suicide the day before she was found dead. Was there the possibility of murder?

Flora had heard that Lily had fallen in love with Henry. And if this were true the unfortunate girl had definitely made herself the target of Jessica, who had a most unnatural affection for her brother, and even for Madge, who was also clearly in love with her handsome neighbor. Either woman might have conspired to have brought about Lily's death. Suppose among the other dark shadows that lay over Armitage House there was one which concealed the murder of the unhappy Lily?

That question was going to continue plaguing her. She could not simply dismiss it. And yet she didn't want anything to happen to send her away from the old mansion. In spite of its tense atmosphere she wanted to remain with Enid. The poor child sorely needed someone. Flora knew there was little for herself in the great city of London but perhaps a return to William Booth's mission. She desperately needed the post.

What really upset her was that no one had told her frankly about Lily. She had been forced to find out the truth in roundabout fashion. Even Enid had evidently been warned not to say anything. Everything tended to make her suspect there was more to the girl's death than they wanted anyone to find out.

She walked back to the house slowly, wondering what

she should do. When she arrived, Enid was waiting to take lunch with her on the sun porch.

Enid was in a talkative mood and asked her, "Have you ever seen a marionette show, Miss Bain?"

She smiled from her side of the table. "Yes. One used to visit Rye every summer. It had a very colorful red, yellow, and gold wagon and four dappled gray horses with red pom-pons in their head harness. The proprietor would lower a platform at the rear of the wagon and set his stage there. Between the acts of the marionette show assistants would go through the crowd and collect money."

"It sounds marvellous fun!" Enid said enthusiastically. "Father took me to see a marionette show in London but it was performed in a regular theatre and I don't expect it was nearly as much fun as the one you saw."

"I'm sure it was more elaborate," she said. "But I doubt that it was more entertaining."

"What other shows did you have?" the ten-year-old wanted to know.

"We had traveling circuses."

"Did they have an elephant?" Enid asked excitedly. "Father took me for a ride on an elephant's back at Regent's Park!"

"I'm afraid trained dogs were the best our little circuses could offer. Occasionally they had trained donkeys and even an occasional wild animal. But mostly we had trapeze and rope walking artists."

Enid's face clouded. "The last time we went to Regent's Park my father had Lily come along. She enjoyed the ride on the elephant as much as I did."

"Did she?" Flora said, at once aware of the sudden change in the child's mood. Now she looked depressed.

"Lily was my favorite governess until you came along," Enid told her.

"That's a nice compliment," she said. "I hope I can live up to it."

"I know I'm going to like you," the little girl said seriously. "And I'll study hard so my father will realize you are a good teacher."

169

"That will surely help," Flora said. "I wonder that you let Lily go if you liked her so much."

Enid's eyes grew large with fear. "I don't think anyone could do anything about her going."

"No?"

"No."

"I'm afraid I don't understand you," she said. "Why did Lily give up her post as governess here?"

The black-haired little girl shook her head. "I can't tell you."

"Can't or won't?" she asked quietly, sure the child would tell her what she knew if she kept pressing her.

"I'm not to discuss it," Enid said with a tremble in her voice. "I was told not to."

"Miss Bain!" It was Jessica who called out her name sharply. She was standing in the doorway to the porch.

"Yes, Miss Armitage?" Flora said respectfully as she rose.

Jessica, wearing an attractive green afternoon dress, came out onto the porch. "I want to have a short talk with you, Miss Bain," she said. "Can you assign Enid to some task so we may have a few minutes privacy?"

"Yes," Flora said, aware that she was about to have a difficult confrontation with the redhead. She turned to Enid, who had finished her lunch. "Enid, I want you to take your arithmetic book outside to the garden and do all the multiplication tables I marked for you this morning."

"Now?" the girl asked, rising reluctantly.

"Yes, now," she said. "I'll go out and join you after a little and we'll then do your French lesson."

Jessica gave the girl a nod. "You heard your governess. Go on and do what she says without any argument."

Enid gave a deep sigh and slumped her shoulders. "Well, if I must!" she said. And she left the porch and went on into the house.

When they were alone Jessica stepped across to face Flora. With an angry look on her lovely face, she inquired, "Why were you questioning the child in that fashion?"

She pretended innocence. "I don't understand."

"I'm sure you do," Jessica insisted. "Don't bother to lie about it. I heard you."

Flora's face flushed. "I'm not a liar by habit."

Jessica looked her most arrogant. "Really?" she said. "I'm afraid one might think so."

"Miss Armitage, if you continue to indulge in such personal vilification I shall have no alternative but to inform your brother."

"How high and mighty we are! And yet you have only a few days between you and the London streets and William Booth's mission. You had better tread carefully or you may find yourself back being threatened by brothel keepers once again!"

Flora battled to hold her temper.

"I do not wish to quarrel with you, Miss Armitage."

"I will ask you once again. Why were you questioning Enid so about Lily? Why should you be so interested in why her previous governess left? It is none of your business."

"I feel it might be," Flora said evenly. "Particularly because all of you have kept the truth from me. I know that this dress I'm wearing belonged to a dead girl. I know that Lily was drowned in the pond!"

She said sharply, "Who told you that story?"

"It doesn't matter. I found out for myself. I know what happened."

"I suppose Father told you!" Jessica said angrily. "That poor old man is in his dotage and you took advantage of him just as you're trying to take advantage of that poor child."

Flora felt sure this was a ploy to pry the truth from her and she was determined not to give Madge away.

She said, "How I found out is not all that important. The thing is that I did find out. Why have you all tried to keep that young woman's death a secret from me?"

Jessica's head was held high. "We do not enjoy having a scandal here. We felt it in good taste not to mention the affair."

"I question that," she said.

"You have no right to question anything," Henry's sister

informed her. "You are here as an employee. One of the other reasons for keeping silence on the matter was to avoid upsetting you. Both my brother and I felt you might become uneasy if you knew of Lily's suicide and not wish to remain here."

"That sounds much closer to the truth," Flora said.

"We even asked Enid not to mention it. Just now you put her to a vicious test. After hearing you I'm no longer sure I want to entrust her to your care. She should be in a proper boarding school where she would receive more balanced attention from a proper staff of instructors."

"That is what you've been wanting, isn't it, Miss Armitage? And now you see a chance to push your idea. I'm sorry to have given you the opportunity."

Jessica smiled coldly. "Perhaps your bad behavior may be put to a good use after all."

"I meant Enid no harm. But I wanted to hear the truth from her. I wanted to find out why she'd been told to be silent."

"Well, now you know!"

"I'm not entirely sure," she protested. "I'm afraid much of what happened still remains a mystery. Why did this girl drown herself?"

"Frankly, I consider that none of your business, Miss Bain. You wanted to know the truth of what happened to her. Now you know. And it seems you are still not satisfied."

"I've only heard a sketchy outline of it all," she said. "I find it hard to discover a motive for the girl's suicide."

Jessica's eyes were ice cold. "There was one, Miss Bain. Never fear!"

"Then I must merely take your word for it."

"I fear that is the case," she said nastily.

Flora said, "Then I, for my part, must decide whether or not to remain here, Miss Armitage."

"For one, I'm not wholly certain you are the right person for the position, Miss Bain. I intend to speak to my brother once again about sending Enid to a boarding school. If I'm able to make him see things my way we shall certainly be able to dispense with your services."

Flora said, "Until such time as I am dismissed by your brother I shall continue to devote myself to Enid."

Jessica smiled icily. "Do not count on my giving you any sort of recommendation when you do leave. I think it might be best if you had another short course of experience in the London streets. That might cure you of the superior airs you seem to have picked up as a vicar's daughter. Your behavior is far above the range of your station in life. Too bad you haven't parents to inform you of that."

She could listen to this threatening talk no longer. She hurried to the door leading into the main house and left Jessica still standing there.

Jessica's belligerent attitude went a long way in convincing her that there was more to be learned about the girl's death than had come out. She was upset that Jessica had discovered she knew about Lily so soon, but on the other hand it was now all out in the open. Jessica would surely go to Henry when he returned from London with some trumped-up story. She could only hope that he would be fair and give her a chance to present her side of it.

She left the house by the front door and found Enid bent over her arithmetic table book on a bench in the garden. The girl glanced up at her questioningly as she neared.

"What did Aunt Jessica say to you?" Enid wanted to know.

She sat beside the child. "Nothing important."

"I know better," Enid said. "She was angry about you asking me about Lily."

"Maybe."

"She was! I'm sure!"

"How can you be?"

A mischievous look crossed the ten-year-old's face. "I know because I waited and listened from the hallway. I heard you both."

"That was wrong, Enid."

"I know. But all's fair when it comes to dealing with Aunt Jessica. You're going to find that out."

"It may be," she agreed. "Where's your parasol? The sun is very strong now."

"I have it here at the end of the bench," Enid said, as she found it and opened it to hold over them.

"Thank you," Flora said, grateful for the shade.

"I did like Lily," the child went on. "I was broken-hearted when she drowned herself in the pond."

"Did you ever guess it was going to happen?"

"No. But sometimes when I went to find her in her room she was sitting alone crying. I don't think she was happy."

"What made her unhappy?"

The child hesitated. "I guess it had to be Aunt Jessica."

"Oh?"

"Yes."

"Go on," she urged the child. "Explain."

"Aunt Jessica had a terrible argument with Lily one day," Enid said. "I happened to overhear them. I was supposed to be playing at the stables but I came back to find a ball and so I heard them."

"That seems to happen pretty often with you," Flora told her.

"I really did come back for the ball," she said seriously. "They were shouting at each other so loud I couldn't help listening. They were saying awful things. Jessica told Lily that she was trying to get my father to marry her. And Lily shouted back that Jessica didn't want him to marry anyone but to always live here with her."

"They actually said those things?"

"Yes. I can remember nearly all they said," Enid went on. "And the next thing Lily said was she wasn't the only one who wanted my father to pay attention to her. She said that Madge Waring was in love with him and maybe Sir Thomas ought to be told!"

"What did Jessica say to that?"

Enid shook her head at the memory. "It was awful! Aunt Jessica said terrible things. She promised Lily she would pay for such talk and that she would tell my father. Then I got frightened and ran back to the stables."

"That was much the best thing to do," Flora told her.

"I don't believe any of it," Enid mused. "I liked Lily and I'm fond of Madge. I think maybe the only part of it that was true was that Lily was secretly in love with my father. He's so nice you couldn't blame her for that, could you?"

"I don't suppose so."

Enid's eyes questioned her. "Don't you find him nice?"

She blushed. "Yes. He's very nice, but that is another matter. And it was after this quarrel that Lily took her life?"

"A day or two after."

"Did your Aunt Jessica report it all to your father?"

"I don't know."

"So you just guess that Lily became so unhappy she didn't want to live. She didn't give you any idea she was going to kill herself, did she?"

"No."

Flora sighed. "I'm afraid I'm the one your aunt will be reporting to your father now."

"It won't do her any good."

"Don't be too sure."

"I'm sure. My father likes you. I can tell by the way he looks at you and talks to you. And he wants me to have someone to teach me here rather than sending me away to school."

She smiled wanly as they both sat in the shade of the parasol. "I hope you're right."

"I'm sure I am," the youngster said. "There is just one other thing you ought to know."

"What?"

"Lily's ghost comes back to haunt the house," Enid said solemnly. "I have seen her in my room. Almost always on moonlit nights!"

Chapter Fourteen

ENID'S STATEMENT was a startling one. Flora had not been prepared for it. But even as she considered it she felt that it might be quite possible. From the beginning she had found in Armitage House a macabre atmosphere and strange tensions. Perhaps part of the strange menace of the ancient house came from the fact that it was haunted. Haunted by the ghost of the drowned governess!

Still, she did not want to encourage Enid in morbid thoughts so she forced herself to say, "I'm sure you must be mistaken! It is your nerves that make you think you have seen and heard a ghost."

"No," the little girl protested. "I have seen her."

"Where?"

"In my room. She opens the door and comes into my room and stands at the foot of my bed. She wears a cloak and hood so I'm not be able to see her face. But I know it's Lily!"

Flora listened as an icy chill ran along her spine. "You

probably had a bad dream and thought you saw a ghost. It happens even with grown-ups."

"I know it is Lily who comes to my room," Enid insisted. "I've heard her sigh as she stands there watching me, just as she used to sigh when she was alive."

"How many times has this happened?"

The little girl thought. "Maybe three or four times in all after Lily was drowned in the pond."

"Have you told your father or anyone else about this?"

"No."

"Why?"

"I didn't dare tell my father because he'd mention it to Jessica and she'd want to punish me. She'd say I should be sent away to some boarding school."

Flora knew the sense this made. She was only too well aware of Jessica's tactics. "It was wise to keep it to yourself, Enid."

"You won't tell them?"

"No," she said. "But I am worried about what you've revealed to me."

"If you remain here you'll see the ghost too," Enid promised her.

"I wonder."

"I'm sure you will," the child said. "I think others in the house have seen it but they aren't talking about it."

"Perhaps," she said. She was thinking that the servants might have something to contribute to the ghost story and she wished she could talk to Dolly. Her friend had been in the servant's quarters long enough now to pick up a good deal of the gossip, and she made a mental note to try and contact Dolly as soon as she could.

"I think Lily is unhappy in her grave," Enid said solemnly. "Isn't that why the ghosts of people come back?"

"It's said to be one of the reasons," she agreed. "But I still think you're mistaken. You've seen shadows and heard the wind sighing and your imagination has done the rest."

"You'll find out," her charge said.

Flora changed the subject and soon had Enid engrossed in reading William Shakespeare's *Taming of the Shrew* in

177

an abridged version for children. It ended the afternoon on a happy note.

When Flora went downstairs for dinner that evening she found old Bradford Armitage seated in his favorite chair in the living room with a glass of sherry. He beckoned her to join him.

"You look very attractive in that dress, Miss Bain."

"I very much fear it's borrowed finery. Mrs. Brant found some clothing for me and this blue dress was in the lot. Now I have learned that all the things belonged to the governess who was found drowned in the pond."

"So you have found out what happened to your predecessor."

"Yes."

"Would you have come here as governess if you had known?"

"I doubt that either Mr. Gladstone or William Booth would have allowed me to come if they'd been aware of the facts."

"The facts?" he said with a slight frown. "Who knows them? Who can tell why that poor girl took her life?"

"Her death does cast a shadow over this house."

"Granted. Yet I don't know how we could have prevented what she did. Knowing about her are you sorry that you became governess to Enid?"

"No. But only because of the child. I think she is truly remarkable."

Enid's grandfather looked pleased. "I most certainly agree. And I do hope you'll remain with us. She needs you. There was a time when this was a happy house."

"I'm sure it was," she said, gazing around the living room at the many Oriental treasures. "You have such a fine Chinese collection."

The old man waved a large hand to indicate his priceless collection. "It all began when I first went to China to establish our import business. I liked the Chinese and they liked me. Many of my business associates helped me find the items with which I have decorated this house."

"Tea is the chief import of your company, isn't it?" she asked.

He nodded. "The scholar Kuo Po first included a description of tea in his dictionary in 350 A.D. But the tea he noted was used medicinally. It wasn't until the sixth century that the Chinese came to find tea a refreshing drink."

"I thought it must have always existed," she said.

"No. Yu Lu in 780 A.D. was the first tea expert. He was the one who developed the Code of Tea."

"Who first brought it to this country?" she asked.

"The British East India Company, which held the import monopoly until about a quarter of a century ago. Then some others of us joined in the trade."

"And it has been profitable?"

"Very."

"Have you seen tea leaves picked?" she asked.

"Many times. They are picked by hand during the season of active growth. The best leaves are the ones near the growing tip of the branch. It takes a tree three years before it begins to yield, and then it is good for fifty years."

"How do you sort out the different kinds of tea?"

"The leaves are withered, rolled, and heated. For green tea the leaves are fired soon after picking. For black they are first fermented for about twenty-four hours. For oolong, the intermediate in flavor, the leaves are partially fermented."

Flora found herself fascinated by the old man's knowledge. "My father always preferred orange pekoe tea."

"Then he had good taste," Bradford Armitage said. "I enjoy orange pekoe myself. Teas are classified according to leaf size, you know. Some are named for the district they come from, such as Darjeeling. China produces most of the green tea and the black comes mainly from Japan. In the Tea Ceremony the dried blossoms of jasmine are added to the tea."

"It's an interesting subject," she said. "I had no idea it was typed until now."

The big man looked pleased. "Another time I'll tell you more about it." Changing the subject he asked her, "Did Jessica tell you about Lily's suicide?"

"No," she said carefully. "I just happened to hear about it."

The old man's searching eyes were fixed on her. "I see." But he made no attempt to question her further about the matter.

Shortly afterward Jessica came into the living room with Henry. Flora had the immediate impression that something had been discussed between the two. Henry had a certain withdrawn air that was not native to him. Enid had permission to join them at the dinner table that evening, and as soon as she came down, her father's mood at once improved.

They gathered in the paneled dining room, where they were served an excellent dinner under the supervision of Mrs. Brant. During the meal Enid asked her father, "Will you take Flora and me to London one day?"

"Why this sudden interest in the city?"

"I'd like to visit the shops and see a play," Enid told him. "Lily planned to take me but we never did get there."

At the mention of Lily's name Henry looked stern. "I'll think about it. We can discuss it later." And he at once turned to Flora, changing the subject by quizzing her on the progress of Enid's studies. But Flora had felt the tension that had quickly filled the room. She had also caught a glimpse of the look of fear on Jessica's lovely face and the uneasy expression shown by Henry's father. There had to be something about Lily's death that they were hiding.

When dinner ended Jessica surprisingly invited Enid outside for a stroll. The child accepted, leaving Flora and Henry alone as Bradford Armitage had made his way upstairs immediately after the meal.

Henry formally asked her, "Would you mind joining me in my study for a few minutes, Flora?"

"Not at all," she said meekly.

Nothing was said as they made their way along the dark corridor to the study. She sat in a leather chair while Henry fumbled with the lamp on his desk in an effort to make its flame brighter.

He sat by the desk awkwardly facing her. In the glow of

180

the lamp, he looked more handsome than ever, but somewhat pale and tense. He cleared his throat. "I had a short talk with my sister before dinner. The talk concerned you."

"Oh?" She had been prepared for this.

"Yes," he went on, folding his hands behind his back. "She tells me you questioned her about the facts of Lily's death!"

"That is not completely true," she said at once.

"It isn't?"

"No. I found out about my predecessor's death entirely by chance and from another source."

His eyebrows lifted. "Another source?"

"Yes."

"May I ask from whom?"

She felt she need not hold back the truth from him. So she said, "From Lady Waring."

"From Madge?" he sounded startled.

"Yes."

"Please go on," he said, uneasily.

She went on to explain that Madge had noticed her standing by the pond wearing the dress which had belonged to Lily and had for a moment thought her to be a ghost. She ended with, "Naturally I then questioned her about how Lily met her death."

"She could not tell you that. No one can. We only know she threw herself in the pond. We found her body the morning after she disappeared."

"I see," she said.

"Lily was a neurotic type, I fear," the young man went on. "She suffered from a number of fancies. I can only imagine that in the end her nerves gave way and she took her own life."

"She apparently gave no hint of her intentions to anyone," Flora pointed out.

He frowned. "That does not mean she wasn't a suicide. Many would-be suicides say nothing of their plans."

"The majority are said to warn of what they have in mind," she persisted.

He stared at her. "Are you suggesting that Lily didn't take her own life? That it could have been a murder?"

"The thought struck me."

"Nonsense," he said sharply. "There was no chance of such a thing. Otherwise I wouldn't have hired you to replace her. I would not want to place you in danger if I believed there was a murderer at large in this house."

He continued to look worried. "Jessica suggested you might have some wrong ideas about the incident. Though she did not know where you'd received your information. She was inclined to blame it on my father."

"I know."

"Father has vague spells when he is not himself," the young man warned her. "You must be careful to remember this in your dealings with him."

"I have always found him most lucid," she said.

"Then you have been fortunate. Well, I trust this clears up all your doubts. Jessica felt you had a distorted impression of the tragic event."

Her eyes met his. "I did wonder about it. I still will continue to, I must confess. You are sure she did not meet with foul play at the hands of someone here?"

"Why do you hark back to that?"

"I don't know. Perhaps it is because of this house. It gives me a strange feeling that is hard to explain."

"It is perfectly natural for you to feel oddly, knowing about what happened to Lily, but after a time this will pass. I'm also sorry you had to learn the story from Lady Waring. I would have preferred to tell you myself."

"I understand," she said. But at the same time she knew that he had indeed had many opportunities to tell her and had avoided the subject.

He was staring at her. "Jessica felt you to be so upset as to make it questionable whether we should ask you to stay on here or not."

Thinking of her concern for Enid, she at once replied, "You need not worry. I'm quite ready to stay on here as governess to your daughter."

Henry gave a small sigh which she interpreted as being one of relief. "I'm glad to hear it. I feel you are ideally suited to the role and I'm delighted with the fast progress you've already made in helping Enid with her studies."

"She is highly intelligent."

"You think so?"

"I do."

"Jessica feels I have spoiled her. She claims Enid ought to be sent to a boarding school. But I have many reservations about the idea."

Flora said, "Enid is an unusually bright young girl. I'd say she can benefit much more from private tutoring than in being restricted to the learning pace of a class."

"I quite agree," he said. "I wish you'd point that out to my sister some time."

She smiled ruefully. "I'm not sure it would do much good. She does not seem to take kindly to any advice offered by me."

With a sigh he told her, "Jessica enjoys being difficult at times."

"I'm coming to understand that."

"Well, now that we have this settled I'm sure you'll have no more difficulties."

"I'm fond of Enid," she confessed. "I would like to remain with her a while."

"And so you shall!" he declared. "Why, Gladstone would not know what to think if I told him you were going to leave us so soon. After all the trouble he went to in order to find you for us."

She rose from her chair. "I'm sorry to have occasioned you so much trouble."

"No trouble. Better we should have this out."

"Since your sister believes it was your father who told me about Lily I think it might be better to let it stay that way without drawing Lady Waring into it. I gave her my word I would protect her."

"That presents no problem," Henry said. "I agree that it might be better to let Jessica believe what she likes. Let her assume my father told you."

"Thank you."

"Not at all. Lady Waring and her husband are dear friends of ours. I would not want to risk any trouble between us. And one never knows just how Jessica will react to anything. Well," he said, changing the subject, "Enid spoke to me about taking her into London and having you come along. Did you hear her mention that at the table?"

"Yes."

"I plan to do it one day soon," he assured her. "London is a great city with many educational things to offer. I wish my daughter to see more of it."

He rose from his chair. "Well, I think we have gained from our little talk," he said with a satisfied air.

They went back to the foyer where she found Enid waiting for her. They went upstairs together and Flora stayed with her as she prepared for bed. Enid said, "I know Jessica only took me walking tonight so you could be alone with my father. Jessica hates to walk with me!"

"That's a strange thing for you to say."

Enid was standing by her bedside in a long, white flannel nightgown. There was a very serious expression on her thin face. "I knew what Jessica was up to. And I could tell she was bored all the time we were out in the gardens. She just barely answered my questions."

"Maybe you didn't try hard enough to be friendly."

"No," the ten-year-old said solemnly. "She was just keeping me out there so Father could talk to you. Has she finally persuaded him to send me to boarding school? Is that it? Was he telling you he wouldn't need you any longer?"

"That wasn't it. It is true Jessica did create a problem by repeating something I had said, but I was able to straighten it out and so there is no trouble."

"I'm so glad!" Enid declared, happily throwing her arms about Flora's neck and kissing her on the cheek. "I don't want you to leave!"

"Don't worry," Flora said, touched by the child's show of emotion.

Enid drew back with fear in her little eyes. "You won't even let the ghost frighten you off!"

"I'm not one to believe in ghosts."

"They exist!" Enid assured her solemnly. "You'll see!"

"There's no time for such talk," Flora told her. "In bed

with you. I want you bright for your studies in the morning."

She left the child's room, troubled by many thoughts. As she reached the landing she met the elderly Armitage coming down from his attic workshop where he restored the Chinese antiques shipped to him by his friends in China. The old man was leaning heavily on his cane as he stepped onto the landing.

"Ah, Miss Bain," he said, his head shaking a trifle as he stared at her.

"Good evening, sir," she said.

"Where is the child?"

"I have just seen her safely to bed."

"Watch over her," the old man said with concern. "She needs careful watching."

"Yes," she said, not knowing quite what he meant.

The old man laboriously made his way downstairs and she decided to return to her own room. When Flora entered there it was dark save for a candle burning on her dresser. She moved to the window and saw that the rising moon cast its silver rays over the lawn. She recalled that Enid had told her that it was usually on moonlit nights that the ghost of Lily returned. An involuntary shudder ran through her.

Had she escaped from one danger in London only to be exposed to another more macabre? Only her fondness for Enid made her want to remain in this place. She could not be sure of any of the rest of them, except for old Bradford Armitage.

When she'd first met Henry she'd believed him to be a fine young man in every way. She still wanted to believe this but now she thought he might be guilty of murder or at least of concealing a possible killer.

Slowly she undressed and prepared for bed. By the time she blew out the candle flame the room was completely lighted by the moonlight. All was silent as she got into bed and drew the covers over her. As she lay on her pillow with her eyes fixed on the moonbeams coming in the window, she turned over all her worries in her mind. She was still doing this when sleep finally overcame her.

Her deep sleep was suddenly broken when a haunting, wild shout rang out. She sat up in bed. Still not certain that it wasn't part of a dream she sat there staring across the room.

At once she decided to get up to see if her charge was safe. She slipped out of bed and hastily but quietly made her way to the door of the little girl's room, opening it slowly.

To her surprise the child was standing near the door in her nightgown.

"Enid! What are you doing up at this hour?" she gasped.

The child looked up with fear on her face. "I saw her!" she said in an awed voice.

"Her?"

"Lily!"

"Nonsense!"

"No," the little girl insisted. "I did see her. I heard her cry out!"

"Cry out?"

"Yes. Didn't you hear her?"

She hesitated. "I heard something."

"She screamed from down the hall," the child said. "And then the door opened and she came in here."

"In here?"

"Yes."

"You must have dreamt it!" she protested.

"I saw her," the child insisted. "She looked just the same as before. Lily came back from the dead!"

"You must put such thoughts out of your mind and go back to bed," she commanded the child.

"Don't you want to hear about the ghost?"

"No. I don't believe in ghosts!"

Enid eyed her gravely. "You must! You said you heard her scream! That is why you came here to me, isn't it?"

"I don't know," she protested uneasily. "I just know we shouldn't be standing here talking about ghosts at this hour. If Jessica hears us I shall surely be dismissed!"

Looking concerned, Enid said, "I'll go back to my bed."

"Please do!"

"But I did see Lily's ghost. She stood crouched at the foot of my bed," the little girl insisted.

"We'll talk about it in the morning," she promised. "Just go to bed now."

"All right."

Flora tucked her in and told her, "Now I want you to sleep soundly and not have anymore bad dreams."

Enid looked up at her. "But it wasn't a bad dream. It was real. Lily came back from the dead again!"

"Go to sleep," Flora said sharply.

She turned and left the little girl's room so there could be no more conversation between them. Quietly closing the door, she made her way to her own room. She found the door still partly ajar. Pushing it open a trifle further she moved into the room. She stood just inside the door frozen with horror as she stared at a shadowy gray figure standing in the direct line of the moonbeams.

Chapter Fifteen

FLORA WAS too shocked to utter a sound. As she stood there terrified, the phantom raised a hand and came rushing at her.

As the ghost struck her with something, she realized that she was blacking out. She felt herself drop to the floor before she became unconscious. It was a long while before she stirred and was able to raise herself up to a sitting position. Her head was aching from a bump on the left side.

When she felt a little better she got up from the floor and made her way to the bed. She tried to review what had happened. What annoyed her most was that her own fears had betrayed her so that she hadn't been able to call for help.

Not that this would have likely made much difference. The ghost would probably have vanished before anyone managed to come to her aid. Had it really been a ghost? Or had it been someone pretending to be the dead girl's ghost?

188

She did not dare tell Henry what happened. She couldn't be sure that he wasn't at the bottom of it. So all she could do was wait and hope that whoever was playing this eerie game might soon give himself (or herself) away. She must keep her frightening experience to herself until she knew more of what was going on in the house. Even to confide in Henry might only expose her to ridicule and ruin her chances of protecting the child.

Her head still aching, she got up from the bed to see that her door was shut. There was no bolt on it so she decided to speak to Mrs. Brant about this. Surely the rather formidable housekeeper would be willing to grant her request in allowing her to have a slide bolt for protection.

She also intended to see Dolly and talk to her. She was certain that her young friend might have some interesting news since all the gossip of the house was bound to be circulated in the servants' quarters. At the moment she needed all the information she could get.

The next morning was foggy, cold, and rainy. After breakfast she sought out Mrs. Brant to ask her if she might have a bolt placed on her door.

The housekeeper regarded her suspiciously. "I should have to ask the master," she said coldly. "I would not venture to do such a thing without his permission."

"Surely it's not all that important!"

"No governess has made such a request before. And as a matter of fact there are few bolts on any of the doors in this house."

"Well, there should be!" she exclaimed.

"You may tell Mr. Armitage that if you like. I can't do anything about it without his approval."

"Then I shall certainly speak to him about it," she said.

It was a bad beginning for the day. She went to join Enid in the study and set out some lessons for her to do.

The girl gave her an inquiring glance. "Did you see Lily's ghost last night after you left me?"

She shook her head. "I don't want to discuss that."

"Why not?"

189

"Because I don't think it a suitable subject for us to talk about," she said irritably.

"I think you did see her," Enid insisted.

"Please!" Flora said.

"All right, I won't say anything more if that's what you want."

"That's a good girl," she said approvingly, and left her in the study to continue with her lessons.

In the living room she was gazing out the window at the pond when she heard footsteps behind her. She turned to see Jessica.

"Good morning," she said arrogantly.

"Good morning," Flora replied quietly, wondering what it was going to be now.

"I assume my brother filled you in on the details of Lily's death last night."

"He discussed it with me."

"Then you won't annoy Enid with any other questions about Lily and what happened to her?"

"I wasn't aware that I had ever done that," she said, knowing that Jessica had made this accusation about her to Henry.

"Well, that's not anything we have to discuss at length. I'm sure we understand each other. I only want to protect the child. She has enough childish fancies as it is about ghosts and such." She paused. "By the way, Mrs. Brant informed me you asked about having a bolt on your door. Can it be that you are also afraid of ghosts?"

She felt her cheeks burn as she replied, "I'm a good deal more afraid of the living."

"I suppose because you led such a sheltered life at that Sussex vicarage," Jessica said sarcastically. "But then when you were in the hands of that brothel keeper in London you must have had to face a more exposed existence."

"That was only for a few days," she said. "At home I always had a bolt on my door."

"We do not believe in them here," Jessica told her tartily. "Frankly, I don't think you will have any need of one."

Flora would have liked to have told her that she'd already had one unwelcome night visitor, but she didn't dare. So she was forced to remain silent in the face of Jessica's taunting.

Jessica seemed to take her silence for agreement. "Armitage House is a quiet place. And we have had few crimes of any sort in this community. I think you need have no worries."

"Perhaps not," she said in a small voice, though she made up her mind she would take up the matter with Henry Armitage later. Flora was still suspicious that Jessica had been her ghostly visitor.

"How are Enid's studies coming along?" Jessica said.

"Very well."

"I'm surprised. It's the first good report I've ever had from any governess. I think there are too many distractions for her living here at home. She would do much better in a boarding school. But then you can't convince her father of that."

"I must return to her now," Flora said, anxious to get away from Henry's jealous sister. "I gave her some exercises which should be completed."

She left Jessica in the living room and returned to the study. When she opened the door she saw no sign of Enid. The completed exercises were there on the desk, but the girl was missing. Knowing Enid's fondness for practical jokes, she searched the room thoroughly. There was no sign of the ten-year-old.

Leaving the study, she went to the stairway where she found a maid on her knees polishing the brass facing plates.

"Have you seen Miss Enid?" she asked.

"Yes, miss," the maid said respectfully, getting to her feet. "She ran past me up the stairs."

"Thank you," Flora said. She mounted the stairs and on reaching the landing called out, "Enid! Where are you? I want to speak to you!"

Her words echoed under the high ceilings. Once again she tried, her hands gripping the balustrade of the second floor landing. "Enid! Where are you? Do come to me!" she cried.

There was a moment of silence followed by a tinkle of laughter from the floor above.

Glancing up the stairwell, she cried, "Enid, don't be a bad child! Please come down and let us resume your studies!"

The laughter came again followed by a scuffle of running feet. With a feeling of grim resignation she began mounting the steeper stairway to the next floor in search of her charge. It was the first time she'd ventured up to this area of the strange old house.

Reaching the next floor she heard a door slam closed at the end of the corridor on her left. Trying the knob she found that it turned easily so she entered the room.

It was a musty, cluttered storage room. The first thing she noticed was the dressmaker's form which was probably Jessica's. There were also boxes, trunks, and a fine black lacquer chest with exotic oriental birds painted on it, which attracted her special attention. She ventured over to it and lifted its top. There giggling Enid lay crouched in a corner.

"What an unkind way to pay me back for trusting you!" she reproached the child.

"I finished my exercises and I was bored," Enid said, stepping from the chest.

Flora sighed. "You know what your Aunt Jessica will say? She'll tell your father I have no control over you and you are not attending to your studies."

"That's not true!"

"She'll make him believe it."

"I won't let her," Enid protested, a look of anger on her thin little face.

"You can best avoid trouble by not playing tricks like this on me."

"I won't do it again."

"For both our sakes, I hope you mean that," Flora told her.

"I do," she insisted.

"Now let us go back down to the study again."

"Wait," Enid insisted. "First I'd like you to see the floor

above where my grandfather works on the Chinese antiques."

Flora frowned. "I don't think we're supposed to go up there."

"We don't have to make any noise. No one will know we did go up, not even Grandfather."

"How can you be so sure?"

"He's the only one who goes up there. And when he is working he doesn't pay attention to anything else."

"I think we should have your father's permission," Flora said.

"There's no need," Enid urged. "Let me show you up there and I promise to go straight back to my lessons."

Flora had misgivings about going to an area of the house that was generally used only by Bradford Armitage. But she could tell that Enid had made up her mind to show her the attic, and would not be satisfied unless she did.

With a sigh, she said, "All right. I'll go up there for just a moment if you will then go back downstairs and start studying again."

"I will," Enid promised.

"Very well," she said.

"Come along then," Enid told her, leading the way out of the storage room and along the corridor. When they reached the stairway leading to the attic Enid went on ahead of her. At the upper landing the girl put a finger to her lips to warn Flora to be silent. Then she led her along another narrower hall to an open door.

They stood gazing into the room where Bradford Armitage was working. He had a number of woodworking tools there and was sawing a small board.

Enid tugged at her arm, "See!"

All at once Flora was aware of the unique type of activity in which the big man was engaged. She had heard that he spent his time restoring the antiques that came to him from China. But he was doing no such thing now. The old man was busily engaged in the construction of what could easily be recognized as a huge coffin!

As he went about fitting the sawn board to the side of

the partially completed box, he sang a hymn in a low voice. As Enid had predicted, he was completely preoccupied with what he was doing and wasn't aware of them at all.

Flora decided that he must be working on his own coffin because he felt no ordinary one would take his huge frame. She was sure Enid had deliberately taken her up there to shock her.

Turning, she looked at Enid, who had an impish grin on her face. She firmly lead her away from the door. They walked back to the landing and before they started down she noticed there was a locked door blocking off the other attic corridor.

In a low voice she told Enid, "You took me up there to frighten me, didn't you?"

"I'm sorry," Enid said, at once penitent.

"You should be," she told her. "I'm going to forget all about this as long as you return to your lessons."

Enid was obedient for the balance of the day. In the early afternoon the fog and drizzle vanished and it became warmer. When the grass had dried sufficiently Flora went for a stroll. Enid had completed her studies and was at the stables playing with the coachman's little girl.

Flora once again found herself drawn to the quiet, yet somewhat menacing, beauty of the pond. She sat on the bench at one end of it and observed the gliding swans.

She was so lost in thought that she was unaware of a weird figure hobbling across the lawn towards her. It was Sir Thomas Waring, owner of the adjoining estate.

Leaning on his walking stick, he studied her with a bright gleam in his sunken eyes. "Ah, yes, you are Mr. Gladstone's young woman, aren't you?"

Startled, she said, "Mr. Gladstone found me my position here, yes. We met the other evening at the Armitage House. I'm Flora Bain."

"I know, I know," he said. "Have you seen my wife?"

"Not this afternoon."

"She often walks over here." He stared at the rambling stone mansion with its vine-covered walls. "It seems Armitage House has a great fascination for her. But then it is only normal that she turns to young people of her own age for friendship."

"Your wife is very attractive."

"No doubt of that," the old man said. "But she comes here without knowing the danger of this place."

"Danger?" The word troubled her.

He nodded slowly. "Yes, danger. I have lived next to this house since I was a lad. I know more about it than most."

"I'm sure you do."

"Madge is new here. She doesn't understand," he went on. "She was a great friend of the young woman who was governess here before you. What was her name? Nelly?"

"Lily," she corrected him.

"Yes, Lily. She thought her a very sensible young person. They often chatted." He stared at Flora. "Have you become a friend of my wife's?"

"Not really," she said. "I've been here only such a short while."

"You know the shadow over this house?"

She said carefully, "I know it is not a happy place."

"It is cursed!" he said flatly.

"Why do you say that?"

"Because I know." He leaned towards her, the weight of his right hand still on his walking stick. "It all began in China."

"In China?"

"The curse came directly from there," Sir Thomas declared. "Since then the house has known a long history of violence and tragedy."

"Ending with the death of my predecessor, Lily," she said.

"Not ending," the old man corrected her. "The curse will go on."

"You think so?"

"I know it," he said. He pointed to the pond with his walking stick. "You know that Lily ended up in there?"

"Yes."

"If you're wise you'll leave before something of the sort happens to you," was the old man's warning.

She rose from the bench in dismay. "You can't be serious!"

"I most certainly am," he assured her. "And I beg that you listen to me."

"Why do you think my life in danger?" she persisted, hoping that if he knew more he would tell her.

"Because of what I know about Armitage House. There is violence and madness there, brought to them by that curse from China."

"You're speaking so vaguely I can't follow you," was her complaint. "But I have an idea I know what you're getting at. You think I will be killed by the same person who killed Lily if I remain here?"

There was fear on the old man's face. "I didn't tell you that Lily was murdered."

"That had to be what you meant," she persisted. "I have been told that Lily was a suicide but I have never believed it. What do you know about her death?"

"Nothing! Nothing!" the old man said in a panic.

She advanced to him. "Please!"

"I have told you all that I can!" was his protest. "Don't plague me with more questions! Just be wise and leave this cursed place!"

With that he turned and hobbled away from her. She watched as he made a path along the side of the pond to the opening in the woods. He used his walking stick to move along at a speed rapid for a man of his age and frail state.

She had almost had the secret from him but at the last moment he held back. Her suggestion that Lily had been murdered seemed to terrify him. Flora wondered why as she walked back in the direction of the towering mansion.

When Henry Armitage returned from London that evening he seemed in a gray mood. He spoke little at the dinner table and when he had an evening chat with his little daughter he was much more grave than usual. Flora noted this and so did the child.

As Flora prepared her for bed, Enid complained, "My

father didn't seem at all like himself tonight. He didn't laugh once."

"Perhaps he worked very hard in his office today."

"He's hardly ever like he was just now," the girl said worriedly. "Do you think my father has been troubled by Lily's ghost?"

She stared down at the child. "What an odd thing for you to say!"

"I mean it! The ghost haunts me and maybe she does the same to him! She must hate us all!"

"Why should she hate you all?"

"Because," Enid said seriously, "I heard my father and Jessica talking downstairs one night before Lily was found in the pond. And Jessica was saying that Lily should be sent away because she'd come to hate us all."

"You must have made a mistake. Heard her wrong."

"No. She said it. And my father said Lily was confused and to give her a chance."

"You mustn't dwell on such things," Flora advised her. "And you needn't worry about your father. He's merely tired."

Flora was not as easy in her mind about what she'd heard as she pretended to be. After she left Enid's room she began to consider again what her charge had said. It seemed there must have been some kind of a confrontation between Lily and the members of the Armitage family before her death.

What about? Had Lily shown her affection for Henry in too obvious a way and so brought about a reprimand from him or some of the others? Had she learned some dark secret about the grim old house and been attempting to use it against them?

She moved slowly on to the landing amid the shadows with these questions filling her mind. Just as she reached the landing a strange feeling of danger came over her. She could almost sense spying eyes hidden in the darkness.

Part way down the stairs leading to the ground floor, a single candle flickered in a wall holder, giving the stair area its only light. By the faint glow of this candle she was able to study the portrait on the landing. The portrait of

Bradford Armitage's dead wife who had bequeathed her good looks to Jessica in a startling fashion.

Standing there in the eerie shadows studying the beautiful woman, she had this strange feeling she was being watched. Then from somewhere in the darkness there came a distinct, ghostly sob.

Chapter Sixteen

The sob had such a phantom quality that for a long moment Flora suspected that it must have come from the ruby-red lips of the beauty in the portrait. Then she heard a stirring on the steps above her and glanced around quickly to see the gaunt figure of the housekeeper, Mrs. Brant, slowly coming down the stairs.

She waited until the housekeeper had joined her on the landing, then she said, "I thought I heard a sob just now."

The thin woman in black stood there stiffly. "You probably heard me cough, Miss Bain."

"It was not a cough I heard," she protested. "It was a sob!"

Mrs. Brant's face showed no expression. "Either your hearing or your imagination must be at fault," was her comment.

Having said that she moved past her and went on down the stairs leaving Flora alone. She stared after her, certain that she had lied. Flora knew she'd heard a sob and she had also noticed the housekeeper's eyes were suspiciously red as if from weeping. For all her stony façade her tear-stained eyes had betrayed her.

She slowly followed the housekeeper down the stairs. As she reached the bottom she heard the front door bell ring. Then Mrs. Brant answered the door and there were the voices of Sir Thomas and Lady Madge Waring as they entered. Armitage House was having company.

Later she joined the others in the living room as Jessica sat at the piano playing and singing for them. She had a sweet-lilting voice and the sad ballad she sang suited her talents. Henry stood by the piano turning the pages of the music for his sister, an admiring look on his face.

Nearby Bradford Armitage sat hunched in a big chair. Opposite him sat Madge Waring. Her expression was tense and preoccupied. Her husband sat at her side with a complacent look on his emaciated face. He continually nodded his white thatched head in time to the music.

Jessica came to the end of the selection and there was a mild applause led by Henry and joined in by all the others.

"A most touching ballad," Sir Thomas said in his reedy voice. "You have a fine voice, my dear Jessica, one worthy of no less a theater than Covent Garden!"

Jessica turned to him, obviously pleased. "You flatter me, Sir Thomas."

Henry smiled. "My sister does have a fine soprano voice but hardly one worthy of Covent Garden."

Madge said impulsively. "You sing so nicely, Jessica. The song truly touched me."

Jessica's father raised himself in his chair and said, "Covent Garden was burned down in fifty-six. Thought everyone knew that. Stood there for nigh on fifty years and now it's a burned-out rubble!"

Sir Thomas Waring gave his contemporary a look of distress. "Have you forgotten, Bradford? The theater was rebuilt in fifty-eight! They've had several seasons in the new house, which is even finer than the old one."

The elder Armitage blinked at him. "The Garden built over again? I don't seem to recall it."

From his stand by the piano Henry told his father, "You have not left the grounds of the estate for more than five years. You have no idea of the things that are happening in London."

Bradford Armitage grunted. "Better off not knowing! It's become a city of slums and rogues!"

"I don't think it's all that much worse than it's ever been," Madge Waring said.

Jessica addressed herself to Sir Thomas. "Have you heard the new coloratura soprano, Adelina Patti? They say she is simply wonderful."

"Yes," Sir Thomas said. "She's remarkable. Began her operatic career at sixteen and she can't be more than twenty now. Already she's been featured in several of the Covent Garden operas."

Jessica said, "She's Italian, isn't she?"

"Yes," Henry spoke up. "But she was born in Spain. I hear she has at least one other sister who is equally talented."

"Give us another tune!" her father said.

"No!" Jessica got up from the piano seat. "I have sung enough for one evening. I don't want to bore our guests. Instead I shall have Sir Thomas tell me the latest news of Covent Garden. It is so refreshing to have one cultured man in our group."

Flora moved toward Bradford Armitage. She said, "The music was a treat."

He sighed. "I used to attend the theater when I was active in business. Now that things have changed I've gone to seed."

"There is no real need for that," she challenged him. "You have the time and you are not locked in this house."

"That is where you are wrong. I am a prisoner here."

"I'm afraid I don't understand."

He waved a big hand in a gesture of explanation. "Don't we all become prisoners of the kind of lives we shape for ourselves?"

"To a degree. But there surely is no need for you to limit yourself to living the rest of your life on the grounds of Armitage House."

"It is my world," he said in a resigned tone. "I have my antiques and my art collection. It is enough."

201

She was about to argue this point when Henry and Madge came over to join them. Apparently the two felt that if they talked privately too long attention might be drawn to them. Madge at once engaged the old man in conversation.

Flora turned and said to Henry, "Enid was a little depressed tonight when I put her to bed. She felt that you were in a bad mood."

His eyebrows lifted. "The child noticed that?"

"Yes. She's extremely sensitive."

"She must be," Henry Armitage said with a frown. "It is true that I came home tonight feeling troubled. I'm sorry that I upset her."

"I thought I should tell you."

"Thank you. I'll try to do a better job of concealing my feelings in future."

"Or at least let her understand why you happen to be in a poor mood. That might help."

He frowned slightly. "Not in this case. The thing that put me in a poor frame of mind would best not be spoken of to her."

"Oh?"

"Yes," he went on. "I had callers at my office today. The parents of the late Lily Marsden. It seems they have been talking to their lawyers and they feel I am legally responsible for what happened to their daughter."

She stared at him in surprise. "How can they possibly blame you for her suicide?"

"I pointed that out to them but they were most obstinate about it. I think they are less concerned over the loss of their daughter than in getting money from me. I suspect their lawyers to be thorough rascals."

"Did they ever complain to you before?"

"No. I saw them at Lily's funeral and they were unable to talk at all. It seems that now the first shock of sorrow is over they are thinking of the financial loss they may have had in losing Lily."

"I still don't think they have any legal case against you." At the same time she was wondering if the girl's parents might now have decided that their daughter had not taken her own life but had been the victim of foul play. Henry's next words confirmed her idea.

"We had a most difficult session and before it was over the father was hinting that he didn't believe his daughter would take her own life. That someone might have throttled her and put her body in the pond to make it seem a suicide. During all this the mother was in tears. I finally got rid of them by pleading that I had another important appointment away from my office. They left hurling threats after me as they went."

"How awful," she said. "Do you think they mean to make more trouble?"

"I don't know," he admitted. "I can only imagine the scandal it could cause. It's not a pleasant prospect."

"What are you doing to protect yourself?" she asked.

"I went directly to my lawyer's chambers in Regent Street and presented the whole problem to him. He's a careful fellow. He asked for the night to think it over. He's promised to come by my office tomorrow with some suggestions."

"I can understand now why you were not quite yourself this evening."

"This trouble could go on for a long while if we aren't able to reason with the parents. And if they hire some firm of rogue lawyers there's no telling where and how it could end."

The conversation between them was brought to an abrupt conclusion as arrogant Jessica sauntered up to them saying, "My! You two are behaving like conspirators!"

Henry's face flushed. "Really?"

"Really!" she told him mockingly. "One would think you are exchanging deep, dark secrets."

"Nothing as exciting as that," Flora was quick to assert. "I was just talking about Enid and the fact that she is a sensitive child."

Jessica's lip curled. "That comes from her being brought up in this grim old house with no other children for company."

"She has the coachmen's little girl and the children of some of the other servants to play with."

"That doesn't help. It's not the same thing as growing up with children of her own class."

Henry scowled at this. "I think it is healthy for Enid to make friends with all sorts of youngsters. It will make her better able to face life. I don't want her to be a frightened, protected product of some supposedly high-class boarding school."

His attractive sister smiled coldly. "The thing is, Henry, you are not thinking of her good but of your own. You are selfishly keeping her here because you want her near you. It's as simple as that."

"Is there anything wrong in my loving my daughter?" he challenged her.

Jessica shrugged. "You made a mistake in marrying her mother and now you continue compounding that first error. You enjoy the role of martyr."

"I don't care to continue this argument," Henry replied, turning his back on his sister.

At that moment Sir Thomas Waring rose from his chair and announced that he and his wife must leave as they had to make an early trip to London the next day. There was a general exchange of good nights. In the general activity Flora managed to dislodge herself from the group and make her way upstairs.

The reveleation offered her by Henry Armitage had increased her fears that he might be in some way involved in Lily's death. She found it hard to see him as a possible killer, but she worried that he might know who had been responsible. He might be trying to protect the guilty party. She realized with some dismay that she was gradually falling under the charm of Henry and could not think him guilty.

As she reached the door of Enid's room she decided to see if the child had gone to sleep. She realized as she quietly opened the door that she'd forgotten to speak to Henry about the bolt she wanted. She promised herself to do this at their next meeting.

Moving into the room she saw that Enid was in bed. Her gentle, even breathing indicated she was peacefully asleep. Without pausing by the bed she continued to the connecting door that led to her own bedroom.

No sooner had she stepped into the room and closed the door after her than she had the eerie feeling that she was not alone. She glanced around quickly and saw someone with a back pressed against the door to the corridor.

A low whisper came from the figure. "Lor', you gave me a fair shock!" It was Dolly.

She hurried over to greet her friend in an excited whisper. "Dolly! I've been wanting to talk to you. And I sort of sensed there was someone in here but I didn't realize it was you until you spoke. Come sit with me on my bed and we can talk."

"I had to sneak my way up the back stairs," Dolly said as they crossed to the bed and sat down. "That cook has eyes like a hawk!" she lamented. "And she seems to enjoy getting double work out of me."

"I'm sorry you're finding it so difficult."

"Life is never easy for the poor and honest," Dolly said with a touch of her old swagger. "How is it with things up here?"

"Enid is a lovely little girl, if a trifle mischievous. I'm devoted to her and she's fond of me."

"Well, that sounds good!" Dolly said.

"But there are tensions and mysteries that worry me. And Jessica is a cruel and arrogant person."

"Ha!" Dolly said knowingly. "I've heard all about her from the others. They say she's crazy jealous of her brother. That she made life miserable for his poor wife when she was alive and now she's even jealous of the little girl."

"It's true."

"And that's not all," Dolly went on triumphantly. "They say that Jessica was madly jealous of the girl who was governess before you, as well as of Lady Waring. It seems Henry Armitage once considered marrying her but something broke it up. She doesn't want to share that handsome brother of hers with anyone! It's the scandal of the kitchen!"

"And what else are they saying below stairs?"

Dolly sat there in the shadows and gave a deep sigh. "They're wondering about you and how long you can last. They all think Jessica will find a way to get rid of you. They say you're much too attractive for her to allow you to stay on here."

"I'm afraid she's doing her best to make me leave," Flora agreed.

"No surprise," Dolly said. "But better get ready for a shock. They also say below that they don't think Lily drowned herself at all, but that someone attacked her and shoved her in the pond."

"I've already thought of that on my own."

"I thought you might. They think that either Jessica or Madge killed Lily. And a few of them say it could have been Mr. Henry himself."

"Surely not!"

Dolly gave her a sharp glance. "You can never tell about those fancy-talking gents. Remember how Nelson Reed pulled the wool over your eyes and you wound up locked up with me in that brothel."

"Henry Armitage isn't another Nelson Reed."

"Don't be too sure," her young friend warned. "Fancy spats and top hats don't make the gentleman, they merely decorate him."

She sighed. "What else are they talking about?"

"A good deal," Dolly told her. "Especially the ghost. Most everyone in the house has seen it. They all claim it is Lily's, though some of the older ones say it was here before she was drowned."

"The ghost came in here and attacked me," Flora told her. "I don't think it's a ghost at all but Jessica pretending to be one."

Dolly gasped. "Why would she do a thing like that?"

"It's hard to say. Maybe she wants to do some wicked things and have them blamed on the ghost. I think she is a little mad, so you find it hard to tell what she's capable of doing."

"I call it a strange house." Dolly shook her head. "What do you make of the old man?"

"I think he's eccentric but his mind seems sound enough. He is building himself a coffin in the attic."

"I heard that," Dolly agreed. "He won't let any of us go up there to clean. But some of them have taken a sneak up there. They claim he has all kinds of heathen statues that he worships."

"I think that's idle gossip."

"I don't know. He's pretty strange. They say he burns incense and bows before the statues. They also claim that he started this in China and that was what drove his wife crazy and made her do away with herself."

"Because he turned to the worship of Buddha?"

"I guess that's it."

"It sounds pretty fantastic. I heard that his wife had been in ill health, so to escape pain she took her life."

"Well, anyway he is funny about the attic. He tends to it himself, keeping it mostly locked up. Only one he allows up there is that Mrs. Brant, a real nasty one!"

"She does appear cold," Flora said.

"Always upbraiding somebody and making them do extra work," Dolly said. "She's the main reason I'd have for leaving if you weren't here."

"Do stay on," Flora begged her. "I'd feel lost if you didn't."

"I'll stay while you're here," Dolly promised. "Only thing is I want you to watch out."

"Watch out?"

"For trouble. You could be in it any time. Especially if that Jessica or Madge thinks your pretty-boy Mr. Henry is taking a fancy to you."

"That's not likely!"

"You never can tell about these toffs!" Dolly warned her.

"I'll be very careful."

"You want to be," Dolly said. "They talk about that Lady Waring and the pranks she plays on that poor old husband of hers. Talk is she comes over here regularly on the sly to meet and make out with your fine Mr. Henry."

"I'm sure they're just good friends," she said, defending them even though she had wondered about this herself.

"Friends!" Dolly jeered. "Some of the maids downstairs has another word for it."

"Their gossip gets out of hand at times," Flora told the girl.

"Don't be too sure. They've been here a while longer than we have. They claim poor old Sir Thomas has a broken heart and he is failing away because of it."

"He's failing away mostly because he's a very old man," she said.

"Cook thinks that's only half the problem. She says Lady Waring only married him for the title and the money that went with it. She didn't think Henry Armitage was wealthy enough so she left him. Now she wants to have her cake and eat it too!"

"Some of these things may be true," Flora said. "But you can't accept every bit of gossip as fact."

"And now, what about the ghost attacking you?" her friend asked.

"That was something else," she said. "I came in here from Enid's room and the ghost was here waiting for me. Before I could say or do anything it came at me and I blacked out. When I came around I had a bad blow on my head."

Dolly stared at her. "Did you get a good look at it?"
"No."

"See anything at all?"

"Just the outline. Very gray and shadowy," she said, a chill running through her at the remembrance of it. "It seemed to be a woman in a kind of hooded cloak."

"That's her! That's Lily's ghost!" Dolly agreed. "Maybe a half-dozen servants has seen her. Couple of them say she called out to them in a kind of moaning voice."

"Until now I've never believed in ghosts."

"I've always believed in them."

"I don't know what to think," she worried.

"I wish I was back at the mission," Dolly said sorrowfully. "That Mr. Booth wanted us to stay and I liked it there. And then there was that young man who took a fancy to me."

"Shanks?"

"Yes," Dolly said with a sigh. "He was a proper scarecrow with his skinny, gangling body and those funny ill-fitting clothes. But I liked him."

"I'm sure he liked you."

"I wonder if he's still at the mission?"

"I'd think so. He said he'd given up his life of crime. I'd say he had reformed."

"You never know. Those that talk about it the most are always the first to backslide," Dolly pointed out.

"He seemed to enjoy the mission. I doubt very much if he'd think of leaving it. He wants to be an officer when Mr. Booth forms his army against sin and poverty."

"I wish I was going to be in that army," Dolly said with another deep sigh.

She gave her young friend a concerned glance. "If you really do want to go back to the mission I'll speak to Mr. Armitage and I'm certain he can arrange it."

"No," Dolly said. "I didn't really mean that. I'll stay on here until that housekeeper gets too much for me."

"Let me know how you're making out," she said. "I'll do anything I can to help you."

"I know," Dolly said, rising. "The only thing is that it could be you who needs the help."

"I'll be extra careful."

"I'll get back downstairs now," Dolly whispered. "If I'm lucky no one will have missed me."

"We have a right to chat," she said. "If there is any fuss about your coming up here let me know. I'll see you're not punished for it."

Dolly smiled at her. "Don't worry about me! I'm too slick for that crowd below. Just so long as I don't run into that ghost along the way. I don't pretend to be a match for any ghosts."

Flora saw her to the door and waited until she was out of sight in the dark hall. She then began to prepare for bed and in a short while slipped between the sheets.

Dolly's gossip had left her in an excited state and she was quite awake. But her eyelids eventually closed and she sank into a deep sleep.

She was suddenly awakened by a series of sharp screams. It took her a moment to rouse herself fully from sleep and realize the screams were coming from the adjoining room—that it was Enid's terrified cries she was hearing.

Chapter Seventeen

FLORA LEAPT out of bed and ran to the adjoining room. There she saw Enid standing up in her bed hysterical.

"Enid, love!" Flora cried out and ran over to the girl.

Enid extended her arms to her and sobbed, "Flora! Save me!"

"It's all right!" she crooned as she held the thin figure close to her. "You don't need to be afraid now. I'm here!"

"The ghost!" Enid sobbed.

"Easy now," she said soothingly.

"The ghost came and touched me. Its hands were all wet and clammy. Just like Lily's hands when they dragged her out of the pond! I saw her! All pale and wet!"

Flora held the child so close she could hear the beating of her small, terrified heart. "You mustn't think about that. You must forget all about it."

"I can't help it," Enid sobbed. "Lily came after me just now. She tried to take me with her."

"You've had a bad dream! A nightmare!"

"No! I woke up and saw her!" Enid burst into sobs again.

"Just don't talk about it. Now do try and calm down like a good girl."

"You won't leave me?"

"No."

"Promise?"

"I promise."

The frightened child's body eased a little. "Lily came back from the grave!"

"No. It was a dream."

"It couldn't have been! I felt her wet hand!"

Flora was going to try to reason with the youngster but at that moment she heard the door from the corridor creak open. She looked around in surprise. There, standing in the doorway with a lighted candle in her hand, was Jessica.

Eyes flashing angrily, she demanded, "What sort of pow-wow is going on here?"

"It's nothing," Flora protested feebly.

"I saw a ghost," Enid said, wiping away her tears with small fists.

"A ghost!" Jessica said with disgust. "You made enough noise to rouse the entire household. I marvel that I'm the only one who heard you!"

"I came as soon as I heard her," Flora said.

"Did you?" Jessica said with sarcasm. "It's too bad you couldn't instill better judgement in her. We can't have her waking the house every night with her fear of ghosts."

"I did see Lily's ghost," Enid insisted.

"Don't tell me any such lies!" Jessica hissed, her lovely face distorted with anger in the candle's glow. "I shall discuss this with your father in the morning."

"He won't listen to you!" Enid taunted her.

"We'll see about that!"

Flora told her, "I'll stay in here with her the rest of the night."

Jessica took a further step into the room. "No," she said. "I forbid it!"

Flora was stunned by Jessica's behavior. "Why?"

"I will not have Enid coddled in such a silly fashion."

Enid began to cry again. "I won't stay here alone."

"You will do just that," Jessica informed her coldly.

"No!" Enid cried.

"You heard me!" she said in a acid tone. To Flora she added, "And so have you! You are to remain in your own room."

Having delivered herself of this Jessica marched out and closed the door on them. Left in the darkness again Enid turned to Flora bleakly. The little girl was still standing in the middle of her bed.

"What are you going to do?" Enid asked.

"What can I do?" she said. "If I don't stay in my room she'll try to cause trouble with your father."

"How can she know?"

"She's likely to come back and spy on us."

"You think so?"

"I'm almost sure of it. She wants to find an excuse for dismissing me and sending you to school. She might make a case out of this."

"I'm afraid to stay in here alone," Enid said, trembling.

"I know."

"What can we do?" Enid asked.

Flora thought for a moment. Then she said, "I'll stay in my room but I'll leave the door between our rooms open. And I'll also leave a candle burning on my bedside table. Then you'll be able to see me all the time just as if I were in the room with you."

"Yes," the child said. "Just as long as I can see you and call out to you."

"You'll be able to," she promised. "Never fear."

"Aunt Jessica can't stop that."

"No, she can't," Flora said grimly. "There was nothing in her instructions to stop us leaving the door open and a candle burning."

A smile crossed the girl's face. "We've gotten the best of her!"

"For a while at least," Flora said with a weary smile of her own. She hugged the child again. "Now get back into bed and I'll see you safely tucked in."

Then she went back to her own dark room. As she reached her bedside table, with trembling fingers she lit the candle in the holder. She got into bed and then called through the open door to Enid.

"Try and go to sleep at once. I'll be watching you."

"I will," the child said. "Good night, Flora."

"Good night."

Then she lay back on her pillow. It was another strange experience. What interested her a good deal was how quickly Jessica had shown herself. Also that the auburn-haired girl had been the only one to have heard Enid's screams.

This all added up to her suspicion that Jessica was playing the role of Lily's ghost. If it were true then it was almost certain that Jessica's mind was unbalanced. No one but a madwoman would stoop to such a terrible trick.

Flora knew that her suspicion of Jessica would be difficult if not impossible to prove. It was again a matter of waiting and watching and hoping the guilty person would become overly confident and make a slip that would give him or her away.

She waited for Jessica to return and storm about the neat arrangement she'd worked out for watching over Enid without breaking the ruling. But she did not come back to spy on them. Eventually Flora fell asleep.

When she woke up it was morning. Sunshine was pouring through the draperies. Enid was stirring in her bed in the other room.

When she finished dressing and checking on Enid to be sure she was ready for the day, the youngster asked her, "Did Jessica come back again last night?"

"I think not," she said.

Enid smiled up at her conspiratorially. "We fooled her, didn't we?"

"That isn't important," she warned the youngster as she buttoned her into a pretty print dress with a ruffled collar.

The wistful face of the little girl took on a knowing expression. "You don't want me to say anything about last night?"

"We'll talk about it later," Flora said. "But not a word about it now. We don't want to upset Jessica or your father. It will only make things worse."

"Very well," the child said.

They went down and joined the others at breakfast. Bradford Armitage said grace as usual. Jessica said little but looked annoyed. Henry's handsome face was tense. Flora thought that Jessica must have been up early complaining to him.

As she left the breakfast table Henry asked her. "Would you mind stepping into my study for a moment, Flora? I'd like to speak to you before I go in to the city."

Flora walked down the long hall to the study debating what Henry Armitage was going to say to her. She was unable to decide whether she should make accusations against Jessica or not. Although Henry was aware of his sister's bad disposition he was all too liable to dismiss it as unimportant. There was a deep bond between the two which would be difficult to break. She had to keep this in mind.

There was the business that Henry had confided to her the previous night, the problem of Lily's parents being ready to sue him for negligence in their daughter's death. On top of this she'd heard Dolly's story that there were whispers Henry might himself have murdered Lily for some reason. She didn't want to believe this but the suspicion lingered in her mind, making her uneasy about taking any stand with the young man.

She stood waiting in the study for a few minutes before he came walking swiftly into the room, closing the door behind him. He looked more handsome than usual in his black suit, gray vest, and black tie.

Standing directly before her, he said, "I believe there was some small disturbance last night."

She was wary. "Yes?"

His slender face was pale. There was a barely perceptible twitch in his left cheek. Impatiently, he said, "I haven't time to play games, Flora. Jessica tells me that Enid woke up in a fit of hysteria during the night."

"She did wake up and cry out."

He said, "Screamed loudly a number of times and raved on about seeing a ghost!"

Flora knew she could not deny this. "I think it may have been the result of a bad dream."

"You didn't see anything of this ghost?"

"No."

"But Enid was sure she'd seen it?"

"Yes. I think the child is nervous. The drowning of Lily must have been a bad shock for her. And from what she told me she was there when the body was removed from the water."

Henry looked unhappy. "I remember. It was most unfortunate. As soon as I discovered she was there I had her taken away."

Flora told him solemnly. "I fear you are paying the price for her presence there now."

"So it would appear," he said. "You think this spell she had was caused by a nightmare?"

"I prefer to believe that."

His eyebrows lifted. "Are you saying that you believe Lily's ghost does haunt this house?"

"I have heard the stories."

"There has been too much loose talk," he said angrily.

"I know," she agreed. "And it would be impossible to keep all of it from your daughter."

Henry Armitage fixed a stern gaze on her. "What is your personal opinion about this ghost story?"

She knew that Jessica must have described her as unfit to continue tutoring Enid because of her own emotional instability. But she could not force herself to lie about such an important matter.

She said, "Until I came to Armitage House I had no belief in ghosts."

"Does that mean you have come to believe in them here?"

"Maybe. I'm not sure. One night I saw a figure in my room. It came towards me and I blacked out. I was struck by something the phantom carried in its hand. I can't be sure of anything since it was gone by the time I came to."

Henry looked shocked. "You have never spoken of this to me before!" Why not?"

She shrugged. "As I've said, it is all very mixed up in my mind."

"Did you tell anyone else of this experience? Enid for one?"

She shook her head. "No."

"You have never encouraged her to believe that Lily's ghost may be returning here?"

"No. Why should I?"

He bit his lower lip nervously. "It seems to be Jessica's belief that you have."

"Then she is being unfair."

Henry clasped his hands behind his back and walked away from her to stand before the fireplace. He faced the fireplace in silence for a short moment before he turned around to gaze at her again.

He said, "Jessica gave me a very bad report on your conduct last night. She suggested that you were encouraging Enid in her hysteria. When she reprimanded you the result was impertinence on your part."

"I wanted to remain in your daughter's room until she was calm. Your sister seemed to think this wrong and ordered me not to. In the end I gave up arguing about it and she left."

"That was all?"

"That was all," she assured him. "I solved the problem by allowing the door between our rooms to remain open. I also left a lighted candle by my bedside so Enid could see me and call to me if she became upset again. There was no more disturbance the rest of the night."

Henry Armitage listened to all this with an air of interest. When she had finished, he said, "I'd say your solution to a nasty situation was a good one. I'm sorry that Jessica was so abusive of you and that I have taken your time in bringing the matter up."

"I'm glad that you did. I think the matter is better aired. Your sister is very difficult at times. I do not blame Enid for her hysterics. I think many of our problems could be solved by having bolts installed inside the bedroom doors. It would give all of us more of a feeling of security."

His brow furrowed. "Ah, yes, the bolts for the doors. You brought the matter up with Mrs. Brant earlier if I'm not mistaken."

"I did," she said. "But nothing came of it."

"I'll think about it," he said. "It would be a departure in this house. We have never felt barred doors necessary. But under the circumstances perhaps we should consider them."

"I would feel more at ease," she said frankly. "And I think Enid would be less fearful."

"Let me give it a day or two's thought." He took his watch from his vest. "My, it is later than I guessed. I must get on to the city."

This ended the interview with nothing really settled. She had an idea it was Jessica's attitude towards bolts on the doors that was keeping him from installing them. It was clear that while he was aware of his sister's shortcomings in temperament he did not like to oppose her unless necessary.

Flora walked along the hall with him. In the foyer they were joined by Enid. The three of them went out to the front steps where the coachman had a carriage waiting to drive Henry Armitage to London. He bent down to lift up Enid in his arms and gave her an affectionate hug and kiss before bidding her goodbye.

Flora and Enid stood on the steps while the carriage drove off. Henry leaned forward and gave a final wave before it turned up the gravel roadway. Flora again found it hard to think of him as a possible murderer, not even if his motive might have been to protect someone else. Yet one could never be quite sure; there would always be a small doubt.

Because the morning was bright and sunny, Flora took Enid out into the garden to conduct the regular study session. Flora talked of the glories of nature with the child. They had a long discussion about plants and flowers that were common to the neighborhood as well as to Sussex, where Flora had spent her childhood. Flora gathered up the study books as they'd finished for the morning. Enid had turned her glance to the direction of Armitage House exclaiming, "Here comes Grandfather!"

The old man was making one of his infrequent tours of the garden, hobbling towards them with the aid of his walking stick.

Flora rose to greet the old man.

"Isn't it a lovely day?"

Bradford Armitage nodded. "I couldn't resist treating myself to some sun," he told them. "My old bones are aching after all that fog and cold."

Enid was also on her feet. "Come sit with us, Grandfather," she begged him.

He slowly came forward and settled himself on the marble bench with a sigh. "When I was in China I spent a great many of my days outdoors."

Enid snuggled down on the bench next to him, taking his huge hand in hers. "Tell us a story about China, Grandfather! You know so many wonderful ones!"

His face showed pleasure. "You've heard them all!"

"Miss Bain hasn't!" the child protested. "And I'd like to hear one of them again."

He gave Flora an inquiring smile. "Are you willing to suffer through one of my recitals?" he asked.

"I'd enjoy it very much."

"There you are!" Enid exclaimed. "Tell us about the Chinese New Year."

The old man cleared his throat. "Of course you know that New Year's is the most important holiday for the Chinese. It is equal to our Christmas, birthdays, and other holidays all rolled into one! When I lived in Canton they often took one or two weeks to celebrate the festival."

"Tell us about the foods they have," Enid said, her eyes bright with interest.

"Dried mushrooms, squid, shrimp, birds' nest, lichee nuts, oyster sauce, and sesame seed oil were among the many musts. The house is specially prepared for the occasion with all the women working overtime cleaning and cooking."

Flora said, "What about the men?"

Bradford Armitage smiled. "They aren't idle. The head of the household goes over all his accounts and sends out notices to all who owe him money. And he has to repay all his own debts. Every reputable Chinese starts the New Year with a clean slate."

"Tell us about the dragon dance," Enid coaxed him.

"The dragon dance is conducted by the young men. The girls keep busy making themselves colorful new clothes while the boys rehearse the dance. They use a big head of an imaginary dragon with large and shiny artificial eyes. The dragon has an open red mouth, big enough to swallow a man, and a big, flapping tongue. The body and tail are made from some soft material painted with brilliant colors and studded with fake jewels. A youth dressed in flashy clothes takes over the head, and in the rear is another young man in a similar outfit. They perform the dragon dance until their places are taken over by two other lads. The dance goes on a long while."

Enid said, "Tell Miss Bain about the cooking."

"At least a week ahead the Chinese ladies gather in each other's houses and prepare every variety of sweets and other spicy taste treats. Then on New Year's Eve the fun begins. There are ceremonies with incense honoring the kitchen god. The men and boys go off for vegetarian dinners at various clan groups. At midnight, from everywhere there comes a colorful explosion of fireworks. The dragon dance continues while many men stay up all night playing cards and generally making merry while the women provide more food for them. Then on New Year's Day there is the big family feast. After that the men play Ng Ga Pei, a finger challenge game in which the loser has to down a drink of strong rice spirit.

"In the evening everyone attends the opera. The men sing the women's roles in a high falsetto. The company is often an expensive professional one brought to the town for the occasion. Often the opera can't be completed in one evening but the Chinese don't worry about this. They are perfectly willing to return another night. Because the New Year's celebration continues so long, they have plenty of time to do this." The old man sat smiling, making it clear he'd finished his account of the Chinese New Year.

"I'd like to see China one day," Enid said. "Do you think I ever will?"

"If the family continues to import from China it is almost certain you'll visit there one day," her grandfather told the girl. "I can't see your father giving up the business at this time."

Enid rose from the bench and asked Flora, "May I go to the stables and play with the children there until lunch time?"

She nodded. "Very well."

"Thank you." She gave her grandfather a quick kiss on the cheek. "Thank you for the account of the New Year in China, Grandfather. Tell Miss Bain more about it!" And with this she ran off in the direction of the stables.

Bradford Armitage watched after his grandchild. Then turning to Flora he said, "I can see that she becomes more like her mother every day."

"They say she resembles her in looks."

"Very much," the old man agreed.

Flora said, "I don't believe I have ever seen a likeness of Enid's mother."

"You haven't," he said grimly. "Just after her death Jessica removed all likenesses of her from the house."

"Why?"

The old man held his walking stick before him and rested his hands on it as he gazed bleakly at the old manision. "You must know by now how jealous Jessica is. She hated that poor girl from the day she married Henry. I think she was actually delighted when Enid's mother died."

"I find that hard to credit," Flora said.

Bradford Armitage said, "You must be aware of the lengths to which Jessica will go to keep Henry under her influence."

"I know something of it," she said cautiously.

"You are much more discreet than our last governess was," the old man went on. "Lily was foolish enough to fall in love with my son and made no secret of it."

"Perhaps she did not realize this could place her in danger," Flora said.

The big man scowled. "I took it on to myself to warn her once. But I don't think she properly understood me," he said. "She listened, but when I finished she replied that she was in love with Henry and nothing else mattered."

"Was that long before she took her own life?"

"Not too long before it."

Flora studied him as she asked, "Did she give you any hint of suicide plans then?"

"I can't say. I wasn't looking for anything of that sort. But I do know it wasn't too many days after that she and Jessica had a most bitter quarrel. Henry had to come between them to make peace. I expected Lily would be dismissed that day. But Henry refused to do it."

"Perhaps it would have been better if he had let her go. She might still be alive," Flora said pointedly.

An uneasy look crossed his face. "Are you saying that Lily was the victim of some sort of foul play here?"

"I have heard whispers of it," she admitted.

"You mustn't pay any attention to such stories," the old man said nervously.

"I try not to," she replied. "If I had believed them I probably wouldn't have stayed on here."

"I'm glad that you have. You have done wonders with the child and she needs you."

"I tell myself that," she agreed. "I've grown terribly fond of Enid."

"And she of you. You must not desert her, whatever happens." He rose from the bench with some difficulty. Gazing down at her with the giant head shaking a little he said, "Some think of me as a mad old man, obsessed with my treasures locked in the attic. A mad man who spends part of his hours building himself a coffin. But however strange my actions may seem, believe me they have a purpose.

"I have tried to combat the tragedy of Armitage House as best I could," he continued. "If I have failed at times it doesn't mean that I haven't battled for the benefit of everyone under its roof."

"I have always regarded you as the single person here upon whom I could depend."

"And you may continue to believe that. There are dark shadows I cannot dispel, much as I would like to. Grim secrets which I must keep hidden for the good of all. Neither my son nor my daughter completely understand this."

With a parting nod he headed towards the great stone house. She had listened to his rather jumbled attempt to justify his behavior with some interest. Once again she felt that he was hinting of some crime he'd kept hidden. It seemed almost certain that the crime surely be the murder of Lily.

She rose from the bench and began walking away from the garden in the direction of the pond. Despite its dark history it had a certain quiet beauty that attracted her.

Standing under a giant elm, she stood very still, staring at the pond with its bird house, swans, and water-lilies. The sun was bright now at midday and she remained in the shadow of the great tree. In the distance she could hear the occasional happy shouts of Enid and the other children.

Then without warning something shot by her to lodge quivering in the thick trunk of the tree behind her head. Stunned, she turned to see what it was. She reached out her hand to touch a slender arrow whose head was buried at least an inch in the tree.

Chapter Eighteen

STARING AT the arrow in disbelief, Flora saw that only good luck had prevented it from imbedding itself in her rather than the tree trunk. An involuntary trembling took hold of her as she realized that she'd been so close to death. And now she turned around to see who had shot the arrow and menaced her life.

Standing about twenty feet distant from her was Lady Waring. She was dressed in a gray suit and wearing a black hat with a tiny white plume in it. In her left hand she carried the bow that had sent the arrow speeding across the lawn. She looked pale and shocked.

She came running over to Flora. "I'm most terribly sorry. I was aiming at the tree trunk and I didn't see you."

Flora found her voice. "No?"

"You must believe me," Madge went on unhappily. "Not until after I dispatched the arrow did I notice you when you moved a little."

She listened with some doubt. It didn't seem likely that she could have been so invisible, and yet she supposed it was possible. "Isn't it risky practicing archery this way on someone else's property? Anyone could accidentally stumble across your path and be hit."

Madge looked guilty. "I know I shouldn't have come over here and I also shouldn't have picked out that tree as a target. But I become bored at our place with the usual bull's-eye target set up for practice."

Flora was gradually recovering from the initial shock. She studied the other young woman closely as she said, "Even so I'd hardly risk this shooting at random over here. There are the children to be considered, Enid and those of the servants."

"I know," Madge said contritely. "Believe me I have learned my lesson. This won't happen again."

She stepped up to the tree trunk and withdrew the arrow, which was firmly imbedded in the tough wood. Flora wondered whether the incident had been accidental or deliberate.

Lady Madge stood there tensely with the bow and arrow in her hands. "Sir Thomas does not approve of my archery," she said awkwardly. "He considers it an unladylike pursuit."

"Really?"

"Yes," the other young woman went on. "There are times when I find life very difficult. I feel so frustrated and shut away from the world. My husband is content to rest a lot these days and reflect on the past."

"Of course he is quite old and not in good health," Flora said. She could not feel much pity for Madge at this moment. The young woman had married for money and position and still wanted the man she really loved to give her all his affection.

Lady Madge's cheeks flushed at this comment. "There is a great difference between my age and my husband's, but I had hoped his health would continue to be good. It hasn't turned out that way. He has been ill almost since the day of our marriage."

"That is too bad."

Madge raised her eyes to meet Flora's. "Please promise me that you won't tell anyone about what happened just now. My husband would be enraged and I'm sure Henry would think me terribly careless. I also wouldn't presume to guess what Jessica might have to say about it."

Flora said, "I'll only make the promise if you will guarantee on your part not to practice archery over here again."

"You have my promise!" Lady Madge said at once.

"Very well."

The young woman hesitated as she was about to leave. "I have the feeling that you don't approve of me."

"I don't know why you say that."

"I somehow sense it," Lady Madge blurted out. "You know that I was to marry Henry and broke up the engagement to marry Sir Thomas. What you don't know is that Jessica behaved so very badly towards me I gave up any hope of a happy marriage with Henry. I broke the engagement in despair."

She listened to this impulsively offered explanation, aware that there could be important truth in it. She had no desire to judge this young woman unjustly. "You really needn't explain to me."

"I want you to know."

"Very well. I'm sorry you allowed Jessica to stop you from marrying the man you loved."

Lady Madge looked bitter. "She not only broke up our engagement but she means to keep Henry for herself no matter who else comes along. Poor Lily is an example of that!"

Her words gave Flora a start. "What do you mean?"

The other girl hesitated, then rather lamely, she said, "I think she contributed to Lily's death in one way or another. And if she decides that you are romantically interested in her brother your life will also be in danger."

"That's a rather strong statement," Flora said.

"I think you deserve a warning."

"Jessica will have no cause to plot against me. There is no romance between my employer and myself."

"Perhaps not," Madge said dryly. "But I have seen the way he looks at you and listens to you. I believe a romance could grow between you."

Flora felt her cheeks burn. "I'm sure you're wrong!"

"Let us wait and see," the other young woman said with meaning. Then she slowly walked back to her own estate. Madge had left, giving Flora a good deal to think about.

She still wasn't sure that Lady Madge hadn't been deliberately trying to kill her. It would have been another unhappy incident like Lily's supposed suicide. This could be Madge's way of dealing with would-be rivals for Henry's love. Or it could have truly been an accident.

She would keep silent and give Madge a chance. There had been something pathetic and sincere in the girl's burst of revelation. Knowing Jessica it was not difficult for Flora to believe that Henry's jealous sister had made the engagement a nightmare for Madge. With this decided, she left the pond to return to the house.

On the way upstairs she paused before the portrait of Jessica and Henry's mother on the first landing. The mother had the same auburn hair as her daughter, the identical strong features, and those hypnotic, almost forbidding eyes. She wondered what this woman of another era had been like, whether she'd had the same uncertain temperament as her daughter.

Mrs. Brant came down the stairway from above. She seemed to have no intention of pausing to speak with Flora.

Deciding to take the situation in her own hands Flora turned to her and said, "One moment, Mrs. Brant."

The stern woman halted amid the shadows. Staring at her, she said, "Yes?"

"You knew the late Mrs. Armitage, didn't you?"

"Who told you that?"

"I believe it was Mr. Bradford Armitage," she said. "He mentioned how fortunate it was that he'd engaged you so shortly before his wife died."

"I had been employed with the family about a year at the time."

"So you knew them all."

"Yes."

"You must have known her well."

"I did," Mrs. Brant said.

"What was she like?"

"She was a great lady," she said reverently.

"I'm sure of that," Flora said. "I'm interested in her as a person. Was she much like Jessica in manner?"

"I have never attempted to observe the manners of my employers or to comment on them," was her reply as she continued down the stairs.

The balance of the day went by without adventure. By the time evening arrived and Henry Armitage returned from London in his fine carriage she'd almost forgotten the archery incident. She had worked hard to eliminate it from her mind by concentrating on her work with Enid.

When dinner ended Henry Armitage drew her aside. "I must talk with you. Let us take a stroll in the garden. It is a lovely evening."

"Very well," she said.

When they were a distance from the house he turned to her and asked, "How did Enid do with her studies today?"

"As well as usual."

"She showed no sign of upset from her hysteria of the night and her belief she'd seen a ghost?"

"I have forbidden any discussion of those things," she told him.

He nodded approvingly. "An excellent idea. She should not be encouraged to dwell on such morbidity."

They changed direction and walked more in the area of the pond. He halted at last staring down at their reflections in the green water. Then after a moment he said, "I have asked you out here tonight to tell you of a sudden decision I have made."

"Oh?" She worried that he might be going to tell her he no longer required her services. Jessica might have at last managed to turn him against her.

He frowned slightly. "I talked to my lawyer today. He feels that legal action may be taken against me by Lily's parents, and the best way for me to avoid a great deal of needless unpleasantness is to get out of the country for a while."

"Then they feel they have evidence to take their charges to the courts?"

"It's this wretch of a lawyer who has taken over their case," he said impatiently. "They haven't the funds to fight a long suit or wait any time to place the action against me. This lawyer fellow is looking for money now and he will be in a much more reasonable frame of mind to accept some sort of offer from my lawyer if I'm out of England."

She found this all rather worrisome. "But if you honestly know Lily's suicide can not be in any way blamed on you or anyone here why not go into court and prove the charges unfounded?"

"I would prefer to do that but my lawyer advises against it. Also, I feel I ought to make some restitution to Lily's parents. By settling the case out of court I may do so. Though it is hard to say how much they'll actually get after this shyster lawyer finishes with them. I suppose it serves them right!"

She found his explanation rather weak. If he were planning to leave the country to avoid the case, he was doing so to either protect himself or someone else whom he knew or feared might have guilt in Lily's death.

She said, "So you will be going away."

"Almost immediately," he told her. "It so happens that I have some business problems at our main office in Canton. I am needed there and since it is at a good moment for me to leave England I shall make the voyage. It means I'll be away some time."

"And Enid?"

"I have thought about that," he said. "And I think I ought to take her along. She has a good, questioning mind and she has always been very interested in the Orient. I think the trip would be an education for her."

"I'm sure she would not want to be parted from you."

"Probably not. And since my sister is going to make the trip there is no reason why the child should not come with us."

"No reason," she agreed in a small voice. So Jessica was going along. She might have known. Henry's sister would not let him out of her sight for a year or more. She was much too jealous of him for that. Flora knew that next Henry Armitage would be regretfully advising her that he would no longer require her services.

"And now about you, Flora," Henry Armitage said in a kindly voice. His eyes met hers with a look of sincerity. "In the short while you've been with us I've come to be much impressed by your qualities. I beg you to come along as one of our party on this expedition to China. It will have many advantages for Enid if you agree. Her studies need not be interrupted and you will be on hand to watch over her. Jessica is neither fond of the child nor a good surrogate mother. Will you be one of our group?"

It was exactly the opposite of what she'd expected him to say, so she was caught in surprise. After a slight hesitation she said, "You really want me to go along?"

"I most certainly do. I'm sure that Enid will be most upset if you don't agree to accompany us."

"What about your sister?"

He furrowed his brow. "Jessica manages to be difficult about whatever I do. But she does not want the responsibility of Enid during the long voyage and in a strange country, so you can rest easy in the knowledge she will want you for a convenience."

"Then I will be tolerated by her."

"You need not worry about that," he said. "I don't want to rush you but I would like an immediate answer. There are many things to be settled and we shall be leaving shortly."

She took a deep breath, making a decision that she somehow felt might well change her entire life. "All right," she said. "I'll go."

"Wonderful!" the young man said with genuine enthusiasm. "I'm leaving Father here in the care of Mrs. Brant and the rest of the servants. It would be pleasant to have him come along but I doubt that his health would withstand the rigors of the voyage and the change of climate."

She said, "When do you expect to leave?"

"The *Orient Queen* sails in four days. With good luck

we should all be aboard. It voyages to the Canaries, around the Cape of Good Hope, pauses at Singapore and Hong Kong, and reaches it final destination at Canton where my father's business partner Yenn Li will be expecting us."

"I shall be seeing at least half the world. It is the kind of a journey I never expected to make!"

"With good luck you should enjoy it," he said. "Our big problems will be the weather and the danger of pirates. There are plenty in the China Sea. Now that the opium trade is thriving the Orient can be dangerous for Western shipping. We have always avoided dealing in the opium traffic but we suffer from the lawlessness it has brought about."

"Then the voyage could offer danger," she said.

"Without question. But no more than the ordinary hazards suffered by any traveler in Asia. Her Majesty's flag and government are respected out there and one is never far from some help. Our ship will carry a quota of military for our protection and she is lightly armed for combat in preparation for chance meeting with one of the pirate junks."

His words conjured up an exciting world. She had seen pictures of Chinese junks and knew they plied the inland and coastal waters of that great country. But she had not realized until this moment that pirate junks existed.

She said, "You make it sound most exciting."

"Let us trust it will be both pleasant and exciting," he amended her statement. He glanced to the other end of the pond where the path led through the trees to the estate of Sir Thomas Waring. "I must go visit Sir Thomas and Madge this evening. I want to let them know my plans. I'm sure they'll be sorry to hear of us leaving for a time."

She gave him a knowing glance. "I'm certain of it."

His handsome face crimsoned as he quickly added, "I mean because of the frailty of Sir Thomas. He could be dead before we return. It is a most lonesome life for his wife."

The next days and nights were among the busiest she'd ever known. There was a hurried excursion into London to buy some needed clothing and other articles, followed by packing for the long trip. Enid was excited to the point of ecstasy but Jessica had a much cooler attitude towards the adventure.

On the final evening before they left Armitage House a small party was held for them. Sir Thomas and Madge Waring were among those attending and Flora had never seen Lady Madge looking so sad. Henry devoted a lot of his time to the forlorn Madge during the party.

She found herself seated next to Bradford Armitage. A deep sigh escaped from his lips as he told her, "If I were ten years younger and in good health I'd be on the *Orient Queen* with the rest of you."

"I know you would. But someone must stay here to look after Armitage House," she said. "So you'll be doing that."

"I shall take care of things, but my heart will be in China with you."

She smiled. "The time will pass quickly and we'll soon return."

"I hope so," he said. "Things ought to be relatively quiet out there compared to what it was in my day."

"As I understand it we are to be the guests of your business partner, Yenn Li, and live in his house."

"Yes. You will find Yenn Li a most honorable person. He was educated in Hong Kong by British tutors and he had a British wife, though he's a widower now. You will enjoy his hospitality. He has a daughter, Han Li, a lovely Eurasian girl. And according to the last letter I received from him his nephew, a young man named Chen Li, also has joined the business. He was educated here in Britain.

"Yenn Li is firmly convinced that China must learn to live with the Western World if the country is to survive and prosper. Most of his compatriots don't hold the same view, unfortunately."

"I think the journey will be good for Enid."

He nodded. "And for my son. It will do him good to

get away from this house which has known so much tragedy. He is badly in need of a change."

He glanced across the room where Jessica was engaged in talk with Sir Thomas. In a low voice he said, "One word of warning. Be as cautious where Jessica is concerned as you have been here. She is a strange girl whom not even I properly understand."

"Thank you," she said. "I will remember."

"And watch the child," he went on in the same tone. "There have been moments when I feared for Enid's safety at the hands of Jessica. My daughter has an uncontrollable temper."

The old man took a sip of his drink. "Well, enough of that. In spite of everything I'm sure you will enjoy the voyage and your stay in Canton."

The next day their baggage was sent ahead to the ship. They followed in a second carriage. It was late afternoon when they arrived at the busy docks to find the crew laboring over loading the last freight to the majestic *Orient Queen*.

Even at dock the great ship looked imposing. She was still equipped with sail although she also had steam power. By deft use of one or the other and sometimes both, she had gained the reputation of being one of the fastest vessels in the China trade.

As they mounted the gangplank Enid saw the half-dozen or more red-coated marines lolling about the upper deck and cried out her pleasure. "Miss Bain! See the soldiers in their bright uniforms!"

She smiled at the child and told her, "It isn't ladylike to point and shout!"

Henry was busy with the purser of the vessel checking on the freight which had been brought aboard. Jessica requested that she be shown to her cabin at once and did not reappear again until after the big ship was underway. Flora had a look at the pleasant cabin in the forequarters of the vessel with bunks for herself and Enid. After that they went up on deck to watch the ship sail and note the motion of the Union Jack fluttering high on one of the masts as the ship slid gently away from the dock, leaving England behind them.

Henry joined them on the upper deck. He placed a hand on Enid's shoulder and smiled as he said, "Well, this is the last look we'll get at the tight little isle until we've traveled many miles."

The weather was fine, the sea calm. The *Orient Queen* soon was rolling gently on its way with the land showing smaller and smaller in the distance until at last it vanished altogether. Flora felt a small lump in her throat when land was no longer in sight. It was the first time she'd ever left England.

That night they ate at the captain's table in his quarters. The *Orient Queen* was not normally a passenger vessel, though she did carry a small complement of them. In addition there were the Royal Marines on board to guarantee the safety of the ship. So dinner was served in the Captain's quarters for Henry Armitage and his party.

Captain Ned Christie was a tall, burly young man with a full black beard, a prematurely bald head surrounded by a rim of heavy black hair, and a weathered, jolly face. Jessica appeared for the evening meal in a new print dress and at once gave all her energies to winning over the captain.

The rather naive Captain Christie was not used to such attention so he was an easy conquest. During the meal he drank the health of his guests. "A great pleasure to have you on this voyage. I am truly honored."

Henry Armitage responded in a suitable vein and it was a happy occasion.

Jessica had been invited to the bridge by Captain Christie and had smilingly availed herself of the offer. Flora took Enid below and helped her prepare for bed. She gave the child the lower bunk.

Staring up at her from her pillow Enid asked, "If it gets stormy and rough do you think I'll fall out?"

Flora laughed. "If there seems any chance of it we'll tie you in."

After Enid was properly settled for the night Flora made up her mind to go up on deck for a final look at the stars before she retired. She mounted the rather steep wooden stairway, finding her long, voluminous skirts troublesome in these strange surroundings.

When she reached the deck she sought out a spot along the railing near the bow. The air was cool and the vessel seemed to be moving along at a good speed under sail. She studied the stars, which had never seemed so bright.

Suddenly she felt an arm placed around her. As she turned she looked up into the face of a mustached Royal Marine. He had looked at her with an interested eye and now he was brazenly taking her in his arms.

"Please!" she begged him.

The young marine chuckled. "Don't play fancy lady with me. I spotted you out careful like. You're the lady's maid. So don't put on airs."

"You must let me go!" she cried.

"Not until we've gotten to know each other," he said, holding her close so that she could smell the heavy odor of rum on his breath. "Let's have a nice ripe kiss, luv!"

She pressed her hands against him, screaming out in alarm. Before he could force his lips on hers the young marine was pulled away from her and thrown to the deck. Above him was Henry Armitage.

"Don't try any tricks with the ladies of my party. I should report you to your officer but I'll be generous and let you go with a warning this time. Do you appreciate that?"

"Sure, guv'nor," the marine said, rising dejectedly. "I didn't properly understand. You don't need to worry no more."

"I know that," Henry said sternly. "Now get on your way!"

The marine vanished in the darkness of the deck and Henry turned to her. "Are you all right?"

"Yes," she said, still slightly trembling. "You came along just in time."

"I can't imagine what got into that fellow," Henry said staring down at her.

"He saw that I was a servant of some sort and felt I might be open to friendship with him."

"You are not a servant, Flora," Henry Armitage said sternly, "and only Jessica tries to make you seem like one. I regard you as a valued associate and the equal of any of our group."

"Thank you," she said quietly.

Then he did a most surprising thing. He reached out, took her in his arms, and kissed her gently on the lips.

Chapter Nineteen

FLORA SCARCELY had time to savor the kiss before he let her go. "Forgive me," he said, "I'm no better than the marine."

She gave him a small smile and told him, "I do happen to know you somewhat better."

"That was no excuse for my taking advantage of you," he said unhappily. "I can only say that I had a deep longing to hold you close to me. To protect you."

"No apologies are required."

He touched her arm tenderly. "You have come to mean a great deal in my life, Flora. Don't think I'm not grateful to you."

"And I owe you a good deal," was her reply.

He looked around the dark deck. "I don't think you'll be bothered again. I shall mention this incident to Captain Christie as I want no repetition of it."

"I doubt that there will be. That young man simply didn't understand my position."

"Had you been a servant girl like Dolly I still wouldn't have wanted him to behave that way towards you."

"Dolly would have known how to handle him," she said lightly. "I'm sure she'd have sent him on his way."

"What about Dolly?" he said. "I'd almost forgotten her until now. Did you talk to her before we left?"

"Yes. I asked her to remain at Armitage House until I came back and I hope that she will. But she doesn't get along well with Mrs. Brant."

"I'm not surprised," he said. "Dolly is a rebel and I fear Mrs. Brant does not take kindly to rebels."

He accompanied Flora back to her cabin and said good night. She prepared for bed as Enid slept peacefully. She felt that in spite of everything the voyage had gotten off to a good start. The incident on the deck which might have turned out to be ugly had actually led to Henry Armitage taking her in his arms for the first time.

While she wasn't prepared to begin a romance with the man she thought it was time that they grew to know each other better. Tonight had established a new closeness between them which she felt was good. She only feared that Jessica's jealousy might get out of hand if he paid a lot of attention to her.

That first night at sea she slept well without any dreams. And in the morning both she and Enid were able to eat hearty breakfasts. They were far out at sea now and the big shop rolled and heaved with the giant waves but they were not bothered by this. Later in the morning they sat out on the rear deck to work at Enid's lessons.

Later in the day, when Flora had finished with Enid, Henry joined her and insisted they go up to the bridge together. There he showed her the charts and explained the mechanics of the wheel to her. It was fortunate that Jessica was taken up with her conquest of Captain Christie. She didn't notice the extra attention her brother was paying Flora.

At the dinner table that night, Captain Christie told them, "Our first stop will be for fresh water and supplies in the Canary Islands. We'll touch at Santa Cruz where Nelson met one of his few defeats."

Jessica smiled across the table at the young captain. She asked, "What are the chief products of the islands, Captain?"

"The Canaries were famous for their grapes until the blight of 1853," Captain Christie said. "Now they're turning to sugar cane."

"A sound commodity," Henry said.

The black-bearded captain laughed. "Almost as good as the tea you import. I believe our government now gets more revenue from taxes on tea than from any other single source." He turned to Flora. "We haven't heard much from you this evening, Miss Bain. Don't you have anything to contribute to our conversation?"

"I can only say that I'm enjoying the voyage tremendously," she replied.

"Good," the captain said. "When we get further east and stop at the various ports you'll have plenty of fresh experiences. One's first visit to the Orient is bound to be a thrilling adventure."

After dinner the table was cleared and moved away to provide an open space for dancing. Two members of the crew who played an accordion and a violin came up to provide the music. The weathered veterans of the forecastle played with gusto. Soon everyone was joining in the fun.

Jessica and Captain Christie led the dancing. Henry danced with Enid, who thoroughly enjoyed herself, pleading with her father to dance with her once again.

Henry laughing and mopping his brow told her, "I must give some of my time to Flora."

"Let her dance with Mr. Maple," Enid told him.

And she did do exactly that. Mr. Maple had come late to join the party. He was the first mate of the *Orient Queen* and a portly young man with a ready laugh. His round face nearly always showed a smile and he had rust-red hair and freckles.

The party went on until bedtime. Flora said good night and escorted her charge back to their cabin. Once again they were both tired enough to sleep well straight through the night.

The next day the weather was a little warmer so they spent more time on deck. In the afternoon Flora found herself seated on a huge coil of rope amidships with Henry at her side. He gave her a warm glance. "Getting away from England has done me a world of good. I feel much easier in my mind."

She studied his handsome face and saw that it indeed had lost much of its careworn expression. Under the circumstances she did not have the heart to mention the legal action about Lily's death, which had been his primary reason for seeking escape from England.

"Enid is having a wonderful time. She's up on the bridge with Jessica and Captain Christie now."

Henry nodded. "The last time I was in China she had not yet been born. Her mother was with me on that trip, of course. Jessica was also along and she and my wife continually bickered. Naturally it was Jessica's fault."

"Too bad," she said.

"Espcially since my wife was soon to die in childbirth. She was carrying Enid during the voyage home. We were all so very young then. I can't believe we were ever that young. My father was along and I merely acted as his assistant."

"Times have changed," she said.

"Yes," he agreed. "Though I'm not sure that Jessica has. Thank goodness Captain Christie is keeping her busy. I'll miss him when the voyage ends."

She smiled. "We can only hope that Jessica will find some other man who interests her."

"Which happens so infrequently," he said, staring out at the ocean with a doleful look. "My first trip to China was when I was just a youngster. It was on that voyage back that my mother took her life."

"How tragic for you."

"I remember it clearly in an odd way. Mostly in bits and pieces."

"I assume from her portrait that your mother must have been beautiful."

"She was," he agreed. "I can still see her face as she lifted me into her arms. She had a wonderful smile."

"Then she became ill."

"It happened while we were in China. I had a native nurse, or amah, and I remember hearing my mother groaning and screaming in her room. My amah hurried me to another part of the house where I wouldn't hear her. Apparently she'd contacted some sort of especially vicious fever.

"Finally my father decided she was well enough to travel. He felt that English doctors might bring back her health more swiftly.

"I remember us getting into a donkey cart to ride down to the vessel. I was very young but I can recall the sing-song voices of the Chinese servants, the black robes and skull caps. My mother had changed terribly in a matter of months. All her beauty faded with the fever.

"I tried to talk to her but she just looked sad and refused to listen to me. Her skin was yellow and she was so thin she didn't look like my mother. Being a child I may even have been cruel enough to have told her that. I don't remember.

"I think she probably became worse on the voyage home. She and my father had always been very happy together. They laughed and talked a lot. But now he seemed no more able to reach her than we children were.

"My mother wandered alone on the ship like a kind of wraith. She spoke to no one and seemed to hear no one when they addressed her. Her meals were taken to her cabin but she wouldn't eat."

"When did you last see her?"

"One night before I went to bed. There was a storm blowing and my father took me to her room to say goodnight. I can still see her sitting there not paying any attention to us. The storm grew worse. I was kept awake most of the night by the pitching of the ship and the howling winds. In the morning the weather changed, the sea calmed. Then my mother was discovered missing."

"Did you realize what had happened?"

"I was too young to fully understand," he admitted. "But my father did tell me that she had thrown herself over the side into the sea since she could no longer bear the pain of her illness. He tried to make me understand that she was better off but I could not believe it. And I recall Jessica crying long and bitterly."

"Perhaps that experience may have had something to do with the way Jessica is today," she suggested.

"Maybe so," Henry said with restraint. "My father's hair turned white almost overnight. He had my mother's cabin sealed for the rest of the voyage and he would not let anyone enter or touch her belongings. I was told he sorted through them later after the ship docked in London. According to him Armitage House was never the same after my mother's death. I grew up there in an atmosphere of mourning. Father still spends much of his time dreaming of the past. It has made him slightly mad. There are times when I worry greatly about his behavior."

"Being alone and fully responsible for the house and the business in London may be beneficial to him."

"I only hope it isn't too much of a strain," Henry worried. "He will have to journey in to London at least twice a week to spend some time in the office. He hasn't done that in years."

Their discussion was cut short when Enid came running to tell them that Captain Christie said they would reach the Canaries the following morning. As proof he had pointed out seagulls from the islands that were already following the ship for the garbage which was daily thrown overboard in the wake of the big vessel.

The next morning the *Orient Queen* docked at the Canaries. Flora had her first glimpse of the high chalk-white cliffs. It seemed as if there could be little vegetation on the islands but Captain Christie assured her the natives managed to extract good crops from the almost barren soil.

Natives in colorful garb came down to the docks to stare at the ship and those who appeared on deck.

They remained at the dock only long enough to take on

fresh water and provisions. Then it was out to sea again to sail down the coast of Africa and around the Cape of Good Hope. The days and nights in these warmer waters were fairly uneventful. Jessica had tired of her conquest of Captain Christie and began to spend much more time with Henry again.

She also became more critical of Flora. She halted her on deck one day to deliver a lecture.

"Just because we're away from Armitage House don't assume that the rules have changed."

Flora said, "I didn't believe that they had."

"You have neglected Enid to be with my brother," Jessica said in a biting voice. "Don't think that I haven't been aware of it. Don't make the same mistake that Lily did."

"What do you mean by that?"

"Lily was silly enough to imagine Henry in love with her. And he didn't have the slightest interest in her. I can only warn you against making the same mistake."

"I'm not liable to."

"Signs don't indicate that."

"You may have read them wrong. I am not the type to easily succumb to romantic notions. I value your brother as an employer and friend. That is all."

Knowing Jessica's mood she avoided her as much as she could. This was not easy even on as large a ship as the *Orient Queen*. One saving grace turned out to be the first mate, Mr. Maple. It was difficult for anyone, including Jessica, to be unpleasant around the jolly fat man. And he had taken a liking to Flora and kept in her company whenever he could.

On the foredeck one morning after they had left the Canaries far behind he jokingly told her, "If I had a teacher like you I could soon obtain my captain's papers. I grew up without a mite of book-learning."

"But you read very well now," she pointed out.

"Had some good skippers along the way who took an interest in me. Picked up a little education here and there. But I still need more before I can get a ship of my own."

"I'm sure you have the ability."

He winked at her. "I need a wife who'll stand behind me and push me ahead."

She laughed, "And that shouldn't be any problem for you either. You've such a wonderful disposition."

Mr. Maple sighed. "They say that everybody loves a fat man but I can tell you that at the same time they don't take you seriously. That's my problem."

"You'll solve it," she said.

The first mate glanced up at the billowing sails above them. "We're nearing the Cape and a blow is coming up. It could mean bad weather."

"Do you really think so?"

"I'm afraid of it," he said seriously.

His prediction proved true. Before the day was out the sky had blackened, the great vessel was pitching and heaving like a cork on the giant waves. Captain Christie warned all who could to remain below decks. He and the members of the crew required to handle the ship in the storm had to remain at their posts.

By late afternoon the sky was as dark as night. Flora and Enid huddled together in their cabin as the angry waves crashed at the porthole. The corridor outside their cabin door was an inch deep in sea water as a result of the sea washing across the decks above. The storm seemed to go on endlessly.

It was dawn the next day before the wind began to ease a little and nightfall before the sea calmed and the *Orient Queen* was able to proceed normally once more.

Sunshine and warm weather returned and the spirits of those on board rose accordingly.

Their next port of call was the island of Hong Kong. Here Flora had her first real taste of the Orient. She admired the beautiful sight. Sailing ships were gathered from all over the world in the vast harbor, loading or unloading freight. There were also native junks and the endless array of houseboats in which families lived and died. The blue mountains of the mainland and the verdant green hills of the island of Hong Kong set off the colorful streets of the city, which were narrower than any she'd seen before.

She marveled at the noises of the city: the cries of the rickshaw boys, the piteous pleading of the street beggars, mixing with the sing-song incantations of vendors offering their wares from open store fronts. Henry hired rickshaws and took them all on a tour of the local sights of the busy city.

After an hour or two they found a quiet spot in a tea house on a hill overlooking the harbor. The owner of the place, a colorful figure in his orange and red silk jacket and skull cap, served them. The tea he served was flavorful and the tiny cookies that accompanied it had a delicious nut flavor.

They left the teahouse, returned to the rickshaws, and were quickly taken back to the dock where the *Orient Queen* had made fast. The next morning the vessel slipped out through the crowded harbor again to begin its final journey to Canton.

Now they were sailing near the island of Macao and in the general area menaced by the coastal pirate ships. These sea criminals would not venture far afield but they'd lay in wait for passing ships. They would come out the short distance from the shore and attack the merchantmen. It was a familiar trick well known to veterans of the coast.

Captain Christie remained constantly on the bridge in this dangerous stretch of water, repeatedly scanning the horizon for any sign of the pirate junks. On the deck the marines had prepared the one cannon remaining and taken their places. The passengers had also been warned of the criticial area and most of them had gathered on the bridge to hear any news.

Mr. Maple came puffing up the steps to the bridge and informed the captain, "Everything is in order down below. Is there any sign of anything?"

Captain Christie put down his telescope. "Not a hint anywhere, and yet I have the feeling."

"Aye, sir, and so do I."

Jessica glanced at the captain with a wry smile. "What does that mean?"

"It means, Miss Armitage, that we sort of feel the enemy in our bones. You get a kind of special sense in this game. I'd be willing to swear that somewhere just beyond the horizon there are one or two pirate junks waiting for us."

Henry Armitage asked, "How long before we are out of the danger zone?"

"Four or five hours," the captain said. "We'd be out of it now if one of Her Majesty's men-of-war should hail into sight. But the queen doesn't have enough such ships patrolling these waters since the treaty was signed."

"I see," Henry said. "Then it's largely a matter of luck."

"That's about it," the captain agreed, placing his telescope to his eye again.

Enid clasped Flora's hand and asked her, "What do you think the pirates look like?"

First Mate Maple told her, "I'll tell you what they're like. They're the biggest China fellers you'd ever want to see. Their heads are shaven except for a tied-up black pigtail and they have long drooping mustaches and black arched brows to decorate their ugly faces. Most of them go stripped to the waist and they carry big swords what can lop off a man's head as quick as you can wink!"

Jessica gave the fat man a look of rebuke. "Please! We don't want the child to have hysterics!"

He chuckled good-naturedly. "Nor you either, miss, beggin' your pardon. But better she knows what she may see. Those rascals are a sore sight for the eyes if you're not expecting them. I know them and I've fought them and I've seen them run scared!"

Enid said, "If there's a battle can I watch?"

Her father patted her head. "If there's any trouble I want you safely below with Flora."

"You make me miss everything," Enid complained.

As she spoke Flora noticed that Captain Christie had become rigid.

"There's no doubt now! I can see them ahead! At least two junks up there just waiting for us!" he cried out suddenly.

Chapter Twenty

Jessica became alarmed. "Surely you must be mistaken, Captain!"

"Nay, he's not!" First Mate Maple said, straining his eyes as he studied the distant horizon. "I can see one of the pirate junks clear with my naked eyes."

Flora now saw the tiny outline of a junk against the sky. She could not judge its movements but guessed that the pirates would try to cut them off.

Captain Christie muttered, "I swear there are more than two. Maybe four or five! They always strike in packs!"

"What will your strategy be?" Henry asked, moving close to the captain.

"We'll keep straight on our course and be the aggressor. I'll have some rounds fired at them before they try to hit us." And he turned to give the helmsman some detailed instructions.

Jessica looked very pale, as if she might be ill at any

moment. "Surely it would be better to turn around and head back for Hong Kong!"

The captain gave her a grim smile. "We'd never manage it, miss. The only thing we can do is meet fire with fire. We have to bluff them out of attacking us if we can."

"Will that be possible?"

"No one can predict that yet," the captain replied tersely, moving away from them.

Henry turned to his sister. "You mustn't bother him now."

"I'm terrified," Jessica said weakly.

Henry told her, "Go below and remain there until this business is over!"

Mr. Maple nodded his head solemnly. "Your brother is right, Miss Armitage. The deck will be no place for women and children."

Flora took Enid firmly by the hand and said, "We'll go down to our cabin at once!"

Enid gave her father a pleading glance. "Must I, Papa?"

"Yes," he said. "Flora is showing good sense. You can't stay up here."

Jessica turned to her brother. "What about you?"

"I'll remain here. If I can be of any service in defending the ship I'll do whatever is suggested to me. If the captain thinks I'll be in the way I'll join you below."

"We shouldn't have come into these waters without a naval escort," Jessica said brokenly.

"That is sheer nonsense! How many warships do you think Her Majesty's Navy has? They can't spare escorts for every merchantman in these seas."

Flora hurried Enid down from the bridge to their cabin. Jessica followed after them but said nothing. Flora took a position at the porthole, which offered a view of the approaching junks.

"You can see the pirate craft from here!"

"Let me see!" the child cried, clambering for a place at the porthole.

"See. They are getting closer now and there are four of them!"

"What funny-looking ships they are!" Enid exclaimed. "Do you think they'll come on board and behead us all?"

Flora put an arm around the little girl. "I hope not!"

"That's what pirates do!" Enid reminded her, forgetting in her excitement that they were possible victims.

"Watch!" Flora said, her heart pounding.

It was a fascinating spectacle. The Chinese pirates were manipulating their junks carefully, gradually moving across the path of the *Orient Queen* so that within a short time they would be close to her, two of them ready to make an attack on either side.

They were close enough now so Flora could see them lining the side of the junks with their great swords in hand, ready to make contact with the British vessel and swarm aboard. Suddenly there was a roar from the deck above as the cannon went off for the first time. There was an explosion in one of the junks on the left at the water line. Wood splintered, smoke rose in the air, and the pirates fell back from the side of the ship. As the smoke cleared, the men on that junk raced about the deck in an attempt to gauge the damage.

Now the pirate crafts were ominously near the *Orient Queen* and the cries of the pirates came plainly across the water. The junks were not without arms and a small cannon on one to the right was fired. There was a shudder from above, indicating that the shot had found its mark.

Flora clutched the excited child at her side tighter and cried, "We've been hit!"

"Yes!" Enid agreed. "I could feel it!"

The *Orient Queen* opened fire on the junk with the cannon. There was an explosion amidships of the junk followed by a great roaring blast and flames. The powder kegs aboard the junk had been set off and were blowing up in a succession of explosions. Cries rang in the air as the pirates were leaping into the sea to escape the inferno of their sinking craft.

All this time Captain Christie had kept the ship under full steam and now it was passing the junks. Flora watched with wonder as they slowly began to swing to the rear of the *Orient Queen*. The cannon above roared out again and she saw that a third junk had been hit and that the other one seemed to be turning away. The test under fire was over.

Enid's eyes were wide with excitement. "Let's go up on deck," she begged.

"No," Flora said. "Best to wait. There may be serious damage and injured men up there. We were hit, you know."

The door of their cabin opened and pale Jessica joined them. She said to Flora, "I wonder if anyone was hurt when we were hit. Henry must still be up there. I thought he had come down here. Why don't you go up and see if everything is all right? I'll stay here with Enid."

"I'd like to go up and see my Papa," Enid said at once.

Flora turned to her. "No. You stay here with Aunt Jessica. He might be angry if you went up above. There could still be danger."

She left Jessica and Enid below and made her way up to the deck. For a moment she could only smell the gunpowder in the air. She didn't see the damage that had been done. Then as she moved forward she saw the gaping hole in the railing and the splintered deck and side of the section given over to the Captain's quarters.

Captain Christie was in his shirt sleeves on his knees beside a badly wounded marine. There were several other injured reclining near him on the damaged deck. A small knot of onlookers had gathered as the captain labored to staunch the flow of blood from the stump of a leg which had been blown off by the cannon fire from the junk. Flora pressed a hand over her mouth to restrain a moan and leaned against the side of the cabin. Mr. Maple came quickly towards her.

"This is no fit place for you, miss," he said as he joined her.

She closed her eyes for a moment fighting the desire to faint. "It is all right," she said.

"Don't look at what's going on there, miss," he warned her and at the same time placed a supportive arm around her.

She fought to control her panic and nausea. Opening her eyes, she asked him, "Where is Mr. Armitage?"

"He's a brave man! He stayed right up here with the rest of us. Ready to do his bit if we were boarded!"

Something in his tone frightened her. "Is he all right?"

Mr. Maple hesitated a second. Then he said, "Yes, miss. His shoulder was grazed and he's waiting his turn with the doctor, but he'll be all right!"

"Take me to him!" she cried at once.

"Whatever you say, miss. But don't try to look around you. Just let me show you the way."

"I won't faint," she promised him weakly. And it was true. All she could think of now was Henry.

He guided her along the deck past the kneeling doctor and an unfortunate marine whom he was trying to help. After they had passed the circle of watchers they came to the less seriously wounded. Henry was sitting with his back against the side of the cabin. His white shirt was torn and bloodstained at the left shoulder.

"Henry!" she said with a sob.

He looked at her kind of dazed, but he seemed in complete possession of all his senses. "It's nothing," he assured her. "A small shoulder wound. Some of the others are badly hurt."

"You've bled so much."

"Not really. It looks worse than it is. The Captain will be around to look after me soon. Don't let Enid or Jessica up here until I've had my wound attended to."

"I'll see that they're kept below," she promised him.

He smiled wanly. "At least we saved the ship. Considering that we paid a small price."

Mr. Maple looked down at her. "The doctor will be coming to fix his shoulder any minute now. I think I'd best see you back to your cabin."

"He's right," Henry urged her. "Do go now. Tell the others I'm all right. I'll come to you as soon as I can."

"Very well," she said, and on impulse she bent closer to him and kissed him on the cheek. His skin was burning hot to her lips. He smiled at her as she rose to leave.

Mr. Maple saw her to the door of her cabin and it was

then she had to put on a first-rate acting display. She gently conveyed that Henry had been wounded but assured his daughter and sister that the injuries were of a minor nature. Jessica became slightly hysterical.

"I'm going to him!" she cried and started for the cabin door.

"No, not yet!" Flora told her, blocking her way.

"What?" Jessica stared at her in anger.

"He doesn't want you up there yet!"

"You can't stop me!"

"You mustn't go!" Flora implored her.

"How dare you tell me what to do where Henry is concerned," Jessica screamed in a rage, making an attempt to push Flora aside.

Then Flora did something that she hadn't anticipated or would ever have expected to do under any ordinary circumstances. She raised her hand and slapped Jessica hard across the face. She stumbled back with a look of utter shock.

"I had to do that," Flora said at the same time.

Jessica reached up to her face and then she unexpectedly broke into tears, slumping down on the side of the bunk with her face buried in her hands. She went on crying involuntarily for several minutes. Enid edged away from her and went to stand in frightened silence at the other side of the cabin.

When Jessica stopped crying, she sat staring down at the cabin floor. Flora remained standing, feeling the strain of the situation.

At last Jessica asked her without looking up, "How badly hurt is he?"

"His shoulder was injured but not badly," Flora told her. "It's nothing to be alarmed about."

"That's all?"

"Yes. Just his shoulder."

"Oughtn't he be ready to see us by now?" Jessica asked.

"I say we should wait until he comes to us," was Flora's reply. Then she went over and gave Enid a gentle smile of encouragement and touched a hand to her shoulder.

It was perhaps a half-hour later that Henry Armitage

arrived at the cabin. Since Flora had seen him his shoulder had been bandaged and his arm was in a neat sling. He had a fresh shirt on and his jacket was draped over his shoulder. Looking pale, but in no great pain, he kissed Enid and hugged her with his free arm.

Jessica showed tears of relief and joy. It seemed that the crisis had ended but Flora noticed that when Jessica finally left the cabin she said nothing at all to her. She walked past her coldly without even glancing at her.

Flora knew how touchy the high-spirited young woman could be. She guessed that Jessica had no intention of forgiving her for having slapped her face. She was bound to hold it against Flora and keep a needless feud going on between them.

The rest of the short journey to Canton was without incident. They reached the harbor at night, anchoring offshore until the morning.

Flora was standing on deck, gazing across the water, wondering what Canton might have to offer, when Henry Armitage came out of the shadows to stand beside her.

"So our voyage is nearly at an end."

"Yes. I was thinking just now how far I've journeyed from quiet Sussex."

"The other end of the earth."

"That's true in more ways than one," she mused.

"Canton is an interesting city," he told her. "Less busy than Hong Kong and truer to the Chinese tradition."

"I'll welcome a stay on land again."

"It has been a long voyage," he agreed. "I wonder how things are going back in England. Sometimes I think I shouldn't have left without settling with Lily's parents. They may think I have some guilt to hide, running off the way I did."

"It was your lawyer's decision that you should handle it in this way."

"Are lawyers always right?"

"Probably not."

"I fear mine may have made a hasty judgment in this case," he said worriedly. "But it's too late to do anything about it now. And anyway he's probably settled everything satisfactorily by this time."

"Most likely."

He sighed. "I've noticed that Jessica hasn't been speaking to you lately."

Turning away from him, she murmured, "Don't let it bother you."

"But it does," he persisted. "What does it mean?"

"It's nothing. Just something she has against me. It happened the day you were hurt."

"What happened?"

"She insisted she was going up on deck before you had your wound attended to. I knew if she went Enid would insist on following her and I couldn't let her up there to witness that scene of carnage."

"You were quite right."

"I tried to reason with Jessica but she wouldn't listen. She became hysterical and shoved me to one side. I slapped her face and blocked her from leaving the cabin."

He gave a low whistle. "So that's it! I knew there had to be something. Jessica is not one to forget anything like that, even though she was in the wrong. I'll speak to her," he promised. "Tell her to quit her childish behavior."

Flora turned to him again. "How is your shoulder?"

"Better, but there's still an intermittent pain, like a toothache," he confessed. "I discussed it with the captain. He thinks a nerve may have been injured. That's what gives me the occasional trouble. The captain has a fair knowledge of surgery and he thinks it will disappear after the wound heals."

"Maybe you can consult a doctor in Canton."

"Maybe. But I hope it will clear up by itself before long."

She glanced at the distant shore. "Somewhere over there is the house where we'll be living, the house of Yenn Li. It should be a wonderful experience for Enid."

"I'm sure it will be," he said with a smile. "And I hope it gives you a taste of another world as well. You look very lovely tonight, Flora."

She smiled. "The shadows enhance me, perhaps."

"No, you look equally well in the sunlight. I have noticed. The voyage has done you good. You look much more healthy than when we left England."

"I feel better," she admitted. "I came to Armitage House soon after having had some grim experiences."

"That's true," he agreed. "And the atmosphere there isn't very soothing. Let us hope that from now on things will be better." Henry sighed. "Well, time to turn in, I suppose. We'll be docking fairly early tomorrow."

"Yes, it's time to turn in," she agreed. "I'm so glad your shoulder is improving."

He looked at her fondly. "I'll not forget that day you came to me on the deck. When I was stretched out there in pain."

"I'm afraid I didn't help much. I'm sure I'd have fainted if it hadn't been for Mr. Maple."

"Just seeing you made me feel better. I knew I could depend on you to keep Enid and Jessica out of the way. And you did."

"I was worried only about your injury," she said.

"That is typical of you," he said as they left the dark deck to go down below. He saw her to the door of the cabin she was sharing with Enid and said good night. As he did so he took her in his arms and gently kissed her.

Just as he released her she saw the door of Jessica's cabin across the corridor close. She realized it had been partly open and Henry's sister had been spying on them. She did not let on to Henry but she knew this would not make Jessica any fonder of her.

Enid was up at dawn when the *Orient Queen* began to move into the Canton harbor. The youngster gave Flora no peace until she also rose from her bed and dressed. They both had breakfast and were on deck to watch as the great vessel slowly moved in to the wharf.

There was the same noise and excitement as when they'd docked at Hong Kong. Sampans moved around the big vessel, dock workers screamed, dogs on the wharf barked, coolies shouted, and there was a continuing, tumultuous confusion. She scanned the surrounding shore.

Beyond the colorful pattern of the city, she saw great granite cliffs, and matted greenery leading to high blue mountain peaks.

Enid tugged at her arm. "I see a man splendidly dressed in green who has just arrived in a rickshaw. He seems very impressive. Do you think it could be Yenn Li?"

She searched the wharf to find the man whom the little girl had so carefully described. She saw him as he was having a grave discussion with another older man who looked as if he might be a port official of some sort.

She said, "I don't know whether he is Yenn Li or not but he surely is the type."

Now the business of disembarking began. Henry told them they'd be leaving for Yenn Li's house in a half hour. He even pointed out his father's business partner standing on the dock. It was the same man whom Enid had first noticed.

They went below to pack their things after the first excitement of arriving was over. Seamen came to take their luggage and Henry and Jessica joined them in waiting to step down the gangway.

Henry was the first on the wharf, greeted by the imposing looking man dressed in rich green silk. Henry introduced them in turn to Yenn Li, who announced that rickshaws were waiting for all of them at the other end of the wharf.

Henry and Jessica went first, with Yenn Li as their guide. Flora and Enid followed behind. The native peasants and coolies were laughing and pointing at them.

"They seem to find us strange," Enid said.

Flora laughed as they pushed through the crowds. "We are a novelty to them."

"I say they are the odd ones," the ten-year-old insisted. She was taken by the colorful clothes worn by the people, the narrow streets with confusion of stores and houses, and the yellow faces and almond eyes capped by round straw hats.

They sat back in the third rickshaw as the coolie between its shafts trotted along quickly. He miraculously found a channel through the milling street crowds and kept in sight of the rickshaw in which Enid's father and Jessica were seated.

At last they left some of the noise and confusion behind, coming to an area of imposing houses set far in off the street and fronted by quaint gardens or walled areas.

"They're turning in ahead," Enid exclaimed leaning forward in the jogging rickshaw.

"Yes, they are," she agreed. "We must have reached the house of Yenn Li."

And so they had. The rickshaws came to a halt in a line before the door of a white and crimson mansion. As Flora stepped out onto the gravel of the walk fronting the majestic house she saw two younger people emerge from within it. One of them was a serious-looking young Chinese man. The other was a girl with perfect European features and jet-black hair. She was wearing a lovely white Western dress not unlike her own.

This breathtakingly lovely girl was introduced to Henry by Yenn Li. When Flora saw his pleased reaction she knew that the girl must be the daughter of the house, Han Li.

Book Three

The World of Han Li

Chapter Twenty-one

THEIR WELCOME to the home of merchant Yenn Li was a very warm one. Introductions were made, Jessica was behaving in her most charming manner to impress the Li family, and Flora felt that they had made a good beginning of their stay in Canton. She was introduced to the lovely Han Li, who spoke perfect English and had a wide familiarity with affairs in Europe. Flora also met and chatted with the serious Chen Li, cousin to Han, who had received his education at Oxford.

The house interested her greatly. It was constructed in the traditional Chinese style—a compound of three successive courtyards with a number of rooms around each. There were large spacious rooms in the first house for the use of Yenn Li and his family, the second courtyard and the smaller rooms served for guests, and the third courtyard in the rear offered rooms for kitchen, storerooms, and servants. Surrounding the rambling structure was a high wall which had one gate only, in the front.

Chen Li joked, "If this house were not owned by someone as Westernized as my Uncle Yenn, the central court-yard of the house would be given over to his concubines and their children."

"But your uncle married only once, didn't he?" she said.

"That is true," the young man agreed. "And his wife was British like you. That is why Han Li is so strikingly different from our native women. My uncle had no inter-est in marrying again. He has remained a widower and de-voted himself to the upbringing of Han Li."

"I'm amazed that she keeps up so well with what is going on in Europe."

"My cousin spent considerable time in England and she also toured the Continent rather widely. And she receives mail and newspapers on almost every ship that calls here from England."

As the days passed Flora was to discover how deeply interested in things British the lovely Han Li was. It also became very apparent that Henry Armitage charmed the young girl. Her attentions to him could not be missed by those in the party. Jessica was especially aware of their growing attraction for one another and was becoming ex-tremely cool towards the beautiful girl. This jealousy made her suddenly forget her feud with Flora, who she now turned to as a friend and confidante.

"That girl is making herself ridiculous mooning over Henry," Jessica said angrily on one occasion when she and Flora were standing in their courtyard alone.

"I don't think she has met many European men," Flora said.

"She acts as if she hadn't," Jessica said with disgust. "I'm sure she considers herself in love with my brother. I can only hope that he keeps his senses! I'm sorry we ever made this journey!"

Flora offered no comment. She had also been watching Han Li and Henry. It was her private opinion that he was as much taken with the Eurasian beauty as she was with him. In fact he spent all his free time with her, aside from working hours with her father and short periods with his daughter.

Enid was living quite a different life as a guest of the house. Han Li's ancient amah, who had lived in England for a time and spoke the language well, was still in the employ of Yenn Li. Han Li insisted that the amah take charge much of the time to give Flora more freedom. Since the arrangement pleased Enid and the amah, it turned out very well. Whenever the old amah took Enid on excursions to the city, she came back with sweets, tiny dolls, and other native novelties.

This gave Flora a chance to do some independent exploring of the busy city. She also had an opportunity to mingle more freely with the adults in Yenn Li's mansion. The weather was warm and pleasant and she enjoyed every moment of it.

One day young Chen Li suggested that she join him on an excursion to the Buddhist monastery of the Lilting Bell. He said, "I think it is something you should see before you leave China, and I have the day to myself."

"Very well," she said. "What time can we expect to return?"

"By nightfall," he told her. "There are inns along the way for food and refreshment. It will be an easy journey."

She went inside to let Enid know she'd be gone for the day and found her seated with the amah in the middle courtyard.

Enid smiled. "It doesn't matter. The amah is taking me to a street bazaar we've never been to before. It will fill in all my afternoon."

"Very well," Flora said. "Finish the studies I assigned you before you go and have a good time."

She changed to a dark dress which she thought would be more suitable to the excursion than the one she'd been wearing. She found a bonnet of a similar shade to go with it and then hurried out to join Chen Li. He helped her into a waiting rickshaw.

He apologized, "The rickshaw will only be able to take us part of the way."

"I'm prepared to do some climbing," she said. "I changed my clothes."

As the coolie between the shafts of the rickshaw trotted

along, Chen said, "I do not want you to leave my country without seeing all sides of it. There is more to China than squatter's hovels, skeletal coolies, scabby orphans, brazen smugglers, and back street smells. More than rich merchants conducting their businesses by day and then having all-night sessions of mahjong."

"I know China, like all countries, has its good and bad sides," she agreed. "Believe me, I have known something of the dark side of London."

"So Miss Jessica has told me," the young man said in his serious way, his green eyes fixed on her. "I heard from her that you were a prisoner in a brothel when her brother rescued you."

"It is partly true," she said. "Jessica has a way of twisting everything to suit herself."

The young Chinese nodded. "Miss Jessica is an arrogant person."

"So you've noticed that!"

"Not only I," Chen said, "but my cousin Han Li and her father have also been aware of her shortcoming."

Flora said, "She began here on her best behavior, but now I think she has grown jealous of your cousin."

"Han Li is a fabulous beauty."

"And Henry Armitage is very much taken with her."

The young Chinese nodded. "Her father has noted this and he approves. It has always been his hope that his daughter would marry one of her mother's countrymen."

"Oh?"

"Yes. It may be that she has found a suitable husband in Mr. Armitage."

"Perhaps," she said. Until now she hadn't realized that the affair might be all that serious. But it seemed that it was, at least on the part of Han Li and her father. She realized that she herself was a trifle jealous of the Eurasian girl.

Chen was watching her. "You do not fancy such a marriage?"

"The idea is new to me," she confessed. "I hadn't thought about a match between my employer and Han Li, although I have seen their friendship develop."

"My Uncle Yenn hopes that the young man will ask for Han Li's hand before he leaves," Chen said. "The distance between Canton and England is great. He would like to see the marriage performed here."

"Wouldn't your uncle miss Han Li greatly?"

"Yes. But her happiness is his first desire."

"Of course," she agreed. "And how do you feel about it?"

He looked more grave than ever. "I fear I am not the one to ask."

"Why not?"

He turned to her as the rickshaw continued on and in a sad voice said, "Because I have my own feelings. I have always been in love with Han Li."

"I see," she said, feeling sorry for the young man.

"I have tried to be more British than the British in the hope of winning her. But it is useless. Her father sees me as his nephew and not as a possible son-in-law. And when I look in the mirror I know that I am a Chinese and that Han Li will never be impressed by my adopted English ways."

"Perhaps she could love you for yourself. Marrying someone English may not be the marvelous thing she has come to expect."

He shook his head despairingly. "It is hopeless. Her father will never allow her to marry me. He can only think of having an Englishman as his son-in-law. He was greatly in love with his wife and he feels this would restore the British in his family. I have given up for myself," he said. "Now I only wait to see if Han Li and Mr. Armitage decide to marry."

"What then?"

"I shall give up working for my uncle. I would prefer to go elsewhere but I cannot pull myself away from Han Li. If she marries and leaves there is nothing to keep me here. I may even return to England myself."

She said, "If you do we might meet again."

He nodded gravely. "That would be most pleasant. I like you and so does Yenn Li."

The rickshaw halted and the coolie boy put down the

shafts of the vehicle. They were at the bottom of a hill and a path ahead led up through a wooded section.

Chen helped her out and said, "I fear that from here on we must journey by foot."

"I'm ready," she told him.

Chen talked to the coolie for a few minutes in their native tongue. After some discussion he turned to her and said, "I have arranged for him to be here and meet us later. Now let us be on our way."

They started up the path with Chen leading the way. She felt sympathetic to him after having heard of his hopeless love for Han Li. She was almost in the same boat. If she were deeply in love with Henry Armitage she could do nothing but suffer about it. He was aware of her only as someone who had been kind to him and to Enid, and Jessica stood by as an almost insurmountable barrier to anyone trying to win her brother's love.

Would Han Li be able to win Henry's affection despite his jealous sister? If she did it could be a hollow victory. If Han Li returned to England and Armitage House as Henry's wife she might find it a frightening experience. Besides the arrogance and hatred of Jessica the Eurasian girl would have to cope with the menace of the ancient house. The ghosts which had tormented them all could well turn their attention to Han Li, and it might turn out disastrously!

She filled her lungs with the tang of young camphor as she followed Chen up the rocky path. She saw the new leaves of the trees with their scarlet stain and heard the song of the bright-plumaged bulbuls from the bushes. At last they came out on a grassy slope looking far down to the harbor where the *Orient Queen* sat by the wharf loading for her return voyage to England.

"Just a little farther," Chen encouraged her.

"I'm not tired," she said.

He moved still higher up until at last, above them in the gray cleft of a cliff, she saw the clear form of a white granite arch. It looked like the entrance to a kind of mountain paradise.

Chen turned to her with a smile. "That is it! That is the Monastery of The Lilting Bell."

They continued on up to the entrance of the monastery where they were greeted by yellow-robed monks with shaven heads.

"I wish you peace," the monk said, bowing to them.

They passed through a moon gate to a stone-paved courtyard with cloisters around it. Chen told her, "I visit here regularly and they know me."

At the end of the courtyard they entered a common room where a kettle boiled on a brazier. Another monk showed them to a corner of the room where they sat on huge cushions at a low table. Tea was brought to them along with tasty little cakes. In the distance she could hear the tinkling of tiny bells, almost a faint whispering of bells, a sound that seemed nothing more than part of the magical background of the place.

"This is wonderful!"

"A little remote from the regular daily routine. I have always found solace here."

"It is so beautiful and serene."

"I have brought Han Li here, but she thinks it too Chinese. She thinks life is much better in England."

"I'm afraid she is one day apt to suffer a dreadful disillusionment."

"I hope not," Chen said.

She let her eyes wander to a tapestry that hung on a nearby wall. "What is the scene depicted on that tapestry?" she asked him.

He looked at it. "The flight of Kwan Yin, who left the world to live in the Nunnery of the White Sparrow."

"One of your legends?"

"Yes. Shall I tell it to you?"

"Please, do," she begged him.

"Very well," he said. "Ages ago the Emperor Po Chia and his empress were distressed because they had no children. They went to a certain mountain and prayed that they might be blessed. Children were born to them, but they had three daughters and no sons."

"A tragedy in China," she commented.

"Especially for an emperor and empress," Chen agreed. "The emperor decided that when his girls grew up and married he would have one of his son-in-laws succeed him. Miao Shan, his favorite daughter, was the youngest and he planned to make her husband the next emperor. But Miao Shan didn't want to marry. She told her father, "I wish to sit alone and pray for perfection. I would like to care for the ill and help the poor. I do not want to marry."

"So what did the emperor do?"

"He became angry. He allowed her to enter a nunnery after a time of great anguish between them. But he planned to discourage her from being a nun by seeing that the mother superior ordered her to do all the worst menial tasks. But she cheerfully carried out these tasks. In a rage he ordered the nunnery burned. But when it was set on fire a great rainstorm came and put the fire out. His anger knew no bounds and he decided to send soldiers to behead her. But his wife, the empress, thought of another plan.

"The empress suggested winning her back to their way of life with music and feasting. But Miao Shan was not to be tempted by luxury. The emperor then had her seized and ordered to be executed. At her execution a miracle took place. The moment the axe touched her neck it broke into splinters and a spirit in the form of a tiger took Miao Shan to the underworld. When she prayed she brightened the underworld and made it a good place. She then returned to the regular world, to the island of Pu To, where she meditated for nine years. By thinking only pure thoughts she became perfect. She was ready to enter the Gates of Heaven."

Flora said, "So she did reach her goal."

"No," he said. "Just as she was ready to enter the Kingdom of Heaven the cries of the poor and troubled on earth reached her ears. She turned back and decided to remain on earth to help them. Because of her great goodness, her name was changed to Kwan Yin, which means the-one-who-hears-prayers."

She smiled, "A happy ending after all. It's a touching story. I must tell it to Enid."

He sighed. "I fear we must return now or we shall be late for the evening meal at Yenn Li's house."

The afternoon had been enchanting. The return trip was quicker than the long climb up the mountain. When they reached the bottom they found the coolie with his rickshaw waiting for them.

As they jogged along the streets of Canton to Yenn Li's house, Chen said, "The *Orient Queen* will soon be ready to leave."

"Oh?" she said. "I wasn't sure when it would be fully loaded."

"Cargo has been stowed aboard her every day during the past week," Chen said. "That means a sailing within the next seven to ten days."

She said, "This has been a wonderful holiday. I shall miss China."

"And we shall miss all of you," he assured her with true Oriental politeness.

They reached the mansion and went in through the front gate. As they stepped inside the house itself they found Yenn Li, Henry Armitage, and Han Li gathered in the living room. She at once felt a certain excitement in the air. Henry Armitage came over to her with a happy look on his handsome face. "I have some great news, Flora. I have asked Han Li to be my wife and she has accepted."

Flora was a trifle stunned by the announcement but she fought hard to hide her shock. She smiled and said, "I had no idea. I hope you'll both be very happy."

"And I," Chen said, extending a hand to Henry. "I trust your marriage may be a perfect one." His face showed no expression as he said this.

Flora was impressed at the way Chen carried this off since she knew from what he'd said to her that this must be the worst possible moment for him.

Han Li, in a lovely yellow gown, advanced to Flora almost timidly and said, "I shall depend on you, Flora. I shall need your help in the time ahead. You are so good with Henry's little girl."

"You'll have no trouble making her love you. The child

needs a mother. I'm glad you will be taking over that role."

Han Li said, "But Henry and I have agreed that we still will want you to be Enid's governess. She needs you so much it would be a shame to break the relationship."

She evaded this by saying, "That matter can be settled later." Privately she was thinking that since Henry had found a wife she would no longer be bound to Armitage House. Enid would have a mother and she could look elsewhere for a post. The prospect of remaining at the old mansion with its dark secrets and ghosts did not appeal to her.

Yenn Li was beaming as he spoke up. "Tonight we shall have a feast and plenty of nice wine to celebrate this happy event. And when my child and Henry Armitage are married before the *Orient Queen* sails next week we shall have a proper wedding party! My house has never been so honored as on this day!"

Henry linked his arm in the frail and lovely Han Li's and said, "Now I shall feel closer to China than ever. I have promised Han Li that we shall return at least every two years."

"Have you told Enid the news?" Flora asked.

"Yes," he said. "I went to her as soon as Han Li had accepted me. She seems very happy about it. Just now she is at a neighbor's house with the amah. I believe they are to remain there for the evening. She enjoys playing with the children."

"I see," she said, glad that she had been relieved of the task of telling the child. One could never predict how such news would be received.

Han Li gave her a knowing glance. "We have also told Jessica."

"Oh?" she said.

Henry frowned. "Jessica is not feeling well so we didn't spend long with her. She is in her room with a headache."

Yenn Li spoke up, "Perhaps she may recover in time to join in the feasting and drinking later on."

"I wouldn't count on it," Henry said.

Chen said quietly, "Nor would I."

Flora made an excuse that she must change her dress before dinner and fled the room. She was still surprised that the affair between the two had advanced so far without her realizing it. Now it was no longer supposition; Han Li and Henry would be married before the *Orient Queen* sailed. He would be taking her home to England with him as his bride.

Feeling somewhat lost and knowing this was going to make a change in her future, she went through the courtyard to her own room and washed up. She changed into an evening dress and was searching the dresser top for a suitable fan when the door of her room was swung open.

Jessica, distraught, stood there in a dressing gown with her hair loose and tumbling over her shoulders. It was clear by the redness of her eyes that she had been crying. She gave Flora a despairing look.

"You have heard the news?"

"Yes."

"What a fool Henry is."

"He and Han Li are in love," she ventured rather weakly.

"In love?" Jessica demanded angrily. "Do you really believe that?"

"I think so."

"Well, I don't!"

"Then why would they plan to marry?"

Jessica took a step nearer her. "I'll tell you why. That scheming Yenn Li has been working on this from the moment we arrived. He wants his half-breed daughter to marry an Englishman. And so he's tricked Henry into becoming his son-in-law!"

"Surely Henry wouldn't ask Han Li to marry him if he didn't love her."

"How can he love her? He scarcely knows her. None of us know much more than her pretty face and her meek voice. Henry has fallen for a pretty face again."

"But he did love his first wife."

"That's what you think!" Jessica raged. "This is typical of him. He's so weak where women are concerned I can't believe it. He married Enid's mother because he thought he

271

could make her happy. She died in childbirth, the silly creature. Not strong enough for it, he said. She wasn't strong enough for anything."

Flora protested. "I don't think you should go on this way."

"I'll say my say!" Jessica warned her, not considering that Flora might be a reluctant listener.

"You're only upsetting yourself."

Jessica ignored this. "Then there was Lily. A nice mess of trouble we had with her. If she hadn't ended in the pond she would likely have been the mistress of Armitage House. She was getting around Henry. I could tell."

"How can you tell?"

"The signs are obvious," Jessica said indignantly. "In spite of my trying to protect him he opens himself to affairs with young women completely unsuitable to him."

"By your standards, but perhaps not by his own."

Jessica glared at her. "You are not blameless. I have seen you play up to him. And I caught you two kissing several times."

"Then you must have been spying on us."

"Spy!" she said disgustedly. "I don't deny it. Of course I'll spy any time it's likely to save my brother from himself."

"Why are you so concerned? He's an adult. He can decide his own affairs," she retorted.

"No. He's never been capable of judging women. It's a blind spot with him. I'd rather have seen him married to you than to that Eurasian creature. It will cause a scandal. Wait and see."

"I doubt that. Han Li looks very much like any English girl."

"But you can tell she's different. Her hair. Her eyes. To think that I sat by and let that Yenn Li bring this about. What will my father say?"

"He'll probably bless the match. He has a high opinion of Yenn Li."

"Which I don't share!"

Flora tried to placate the upset young woman. "You can't stop the marriage now. There's no good causing a scene. You'd do best to pretend you don't care one way or another."

"But I do care!"

"You mustn't allow the others to know that."

"I shall not take part in any of the festivities," Jessica informed her. "I shall be ill until the *Orient Queen* sails."

"That is being unfair to yourself."

Jessica raised her chin in her arrogant fashion. "I know what is best for me. I should have realized I wouldn't get any sympathy from you."

"I don't see that sympathy is called for," she protested.

"You can't be that naive," Jessica snapped, and left the room as abruptly as she'd entered it.

Flora stood there unhappily. She knew that many of the things the other girl had said were exaggerated. Henry wasn't the simpleton his sister was picturing him to be. Indeed, he was an astute young man. It was nonsense to suggest that he couldn't pick himself a proper wife.

This rage she'd witnessed was all a product of Jessica's abnormal jealousy. It had been bad enough before but she could see that it might grow more serious now. She felt sorry for Han Li having to return to England and the dark shadows of Armitage House.

She tried to put the unhappy scene from her mind as she went out to join the others. Yenn Li had the celebration already underway. He had hired a trio of musicians who had arrived and were now playing in the first courtyard. Tables had been set out there and gaily colored paper lanterns served to light the courtyard.

It was a mild night, suitable for an outdoor feast such as this. Servants scurried back and forth setting out great trays of food. Rice wine was served, and both Henry Armitage and Han Li, seated in the middle of the group, seemed extremely happy. Toasts were drunk to them and Henry responded in gallant fashion. He was no longer wearing his arm in a sling though he favored it and complained of it aching at times.

Flora was seated next to Chen Li. When there was a lull in the jollity and everyone was busy eating she turned to him and said, "You handled yourself very well when you heard the news."

Chen shrugged as he hesitated over his chopsticks and the bowl of food before him. "It was not entirely a shock to me as you know. I had predicted it to you."

"So you did."

He gave her a questioning look. "What about Miss Jessica?"

"She is in a rage. She came storming into my room."

He looked concerned. "Do you believe she will continue her hositility to Han Li after the shock of hearing about the marriage has passed?"

"Yes."

"That worries me," he said. "Han Li is my beloved cousin. She will be a stranger in England for all her knowledge of the country. I would not like to think of her being abused."

Flora said, "Jessica lives with Henry as you know. Their father is also in the same house. He is a good man but he is getting old and eccentric. There is not much he can do."

"So Jessica will be in a position to torment my cousin daily?"

"If she so wished."

"How have you found it living in the same house with her?" Chen Li asked.

She sighed. "I do not like Armitage House. It has a weird atmosphere. I could almost say that I hated it. I have remained on there only because of Enid."

"Will you stay on there now that Han Li has married your employer?"

"I don't know. I haven't made up my mind yet. I think I may give up my position eventually because of my fear of the house."

Chen was staring at her. "Why do you hate it?"

"Some dreadful tragedies have taken place there," she said. "One of them was the death by drowning of my predecessor, a young woman named Lily."

"Indeed?"

"She was said to have taken her own life but many people have doubts. She had shown a liking for Henry Armitage."

"Do you think the woman was a suicide?"

"I don't know," she said unhappily.

"I see," Chen said quietly, and he turned to stare with troubled eyes at his lovely cousin sitting in the center of the group looking so ecstatically happy.

Chapter Twenty-two

IN THE days following the wedding announcement there was a constant flurry of preparations and joyous celebrations. Even Enid was caught up in the spirit of happiness which seemed to fill the house of Yenn Li. But Jessica studiously avoided the festivities and kept strictly to herself.

Another minor cause of worry was the pain that had lingered in Henry's injured shoulder. He complained of it often and he was still unable to make much use of his arm.

One morning after Flora had finished working with Enid on her lessons Han Li came out to the second courtyard and sat on a bench with her.

"I am troubled by Henry's shoulder injury. He has been complaining more about it lately," she said.

"Perhaps he can have it treated when he returns to England," she suggested.

"I wonder. I fear that the pain might get worse on the

voyage. There is a doctor here in Canton I think he should see."

"Why not suggest that to him?"

Han Li looked worried. "I'm afraid he may make fun of me for suggesting one of our doctors."

"You must not feel that way," Flora counseled her. "You are going to be his wife, not his servant. You must feel you are his equal. Your ancient culture is as good as anything we have to offer in England even though it may be different."

"You are so bold!" she gasped.

"I'm trying to give you good advice."

"But England is such a land of progress with your railway trains, your great factories, and your gas lighting and heating. It is a place of modern miracles."

"It is also a place of great poverty, drunkenness, crime in the streets, and a generally backward attitude towards the calm, artistic culture which you have perfected."

"You are just saying that," Han Li protested.

"It is true," she insisted. "I don't think you should carry your worship of things British too far."

"My father believes that the British are the greatest people on earth."

"We have our virtues and our weaknesses," Flora said. "Your father is unfairly prejudiced because he knew a time of great happiness with your British mother. Thus he has come to revere all things British in her name and memory. That is a mistake on his part which you must not share."

Han Li looked baffled. "Don't you think I will be happy with a British husband?"

"I know that Henry Armitage will try very hard to make your life a happy one. But do not think that merely having a British husband is a guarantee of happiness. It isn't."

"Now I am confused," Han Li said.

"You mustn't be," she told her. "I merely am trying to make you proud of your own heritage."

"You are so good. I am glad I shall have you as my friend at Armitage House."

"You will find living there very different."

The girl nodded. "Jessica will be there."

"You simply must overlook her jealousy of Henry. It is a sick thing. Try to ignore it and get along with her as best you can."

Han Li glanced in the direction of Jessica's room. "She refuses to attend any of the feasts in our honor. She is very angry."

"You can always hope she'll get over it. England is a long distance away. The voyage will give her time to change her mind."

"I wish to be friendly with everyone," Han Li said.

"I know that and surely Jessica must eventually realize it. With some luck this unpleasantness will blow over."

"If only it would," Han Li said devoutly. "If I speak to Henry about going to see the Canton doctor will you come along with us?"

"Why?"

"I think it would be an interesting experience for you," the girl said. "The doctor is very old and wise. You might even like to ask him some questions about yourself."

Flora laughed. "I doubt it. I feel quite well. But let me know and if I can I'll be glad to go along."

"I shall speak to my father," Han Li said. "He is a good friend of Dr. Kang. He will arrange for him to see Henry."

Flora forgot completely about the conversation until the following afternoon when Han Li came to her room to tell her that she'd been in touch with the eminent Dr. Kang.

"We are to meet Henry at the business address of my father. Then we shall proceed from there to Dr. Kang's."

"Right away?"

"Yes."

"You're sure you want me along?" Flora asked.

"Yes," the lovely Chinese girl said. "And Henry expects you to come."

"All right," she said. "Give me time to put on another dress."

A little later she met Han Li out by the gate. They got

into a rickshaw that took them through the busy, winding streets of the ancient city to the white building with dark green shutters that houses the tea business.

Henry was waiting for them and quickly summoned another rickshaw. He said, "I'll follow after you two since Han Li knows the way."

When they arrived at the lavish red gate of Dr. Kang's house Han Li got out of the rickshaw with Flora and Henry joined them. He looked up at the huge gilt letters in Chinese across the top of the red gate and asked Han Li, "What is that written up there?"

She smiled. "It says this is the Temple of Better Healing."

Henry looked amused. "I hope Dr. Kang lives up to his sign."

The gatekeeper greeted them with a nod, murmured something to Han Li, and rang a gong just inside the gate. He then waved them to the granite steps leading to the verandah. The balustrade was decoratively planted with petunias, ginger, gardenias, and hibiscus.

In the main hall an attendant greeted them and waved them on to the waiting room. Henry whispered to Flora, "There is more ceremony here than at the best Harley Street physician's."

There was only one wizened old woman in the waiting room ahead of them so they all found chairs to sit in. The doctor's assistant opened the door of the examining room and shouted to the old lady to come in. The crone was apparently half-deaf.

After a short wait the door opened again and the assistant called to Han Li in Chinese. She got up and told them, "We are to go in now."

Flora followed after Henry and Han Li and found herself in a good-sized room which smelled strongly of herbs.

Dr. Kang sat at a cluttered desk. He was a large, stout old man with a thin gray beard and a completely bald head. He wore a robe of black and gold and a black mandarin cap with a gold crown.

"What may I do for you this fine afternoon?" he asked, studying Han Li with mild eyes.

"I have brought the man I am to marry and a member of his household to see what a fine physician you are, Dr. Kang."

"The compliments flow from your lips like fragrant petals dropping from trees but I fear the only way to convince anyone of medical talent is to offer them a cure."

Han Li said, "I hope I may have you show your skill by doing this for my husband-to-be. His arm was injured at the shoulder when pirates attacked his sailing vessel.

"Ah!" Dr. Kang sat back in his chair, stroking his thin beard with a delicate, slim hand.

"You will help ease the pain," she begged him as they stood before the old man's desk in a semi-circle, Henry in the middle.

Dr. Kang went over to the shelves where jar upon jar of herbs and other medicinal products sat. He indicated the more than a hundred jars, bowls, and flasks with a gesture. He said, "This is not a case I can treat with a bit of dried fungus, with the red galangal ginger of Hainan, or with cinnamon bark. It is a far more serious problem."

"Then you must use your other skill, Dr. Kang," Han Li suggested.

"Ah! So you are suggesting that I turn to the ancient art of acupuncture."

Han Li nodded. "My father says you are better at it than anyone in Canton."

"But do these Westerners have any confidence in this healing art?"

Henry spoke up, "I don't know anything about it, Doctor."

"We insert needles to diminish an abundance or to replace a deficiency," Dr. Kang said. "It is one of the ancient healing arts of China. Not all our doctors believe in it, but those of us who do believe in it strongly."

Han Li turned to Henry and said, "Long ago Dr. Kang cured the gout in my father's left foot by acupuncture."

Henry said, "And you think he can cure the pain that keeps returning to my shoulder?"

"Why not?"

"I think a nerve has been damaged," he said. "I don't see that sticking a needle in it will help."

"It is most necessary that you have belief in your physician or he cannot help you."

Han Li turned to Henry again. "Please, try it!" she begged him.

Rather flustered he glanced at Flora. "What do you say to all this?"

"I doubt that you can suffer any harm. You are in pain. I'd say anything is worth a try."

"Well, let us give it a try. Explain what you are going to do."

"In a moment," Dr. Kang said. "If you will first be kind enough to remove your jacket and shirt so that I may study your bare shoulder."

With Han Li's help Henry removed his jacket and shirt. The scar and red tissue where the shoulder had been wounded was now exposed. The old doctor went over to him and carefully examined it.

"You had a narrow escape, young man," he advised him. "Had the wound been a little lower you would have lost all your bone in that area."

"I know," Henry said.

Dr. Kang went to his desk and opened a drawer. From it he drew out a silver case, which held nine needles of various sizes. "These various styles of needles were invented long ago by the Emperor Huang-ti. The earliest needles were made of flint. Later they were made of iron, gold, silver, and copper. I prefer those constructed of copper. Each shape is designed for a specific type of treatment. I shall use the Yuan-Li needle on you." He lifted it from the case and held it up before Henry.

The young man stared at it. "It is one of the heavy ones."

"That is so. Its point is round and slender. It is applied to replenish vascular emptiness, to cure paralysis, rheumatism, and stagnation in the arteries. If I am successful I shall be able to remove your attacks of pain."

"Then get along with it, Doctor, for the pain has returned at this very moment."

"You will please be seated," the old man said, leading him to a chair. "I am going to treat you at the two vital points for your ailment. I shall work in the lung meridian, but first I shall administer Chung Fu, which means the needle is to be inserted in a spot near the center of your chest."

"Go ahead, Doctor," Henry said.

Dr. Kang placed the needle in the center of Henry's chest and quickly spun it around. It had sunk into the flesh and it seemed that the spinning might produce pain and blood, but it did neither. It was evident that Dr. Kang was a specialist in his field. He allowed the needle to remain in place for a little and then he removed it.

"That didn't hurt much," Henry said, "but my shoulder still is paining."

"Patience!" Dr. Kang said. "We have not completed our treatment."

Han Li's pretty face showed sympathy for what Henry was enduring. Flora found herself terribly excited as the moment for the second part of the treatment drew near.

"Next I shall use the point K'ung Tsue, which is three quarters of the way up on the inner side of your injured left arm. This spot has to do with the movement of the shoulders, and of reaching over your head. It may also be used for sore throats and headaches."

Dr. Kang inserted the needle in the lower left forearm and once again spun it around expertly. He allowed it to remain in Henry's arm for a little more than the count of ten and then he removed it. "Well?"

Henry was astounded. He got to his feet and stared at them in wonder. "I don't know how or why but the pain is gone!"

Dr. Kang smiled happily. "Then we have succeeded!"

Henry said, "It's only a temporary fluke, isn't it, Doctor? The pain is bound to return?"

"No. I have reached the seat of the pain and effected a cure. You will not be troubled by the ache again."

"I want to believe you, Doctor," Henry said. "But it is almost too much to hope for."

Han Li ran over to him and happily held his good arm. "I believe. I know you are cured."

They left the doctor's and returned to the house of Yenn Li. Henry's shoulder pain did not return. That night the feasting and celebrating were partly to mark his cure.

Later that evening a newcomer entered their lives who was destined to play an important role in the days directly ahead. Dinner was still going on when one of Yenn Li's servants announced a visitor. The servant had brought a card and now the merchant read from it aloud.

"Colonel Noel Tarrant," he read. He inquired of Henry, "Is he some friend of yours come to join us in our celebrating?"

Henry said, "I've never heard of him before." The name was unknown to all of them.

"Perhaps he is some Britisher who has heard of the wedding. It can do no harm to allow him to enter and give him a hearing."

"If you like," Henry said. "Though I can't imagine why he should be interested."

Yenn Li gave his servant instructions to show the man in. A few minutes later a remarkable character presented himself to them. He was short, slender, and wore a linen suit that had once been white but was now dirty and soiled. His sun helmet, which he quickly removed, was also filthy. He was middle-aged with gray hair a bronzed, hawklike face. His eyes were smallish and a shifty blue.

"A jolly good evening to you," Colonel Noel Tarrant said in a caricature of an English gentleman's manner.

Yenn Li stood to greet him. "To what do we owe the pleasure of your company, Colonel?"

"Ah, yes," the colonel said. "The truth is I have fallen upon difficult times through no fault of my own and I have come to this house for aid."

"Indeed?" Yenn Li said coolly as they all watched in silence.

"Yes," the colonel said jauntily. "I have just learned that the *Orient Queen* is returning to England shortly. I have come to ask to be taken aboard her as a passenger."

Yenn Li said sternly, "For business of that sort you should have called at my office rather than intrude on my home."

Captain Noel Tarrant chuckled. "That wouldn't have done any good, sir, if you know what I mean. The clerks in your office would never have allowed me to get by them."

"Isn't it likely they'd be right?" Yenn Li demanded.

"That is exactly right."

"You are unable to pay your fare to England?"

"Had I been able to I could have shipped out of here many times," the man said with some bitterness. "Even though I have friends high in the army and politics back home no one will stake me to a passage. It would merely be a loan. I can pay as soon as I reach British soil and am able to contact certain friends there."

Henry said, "We'll be sailing in a few days. I'll speak to Captain Christie and see that room is made for you."

Colonel Tarrant smiled happily. "Thank you, Mr. Armitage, you are truly a gentleman. And I wish you and your bride-to-be every happiness."

Han Li seemed touched by this tribute. She rose and said, "You must stay for some food and drink, Colonel. I'm certain that is the wish of my father and my fiancé."

Yenn Li, apparently feeling an awkward situation, made a broad gesture. "By all means join in our celebration, Colonel."

"Thank you," the colonel said with a bow. Then he came over and sat next to Flora while he received a heaping plate of food from one of the servants. He glanced at her over the plate. "You're one of the party returning to England?" he asked as he began stuffing the food in his mouth. He ate ravenously as if it could have been some time since he'd had any sort of a decent meal.

"I'm the governess to Mr. Armitage's ten-year-old child," she said.

"Ah, so he has been married before?" the colonel said, his mouth full.

"Yes," she said, feeling some distaste at his table

manners. It was unpleasant to watch him even though
she knew he might have been famished.

"Who else is in the party?"

"Mr. Armitage's sister," she said. "But she is not here
tonight." At the moment she hadn't thought anything of
the question but later, when she reviewed it in her mind,
she would think that he'd been quizzing her too much.

"So he has a sister traveling with him as well."

"Yes."

"Armitage is a famous name in Canton," the colonel
continued with his mouth still full. "They say the family
has one of the most successful tea firms in existence."

"I wouldn't know."

"Fortunes have been made in tea and they will be
made again," the colonel informed her. "I have an idea
how the business is conducted. I've spent a good deal of
time in the Orient."

"What have you done for a living?" she asked.

"Mostly the army in India," he said. "I moved to the
China coast after I'd retired from my regiment. A bout
of ruinous gambling put me on my uppers and in a spot
where I have to beg English visitors here for a passage
home. Only as a loan mind you, I can pay back the
money when I get back."

The presence of the rather odd Englishman beside her
took away much of the pleasure of the occasion. Most
of the others had returned to talking and laughing among
themselves but she noticed that young Chen Li was staring at the English stranger with hard eyes. She wondered
whether Chen might know anything about him. The
young man was very familiar with the people in Canton.

Having stuffed himself with food the colonel was now
quaffing down cups of wine. He glanced around him and
said to her, "This is a posh place! I vouch it took a lot of
thieving on Yenn Li's part to find the money for this
kind of mansion."

She eyed him indignantly. "Yenn Li is our host and my
friend. I cannot allow you to call him a thief."

"Sorry," he said at once, studying her from under the

heavy lids of his snakelike eyes. "Just a joking reference of mine. Didn't mean anything at all."

She got up and walked over to where Chen Li had sat. As she joined him, she said, "I couldn't stand that foul man any longer."

Chen nodded. "I can't imagine why my uncle invited him to join his guests."

"He didn't want anyone to think him inhospitable," she said. "He was put in an awkward situation."

"True," Chen agreed.

"But he was placed in the difficult spot by an expert. I don't know the whole story of Colonel Noel Tarrant, yet I'm positive he is not all that he pretends. I noticed you staring at him and wondered if you knew him," she said.

"I can't say that I recognize him," Chen was ready to admit, "but he is a type that immediately puts you on your guard. There are many Colonel Noel Tarrants along the China coast. Some of them have dark histories. Most of them are remittance men."

"Remittance men?"

"Yes. Black sheep of good families who have been sent out here so their behavior does not disgrace their people. They are supported by monthly stipends sent them through the mails or the local banks. Remittance men have been a nuisance out there for some years, but I doubt if our colonel is in that group. I don't see him as a man having a wealthy background."

"No," she agreed. "He claims he has no money now at all. Judging by the way he's been helping himself to food and drink he hasn't been living too well lately."

"I shall make enquiries about him," Chen promised.

"I wish you would," she said worriedly. "I can't imagine why Henry Armitage so impulsively invited him along on the *Orient Queen*. He is one passenger I could do without."

When the colonel finally left he was unsteady on his feet from his heavy after-dinner imbibing. He said good night to everyone and made it a point to spend a moment with Flora.

Henry Armitage came over to Flora. "I saw that the colonel made a special point of talking to you before he left. What do you think of him?"

"I don't trust him."

Henry raised his eyebrows. "I know he isn't all he pretends, but maybe he's not a bad fellow and just down on his luck. You feel that strongly about him?"

She sighed. "I don't know. Perhaps my frightening experiences have finally left me with an instinct for unsavory people. I don't like the colonel, though I really know little about him. I think you made a mistake asking him along on the *Orient Queen*."

Henry frowned. "I certainly hope not. I was in a good humor and unthinkingly felt sorry for him. But there's little I can do about it now. I publicly invited him to join us."

Chapter Twenty-three

MUCH TO Flora's dismay Colonel Tarrant became almost a regular caller at the house of Yenn Li. The servants took it for granted that he was one of the English visitors and so he had no trouble gaining entrance to the mansion. He exuded an oily friendliness, so that it was hard to turn one's back on him, but Flora still felt he was not to be trusted.

Then one noon when she and Enid returned from a walk she was surprised to come upon the colonel and Jessica engaged in a serious conversation in the second courtyard. Neither paid any attention to her as she went on to her own room. She could see that Colonel Tarrant had made some sort of impression on Jessica as she'd been listening to him with the greatest interest.

This marked the beginning of an odd friendship between the two. Jessica returned to joining in at the wedding celebrations and the colonel usually was quick to rush to her side. They made a strange couple, but since everyone was desperately anxious to have Jessica forego her hostility towards the rapidly approaching marriage, it was generally considered fortunate that Colonel Tarrant had turned up.

At the first opportunity Flora asked Chen whether he'd been able to discover anything about the colonel.

Chen nodded bleakly. "He is known in the city. From what I have been able to learn he was dishonorably discharged from the Indian Army for gambling."

"He said he had retired, but what you heard is more likely the truth."

"My information came from trusted quarters," the young Chinese told her. "Further, since his arrival in Canton he has been used as a go-between by the opium runners for one thing. Also, he has incurred a number of bad gambling debts and been accused of using marked cards. Undoubtedly, he can no longer continue here and feels he can safely return to England to play his crooked games. Maybe some of his associates in the opium trade have invited him to join them there."

"I'll be glad when the wedding is over and we leave," Flora said. "I'm beginning to get edgy."

"You have so soon tired of China?"

"Not of China," she told him, "but of the situation. Jessica is still in far from a good mood and now we have this colonel to contend with."

Chen sighed. "The wedding day is not far off. Yenn Li has decided to have it on the day of the fidelity festival. That is Thursday of the next week."

"So the date has been set."

Chen sighed. "With the marriage of my cousin a world ends for me. I intend to begin a new life away from Canton."

"You really are broken-hearted at her marriage," she said with sympathy.

"I cannot disguise that from you. I have told you of my feelings for Han Li. My only fear is that this delicate blossom may be destroyed by the cruel English climate and the cruel English people around her."

"You're thinking of Jessica."

"I can't help it. I know that Henry's sister hates Han Li

for planning to marry him. She will do all she can to make my cousin's life miserable."

"Let us hope that Henry will not allow that to happen."

"But he seems so blind where his sister is concerned," Chen worried. "He gives her far too much freedom. He even seems to condone this friendship of hers with the colonel."

"Because Jessica has been so troublesome he'll agree to almost anything to placate her."

"A most unfortunate situation," Chen said sadly. He looked at Flora with troubled eyes. "I will hope that you may be able to keep Han Li from harm."

"I will try as long as I'm with her."

"You have other plans?"

"Not really. But I don't think I shall remain at Armitage House after we return to England."

"What about the child?"

"Han Li and Enid get along famously. She can take care of her just as well as I."

"But if something happens to Han Li? Then what about the child?"

"I don't want to think that anything will happen to Han Li," she said.

"Nor do I."

"So let us not suppose such things," Flora said.

"I shall come to England as soon as I can. Perhaps I may be able to help my cousin adapt to her new life. And perhaps we will meet again."

"I hope we do," she said. "I think your coming to England is a good idea."

Chen left her to return to his office in Canton. She wandered out to the second courtyard where she came upon Jessica seated in the sun.

Flora said, "Isn't it a lovely day."

"The weather has improved," Jessica said. "And I understand that fine weather is expected all next week. You know, don't you, that the wedding will be held next week?"

"I found out this morning."

"I say the whole thing is ridiculous. Henry will tire of the silly little thing in a few weeks and then what?"

"I doubt that," she said. "They are so very much in love."

"Love!" Jessica said with disgust.

"You must believe in love!" Flora exclaimed.

"Not between a Chinese and my brother."

"Han Li is only part Chinese and she's so attractive!"

Jessica sneered at this. "I have heard some tales about her father and how he built up his fortune. From all I hear he is no more honest than he should be."

Flora was shocked. "How can you say that!"

"Because I heard it! Yenn Li built up his fortune on a pyramid of crooked deals. It is gossiped in Canton that he has long been cheating my father."

"I think I know who you heard that from," Flora said.

"Do you?"

"Yes. Colonel Tarrant!"

"Little goes on in Canton of which Colonel Tarrant is unaware. When I get back to England I shall tell my father to check on Yenn Li and discover whether he's being cheated or not."

"You must be mad to want to cause trouble at a time when your two families are being united!"

"I think that thieves and liars should be exposed."

"In that case why not begin with Colonel Tarrant!"

"Colonel Tarrant is not a liar!"

"I am sorry to have to tell you that he is," Flora said. "He is also much deeper in vice than you'd dream. He has told you these stories blackening Yenn Li's name because he knows you want to hear them. It is his business to please. He is giving you his loyalty, but it will be for a price. He will want a good amount of money from you."

Jessica jumped up at hearing this. "I don't believe you!"

"All evidence points to the fact the colonel is a scoundrel."

"Then why is he tolerated here?"

"Yenn Li thinks he's harmless, but that is a mistake, as your story has just proven. He's been cultivating your friendship because no one else will trust him."

"Do you consider me some sort of simpleton?" Jessica asked angrily.

"Yes, if you can't see through a cheap adventurer! If you're interested in rumors, the current one about Colonel Tarrant is that he was thrown out of his regiment for shady card playing."

"That's a monstrous accusation!"

"Unhappily I fear it may be true. Talk to the man if he amuses you, but don't believe all that he says. He has a venomous tongue "

Jessica said, "You and the others dislike him because he has gone out of his way to be my friend. I am being treated shabbily by all of you because I've tried to save my brother from a disastrous marriage," Jessica said with a show of self-pity.

"Not so," Flora said. "Your trouble is that you don't want to see Henry marrying anyone. You want to keep him for yourself!"

"How dare you!"

"I say it because I know it's true!"

Jessica laughed harshly. "It's too ridiculous to protest. What is nearer the truth is that *you* are in love with Henry but lack the courage to fight Han Li for his love!"

She winced under Jessica's words but replied quietly, "You opposed Henry showing any interest in me earlier. And whether I love him or not is hardly relevant. He is in love with Han Li and she dearly loves him!"

This time she was the one to march off and leave Jessica standing alone in the courtyard.

Henry Armitage returned earlier than usual from the office that afternoon. Flora and Enid were sitting next to the fountain in the first courtyard and Henry came over and joined them. He picked up Enid in his arms and kissed her. "How have you spent the day?" he asked as he put her down.

"I've worked with Flora on my studies, gone to the sweets bazaar with the amah, and had a fitting for my dress for the wedding."

Henry smiled. "What color is your dress to be?"

"No!" Enid said. "I mustn't tell you. Han Li wants us to keep the colors of our dresses a secret until the day of the wedding. She says that then we'll burst out on you like a rainbow!"

"I see, a conspiracy of women. So I must be patient."

Pigeons often swooped down in the courtyard to waddle about the fountain and drink from the water surrounding it. Now Enid drifted away from them to chase the birds and head them off when she could.

Now that Flora was alone with Enid's father she took the opportunity to warn him. "I have a feeling that Jessica is up to no good."

"No?" he said, seeming surprised. "She's attended the last few dinners we've had. I thought she was coming around."

"Don't count on it. She still hates Han Li and she has been hearing wicked stories about Han Li's father from that dreadful Colonel Tarrant."

"Noel Tarrant has been feeding her lies? So that's how he repays kindness," Henry raged. "The fellow is a bounder!"

"I made that clear to Jessica, but she prefers to believe the stories he has told her about Yenn Li cheating your father's firm. She threatens to repeat the story to your father."

"We'll see about that. I will have a talk with her before we reach England. Yenn Li is one of the most honest men I know. The charges the colonel has made are ridiculous. I should throw him out the next time he shows himself here!"

"That might further enrage Jessica and make her all the more vicious towards Han Li."

"I suppose you're right."

"Tolerate him until the wedding and voyage are over. You need never see him again once the ship reaches England. Then you can send him packing and make sure that Jessica knows that she was lied to."

"What would I do without you, Flora?"

She smiled wanly. "You'd manage very well, I'm sure."

"Not at all. I need you. You understand the people I

have to cope with. I'm afraid Han Li is in for a series of shocks when she comes face to face with dealing with what she feels are the perfect English. I worry about her each day."

She was touched by his words and the obvious agony they concealed. "If you love Han Li you must be strong enough to protect her."

Henry's eyes met hers. "She is the loveliest creature I have ever known in all my life. Yet somehow she is not real to me. She's more a lovely vision than a person. I fear that any ill wind might sweep her away."

"You know the dangers," she said. "You must prepare yourself to fight them."

He nodded. "I intend to try."

Han Li appeared for dinner wearing a gown of pale blue. She had never looked more lovely. It was apparent that Henry could not take his eyes off his bride-to-be. Jessica watched them with a grim expression, probably annoyed because Colonel Tarrant had not yet made his nightly appearance.

Flora was relieved that the colonel was not there to spoil the genuine joy around the dinner table. Yenn Li was wearing one of his richest silver-embroidered robes with a matching mandarin cap. He continually joked about the coming wedding, promising it would be one that Canton would long remember.

Enid had been allowed to join the adults at the table and now she asked, "Are there going to be fireworks for the wedding, Yenn Li?"

"Why not?" Yenn Li said, raising the goblet of wine in his hand. "It is a proper day to celebrate. The fidelity festival comes only once a year!"

"What is the fidelity festival?" Flora asked the dignified Yenn Li.

"Long, long ago in the Tang Dynasty, well over a thousand years ago, a chieftain in Southwest China coveted the beautiful bride of a prince who lived in an adjoining region. So he asked the prince to dine with him and then gave him poison."

"What a wicked man!" Enid exclaimed.

"Without a doubt," Yenn Li said. "Well, this wicked man set out to woo the lovely princess. But she, guessing what he had done, vowed revenge. When the wicked man asked her to marry him she told him that she would accept on the condition he wait a year from the date of her husband's death. She also asked that a wooden tower be built in which the wedding ceremony would take place."

"Did he build it?" Enid asked.

Yenn Li smiled. "The date of the wedding was set on the first anniversary of the prince's death. The two were married. She and the wicked man went up into the room at the very top of the tower, where they were to spend their wedding night. When they were in the room she secretly locked the door and threw the key over the balcony. In the meantime she had ordered her faithful ladies-in-waiting to set the tower ablaze with torches. They followed her orders obediently. When the wicked man saw that he was trapped in a flaming tower he tried to escape, but it was too late. He died in the fire and the princess had her revenge, though she had to die with him to get it."

"What a sad story," Enid said.

Han Li told her, "They claim it is a true one. I first heard it when I was no older than you."

The dinner continued late into the evening, but Colonel Tarrant did not appear. When he did show himself the following night his face was covered with cuts and bruises. He told a story about rescuing an old woman from would-be thieves and Jessica applauded his courage.

Chen Li scornfully told Flora, "The man is lying once again. Last night he became involved in a drunken brawl in the lodging house by the docks frequented by sailors. They threw him out on the cobblestones and left him there unconscious."

Later in the evening Flora received a pleasant surprise when Han Li took her aside and said, "You are to be my one bridesmaid at the wedding."

"I'd rather not," she protested. "You must have other friends. Perhaps you should ask Jessica."

The lovely girl shook her head. "Never will I ask that cruel woman!"

"Your other friends then?"

Han Li said, "This is to be a Christian ceremony. It is my father's wish and mine. He and my mother were married by a missionary long ago. So it will be with Henry and me. We have spoken to the English missionary and he has agreed to come and perform the service. My friends are all Buddhists. They would not feel easy with this other priest. You are different. Your own father was a priest."

"Very well, if you want me, I'll join the wedding party."

At last the wedding day dawned. Members of the crew of the *Orient Queen* and some of Canton's European colony were among the guests. The others were Chinese friends of the bride and her father. They began arriving early from distant points and Yenn Li, dressed in a gorgeous robe, greeted them with great formality.

Captain Christie arrived in his best shore uniform, accompanied by First Mate Maple. The aged Anglican missionary donned his black cassock and white surplice in preparation for the ceremony. Colonel Tarrant arrived in a Prince Albert coat and striped morning trousers that he'd scrounged from someone. He looked extremely warm in his stiff collar but at least he was a lot more presentable than he would have been in his dirty linen suit and sun helmet.

The wedding took place in the first courtyard. Henry Armitage made a handsome groom in his spotless white linen suit and Han Li was the loveliest of brides as her father led her down to face the old missionary.

When the ceremony was over a noisy celebration began. Yenn Li had hired a large Chinese orchestra and a troupe of traditional dancers who executed a ballet depicting the legend of the fidelity festival. After that came the feasting.

As soon as darkness arrived Yenn Li kept his word to Enid and had a spectacular display of fireworks set off. The sky above his house was brilliant with orange, blue, green, and yellow light. It was surely an event no one would easily forget. In the excitement of the fireworks the bride and groom managed to slip away.

Flora knew through Chen Li that they were spending the two days and nights before sailing at a mountain lodge not far from the monastery of The Lilting Bell. She stood watching the fireworks with Enid, realizing that Henry Armitage was forever lost to her. Only on this night of his wedding to the beautiful Han Li was she able to admit finally to herself that she had fallen in love with her employer. All at once she was aware of someone standing beside her. Turning, she saw it was Chen Li.

"Until tonight I was not sure."

"Sure about what?" she asked.

"About you and Henry Armitage. You were in love with him, weren't you?"

"Maybe. I don't know. What does it matter?"

"I saw it in your face after the wedding. So I was not the only one miserable inwardly. It is good to have a fellow in any misfortune."

"We mustn't have such thoughts. We should only be happy for two who are so dear to us."

"That we surely can do," Chen Li agreed and he raised his eyes to watch as there came another splash of brilliant colored lights which after a few seconds quickly melted away. "How glorious the bursts of fire are," he said quietly, "and yet how quickly they fade away."

With the wedding a thing of the past, attention centered on preparations for the voyage back to England. The *Orient Queen* was heavily laden with cargo and waiting only for Henry and his bride to return from their brief honeymoon. Flora had everything packed for herself and Enid. Jessica was complaining of the delay in sailing while Colonel Tarrant had already taken up residence on the vessel as if to make certain that he would not be left behind.

On the night before the sailing Yenn Li spent some time talking to Flora. Suddenly he seemed to have become a much older man. It was plain that parting with Han Li was not going to be easy for him.

He told Flora, "Ever since my wife died I prayed for the day when my daughter might find herself an English husband, a husband of her mother's race. Now that it has happened I no longer am sure that I was right."

"I'm sure Han Li and Henry love each other," she said.

The old man gazed sadly into space. "Will their love be equal to the problems they must surely face? I hope so. I was the one who most encouraged the match. But last night I had a bad dream. I dreamt that my daughter was dead. That she had drowned and they were dragging her body out of some dark green pond unlike any I had ever seen." He turned to Flora. "Do you think my dream may have had some meaning? A warning?"

A cold chill ran down her spine. She thought of Lily and the green pond and the mystery that still surrounded her death. She forced herself to say, "I think it is only that you are saddened by the knowledge that Han Li will be leaving you.

"Perhaps," the old man said with a sigh. "Perhaps that is it."

The next morning everyone departed from the house of Yenn Li and journeyed to the wharf where the *Orient Queen* awaited them.

Yenn Li was typically stoical in his goodbyes with his daughter, but she was Western enough to have her eyes fill with tears. Chen Li was conspicuously absent for the farewells. The *Orient Queen* slowly moved out into the harbor leaving the clamor of the Canton waterfront behind. The lonely figure of the elegantly dressed Yenn Li could be seen waving from the dock for a long time.

Han Li and Henry stood at the rail of the vessel and waved back. Their arms were around each other like the true lovers they were. Flora stood a distance away with Enid and had her last glimpse of the shore. She did not expect she would return to this exotic land again and suddenly a deep feeling of sadness engulfed her.

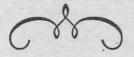

Book Four

Return to London

Chapter Twenty-four

THE RETURN voyage of the *Orient Queen* was considerably less exciting than the journey out had been. They sailed through the dangerous waters of the China Coast without incident. In Hong Kong they remained only a few days before starting out across the rough water which would take them around the Cape of Good Hope. But this time the sea was calm, the passage around the Cape quite uneventful.

By the time they reached the Canaries Flora had decided that nothing at all was going to happen to mar the voyage.

Han Li had seemed to enjoy the trip. She and Henry spent a great deal of time by themselves and the others on the ship respected their privacy. Jessica and Colonel Tarrant continued their friendship.

When they were only a few days from England Enid suddenly became nauseated and ran a high fever. The child had to be put to bed. Flora kept a faithful vigil at her bedside until the mysterious illness had eased. Enid was still confined to her bunk but others were taking turns staying with her.

On this particular morning Han Li had volunteered to keep the child company while Flora went up on deck to get some fresh air and sunshine. She was standing by the railing watching the fairly large waves when Henry came striding down the deck looking worried.

Halting by her, he asked, "How is Enid this morning?"

"Her fever is down and she has no nausea. In fact she enjoyed an excellent breakfast."

"That is very good to hear. What do you suppose brought on her illness?"

"The captain thinks it was a bout of some kind of fever. In Canton she must have been exposed to many native children who'd suffered from various fevers."

"Why would it take so long to show itself?"

"Sometimes fevers are like that. The germ may have been incubating for a long while before erupting into full disease. You mustn't worry so. Enid is a sturdy child and she is quickly returning to complete health."

Henry looked grateful. "A good deal of that is due to the fine nursing she received from you."

"And don't forget Captain Christie," she told him. "He may not be a doctor but he does have a gift for medicine and a good knowledge of it."

"I know," Henry said. "He showed me the various books on the subject he has in his cabin. He even has an illustrated guide to surgery—just studying the plates made me shudder."

"It's imperative that someone aboard know basic medicine," she said. "The voyages are so long."

"I agree," Henry said. He glanced out at the ocean. "I must admit I'm very bored with the water now. I shall be glad to set foot in England."

"So will I."

"I have made arrangements for us to be met at the docks and driven straight to Armitage House," he said. "I wrote a long letter concerning this to my father before my marriage. He should have received the letter by one of the ships which left ahead of us."

At this moment she saw Captain Christie coming over to join them. Judging by the expression on his face he was upset over something.

He walked up to Henry and said, "I have something of importance to tell you, sir."

"Yes?"

Captain Christie hesitated. "May I speak frankly before Miss Bain?"

"I would say so," Henry said. "Unless it is some matter you deem unsuitable for female ears."

"As you may have noticed, sir," Captain Christie said with a hint of embarrassment, "my officers and I have organized some card games to while away the time. This voyage has been a rather tame one."

"I know," Henry said.

"Well, sir," Captain Christie said, "the first and second mate and I have been playing with Colonel Tarrant."

"Yes," Henry said.

"The colonel is a remarkably lucky card player, or perhaps I should say clever. He has been winning almost every night. And winning very respectable sums from us, sir."

"So?" Henry questioned him.

Captain Christie's face was purple. "Well, last night the first mate thought he saw Colonel Tarrant hide a card up his sleeve. He did it very deftly, sir, but Mr. Maple had been watching him as he was a mite suspicious.

"He challenged the colonel about the card and of course he denied it. But Mr. Maple wasn't satisfied, sir, so he took the matter into his own hands."

Henry asked, "In what way?"

"You might say in a direct way," the captain went on with difficulty. "He roared and jumped up, taking the colonel by the lapels of his jacket. Then he began to shake him like a terrier shakes a rat and I tell you, sir, that not one card fell out of the colonel's sleeve, but four!"

"So there is no doubt about it. The colonel is a card-shark."

"I'd call him a thief," the captain said hotly. "I had him locked in his cabin. He's down there now."

"Your prisoner?"

"Yes, sir," the Captain said. "I want that fellow to give us back the money he tricked us out of and be properly punished as well."

Henry scowled at this. "A nasty business! You want me to talk to him for you?"

"If you would, sir,"

"I'll be happy to," Henry said. "We've known from the start that Tarrant has a record but I didn't expect him to try his tricks on us."

"Well, he has."

Henry glanced her way. "This shouldn't come as any surprise to you, Flora."

"No," she said. "I've never liked the man."

"Nor I," Henry said. "Though I did take pity on him and offered him a free passage back to England. In return he intruded on us every night and now he has shown his gratitude by robbing the officers of this ship."

"Perhaps it is fortunate he grew so bold," she told her employer. "I'm sure he has plans of following us to Armitage House and establishing himself there by telling lies about Han Li's father to your father."

Henry exclaimed angrily. "Well, there'll be none of that. No matter how much he pleads innocence I know the truth."

Captain Christie nodded to the aft deck and said, "It would seem, sir, that not everyone on board shares your dark view of the fellow."

Flora followed the captain's eyes. Jessica and Colonel Tarrant were strolling across the aft deck, arm in arm.

"Jessica seems to be hypnotized by Tarrant," Henry said angrily.

"He seems rather a favorite with the ladies," Captain Christie acknowledged. "But what I would like to know is how he escaped from a locked cabin."

Henry gave the captain a knowing glance. "Surely you have had enough experience with criminals to realize it is not all that hard for an expert to pick a lock."

"The nerve of him, sir!"

"Nerve is his strong point," Henry agreed. "The question is how I should approach him with my sister in his company."

"Well, sir," the captain said in a relieved tone. "Then I'll just leave it in your hands."

"I may want you to lock him up again," Henry said. "And if I do we'll have to find a better way to keep him in custody than before."

"I'm open to suggestions," Captain Christie said. He tipped his cap briskly again and returned to the bridge.

Henry sighed. "I might have known we'd not have a voyage without at least some trouble."

"It looks as if Jessica and the colonel are heading this way," Flora said.

When they drew close the colonel bowed. "I saw the captain talking to you," he told Henry. "There was a rather unfortunate misunderstanding last night, and as a result the captain locked me in my cabin."

"You are not down there now!" Henry said sternly.

"Indeed, he is not," Jessica spoke up. "I went to find out why he had not met me at an appointed time and discovered him a prisoner. I at once found First Mate Maple and had him freed in my custody."

"Do you realize he is accused of repeated cheating at cards?"

"I don't believe it!"

Colonel Tarrant laughed uneasily. "The whole thing is preposterous! The captain and the mates plotted this to get revenge on me. I had been winning from them nightly."

"I know all about that," was Henry's grim reply. "I accept what the captain told me and I'm going to be generous with you. First, I will expect you to go to the captain and reimburse every penny you filched from him and the two mates by crooked dealing. And second, I expect you to vanish from my sight the instant the *Orient Queen* docks. I do not ever want to set eyes on your ugly face again!"

The colonel assumed a stance of great dignity, which was rather comic considering his dirty linen suit and battered sun helmet. "Mr. Armitage, I'm not in the habit of being called a card thief or being told what to do."

"I won't have it," Jessica fumed, her pretty face crimson with anger. "I have invited the colonel to come to Armitage House as our guest until he finds himself in England."

Henry glared at the little man. "I don't care where you plan to 'find yourself' as long as it not in my home!"

"Our home!" Jessica exclaimed. "You had better remember that. I shall have something to tell our father about the girl you married and her dishonest parents!"

Henry turned on her. "I want to hear no more of that! All those stories about Yenn Li's dishonesty came from this thieving fraud!"

"How dare you, sir!" Colonel Tarrant demanded. Nonetheless he looked shaken.

"I dare more than that," Henry said. "I have given you my terms. Either you accept them or I shall have you bound in irons for the duration of the voyage and turned over to the courts when we land in London. A term in prison should do you a great deal of good."

Jessica turned to the colonel. "Don't let him frighten you, Noel!"

In a low voice, he told Henry, "Very well. If they are such poor sportsmen I shall certainly return their losses. As for having anything to do with you after I land, I would rather associate with the lowest of scum. I shall be happy to leave your company."

"Excellent," Henry said. "Just one thing. I cannot answer for the tempers of the captain and his friends. And I would say that you might be well not to appear on deck after dark. They might take a notion to toss you overboard and no questions asked."

"You do not scare me, Armitage."

"I had no intention of scaring you," Henry told him. "I'm offering you what I believe is a practical warning."

The colonel turned to Jessica. "Come along, my dear. I do not intend to remain here and be insulted." With that he took her by the arm and led her off.

Henry watched their retreating figures as they went

back down the deck. "I hope that Jessica now sees clearly what that fellow is," he said. "I think we have finally pinned him down. He is nothing but a confidence man."

Flora said, "I fear he has firmly planted malicious lies about Yenn Li in Jessica's mind. Sooner or later they may bear fruit."

"I shall talk to her again after we land," Henry said. "At any rate, I doubt my father would listen to her stories. He and Yenn Li are old friends."

The forty-eight hours were uneventful. Flora noted with some amusement that the colonel showed himself little on deck and in the evenings did not appear at all. It was clear that he had taken Hrnry Armitage's warning seriously.

On the morning of the third day they approached the coast of England. But there was little to see as a heavy fog wreathed everything. Flora regretted that this bleak weather was Han Li's welcome to her new home. The fog made the docking of the *Orient Queen* difficult as well.

Almost the first person off the ship was Colonel Tarrant. He hurried down the gangplank with his bag in hand, never once looking back. Flora was watching from the deck as his furtive figure vanished among the crowds swarming the docks. She fervently hoped that she would never set eyes on the ugly, malevolent little man again.

Jessica, however, sought Flora out on the deck and inquired, "Have you seen the colonel this morning?"

"Yes," Enid said. "He got off the ship some time ago. I think he was the first to leave."

"I can't believe it! Are you sure?"

"I saw him go."

"But he promised to come to my cabin before leaving," Jessica said. "He told me he would give me his London address. The names of friends through whom I could reach him."

"Perhaps he will get in touch with you at home."

"Perhaps," Jessica said dubiously. "However, I feel he might hesitate to do that. Henry was so needlessly insulting to him."

"He did cheat the captain and the others at cards," Flora pointed out as they stood on the damp, cold deck.

"I don't believe it," Jessica declared. "Captain Tarrant is a gentleman. I shall always be of that opinion!"

Flora did not bother to argue with her further. She was too busy with preparations for landing to think about much else.

Henry had arranged for two carriages to move them and their baggage to Armitage House. Flora and Enid rode in the carriage with Han Li and Henry while Jessica rode in the other.

"I shall travel alone," Jessica had sniffed indignantly. "I do not want to ride with Henry and that creature he married."

As their carriage slowly rolled over the cobblestone streets Henry tried to point out places of interest to his bride. But nothing could be clearly seen and Han Li was not able to enjoy the trip.

Henry complained, "On days like this London can be most gloomy."

She patted her hand on his. "You must not worry so. I shall enjoy plenty of sunshine in this country. We have our lives ahead of us."

Enid spoke up, "It is hardly ever foggy at home!"

"True," her father said. "We do not get as much fog as the other sections of London."

At last they reached the stone pillars marking the entrance of the old mansion. The carriage wheels bit into the gravel and within a few minutes they were at the entrance of the great, rambling, stone house.

Henry smiled at his bride. "Well, here we are, though I'm afraid the fog is hardly better than it was in the heart of the city."

Han Li peered out the window at the house. "How vast it is!" she said, impressed.

"It is really too large for us," Henry told his bride. "We don't use all of it."

Enid was in a great hurry to greet her grandfather and jumped out of the carriage ahead of everyone else. Henry gave Han Li a fond smile and told her, "It is our custom to carry brides over the threshold of their new homes. I shall now do this with you." Flora waited for Jessica to join her from the other carriage before entering.

Bradford Armitage was standing there leaning on his cane waiting to welcome them. "Jessica, my dear," he said, opening his arms to his daughter.

"Father!" she exclaimed rushing to him.

The big man embraced his daughter and then turned to greet her. "Welcome back, Flora," he said. "Everyone is looking so healthy I think the trip did you all good."

Jessica put on a long face saying, "Henry fears that the climate here will harm the health of his new bride."

Bradford Armitage gave his daughter a reproving glance. "In that case we must do all that we can to protect her."

Flora was a witness to the exchange. She was almost certain that the old man had intended an extra meaning in his words. At any rate Jessica said nothing more but turned to direct Mrs. Brant in the disposition of their luggage.

Armitage House had not changed, Flora decided as she unpacked her things in her room. She thought that Bradford Armitage seemed as well as when they had left, if not some better.

Almost the instant she had stepped into the cool, shadowed silence of the house she had felt its eerie atmosphere take hold of her once again. All the threat of the unknown which had been there before seemed just as real now that she'd returned. And she thought this boded ill for the lovely Han Li.

After she unpacked and changed into a warmer dress she went downstairs. Enid had hurried off with an armful of presents for the coachman's children so she was on her own.

In the living-room she found Bradford Armitage and Henry standing together with glasses of some sort of liquor in their hands. Henry at once asked her, "Won't you join us in a sherry?"

She accepted his offer and he poured her a drink, passing the glass to her. He said, "Han Li is weary after the long trip and is resting until dinner is ready."

Bradford Armitage said, "She has grown into a beautiful woman, but then she was a lovely child. I was delighted when I heard the news that Henry was going to marry again."

She smiled over her drink. "It is a pity you were not there for the wedding. It was a memorable event."

"I can well believe it," Henry's father said. "I was present when Yenn Li and his English wife were married and that was an occasion I shall never forget. Little did I guess then that the daughter of that union should one day become my daughter-in-law."

Henry said, "We must all return to China for a visit with Yenn Li in the not-too-distant future. I'm sure you could manage the trip, Father."

The old man sighed. "I do not think so. I have been taxed in your absence keeping the business going. I doubt if a long ocean trip and change of climate would agree with me."

"I think you look very well," she told the old man.

"Thank you, my dear," he said. And he told Henry, "Not that I didn't have enough problems here. As I wrote you I had several long sessions with the lawyer representing Lily's parents. At the start he was asking for an unwarranted amount, and I'm sure a major part was for him."

"I didn't receive your last letters. They must have reached China after we left. How did you finally manage with that lawyer?"

"I made him visit me at the London office three times. And I noted on every occasion that his breath smelled strongly of gin. I began to think that he was even more of a scoundrel than we'd first believed, so I made some discreet inquiries about him."

"And?"

"I discovered that he had been all but disbarred several years ago for dipping into a client's funds. Having learned that I called in Lily's parents and had my lawyer tell them the facts about their representative. We discovered then that they had promised to turn over half of whatever he might get in damages to him. My lawyer warned them that their chances of getting anything at all from the rogue were slim. Almost at once the two decided to drop the lawyer and settle with us directly rather than go into court. The sum I paid them was more than what they might have gotten from the lawyer if they were lucky. We were both satisfied."

"I'm glad you did give the parents something. I agree we bore no guilt for Lily's death but I have always felt very badly about it. I'm sure I could not have handled it as well as you did."

"It was a tragic business," the old man said with a sigh. "I hope we never have anything like it happen again."

"I hope not," Henry said quietly, taking a sip of his sherry.

The two men were silent for a moment. Flora could see that Henry was relieved to know the legal action had been settled and she wondered again why he had run away from the affair.

She broke the silence by asking, "How are Sir Thomas and Lady Waring?"

"They are in Italy at the moment," Henry's father said. "Sir Thomas has had a further decline in health and Madge was told by his doctors that a warmer climate might do him a great deal of good."

Henry spoke up in a rather strained voice. "Did you tell Madge that I had married?"

"Yes," his father said meeting his glance with a wise one of his own. "I told her."

"What did she say?"

"She was surprised." He paused. "But then you knew she would be."

"I wasn't sure."

"It wasn't long after that she decided to take Sir Thomas to Italy."

"I see," Henry said, and he turned away to fill his glass again.

Flora suddenly remembered Dolly and asked the old

man, "What about Dolly, the young woman who came here with me and became the kitchen maid?"

"I intended to tell you. Not long after you left she had another misunderstanding with Mrs. Brant and decided to leave. She's been gone for over a month."

Chapter Twenty-five

THE NEWS that Dolly had left Armitage House was a shock. Flora had worried about the hot-tempered young woman and hoped that she would remain at least until her return.

She'd been comforted by the knowledge there was one staunch friend with her. Now she was alone except for the Armitage family.

"I wonder where Dolly went?"

"I can't tell you that," Bradford Armitage said. "But I suggest you ask Mrs. Brant."

"I think I'll do so now if you'll excuse me."

"Of course."

She put down her empty glass and left the living room in search of the housekeeper. As she passed the bottom of the stairs she saw Mrs. Brant coming down.

"I wanted to ask you about my friend, Dolly Wales," she said. "Did she leave any address or message for me?"

Mrs. Brant sneered. "That one? All she could think of was making saucy answers and neglecting her work!"

Flora knew this wasn't true but she didn't want to get in an argument with the housekeeper. "I can't understand her not leaving some message for me!"

"Broke five pieces of our best china," Mrs. Brant informed her. "Done out of malice, I say. I gave her orders to pack and she went. You'd be better off to forget the likes of her altogether," Mrs. Brant stated emphatically as she stomped off in the direction of the kitchen.

Flora strolled slowly to the front of the house again. She fought hard to keep her anger toward Mrs. Brant under control as she did not want the others to see she was upset.

Dinner was a quiet affair. Han Li came down to join them but still looked weary. Jessica was still annoyed that the colonel had walked on her without a word. Henry showed some uneasiness, and only his father and his daughter seemed in a good mood.

The fog still was thick around the house. Han Li peered out the big windows to try and see the grounds. Seeing the pond, she asked Flora, "Is it very deep?"

Flora nodded. "I think so. I believe at least one person has drowned in it."

"We would never have such a pond on the lawn of a house in China. Our pools are very shallow and merely for decoration."

Han Li looked around the big living room. "The rooms here are so immense. And what is done with the upper floors?"

"Very little," Flora said. "Your father-in-law uses part of the two top floors to house his antiques. He goes up there to work on them at times."

"Chinese antiques?"

"Mostly."

"I must go up and look at them."

"There's time enough for that," Flora said, recalling the day she had discovered the old man busy constructing his coffin.

Han Li smiled sadly. "I am very much in love with my husband but already I miss my father."

314

"Of course. That's to be expected."

"And Chen."

"Chen Li is a fine young man," she agreed. "You are lucky to have him as a cousin. He spoke of visiting England soon."

Han Li raised her hands and pressed them together before her in a gesture of happy anticipation. A smile crossed her lovely oval face. "Oh, I hope he does! Maybe he will persuade my father to come as well."

Later that night she lay awake in bed debating how to go about leaving the old mansion. She knew she could not remain in the midst of the tensions and dark rumors surrounding the place. Dolly had gone and so must she. She didn't like deserting Enid, but perhaps this would be better for everyone. Han Li would be occupied giving extra attention to the child, so she would not be so lonely. Enid, on the other hand, seemed to like and respect her stepmother. So there ought to be no problems.

Flora knew she would miss talking with Henry Armitage every day. There was no doubt in her mind now that she had been on the point of surrendering her heart to him. But there was no point in dwelling on that now. Henry was married and lost to her. She needed to get away from both him and the house.

She knew that she must warn Han Li against Jessica before she left. The Eurasian girl knew that Jessica was much too fond of Henry, but she did not know the dark history of the house. She could not be aware that Lily had died mysteriously after having shown a romantic interest in Henry. She had to be put on the alert.

At Enid's urgent request she'd left the door between their adjoining rooms open. She could hear the regular breathing of the child and see her in her bed. She had come to have a strong protective feeling for the youngster but yet she knew that she must leave her. There was no other way if she was to rebuild her life.

If she were lucky she would quickly locate another position as governess in a house not as afflicted with dark passions as Armitage House. She would also try to find

Dolly. But her effort in that direction would depend a great deal on luck.

With these thoughts in mind she dropped into an uneasy sleep. She began to dream. She was in the pond, floating under the green surface. She looked up through the slimy water, knowing she was drowned. Unable to move, just floating idly under the water. Then she saw a shadow above her. Someone was standing at the edge, staring down at her through the murky water. It was Jessica. She tried to shout, but could utter no sound!

Then Jessica raised her hands above the water and screamed down at her in an eerie, witchlike manner. The scream was repeated as she came awake in a welter of perspiration. She sat up in bed quickly, her face full of fear as she realized the screams of her dream were real and coming from somewhere far above in the old house.

And then there was silence. She was trembling as she gazed through the shadows to see that the child in the other room had not awakened. She apparently had not heard the screams.

She could not convince herself they had been part of her nightmare. She recalled the nights when she had heard similar cries and had seen the phantom.

Dolly claimed the servants believed it to be the ghost of Lily. But a few insisted there had been a phantom haunting Armitage House long before Lily had been found drowned. What to believe? Dolly was no longer in the house to keep her advised of what was going on.

With a sigh she lay back on her pillow and attempted to sleep. At last she slept again and did not wake until morning.

Enid was already by her bed with a smile.

"It's a lovely sunny day," the child said. "I'm glad. Now Han Li will see that we do have good weather in England."

"It is nice that the fog has lifted," she agreed. "Do hurry and dress for breakfast."

Flora was dressed and ready to go downstairs almost as soon as Enid. She was determined not to say anything about the weird cries she'd heard in the night but she intended to speak to Henry Armitage at the first opportunity to give him her notice.

The breakfast table was deserted except for her and Enid. She learned from the maid serving them that Henry Armitage had breakfasted early with his father and both men had gone in to their London office. Both Jessica and Han Li were having breakfast in their rooms. Flora was sorry she'd not had a chance to speak to Henry about leaving, but made up her mind she would do it that evening.

It was back to the usual routine. She and Enid worked at the child's lessons in the garden. By noon they had looked after most of the assignments for the day and Enid ran off to play with the other children.

As other times in the past, Flora found herself drawn to the pond. She could not deny that it was a sort of magnet for her. Now she slowly strolled there from the garden. She stood by the bench and watched the swans as they glided towards the small island in the center with its wooden bird house.

Hearing a sound, she glanced up and saw Han Li coming out of the house wearing a lovely yellow gown. She at once crossed the lawn to join Flora beside the pond.

"I hoped to find you," Han Li said.

"I've been in the garden with Enid. We often work at her lessons out there," she said. "Isn't it a nice day?"

"Yes," Han Li said tensely.

"Is something wrong?"

"Is Armitage House haunted?"

"What makes you ask that?"

"Several things," Han Li said. "I have a strange feeling about it."

"It has had its share of tragedies," she admitted.

"I can tell," Han Li said solemnly. "I have a sensitivity to spirits both good and evil. I feel this house is inhabited by an evil spirit."

"Oh?"

"Yes. And last night I was awakened by screams. Henry

slept through them. But they woke me up. I was sure they were the cries of a ghost!"

Flora was upset. She decided she could not be less than honest with the girl.

"I also heard the screams."

"Then we must have been the only ones," Han Li said. "I asked Jessica and she insisted she hadn't heard anything. She implied I might be mad."

"Jessica excels at that," Flora smiled.

"So you heard the screams just as I did," Han Li went on with excitement in her voice. "Did you see anything?"

"No."

"I did."

"You did?" Flora gasped.

"I went over to the window and looked out. Standing by this pond, almost where we are now, I saw a female figure. I could not see her face. But I know that it was a phantom."

"Why?"

"Because as I watched she seemed to vanish. To disappear in the air. One moment she was there and in the next she was gone."

Flora asked, "Did you wake your husband?"

Han Li shook her head. "I could not disturb his sleep. A good wife does not do that."

"He might have wanted you to."

"I think not."

Flora asked, "At least I hope you mentioned it to him this morning."

"No. I did not dare. He would think me a silly female given to fancies. I so badly want his respect."

"I don't know what to say," Flora sighed. "You should have wakened him at the time. That would have been best."

Han Li was solemn. "Tell me about this ghost so I may understand it."

She faltered. "That isn't an easy request. I know very little about it myself."

"You have been here longer than I," the lovely girl told her. "You must know something of the house. Tell me!"

Flora hesitated. Then she said, "This ghost is said by some to be the ghost of Lily, who was the governess here before I came. It seems that she fell in love with your husband."

"Did Henry love her?" Han Li asked.

"That was the pity of it from her standpoint," Flora said. "Henry did not see her in a romantic light at all. One night she threw herself in the pond here. They found her the next morning. It was generally accepted that she was a suicide. But when her ghost began returning as it seems to have done last night, people began to whisper that she'd not taken her own life. They hint that she may have been murdered and thrown in the pond to make it seem a suicide."

For the first time Han Li appeared alarmed. "And is my husband under suspicion?"

"Anyone who was here in the house at that time could be suspect," Flora told her simply.

"I see."

Flora touched her arm sympathetically. "I don't for a moment think your husband had anything to do with it, but you cannot stop people from talking in these cases."

"No," Han Li agreed, staring into the pool with a look of horror in her lovely eyes.

"I have only told you this because I intend to leave here soon and I don't like the idea of leaving without offering you some kind of warning."

"You are not giving up your position as governess?"

"Yes. I have been thinking about it for some time. I would like to remain for your sake and for Enid's but I think you may do better without me. You can be Enid's teacher. It will occupy your time and also bring you two closer."

Han Li said, "I would still prefer you to remain."

"Impossible. I'm sorry."

"When do you plan to leave?"

"The end of the week if your husband agrees. I will go as soon as I can."

"Please give it a second thought. I will feel more alone and in danger without you here."

319

Flora made no promises to Han Li because she was determined to leave. The fact that the lovely Chinese girl had also heard the eerie screams and seen the ghost convinced her that tragedy would continue to stalk Armitage House. She wanted no part of it.

It wasn't until after dinner that night she had a chance to take Henry Armitage aside and ask to speak to him privately. "It is about an urgent personal matter," she said.

"Very well," he said and led her into the study.

Once she was seated she told him, "I wish to leave here. As soon as I can. I don't want to remain any longer than the weekend at the most."

Henry registered dismay. "Why?"

"I need a change."

He frowned. "I think that is a stupid reason for upsetting everything here."

"I must live my own life," she said.

"Where can you go?"

"I don't know. There must be respectable lodging places in the city for young women of limited means."

"And if you find such a place? Then what?"

"I shall look for a position similar to the one I have here. One in a family that is small and has few problems."

He paced up and down before her. "We need you here more than ever."

"Nonsense! You have Han Li. She can act as a teacher to Enid, and an excellent one she'll make."

He stopped his pacing to stare at her. "There's nothing I can do or say to make you remain?"

"No."

"This is a shock to me, Flora," he said. "I have always looked on you as someone on whom I could depend."

"I have been loyal."

"I won't deny it."

"It's just that I feel it best to leave. Of course I would appreciate having your permission to return occasionally and pay a visit to Enid."

"Granted of course," he said wearily. "Things have been very trying today."

"I'm sorry," she said.

"Have you told Han Li of your desire to leave us?"

"Yes. I think she understands."

"She is a kind and understanding person," he agreed. "If you must leave us let there be no ill will on either side."

"That is the way I'd like it," she agreed.

He furrowed his handsome brow. "Where will you stay in London when you are looking for a post?"

"I don't know."

"I think I can help you. Make sure you are in good company and save you from any more threats from the underworld. There is a Mrs. Lingley who is the widow of a man who worked for us many years. She was quite alone at the time of his death as their children had grown up and left home. She solved the dilemma by turning her home into a boarding house."

"It sounds a most welcome suggestion."

"I will see you to the house myself when the time comes."

She eyed him gratefully. "That is very kind of you."

"Not at all. You will find Mrs. Lingley a fine woman. If you find no post at least you'll be in a good home. And you can always return here."

"I'll remember that."

"When do you propose to go?"

She hesitated. "I would like to accompany you when you leave for the city in the morning."

"Aren't you going to discuss it with Enid? You two have had an ideal relationship."

"I shall leave her a note. I'm sure it will be easier for her that way."

"I see," he sighed. "Well, we shall not hire any replacement to take over from you. I'll follow your advice and have Han Li coach Enid. So the post will be waiting for you if you change your mind and wish to return."

"Thank you."

"One more thing."

"Yes?" She looked up and saw that his face was troubled.

"Are you leaving because of Jessica and her general attitude towards you?"

"Not altogether."

He persisted, "But that is part of it?"

"I suppose so."

"I'm not surprised," he said gravely. "And I can promise you if you do change your mind about remaining that I shall see my sister keeps her place."

"There is more than that," she said.

"Apparently," he said with another sigh. "Give it another night's thought."

"I will," she promised, rising.

"What about my father?" he asked as she was about to leave. "He dotes on you."

"You explain to him for me. It will come better from you," she said.

"Very well."

She left the study and went to her own room where she immediately sat down to compose the letter which she intended to leave for Enid. It took longer than she expected and when she reached the end of it and signed her name there were tears blurring her eyes.

Taking the note she went into the little girl's room and set it on her dresser with her name prominently on it so she would find it first thing in the morning. With that done she returned to her own room and prepared for bed.

It still troubled her that Henry had not installed bolts on the doors. But he had not taken well to her suggestion so did nothing about it.

As she thought about it, she realized she'd been able to make very few changes since coming to the house. The sinister atmosphere had defied her and she had lost. Dolly had given up long before her and left. Would she ever see her plucky little friend again? It was doubtful. London was a large place and people got swallowed up in it.

Because she'd made her decision sleep seemed to come to her more easily. There were no dreams, which made it more startling when she all at once came wide awake.

She sat up on her elbow and stared into the darkness trying to find out what had wakened her so abruptly. And then she found out. The handle of her door was slowly being turned! As the door began to open ever so slowly, she heard a weird, heavy breathing, almost like a panting. She was frozen with fear as she waited to see who the intruder might be.

Chapter Twenty-six

IN THE adjoining room Enid stirred and cried out in her sleep. The cry had an immediate effect. The door was quickly drawn closed and Flora heard the sound of feet padding off down the hall!

For long minutes she still sat there in bed with beads of perspiration at her temples. Whatever or whoever it had been, planning to surreptitiously attack her in the night, had been frightened off by Enid's cry. After she recovered from the worst of her fright she went to the door. She gently opened it to gaze out into the hall, but there was nothing but silence and emptiness.

The following morning she awoke earlier than usual, quietly dressed, and packed her bag. Then she went downstairs to have a quick breakfast before leaving for London with Henry Armitage.

Making her way down the stairs she glanced at the painting of Bradford Armitage's wife, who so resembled Jessica. It had been one of the first things that had caught her attention when she'd arrived at Armitage House. She wondered whether if that lovely woman had not died the history of the Armitage family might have been altered. Would they have been a more happy group? Wasn't it possible that the tragedy of her suicide had cast the first shadow over them all? It seemed possible.

Reaching the breakfast table, she found Henry and his father. Both men rose to greet her as she joined them.

Bradford Armitage eyed her sadly. "I'm sorry to hear you're leaving us. I'll miss you."

"I would like to come back and visit Enid," she ventured. "And keep in touch with you all."

"You will always be welcome here," Henry Armitage said. "Isn't that right, Father?"

"We are stupid to let her go," Bradford Armitage said, his palsied head shaking. "What do you want, my girl? More money? Name your salary and you shall have it!"

"It's not that. I feel I must get away from here. It's this house. I can't explain why. I feel depressed all the time."

"That is a strange comment."

"I'm being perfectly honest."

Henry poured himself more tea. "She feels the need of freedom. Perhaps it has to do with the long trip to China and being confined so much with the family. I say let her have a chance to try another job and hope that she will soon return."

Bradford Armitage looked sad. "I do not think she will."

"I might," she told him. "I know I shall miss Enid. Perhaps my ties here are stronger than I realize. But I want to discover that for myself."

"You have a female stubbornness," the old man said. "There is no point in trying to reason with you now. I can see that."

The carriage was ready for them when they emerged from the front door. On the steps Bradford Armitage stood leaning on his cane, waving her a sad farewell as the carriage pulled away.

She was in a strange state of mind. She regretted leaving Armitage House and yet she knew she could no longer stay there. The reasons for her desire to leave were sound.

She knew that since she had left the quiet vicarage in Sussex she had grown a great deal. She was much more experienced and sure of herself. Also, she felt she would now be better able to cope with the city. She had learned a good many lessons.

Henry said, "I shall take you directly to the home of Mrs. Lingley before going to the office."

"You need not take your time to come with me," she said. "Just send me in the carriage."

"No," he replied. "I want to see you safely there and introduce you to the old lady. She is rather deaf and I want to be sure she understands everything."

She gave him a grateful smile. "You're being very kind."

"You have saddened us all by leaving. My father is very upset."

"I know," she said. "I'm sorry. But I will see him when I return to visit Enid."

"I worry about the child," he said with a frown.

"I'm sure Han Li will take excellent care of her."

"Of course."

Remembering the nightly screams and Han Li's account of seeing the phantom, she said, "There is one thing I still think you should do."

"What?"

"Bolts should be installed on the bedroom doors."

He stared at her. "You really think that is important?"

"Yes. People rest better when they feel they have security. I'm positive it would mean something to the child."

"Enid is far too nervous," he agreed.

"It would help. When she wakes up from a nightmare she wouldn't be so afraid."

"I'll speak to Mrs. Brant about it."

Flora said, "I think you should see to it yourself. She is not one to cooperate in any improvements."

He made no reply to this so she could only hope that he would follow her advice. She had no high opinion of Mrs. Brant and she sometimes wondered how much the gaunt old housekeeper might have to do with the strange happenings at Armitage House.

Now they were reaching the busier section of the city, so their progress was considerably slowed down. Henry glanced at her as they inched forward. "Does the city frighten you? I mean, after all your bad experiences."

"No. I have grown in experience. I think I can better take care of myself now."

"I sincerely hope so. If you need anything at all do not hesitate to contact me."

"I won't."

"There is no need of your being alone and friendless any longer. You know where to reach me."

"Yes," she said. What she didn't say was that she badly wanted to be independent. She did not want to have to lean on him for help. He was Han Li's husband now and she didn't want to be the object of any sort of ugly gossip, however unfounded. She would not turn to him for help unless she were really in the most dire straits.

The traffic began to move better when a policeman appeared. The carriage continued on to a less busy residential section of London. They turned into a short street of identical brick houses with single steps at the entrance of each.

"This is where Mrs. Lingley has her boarding house."

"It seems a quiet street."

"I can promise you it is most respectable. She is a lady of impeccable morals."

The carriage halted before one of the houses and they got out. As they crossed the sidewalk she saw there was a brass plate with the name Lingley on the door of the house. At least this made it possible to pick it out from the many other similar ones on the street.

Henry used the brass rapper and after what seemed like an age the door was opened by a young girl in a maid's uniform and cap.

The maid's pinched young face showed curiosity. "Do you want to see the missus?" she asked.

"Yes," Henry said. "Is she at home?"

"Come in. You can wait in the parlor. I'll fetch her."

Henry nodded to Flora and picked up her bag. They followed the maid along a short wall papered in a dismal shade of green. They found themselves in a small parlor dominated by a round table in its center, a number of steel engravings of battle scenes on its walls, and sorry-looking rubber plants placed at various points around it. The maid vanished and they sat down in two of the shabby, ugly chairs that formed part of the parlor furniture. The room had a rather heavy smell, like that of cabbage cooked some days before.

Flora gazed up at an embroidered and framed motto which read, "Virtue is its own reward." On another wall she saw a mate to the first motto, "The meek shall inherit the earth."

Henry gave her an apologetic look. "It is plain but clean. I had a clerk and his family boarding here until they found a house of their own."

"I'm sure it is all right." She knew that on her limited savings she could afford no better place.

There was the sound of someone hurrying along the hall. A moment later a tiny woman in black, with a lace cap on her head and an ear trumpet held to one ear, came into the room.

"Mr. Henry!" she exclaimed in a thin voice. "Now what a fine surprise! I didn't expect to see you, sir."

He smiled and nodded and leaned close to the ear trumpet to announce, "I have brought you a young lady who has been our governess and who wants to seek work in the city. She needs a place to board until she finds a suitable post."

The little woman seemed to understand it all. She nodded. "I have a room." And she named the rent per week. "Including meals of course."

Henry turned to Flora. "Will that be all right?"

"Fine," she said.

Henry shouted into the ear trumpet again. "That will be excellent."

Mrs. Lingley nodded and then she extended the ear trumpet in Flora's direction. "I trust you are a good Christian girl?"

She spoke into the trumpet. "My father was a vicar."

"Oh!" Mrs. Lingley seemed greatly impressed. "My late

husband was a member of Her Majesty's Guards before he retired and went to work for Mr. Henry and his father. My Will was fond of the firm of Armitage I can tell you. Put his whole heart in his work. Died at the job, he did."

"That is too bad," she shouted back.

Henry signaled for the trumpet. "I must go to my office now. You will hear from me later."

The old woman nodded. "Give my warm regards to your dear father," she said.

"I shall," he shouted. Then he turned to Flora with a smiled. "At least your lungs are bound to get some exercise."

"So it seems. Thank you for everything."

His eyes met hers. "Remember, don't hesitate to call me if you have any problems."

Mrs. Lingley saw the young man to the door shouting the praises of the house of Armitage all the while and commenting on what a heroic person her late husband had been. Flora was sure that Henry was glad to escape from the house and Mrs. Lingley's loud rantings.

The little woman came back to her with a businesslike air. "Follow me."

Flora picked up her bag and followed the little woman along the rear section of the short hall and up a flight of stairs to a second floor divided into a surprisingly large number of tiny rooms. These cubicles were furnished identically with a bed, a tiny table holding a washbasin, and a small dresser. Mrs. Lingley led her to one in the rear whose window looked out on another similar window from the house behind it. "This is your room."

Because the two houses had been built perhaps only two feet apart just a tiny amount of daylight filtered in through the worn curtains at the window.

Flora shouted in the old woman's trumpet, "It is not very bright. Do you have any others?"

Mrs. Lingley shook her head. "None. Filled up."

She shouted, "Perhaps later?"

The old woman said, "Maybe. I can't promise. You can pull down the blind for privacy and light a candle. Candles are not provided but I have a supply in the kitchen. You can buy them from me as you need them."

Flora could see why candles were not provided since they would be needed most of the day and night. Mrs. Lingley might lean to virtuous mottos about the meek inheriting the earth but she was proving a sharp businesswoman.

Mrs. Lingley vanished as soon as she'd shown Flora the room. It was evident she didn't want to linger and talk, probably because she was afraid Flora might offer some more complaints. It was a great change from the elegance of Armitage House but Flora felt she could put up with it until she found a suitable position.

The troublesome thing was that for all her plans she really did not know just how she was going to go about finding a job. It was not easy in London without important friends. She could seek out William Booth's mission again and perhaps get help there. Mr. Gladstone had learned about her through William Booth and had found her the job of governess at Armitage House. But she hesitated to bother William Booth again.

Perhaps if she contacted the clergymen at some of the nearby churches they might be able to assist her. It would do no good to see the minister of a church for the poor. She would have to find someone whose church catered to wealthy families who would perhaps know where a governess was needed.

She unpacked her few things and put them in the rickety dresser. Within a short time it was the dinner hour and she went downstairs. When she entered the dining room most of the other lodgers were gathered at a single long table with the deaf Mrs. Lingley sitting at the head of it. The maid was hurrying up and down the length of the table serving.

Mrs. Lingley saw Flora enter and at once went over to her. "I have a place for you," she said. And she led her to a vacant place about halfway down one side of the table.

She sat down feeling awkward between a stout, graying woman and an elderly man with pince-nez who looked like a clerk.

The talk around the table was lively and as Flora got over her initial shyness she noted that she was the only young person seated there. The majority of the other lodgers were elderly women. There was the thin, balding old man who sat beside her and a dour, stocky man with gray hair standing straight up.

The bald man smiled at Flora and said rather timidly, "You are new here."

"Yes."

"I am one of the older residents," he said. "My name is Blair Sweeney. I'm a clerk at the drygoods store in the next block."

"My name is Flora Bain and I'm boarding here until I find a new post as governess."

"Ah, you must be very well educated!" the thin old man said, obviously impressed.

"Just average."

"One has to have a good education to be a governess," Mr. Sweeney said. "I'm a great reader myself. Charles Dickens is my favorite author at the moment. Have you read any of his works?"

"Yes. I've enjoyed his stories."

Mr. Sweeney beamed at her. "Have you read *Dombey And Son*? I greatly enjoyed that."

"I have."

"And his new book *David Copperfield* is surely a gem!"

"I haven't gotten to it yet."

"You must!"

The maid came and served them the main course, which was some kind of pasty stew with hardly any hint of meat in it. Flora regarded her dish for a moment before she tried to eat any of it, though she noticed the others were attacking it with gusto."

Mr. Sweeney glanced at her. "Today is stew day," he said. "Tomorrow it will be codfish. Mrs. Lingley has her set menu from day to day, the pattern doesn't vary. But one gets used to the food and it really isn't all that bad."

"I'm sure it isn't," she said reaching for her fork, and indeed it tasted better than it looked.

The elderly clerk leaned towards her. "Winter is on the

way. You may find the house cold. Buy some extra sweaters and bedclothes if you want to be warm. That's what all the rest of us who can afford it do."

"You mean she doesn't supply proper heat or enough bedclothing?"

"She does according to her standards," the old clerk said. "But her standards aren't very high."

"I see," she said.

"Not that she isn't a good woman," Mr. Sweeney was quick to say. "It's just that she's a mite mean."

Flora thought how different the atmosphere at this table was from that of Armitage House or her own home. From the head of the table she heard the deaf Mrs. Lingley yell sympathetically at someone near her, "Chilblains! I know what they are! They can make you miserable!"

Old Mr. Sweeney asked her, "Have you any position in prospect?"

"No. But I intend to begin looking tomorrow."

He said apologetically, "The reason I asked is because a customer of ours tried to persuade one of the young lady clerks at the store to give up her position to work for him."

"Indeed?"

"Yes. He is a very fine man, a Dr. Timothy Storch, really very distinguished in his manner. He operates a private hospital for those with slight mental illness. I understand his wife assists him in the venture. I believe he is looking for another female assistant who has had some experience with children. Your mention that you have been a governess made me think it might be of interest to you."

She was thrilled. It was the greatest kind of good fortune. She'd been worrying about looking for a job and here was one without looking. And from all that the old clerk said an interesting position in the employ of a fine, upstanding doctor. She said, "Thank you for mentioning it. I hope the job isn't taken. I'd like to seek out Dr. Storch for an interview tomorrow."

"You can come to the store and I'll get you his address.

He always arrives in a fine carriage but I'm sure you can reach his place in an omnibus."

"Thank you," she said gratefully. "I shall surely come by tomorrow for the information."

That evening Mr. Sweeney's prediction that the room would be cold was borne out. She was not able to sleep properly because it was so chilly. And winter was still to come. Somehow she got through the night and the breakfast of thin porridge and stale white bread in the morning.

She knew that Henry Armitage hadn't any idea of Mrs. Lingley's grasping manner of running the lodging house or he wouldn't have sent her there. She was determined to leave the place as soon as possible, so she presented herself at the store where Mr. Sweeney was employed shortly after its doors opened.

Mr. Sweeney was standing behind a long counter, with shelves holding bolts of cloth covering the wall behind him. There was cloth of almost every conceivable type to choose from.

Flora approached his counter with a smile. "I have come for the address," she said.

"Of course," the old man remembered. He called a young assistant to his side to man the counter and then scurried off to the office to get the doctor's address.

The young assistant asked her impertinently, "Is the old goat trying to get you a job?"

She eyed the pimply young man coldly. "You needn't worry. I'm not planning to work here."

Unabashed, he winked at her. "You wouldn't find it so bad. I'm real nice to all the girls."

"That's warning enough," she said, turning her back to him and walking away.

Fortunately Mr. Sweeney arrived a few seconds later with a scrap of paper bearing the address. "I have it here," he said triumphantly. "Dr. Timothy Storch, 9 Knox Street. That is the address of the mental hospital. It could very well be one of the finest in London."

"Thank you so much."

"My pleasure. I will see you at dinner tonight."

She left the drygoods store and went to the nearest crossing where a policeman was standing. She asked him how to get to the address on the paper. He studied it and then advised her how to reach the street by omnibus.

A half hour later she was making her way along Knox Street in search of the mental hospital. It was a narrow quiet street with only a few houses with gardens in front. Mid-way along the street she saw the gate posts with number nine marked on them. The wooden gate was gray with age. It was also a slight bit ajar. As she went in through it she found herself in a large garden with several walks.

In the distance stood a large three-story red brick building. It was plain in design with tall narrow windows at intervals and an unimposing entrance door. In the center of the lawns there were sculptured figures of cupid on pedestals but the faces of the cupids were broken and mutilated. The sight of them gave her an odd feeling. Suddenly, without any warning she was grasped from behind.

Chapter Twenty-seven

CAUGHT COMPLETELY by surprise, Flora cried out in fear. As she did so her attacker swung her around keeping a firm hold on one of her arms. Now she was able to see who it was. He was a youngish man with matted blond hair and a beard-stubbled face with the vacant, odd look of an idiot. Spittle dripped from the corners of his mouth and his round face wore a grin.

"Let go of me!" she cried.

The big man's reaction was a mad laugh.

"Please!" she begged him, realizing she had been unfortunate enough to have encountered one of the patients of the mental hospital.

"Pretty!" he said in a thick, odd voice.

She was about to scream out again when the front door of the big red brick building was swung open and a short, angry-looking bow-legged man came running towards her and the madman.

"Martin!" the short man said angrily. A ring of keys dangled from one of his trousers pockets.

At the sight of the authoriative little man the blond brute quickly released Flora, running off towards the rear of the hospital.

"He got away!" Flora said unhappily.

The short man chuckled. He had the purple face and bulbous red nose of a drinker. "He won't go far! There's an exercise ground for the patients back there. He's returned to it. He's harmless as long as he doesn't get excited. My apologies, miss. I can't be everywhere. This sort of thing don't normally happen. Did you come to see a patient?"

"No," she said. "I have come to see Dr. Storch. Is he here?"

The red-nosed man eyed her with new interest. "Yes, he is, miss. Happens to be in his office this minute. I'll turn you over to the young lady who is his nurse and assistant."

She said, "I thought his wife was his assistant."

The short man chuckled and winked at her. "Lor', miss, you are way behind the times. The doctor's missus isn't up to doing any work these days. She's a patient here same as the rest, though he did give her the best private room. The doc's a gent, I'll say that for him!"

"His wife is now a mental patient here in the very hospital in which she worked?"

"That's right, miss," the bowlegged man nodded. "Too much of the gin bottle did it. She's no better now. Drinks all the day and night. Don't see how she can last long!"

"That's tragic!"

"I agree, miss," the man said solemnly. "But the doc has found himself a good-looking young woman to carry on with him, if you know what I mean. So it all has ended well."

"Except for his unfortunate wife."

"Yes. I'll take you in now, if you like, miss. My name is Oates. If you're around here long you'll see a lot of me. I'm the chief warder. The rest of them are old for their jobs. And we have a half-dozen women attendants, though they don't amount to much."

She followed him into the red brick building and was

taken down a narrow corridor to a good-sized room with a table and some chairs in it. There was a young, golden-haired woman standing there. What immediately struck Flora was that she was pretty in a cheap, coarse way and that she was wearing what might be called an evening gown with a very revealing neckline.

Mr. Oates introduced Flora, saying, "This young lady has come to see the doctor."

The golden-haired one's eyebrows raised. "Has she?"

"Yes, miss," Oates said. "If you'll excuse me I have to go to the exercise yard. I think the gate has been broken open again." Having said this he turned and vanished.

Flora stood uncomfortably before the young woman. She said, "I'm sorry to intrude on you."

"You've come about a patient?" the woman asked warily.

"No. I want to see Dr. Storch about a position here I believe is open."

"You want to work here?"

"Yes."

The girl looked cynically surprised. "I'll ask the doctor if he can see you."

"Thank you."

She went into the adjoining room, closing the door after her. Flora looked around taking stock of the room. It was very plainly furnished. The young woman returned shortly and said, "He'll see you now."

Hesitantly she crossed over to the door and entered the doctor's private office. Dr. Storch was standing there to greet her. He was a very tall man with a concave face showing deep lines. His eyes were sad with great pouches under them. He was well-dressed in a gray tweed suit with a black vest but he looked strangely restless.

He waved a large hamlike hand to offer her a chair. "Won't you sit down, miss."

"Thank you. My name is Flora Bain. I heard from a clerk at the drygoods store near where I'm boarding that you are in need of an assistant. I hoped that the post might still be open."

337

Dr. Storch stood with his hands clasped behind his back studying her with piercing eyes. "The job is still open."

"Then I would like to apply for it."

"Indeed," he said. He had a soft, cultured voice but there was a vagueness in his manner which bothered her. And now she noticed the room was filled with a kind of acrid odor. She supposed it was from some sort of medications he might be preparing.

"I have had training with children. I worked with a well-known family as a governess. I'm certain they would be pleased to give me a recommendation."

He waved a bony hand. "No need," he said. "You know what sort of place this is?"

"It is a mental hospital."

"A private hospital for the insane," he said. "We do not take violent cases if we know they are violent. Unhappily we have gradually built up quite a few of them. Even with careful screening they are put upon us by their relatives. All they want to do is be rid of them, you know."

"I've had very little experience with such matters."

He sighed heavily, his face sadder than ever. "And I have had too much experience. Most of our cases are mild eccentrics. We have private and semi-private rooms for them and a ward for men and one for women. That is a matter of convenience as we are able to offer this accommodation at a cheaper price. The medical treatment is the same for all. Have you had any home nursing training?"

"A little," she said. "My father was a vicar in Sussex. Often when accidents occurred near our home the victims were brought to us until a doctor could be reached. So I learned quite a few of the fundamentals of nursing."

"Excellent," he said. "You have met Kitty."

"Kitty?"

"I should have made myself clearer," he apologized. "Of course I refer to Miss Kitty Derry, the young lady who showed you in just now."

"Of course. The girl with the golden hair."

He nodded. "She is striking, isn't she? Miss Derry makes a fine secretary and is very good at going over the accounts, but she does not like working with the patients. She has not the nerves for it."

"I see."

"My dear wife, before her nervous breakdown, was invaluable as my full-time assistant. Unfortunately she is now under medical care herself so I have been forced to look for other help."

Flora said, "I trust her illness is only of a minor nature." She did not let him guess that she'd already heard from Oates that chronic alcoholism was his wife's problem.

"She has her good days and her bad. I do not dare to actually let myself hope. But I have not given up. Not by any means!"

"I understand," she said.

He took a few steps away from her and abruptly turned around. Fixing his eyes on her, he said, "Do you think you can adapt to the work here?"

"Yes."

"Your position would be that of head attendant with special regard to the women's ward. We have six women attendants who would be under you. And you would work in cooperation with Chief Warder Oates."

"I have already met him," she said.

"Have you?" the doctor asked.

"Yes. When I entered the grounds I was attacked by a blond man named Martin. Oates came to my rescue."

Dr. Storch looked annoyed. "Martin was on the loose again?"

"Yes."

"I have warned Oates to keep a closer watch on him," the doctor complained. "He is one of our more violent cases. I trust that you were not harmed?"

"No. Oates arrived in time to help me."

"A very poor introduction to our institution," he said dryly.

She managed a small smile. "I'm not allowing it to frighten me. I realize this is a hospital for the insane."

"An excellent attitude," the doctor said. "It bodes well for your future here. The pay is four pounds a month and your room and board. In addition there will be yearly increases in salary until you reach seven pounds a month. Is that satisfactory?"

"It seems very generous."

"Remember the work is trying and of a highly confidential nature."

"Of course."

He stared at her for a long moment. "Are you familiar with Bedlam?"

"I believe it is a public hospital for the insane," she ventured.

"You have never visited it?"

"No."

"It is in Lambeth. And I could not commend a visit to you. The patients suffer there in the most unfortunate conditions."

She recalled, "I believe my father once had occasion to visit a former parishioner there. He was greatly depressed by his state and the way the place was operated."

"Exactly," Dr. Storch said. "There is no proper care for mentally ill people in these public institutions. The private hospitals are the only hope the relatives of the insane have. They send us their sick ones and we do the best we can."

"I would consider it noble work."

"Exactly," he said. "I must see that you talk with some of the relatives when they come here to visit. You would make such a fine impression on them. Your training as a parson's daughter stands you in good stead."

"Thank you." She was trying to analyze her feelings about the doctor. He seemed a competent, kindly man, and yet there was something else about him. Something less easy to define. Could it be a kind of suavity? A polish which concealed his deeper nature?

"You will not find conditions here perfect," he warned her. "You may even think some things appalling. I will not be surprised if you do. But we try to do our best. That is all. We have more patients here than our premises can hold with comfort. But cases come and I cannot turn them away."

"That is very good of you."

He made a weary gesture. "One does what humanity demands. Kitty will be happy that I have someone to take over the patient work from her. When can you begin?"

"Almost any time."

"Then why not at once."

"You mean today?"

"We need you here badly."

She was mildly surprised. "I would have to get my things from my boarding house."

"How did you get here?"

"By omnibus."

He frowned. "Omnibus! We can't have members of our staff using such common transport. I shall have the carriage made ready and you'll be driven to your lodging house to pick up your belongings and then brought back here."

"I couldn't impose on you," she protested.

"Not at all," the doctor said. "It is to our advantage to have you begin here as soon as possible. I'll go see about the carriage and while I'm doing that Kitty will show you where your room will be."

"Thank you," she said.

He led her out to the other room where Kitty was flipping through the pages of a penny dreadful. She held it up for them to see. "It's the new Hogarth Gem Novel. *A Difficult Case, or Lady Dudley's Secret*! It's full of thrills."

Dr. Storch eyed her reproachfully. "Kitty! I have warned you about those trashy weekly magazines before. What do you think the relatives of patients will say if they come here and find you reading that sort of stuff in the reception room? What will they think of me and the hospital?"

Kitty stood up boldly. "They'll know I like a bit of action in my reading."

"Its a show of deplorable taste," he said. "I'm going to see about the carriage. I have just hired Miss Bain. Let her see her room."

The buxom blond threw the magazine he'd criticized down on the table beside her with a muttered exclamation.

Fearing the other girl was in a rage Flora said, "You don't have to show me my room now. I can look at it later when I return."

Kitty eyed her coldly. "He said to show you the room now and that's what I'll do."

"Whatever you like."

Kitty crossed in front of her and opened a door at the back of the room which she'd not noticed before. Kitty led her through a dark hall and down a short corridor to a small room opening off the end of the hall. It had an outside window that looked out on some trees and a bit of green grass. The room itself was plainly but pleasantly furnished with print curtains at the windows to match the bedcovering.

Kitty turned to study her. "This is it."

"I think it's nice."

"It will do," Kitty said. "So you're going to take over the patient work from me?"

"Yes."

"I can't stand being near those loonies. You're welcome to it! But remember one thing!"

"What?"

"The doctor don't go with the job. I've taken squatter's rights to him. Understand?"

"Perfectly," she said. She was relieved to hear that what she'd suspected from the start was so. It meant that she needn't fear being bothered by the doctor.

"Then we can get along," Kitty said.

"Isn't the doctor's wife a patient here?" she asked.

"Her!"

"You don't think much of her?"

Kitty said knowingly, "You'll meet her. You decide."

The young woman took her back to the office where she waited for a few minutes until the doctor returned to announce the carriage was outside waiting for her. She thanked him and hurried out to it.

Mrs. Lingley couldn't believe her eyes when she saw Flora ride up to her door in another carriage.

The little woman put her ear trumpet up and observed acidly, "I trust you are not going to the bad, Miss Bain!"

"No," she shouted into the ear trumpet. "I have already found a position in a private hospital and I've come to get my things."

She went up and quickly packed her things, anxious to leave the drab atmosphere of the boarding house as soon as she could. When she came down she paid Mrs. Lingley and asked her to thank Mr. Sweeney for her and tell him that she'd taken on the job at once.

The carriage ride back to the mental hospital was much easier than it would have been in an omnibus. She relaxed a little, content with her good fortune. If the hospital and Dr. Storch hadn't been just as she'd expected she was sure that they would turn out all right.

The coachman took her bag into the hospital for her and she quickly unpacked. Kitty came to the door of her room and knocked. When she opened the door Kitty thrust an armful of clothes at her. She said, "These are the uniforms. I guess they will fit. You can alter them if you like."

"Thank you," she said. Until then it hadn't struck her that she would be wearing uniforms. But she realized the sense of it. One had to be apart from the patients, dressed so they would readily recognize you.

She sorted out the uniforms and found them all to be a drab gray and made of heavy woollen material. This would surely be suitable in the cold weather ahead. She had also been glad to see a plain little fireplace and some wood in her room. At least she need not be cold.

Changing into one of the uniforms she found that it fitted her. It was cut round at the neck with a plain collar, had puff sleeves which narrowed at the wrist, a neat waist and flowing skirt. Only the sleeves were too long and she turned these up neatly. Then she went out to the office for Kitty to inspect her.

Kitty was seated reading her thriller again. She looked up when Flora came into the room. "It fits better than I expected."

"I think it's fine," she said. "The sleeves need turning up but I can do that later."

"Then you're ready to begin?"

"Yes."

"You can go down to the women's ward. The doctor is there now. He'll soon be back because Oates will be feeding the patients."

"I see."

"We eat here in our own dining room," Kitty said. "Just you and I, the doctor and Oates. The rest of them have a room to eat in back in the patient's section."

Flora started down the corridor to the back of the big private hospital. It was shadowy and smelled of carbolic. The first thing to reach her ears were a series of maniacal screams. She forced herself not to be upset by them and continued on.

She came out in another short hallway at right angles to the one she'd just walked down. The door on the right was open. She saw a large room with perhaps a dozen plain iron beds on each side of it not unlike the ward at the mission. Seated on the beds or standing by them in various stages of dishevelment were a number of women. She also saw Dr. Storch and an attendant standing in consultation part way down the aisle between the rows of beds.

Most of the women were in Mother-Hubbard-type dresses, a few in soiled-looking nightgowns. Some of them stared at her with the vague interest of the mad, others ignored her altogether.

Dr. Storch left the middle-aged woman attendant to come to her. "You made very good time," he said.

"Yes," she replied.

He indicated the room around them. "This is the general ward for women. The private rooms are upstairs and the rooms for the violent are in the cellar. You will be an overseer of the whole area along with Oates."

"I see."

"Sedation on the hour!" he said in a stern voice. "That is the secret of a well-organized mental hospital. We have definite sedation periods that must be strictly adhered to. Oates will give you a schedule and I shall depend on you to carry it through."

"How are the drugs administered?" she wanted to

know, since she knew nothing about handling a hypodermic needle.

"We have tablets mostly. For the few patients who require medication by injection I look after it. But you need not worry about that. I'll leave you here for a while with Mrs. Gentry, who will instruct you in our routine. I shall see you later at dinner." He bowed and stalked out of the ward.

Mrs. Gentry gave Flora a kind smile. "It won't be so bad," she told her.

Flora spent a short time in the ward trying to make some of the patients more comfortable. It was a rather hopeless task since they didn't seem to care. Then Oates came to take her on a tour of the rest of the hospital. She saw the men's ward, a replica of the women's only perhaps a little less clean. She had a glimpse of the cellar with its cells. Each cell door had a tiny opening through which clawlike hands with long nails emerged as the mad occupants groped for freedom. It was also from down there in those dungeons of despair the weird wailing emanated.

She shudderd as she and Oates climbed the stairs leaving the dank cellar behind them. "Isn't there anything more that can be done for those poor souls?"

"Lor', miss, we're doing more for them than most would. They are the bad ones."

The upper floor with its private rooms had much better housekeeping. Some of the doors of the patients' rooms were closed while others were open. There was a mixture of men and women who were all much less demented than on the floors below, and much better dressed.

Oates confided in her, "These are the toffs! Some of them are from the best families in England and not much more than eccentric. If they was poor like you and me they'd be out in the streets and no harm done. But because they embarrass their rich and titled relatives they get shoved in here."

She sighed as she spied an old man seated reading in his room. That he was eccentric there could be no doubt since he had a cut-out gold-paper crown on his head. He didn't even raise his eyes from his book as they went by.

"What about him?"

Oates chuckled. "Mild as can be and an educated gentleman. Only thing wrong with him is he thinks he is a king. And that's not so far off since I've been told that his cousin is the Duke of Cumberland."

They moved on down the hall and came to another open door in which a fragile woman with a badly scarred area on one side of her face stood. She had at one time been a beauty but now she had a kind of gargoyle appearance because of the twisted scar tissue.

The woman held a hand out to Oates in appeal. "Did you mail my letter, Mr. Oates?"

"Indeed I did, Mrs. Miller. You can rely on me. You know that!"

Fear showed in the elderly woman's eyes. "You didn't tell the doctor?"

"Never!" Oates said.

Mrs. Miller stared at Flora nervously. "Who is she?"

"New help."

Mrs. Miller worried, "But she'll tell the doctor! He'll find out about my letters!" She was slipping into a panic-stricken state.

Oates shook his head. "No. She is a friend of mine. She won't say a word."

"You're sure?" the woman asked anxiously.

"Positive!"

Mrs. Miller relaxed a little. "Then it's all right."

"Right as rain," Oates said with a wink for the woman.

"You will bring me the answer when it comes?"

"Depend on it."

Mrs. Miller had a hankie in her hands which she twisted nervously. "I have another letter I wish to send out. I will have it ready for you tomorrow. There'll be a pound note with it."

Oates winked again. "Any time, Mrs. Miller. Oates aims to oblige."

Flora heard all this with some amazement. As soon as

they moved on, making their way down another corridor, she asked, "What about Mrs. Miller?"

"Another of the mild cases. I guess she was a beauty in her youth and then her face was half-destroyed by fire. Caught in a blazing barn trying to rescue a favorite colt. After that she became a recluse and wouldn't see anyone or look in a mirror. Her family brought her here and she's improved a great deal. Wants to get out and she's sane enough to leave. But the sad truth is her family don't want her, so the doctor has to keep her on as long as they're willing to pay."

"That doesn't seem right."

Oates nodded gloomily. "I agree. But you'd be surprised to hear we have more than one case like that. A good many. Unwanted people. I cater to her by taking her letters to post."

"Do the members of her family answer the letters?"

He shook his head. "No. Fact is they don't really get sent. I give them to the doctor and I expect he shows them to the relatives if they ever call. But nothing will be done. They don't want her."

"But you're giving her false hopes by lying to her."

"Have to do a bit of that around here," he said with a wink. "These aren't normal people we're dealing with."

The warder's callousness shocked Flora. She was about to reproach him for it but she was stopped by the appearance of a weird apparition staggering down the hall in their direction. It was a very stout woman in a kimono of some kind with her hair sticking out wildly in every direction. One hand was pressed against the wall to steady her as she stumbled along the corridor.

"Oates!" she cried angrily. "You didn't bring the gin!"

Oates at once cringed. "Sorry, Mrs. Storch, the doctor has it. He took it from me and said he'd bring it up to you himself."

"Liars!" the drunken woman stormed. "You're a liar and so is he!"

"I wager he'll be along with it soon," Oates told her.

The stout woman weaved a little. "He'd better be! You tell him I'm waiting and I want my gin! Let him send that floozy he has down there up with it if he can't bear the sight of me!"

"Yes, Mrs. Storch."

"Or is he too occupied with his pipe to pay any attention to you," the gross woman said with a nasty, leering smile. "Tell him he can have his pipe but I want my gin. And I want it right away!"

With that she turned and, using a hand to steady herself, once again groped her way back down the dark hall. Oates spread his hands in despair. "That's the way she is all the time these days. Like as not she has two or three bottles hidden somewhere in her room. The doctor tries to keep her down to no more than a bottle a day."

"She's in dreadful shape."

"Brought it on herself. Kept drinking more and more."

"What did she mean about the doctor and his pipe? I didn't understand that," she said.

Oates gave her a sly look. "You will," he said. "Everybody has a little weakness, you know. Mine is rum. Hers is gin, and Kitty's happens to be men."

"And the doctor?"

"His is harmless enough," Oates said. "You're bound to find out about it. You can smell it in his office. He's partial to smoking a pipe of opium every so often."

Chapter Twenty-eight

FLORA COULDN'T believe she was hearing correctly. It was impossible to accept that the head of the hospital was an opium addict. There was no question but that was what he was telling her, and yet informing her so casually as to make it seem of no importance. A minor weakness in the good Dr. Storch!

She stared at the bow-legged warder. "You are serious about this?"

"It's the blessed truth," Oates told her. "But don't ever so much as breathe it. The doctor would be furious if it got about."

"I should think so. People would have no confidence in him. Opium ruins the health and minds of its victims."

"And so does rum or gin," Oates replied. "But only if you take too much of it. I know my limit and the doctor's missus doesn't. That's what makes the difference. The doctor has been on drugs since first I've met him and I can promise you he's none the worse for it."

"He may *seem* none the worse for it," she corrected him.

"Same thing," Oates said dismissing it. "Best that we forget all about it, miss. It is none of our affair."

When Oates finished the tour of the building, she went to her room for a few minutes before joining the doctor and Kitty in the dining room. The things Oates had told her about the hospital worried her, and the final discovery that Dr. Storch was an opium smoker completely shocked her.

It seemed to her that Dr. Storch must be neglecting his duties. By Oates' account there were many patients in the place who were no more than eccentric but were kept there in return for payment by their relatives. These unfortunates were in a real sense prisoners of the hospital, and the doctor was being well paid to shut them away from those who didn't want to be bothered by them.

The whole thing was very upsetting. She had been so certain of her ability to look after herself in the city and this was where her assurance had landed her. What to do?

She decided she probably should remain for at least a month or two and make some observations. If what she feared were true then she had no choice but to report the criminal activities to the authorities. But would she be able to prove that he was indeed indulging in criminal practices? Would the word of a young woman attendant be taken against that of the doctor? Dr. Storch had a distinguished air and would be able to hornswoggle almost anyone with it. Even she had been impressed.

This meant she must find some means to prove her case if she decided things at the hospital were as grim as they appeared to be. She would need time to think about her course of action. She might call on Henry Armitage or William Booth to help her expose what was going on at the hospital when the time came. Even better, if she could find Mr. Gladstone and enlist his aid, his high political position would make him a strong ally.

She forced herself to appear casual when she joined the motley assemblage of Oates, Dr. Storch, and Kitty at the dinner table. The food served was excellent but she was a little too tense to fully enjoy it. She watched the doctor, covertly noting that his skin had a rather deathly, yellow-ish tinge. Also his eyes were strange, the pupils were distorted. Now she realized these things had bothered her earlier but she hadn't fully understood them.

The doctor pushed his plate away and touched a napkin to his lips. He directed himself to her. "You now have seen the entire hospital, Miss Bain?"

"Yes," she said.

"Do you still feel equal to the tasks demanded of you?"

"I think so," she said. "I find that I have a sympathy for the patients."

"Excellent, as long as you don't carry it too far," Dr. Storch said. "But much better than Kitty's attitude of revulsion."

Kitty glared at him. "I don't see living with a lot of mucking idiots any fine treat!"

"You see?" Dr. Storch said with a sigh. "No sympathy there at all."

Oates chuckled. Ignoring his napkin, he drew the back of his hand across his lips and said, "It takes experience to know how to deal with the loonies. I pride myself that I've got it. You have to know when to bear down."

"Very true," Dr. Storch said absently. "I have great faith in Oates."

Flora felt he had entirely too much faith in the rough and devious Chief Warder. In most ways it was Oates who was responsible for carrying out the hospital's activities. She couldn't help wondering what naive Mr. Sweeney would think of his distinguished doctor and his wife if he knew the truth.

Her room was comfortable enough after she'd built a small fire in the fireplace. Yet she had difficulty getting to sleep. Every so often the wailing from the cells in the basement reached through the walls of her room and she was also tormented by the predicament in which she found herself.

She began to think she would almost have been better off to remain at Armitage House. Menacing as was the atmosphere there she at least felt there were those in the house to whom she could turn. Here there was no one.

She missed Enid and she worried about the fate of Han Li. If only Dolly were with her here. Dolly with her great common sense, buoyant spirits, and ability to get out of difficult situations.

The next morning Flora began her first full day of work at the hospital. Dr. Storch had not exaggerated when he said that sedation on the hour was the rule. The way that Oates administered drugs to the patients shocked her. Most of them were kept in a dazed state all the time so that they could barely answer when they were spoken to.

One of the good features of the place was the exercise yard out back. She took her turn accompanying the female patients out there for a while. It was a sunny day but cool as winter was in the air. Many of the patients were too drugged to keep moving around properly in the cold air.

In the afternoon she devoted some time to the private patients. Her first encounter was with the imaginary king. She had gone in to see that his room was properly tidy when he looked up from a book he was reading and eyed her sternly.

"Maid!" he cried and put the book aside. "You have taken your time in coming to me!"

"What is it?" she asked him.

The old man stood before her in his cardboard gold crown looking every inch a monarch. He thrust out his hands. "Will you please to put my gloves on!" he demanded.

It seemed a harmless enough request. She said, "Where are they?"

"On yon table," he said in an arrogant tone.

She turned to the table and, sure enough, there were his gloves. In fact the table top was covered with a mound of gloves in all shapes, sizes, and colors.

"Which ones do you want?"

"As usual!" he cried impatiently. "Get on with it!"

Not knowing quite how to handle the situation she picked up a pair of leather gloves and put them on the hands of the would-be king. She smiled when she'd finished. "There you are. They look very well."

The old man frowned at her. "Call me sire, scullery maid."

She sighed. "Yes, sire! Now I must go."

"No!" he roared.

She halted, staring at him in amazement. "What now?"

His hands with the gloves on were still stretched out. He ordered her, "Put on my gloves!"

"I have, sire!" she declared, wanting to humor him.

"No! Put on the other ones!"

With a growing feeling of despair she took a pair of woolen gloves from the table and put them on over the leather ones. She was again about to leave when he roared at her.

"Dolt!" he cried. "Put on all the gloves!"

"All?"

"Of course. What a stupid scullery maid you are."

Feeling ridiculous she began the task of placing all the rest of the gloves over his hands. Fortunately they were of different sizes and she was able to stretch them on. When she placed a huge pair of mittens on as the last layer, he was wearing a grand total of eight sets of gloves.

Oates came into the room just as she finished. He roared with laughter. "I see the king has placed you in service."

She nodded miserably. "Yes."

"Come along. You've done enough for him," Oates said as he bowed to the king. "I hopes the gloves keeps your hands warm, sire!" Oates was still laughing. "I should have warned you. It's a daily routine with him. Usually one of the other girls does it."

"Will he keep them on?" she asked.

"Generally for about an hour or so. Then he calls out for someone to come and take them off."

The bow-legged man told her to remain on the women's side of the private rooms in the future, at least until she had some more experience. Then he went back downstairs.

She saw that several of the women's rooms were clean

and neat. As she came to the room of the scarred Mrs. Miller, she saw the older woman was pacing up and down nervously.

The woman halted pacing and stared at her. "You are the new one, aren't you?"

"Yes."

Mrs. Miller came up to her quickly. "You can help me!"

"What do you mean?"

"You know," the woman said impatiently. "I'm being kept here against my will so my brother can use my fortune as he pleases."

"But Oates is taking out your letters," she said, not wanting to get involved in this for the moment.

"Oates!" Mrs. Miller said in disgust. "I know him. He's lying to me and playing along with the doctor. I only keep testing him hoping that one day he really will decide to help me reach my friends on the outside."

Flora stared at the woman and could see no hint of madness in her. With a sigh she closed the door to give them privacy. "Are you telling me the truth?"

"Of course I am," Mrs. Miller said unhappily. "I was merely depressed by the loss of my dear husband when my brother induced me to come here. It was to give me a rest and bolster my nerves. Imagine anyone improving in this cruel madhouse! I've tried ever since to leave but my brother is paying Dr. Storch well to keep me here."

Flora asked, "Are there any others?"

"I can name a half-dozen like myself," the woman said. "And there must be more. Will you take a letter to a friend of my husband's for me?"

She frowned. "I won't promise that. But I will do something for you. I've only been here a day or so. Give me a chance. You have my word I won't forget you."

Mrs. Miller eyed her unhappily. "I think you're lying to me as well."

"No. You mustn't think that. Keep up your courage."

The woman said bitterly, "I've been bribing Oates all along and he has done nothing but destroy my letters. I only have five pounds left. I'll give it all to you if you'll take out a message for me."

She shook her head. "I don't want the money. But I will help you."

Mrs. Miller studied her with new interest. "You'll help me and not take any money?"

"That is what I said."

"You know," the woman said slowly, "I think I believe you. For the first time I have a little hope."

"I'll be taking a great risk. You must not say a word about our discussion to anyone."

"I won't."

"Especially not to Oates," she warned.

"I know him," the woman said bitterly. "He's the one who really runs this place and the cruelty he shows to those poor souls in the cellar is beyond thinking about."

"I have an idea," Flora said. "Now I must go. It will be a week at least before I can act. But then I will do what I can."

"Bless you!" Mrs. Miller said emotionally.

She had made up her mind to so something about the hospital from the start. But after her discussion with Mrs. Miller she was determined to try and save those who were the illegal prisoners of Dr. Storch. She studied the other patients and picked out the ones she felt should be released.

The slovenly, golden-haired beauty became friendly with her in the weeks that followed. It appeared that Dr. Storch was devoting more and more of his time to his opium pipe and less to Kitty. His office smelled continually of the acrid opium smoke and he was more aloof from others than ever before. He walked about the hospital in a seeming world of his own, barely speaking to them. He had reached a point where everything had been turned over to Oates.

Kitty complained to Flora, "I don't trust that red-nosed Oates. He may be soaked in rum but he's out to take the hospital from the doctor."

"Don't you think he's loyal?" Flora asked innocently.

"No!" Kitty said with disgust. "He's a rotter! Just waiting his chance to get full control of this place."

"Can't you do anything?"

Kitty scowled at the door leading to the doctor's office. "How? He's on that pipe nearly all the time. You can't reach him anymore. If I'd known it was going to turn out this way I'd never have wasted my time coming here."

"It's too bad," she said, pretending sympathy.

"I was barmaid at the Three Owls," Kitty went on in a tone of self-pity. "If I do say it myself, I was the main attraction of the place. I had regulars who came back night after night. Then he came in one night with his airs and importance. 'Kitty, I'll make a lady of you,' he says. 'Come and live with me at my hospital and you'll want for nothing!' "

"And now he doesn't care for anything but that drug," Flora volunteered.

"That's how it is! I'll be as mad as the worst of them in the cellar if I stay around this place much longer. His missus is up there drinking herself to death. Never comes down anymore as long as we keep the gin going up to her. I'm going back to the Three Owls if there isn't a change soon. And if I were you, my miss, I'd keep an eye out for a new position."

"You think so?" she asked, still pretending.

Kitty leaned forward conspiratorially. "Unless you want to wind up mistress to Oates. I'll warn you that little drunken bully has his eye on you. He told me so! I'm warning you against him."

"Thank you, Kitty, for being kind enough to tell me."

Kitty shrugged. "You're a pleasant enough little thing. You haven't my sort of figure and you're a modest beauty as far as the face is concerned, but you deserve better than Oates."

"I hope so."

"But he's ruling the roost here now," Kitty went on. "And the roost is not going to be a happy place to remain."

The blonde picked up the penny dreadful she'd been reading. She tapped it significantly. "Right there is where I learn about life. The doctor makes fun of me for reading these but that's where you find out what the world is. I read a case almost like this only a few weeks ago. An evil lawyer stole the estate from a drunken squire and then caused his death. After that he schemed to make the widow marry him. I know what is going on in this evil world because of these stories."

"I'm sure they're very educational," Flora said.

Kitty glared at the significantly closed door leading to the doctor's office. "Him in there stupid with opium and he has the nerve to make fun of me."

Flora was thinking quickly. "If only I could have a day and evening off I could go visit my former employers and perhaps get my old job back. But Oates will never give me the time off."

Kitty did exactly what she'd hoped, rose to the bait. "Take the day and evening off. I'll say the doctor told me to tell you that you could. Oates won't dare question me and even if he goes to the doctor it will be all right. The state the doc is in now he won't remember."

With sincere gratitude, she said, "Kitty you are a warm-hearted, good girl!" And she impulsively kissed the big blonde on the cheek.

Kitty looked pleased. "That's what they always said at the Three Owls."

"You should go back there."

"I have my plans," Kitty said. "And when noon comes tomorrow you take off and stay as late as you like. Overnight if you have to."

"Thank you," she said again.

So it was arranged. Flora was in such a state of excitement that she could barely sleep that night. She knew that normally she'd have been despairing because this job had turned out to be another horrible ordeal. But she wasn't thinking about that at all. Her concern was for the unfortunate victims of Dr. Storch's hospital and how she was going to help them.

Once she escaped from the place she would find someone to listen to her story. She didn't know quite who but she would make some start. She could tell Henry her plight but pride made her want to avoid doing that. She had left Armitage House against Henry's advice and she didn't feel like going to him with the admission that she'd been wrong. Or at least he would see it that way. She would rather find someone like Mr. Gladstone. But how did one locate and talk to Mr. Gladstone?

The next morning she went the rounds of the hospital with Oates and helped him sedate the patients. She also noticed that this morning, as on several others, he came to work with a strong smell of rum on his breath, still a little drunk.

As they finished with the women's ward and were on their way to the men's, the bow-legged man make an awkward attempt to put his arm around her as he lurched against her in the corridor.

She gave a small, startled cry and drew back from him. "What are you thinking of, Mr. Oates?" she asked.

He chuckled and said, "The future, my girl, the future. I need a lady like you to help me run this place. And if you know what's good for you, you and me might make a fine pair."

Pretending to be shocked, she demanded, "What about Dr. Storch?"

"Old opium head!" he scoffed. "He's about ready to move down to the cellar as a patient. And after that it won't be too long before he makes another move to the cemetery. I've got it all planned out."

"I don't know," she said.

He winked at her drunkenly. "Just keep a silent tongue and let me take care of everything," he said. "It won't be long until Oates is the master here!"

If nothing else would have driven her to the authorities with her story this little scene would have made her actions certain. But she'd already make up her mind and this only drove her on more urgently.

She had a short talk with Kitty after lunch. The blonde made sure that Oates had an errand to keep him busy and out of the way so Flora could get out of the place without his being aware of it. She dressed in her best dress and bonnet, put some money in her purse, and then hurried out of the somber red brick building.

When she walked swiftly through the gateway to the street she felt a sense of freedom. Only then did she realize how dreadful it was to work on as a virtual prisoner in the mental hospital.

When she reached the main thoroughfare and stood at the curb to wait for an omnibus she all at once felt lost. With a sinking heart she realized once again that she was going to have a most difficult time getting anyone to listen to her story. She didn't know where to begin. Who would she try and see first? She couldn't take an omnibus to the Houses of Parliament and ask for Mr. Gladstone! They would think her an idiot and send her packing.

The omnibus arrived. She stepped aboard and paid her fare. She sat lost in her thoughts until they were in the section of the city where Mr. Sweeney clerked in the drygoods store. This decided her. She would go and see him. It would be a first step. He had been responsible for her going to the mental hospital in search of work. Now he might be able to advise her in some way.

She hurried off the omnibus at the next stop and made her way to the drygoods store. The store was fairly well filled and Mr. Sweeney had an elegant woman customer, but he caught Flora's eye.

When he completed the sale he walked to where Flora had been waiting for him. Mr. Sweeney beamed at her. "You're looking very well. I trust you are happy in your new position."

"I'm afraid not," she said. "That is what I have come to tell you about."

Mr. Sweeney looked distressed. "What a pity! Can you come over to the counter and talk to me while I rearrange my stock? The floorwalker would not approve of my counter being in such a mess."

She sat on one of the high stools there explaining her problems as he fussily rolled the bolts of cloth and placed them back on the shelves. They both finished at approximately the same time.

"I can't believe that Dr. Storch is an opium addict," he said.

"It's true. But I know it's going to be hard to get anyone to listen to my story."

"Not that I doubt you," Mr. Sweeney hastened to say.

"I need someone with some weight to instigate an investigation into the goings on at the hospital," she said. "A strong crusader. Mr. Gladstone would be ideal but I don't know how to reach him, and I have only this afternoon and evening; then I must go back or Oates and the doctor will become suspicious."

Mr. Sweeney's face filled with excitement. He said, "I think I know the very man! Charles Dickens!"

"The writer?"

"Why not? He is, as you know, my idol. I have followed his books and his personal activities. He has crusaded for reforms in child labor and the workhouses. In most cases he has been successful. I say he's your man!"

"But an eminent man! How does one get to meet him?" she asked.

Mr. Sweeney's excitement continued. "It may not be as difficult as you think. In fact it could all work out very well!"

"I'm afraid I don't follow you," she said politely.

Now the clerk leaned over the counter and confided, "Tonight Mr. Dickens is giving readings from his books right here in London. I have planned to attend. It is my hope that afterward I may be able to catch him as he comes out the stage door and have him autograph my copy of *David Copperfield*. If we could somehow get a message from you to him perhaps he might give you a hearing. He is always interested in social causes. And I might get my autograph from him at the same time!"

Mr. Sweeney's excitement was catching. "I know Mr. Dickens is a powerful writer and a great humanitarian," she agreed. "But how could we go about it?"

"Let me plan it," the bald Mr. Sweeney said. "You can stay in London for the evening?"

"I can," she agreed.

"Excellent," he said. "I am not returning to the lodging

house for dinner after I leave work. Instead I'm going to have fish and chips at a pub I know and then on to the readings. You may join me. It is a very respectable pub. And while we are having dinner we can plan our strategy."

She smiled at him eagerly. "You've given me confidence, Mr. Sweeney. I almost think we'll manage it."

"Just a matter of good planning," the bald old man said. "You can fill in time looking around the shop until it is closing hour. Then we shall repair to the pub, have our meal, and compose some sort of note for Charles Dickens."

"If only we can get it to him," she said.

"I shall work at that when the time comes," he promised her.

Flora got down from the stool and gazed up at him in admiration. "Mr. Sweeney, I think you are one of the most resourceful men I have ever met!"

"Give the credit to Mr. Dickens," the old clerk said happily. "I tell you it is he who inspires me!"

Chapter Twenty-nine

FLICKERING GASLIGHT and jolly laughter set the mood at the pub known as the Fox and Hounds, situated near the Strand in the West End of London. It was to the Ladies' Salon of this busy and popular place that Mr. Sweeney took Flora. He insisted that she join him in a glass of ale and then they ordered tasty plates of fish and chips.

The old man smiled at her. "This is where I come at least one night a week to break the routine of Mrs. Lingley's fine fare!"

Flora laughed. "Knowing her fine fare from experience I can't blame you for wanting to get away from it."

"A most frugal woman. But all in all a good soul."

"This is very exciting," she said, glancing around her at the men and women seated at the other tables. From the bar there came the sound of an accordion being played and someone singing in a gruff voice.

"That's Jocko Gaunt himself," Mr. Sweeney informed her. "He likes to sing. He used to be a professional boxer and I followed the accounts of his fights in the sporting papers. Now he's retired and runs this place."

"I expect he does very well," she said.

"First rate," Mr. Sweeney said. "And sometimes when he passes through here he recognizes me. He calls me the draper because I once worked in a draper's shop."

"I'm glad you have a secret life, Mr. Sweeney," she said seriously. "I'd hate to think of you having nothing but an endless array of days and nights at that bleak lodging house."

Mr. Sweeney was having his third ale and now he looked at her with moist eyes and said, "You are a most remarkable young woman. You have perception, my dear, and so few of the young are blessed with it today. Indeed if I were forty or more years younger I would propose to you at this moment," he exclaimed. "I would be your David Copperfield!"

Mention of the Dickens character brought to mind the reason for her being there. "We aren't staying here too long are we? We won't be late for Mr. Dickens' readings?"

"No. Plenty of time. The readings are to be held at Thurston Hall tonight. I already have my ticket. We'll get you one at the door."

"Will that be hard? I've heard they are well attended."

"Never fear! It happens I am a personal friend of the ticket seller there. He'll find a ticket for you. Sam has never let me down yet!"

She said, "What about the letter we were going to send backstage? We mustn't forget that!"

"You are quite right. I shall go into the main room of the pub and get a sheet of paper and envelope from our good host, Jocko Gaunt."

Flora watched him weave out to the pub rather unsteadily. She had consumed only one glass of ale along with her food, but the three that Mr. Sweeney had taken seemed to have had a strong effect. Now she counted on his being an experienced drinker and trusted that he would be sober by the time of the readings.

As she was considering this the old man returned, still a

little unsteady on his feet, but with a look of determination on his face.

From his vest pocket he produced a pencil. He poised it over the paper. "How shall we begin? Dear Mr. Dickens?"

"Yes. I think we should have a formal opening."

"Excellent," he said. "Dear Mr. Dickens."

"What shall we say next. We must catch his attention."

"Yes. And at a time when he is busily occupied. I think it should be dramatic and very strong."

She nodded eagerly. "I agree."

"Now where are we," Mr. Sweeney said. "Dear Mr. Dickens, . . ." He paused. "How about this? I am in a most fearful plight and may even meet my death at the hands of some very evil men!"

"It's dramatic," she said. "But isn't it a little too much like *Lady Dudley's Secret*? It smacks of the one penny thrillers."

He waved this aside. "No, not at all. Dickens is a man of action and emotion. We must catch him on the wing!"

"That should do it."

"Now," he said writing, "of some very evil men. And I pray that you will see and advise me as you leave the stage door. I have it within my power to expose a great social evil in our city but I cannot do it without the help of a man like you."

"Yes," she said. "I like that!"

"Good," he said, carefully writing it. "Now the conclusion: My life and the lives of others are in your hands. I shall be at the stage door with my friend and your devoted reader, Mr. Blair Sweeney. Please do not turn me away. Your ardent admirer, Flora Bain."

She bit her lip. "Do you think ardent admirer is too strong? And does it matter if he knows you're a reader of his? You could tell him later."

"No. All that is important. Charles Dickens values his readers. Knowing I am one will put him on our side at once. I understand authors. And he has an eye for the ladies as well. So ardent has to be exactly the right word."

"Well, if you think so."

"Perhaps I should order another ale while I read it over and consider it," she said.

"No, I beg you," she said. "Otherwise we are almost sure to miss the readings."

"Well, if you think that. Now we will fold it up and put it in the envelope. How shall we address the letter?"

"To Mr. Charles Dickens, Esquire," she said.

"No, we must do better than that," he told her. "Let us make it it: Charles Dickens, Champion of the Underdog, Urgent!"

"That's awfully dramatic again," she said.

Mr. Sweeney spoke as a man of experience. "It has to catch his attention or that of his dresser. He'll be getting dozens of letters. This one has to stand out."

"It should," she said, already feeling embarrassed. Yet she realized that the old man was probably right. This was a desperate ploy for attention on her part and they had to do everything possible to make it work.

The old man looked at his pocket watch. "Time to leave. The hall is not far from here so we can walk."

They left the friendly atmosphere of the Fox and Hound to make their way along the gaslit street. It was theatre time so the streets were busy in this part of London. Flora kept close to Mr. Sweeney as they made their way through the crowds.

When they finally reached Thurston Hall she was distressed to find a huge crowd of people assembled and a long line at the ticket office. Mr. Sweeney did not seem worried.

"You wait here," he said. "I will go in the side entrance and speak to my friend in the ticket office through the rear door. Don't move!"

Mr. Sweeney shortly returned with a smile, which informed her all was well. "I managed it," he crowed with delight. "I have your ticket and right next to mine in the balcony. Now let us go to the stage door and deliver the letter to Mr. Dickens."

Mr. Sweeney escorted her down a dark, narrow alley which had a small gas lamp over a door at the end of it.

She felt a thrill at the experience. "This is exciting. I have never been to a stage door in my life."

"I have many times," the old clerk said in his man-of-the-world manner. "I collect famous stars' autographs, you know, so I frequent stage doors."

When they reached the stage entrance there was no one in sight. Mr. Sweeney glanced at her and said, "We might as well go in."

"Do we dare?"

"Tonight I dare anything," he said. Note in hand he opened the door for them. They stepped inside and found a small musty vestibule with stairs leading up somewhere.

Almost immediately a large, burly fellow appeared from the shadows. He blocked their way with a scowl on his broad face and exclaimed, "Here, now! What do you two think you are up to?"

Mr. Sweeney removed his top hat and said, "My dear sir, this young woman and myself are dear friends of Mr. Dickens. We have an urgent message for him. Would you be kind enough to see that he gets it?"

The burly man growled, "Two bob will see it gets to his dresser. I can't promise nothing beyond that."

Mr. Sweeney sighed and fished in his trousers pocket. "Two bob is fine. Just do your best." And he drew out the money and paid the stage-door man.

They went out into the alley again and she said, "Well, at least we have tried."

"I'm sure it will get to him if that fellow keeps his promise. We'll come back here after the performance. Now let us enjoy the reading."

They edged their way inside. Hawkers of programs and sweets stood along the way to sell their wares. Mr. Sweeney purchased a program for himself and one for her. Then they were pushed on and squeezed up the balcony stairs. It was with relief they reached their seats in the crowded hall. They were lucky enough to be seated in the very center although they were in almost the back row. The platform with its reading stand and table with a glass of water seemed very distant.

"I'm terribly excited," she whispered to him.

She consulted her program. He was reading from *A Christmas Carol*, *The Cricket on the Hearth*, *The Chimes*, *The Pickwick Papers* and *Oliver Twist*. She had heard that he often ended his program with the great dramatic scenes from *Oliver Twist* and looked forward to this.

Suddenly the great man presented himself. He came out from the wings in a most modest manner, bowed and took his place at the lectern. There was a roar of applause and many people rose to offer their hero a standing ovation. Mr. Sweeney and Flora were among them.

He bowed again and grasped the lectern with both hands and the crowd at once became quiet. A hush fell over the house as he began to read the opening lines of *A Christmas Carol*. It was the most exciting theatrical experience Flora thought she'd ever known.

As Dickens continued he began to act out the various characters, making them clear and distinct for his audience. He had a pleasing voice and presence. He was a man of great dignity.

Dickens completed his first selection to another round of applause. Mr. Sweeney leaned forward in his seat so as not to miss a single word. Dickens moved from one selection to another keeping his audience in tears and laughter. He seemed to produce one as easily as the other.

During the intermission Mr. Sweeney asked her if she would like to take a stroll but she declined, fearing that they would be pushed by the crowds and have to battle again to reach their seats.

He agreed. "Better to remain where we are."

"He was wonderful," she said.

"No one like him," Mr. Sweeney said.

"Do you think he will get the message?"

"We'll know as soon as this part of the show ends," the old clerk said. "We'll hurry to the stage door and wait for him. He is bound to leave the auditorium by that exit."

"Will there be others there?" she worried.

"Of course," he said. "But we shall push our way to the front."

Charles Dickens appeared again. The audience became more emotional in its response. And when he came to the scenes from *Oliver Twist*, depicting the murder of Nancy by Bill Sikes and Fagin in prison, the audience was completely silent. Silent even for a long moment after the reading ended. Then there came such a surge of applause that the building seemed to vibrate. Men stood up, and there were cries of approval from every part of the great hall.

Mr. Sweeney grasped her by the arm and hissed in her ear. "We must go. Have to leave before the others if we're to get to the stage door first!"

She nodded and let him guide her out. People were still in their seats applauding as she and the old man hurried down the several flights of steps out into the street. A slight fog had arisen since the beginning of the evening and it was cooler. Many carriages waited in line along the street in front of the big hall.

They dodged into the alley and made for the stage door. Two or three young people had already gathered there. Then came the vigil. And while they waited others joined them with programs in hand. Autograph hunters ready to descend on Charles Dickens.

Mr. Sweeney whispered, "Often he doesn't stop for autographs."

"I wonder what he'll do tonight."

"We'll just have to wait and see."

It seemed an age before the burly stage-door man appeared. "Stand back! Back and make way for Mr. Dickens and his party!" he ordered them all.

Somehow Flora managed to keep close to the door though everyone was pushing to get her place. Then she saw the outline of a top-hatted figure and a moment later Charles Dickens stepped out into the alley. Shouts of appreciation rang in the alley. Charles Dickens lifted his top hat and smiled. There were two other men with him.

Flora knew if she didn't speak out now it would be too late. She plunged forward and said, "Mr. Dickens, I am Flora Bain!"

"Here now!" the burly stage-door man said, rushing up to grasp Flora and push her back.

"It's all right," Charles Dickens said, lifting a hand to stop him. "I want to speak with this young lady."

She felt a great surge of relief. "Thank you, Mr. Dickens."

"Get my carriage, Stead," Charles told the guard, who hurried off to obey the command. Dickens turned to her again, "We must get out of here quickly. Where is that man you referred to in your dramatic missive?" He said the last in a jocular tone.

"Here, sir!" Mr. Sweeney said, bobbing up out of the crowd.

"Come along with me, both of you," Charles Dickens said.

The great man took her protectively by the arm and escorted her down the alley where a carriage was waiting. Dickens helped her and Mr. Sweeney up into the carriage, then stepped up himself, sitting next to her. The two men with him sat in the opposite seat.

"Where to, Charles?" one of them asked.

"The Trafalgar Restaurant. We can go up to one of the private rooms and have food and some wine. I find myself very weary."

The man leaned out and told the coachman, "The Trafalgar Restaurant!"

As the carriage got under way there were shouts of affection from those gathered in the street. Charles Dickens settled back with a sigh. Mr. Sweeney was on one side of him and Flora on the other.

The carriage rumbled along the street, pausing for traffic every now and then. Mr. Sweeney said, "This is the greatest moment of my life, Mr. Dickens."

The author turned to the old clerk. "So you read my works, do you?"

"Yes, I do. And I have most thoroughly enjoyed them. But never more than I did tonight when you read them from the stage. I shall always remember it."

"Thank you," Dickens said. "I fear it shall remain in my mind as well. I am most dreadfully tired from the chore. Have you the slightest idea of the amount of energy I use in one of those performances?"

One of the men sitting opposite said, "They are too hard on you, Charles, but still you persist in doing them. Why?"

Dickens sighed. "I like the applause and I need the money!"

"Neither reason is good enough for what this is doing to you," the man warned him.

The carriage finally came to a halt before a well-lighted restaurant entrance. They all stepped down from the carriage and one of the men accompanying Charles Dickens went ahead to make arrangements for the private dining room which he had requested. It took only a moment or two. The proprietor of the place came out to greet the famous author effusively and guide their party up a flight of stairs to a paneled private dining room with a fireplace, huge mirror and rich rugs.

Charles Dickens removed his coat and top hat and Mr. Sweeney helped Flora with the cape she was wearing. Then the famous author ordered for them all after which he went over and stood to warm his hands before the logs blaring in the fireplace.

He turned to Flora after a moment and motioned her to sit down near him. With a smile playing around his lips he said, "So you are my ardent admirer, Flora!"

She blushed. "I wrote that very impulsively, please forgive me."

"Your letter was full of the dramatic," he told her. "I'd say you have a flair for words. At least your letter caught my attention. I read it twice before I went onstage."

"Give Mr. Sweeney credit for that. He composed it with the thought that it must be striking or you might not notice it."

Dickens raised his eyebrows and gave the old clerk an amused look. "You have missed your profession, Mr. Sweeney. You should be in Fleet Street."

"I did think of a newspaper career once but I felt I hadn't the learning," the old clerk said.

Dickens chuckled. "I'll promise you that you wouldn't need much learning. Isn't that so, gentlemen?"

The two middle-aged men with Dickens joined him in

laughter. The older-looking of the two said, "I have lately noticed a scarcity of genius in the street."

Charles Dickens now turned to her again. "I trust your letter was not a fraud. That you do have something to inform me about."

"I do," she said.

"Proceed," he ordered her.

Nervously she began her story of Dr. Storch's mental hospital and what was taking place there. She particularly stressed the oversedation of the patients and the fact that many of them were being kept in the institution illegally for the benefit of the relatives who'd placed them in there.

Dickens showed a growing interest as he listened. When she finished he stroked his beard and frowned. Glancing at the other men, he said, "I would say that this is a scandalous situation, wouldn't you, gentlemen?"

"It should be looked into," the older man agreed.

"The police should investigate the hospital at once," the younger man said. "It is important that you get the right officer to take charge of the investigation."

Dickens nodded. "I shall speak to Inspector Field in the morning." He turned to Flora again. "Field is the Chief Detective of Scotland Yard. I know him well. He's the man to deal with Storch."

"Thank you," she said gratefully. "I've very worried about what may happen. I think there is no time to lose. Dr. Storch is deteriorating rapidly and soon the drunken Oates will be running the place."

Dickens said, "I'd expect Field to take action immediately."

At the restaurant waiters arrived with food and drink for the company. Charles Dickens grew more relaxed at the table and asked Flora how she had come to meet Mr. Sweeney. She told him and she also mentioned the other experiences she'd had since she'd left home to join her uncle in London.

The famous author listened with interest. "And so you

371

have been to China along with your other adventures? I would say you've had a most exciting life."

"A little too exciting. Now I find myself still in the midst of trouble."

The talk at the table turned to Inspector Field with whom Dickens had made many excursions into the underworld of London. Dickens seemed to have unlimited confidence in the man he was planning to have investigate Dr. Storch and the hospital.

"Field is a capital fellow! One night I was with him when he visited a tramps' lodging house looking for some wanted criminals. Saint Giles' church clock was ringing as the door to the fetid place was thrown open. The assistant inspector shone a light in and I saw a sight which is still etched in my mind.

"That wretched house was packed with men, women and children. Twenty, thirty. Who could count them! An Irishman in one corner with his wife and eight babes. You could not cross the room for the humans huddled on the floor in sleep. The inspector inquired who the landlord was and a spectral figure rose unshrouded from a grave of rags. 'I am, Mr. Field,' he said, a bundle of ribs and parchment leaning against the wall scratching himself."

"The poor of the city are being crowded into ghettos," the older man with Dickens said.

"My own feeling," Dickens said. "Thus, we make our New Oxford Streets and other new streets, never heeding, never asking, where the wretches whom we clear out crowd."

When they finished at the table Dickens said, "Are you prepared to return to that hospital and remain there until the police come?"

"Yes," she said. "Though I don't want to stay there long. It could be dangerous."

"I agree," Dickens said with a solemn look on his bearded face. "But I can promise you Inspector Field will be there tomorrow. The chances are he will close the operation at once."

"I'm sure he will," she said. "So many terrible things are taking place there."

"I shall plan to see the inspector afterward," the famous author said. "And I want to see you again. I'm presently staying at a hotel in the city. I'll write my address and you can reach me at the hotel if I'm unable to get in touch with you."

"Thank you," she said.

Dickens told her, "I'm sure I can find a person with your qualities a good position, and I know of several places you can live. So you mustn't worry about making a fresh start."

"You're too kind," she told him.

He smiled. "My meeting you has been an unusual experience. Perhaps I shall be able to do some good as a result of your telling me about this hospital. And the story of your life could help me in my future writing."

"That is so, Mr. Dickens," Mr. Sweeney said, speaking up for the first time in quite awhile. "I say her experiences should be set down."

The author smiled at him. "And what can I do for you, Mr. Sweeney?"

"Autograph my copy of *David Copperfield*, sir," the old clerk said. "And continue writing your fine novels."

"Both your requests are easily fulfilled," Charles Dickens said. "Let me have your book."

After he had autographed Mr. Sweeney's copy of *David Copperfield* the supper party broke up. They left the restaurant and returned to the carriage. Charles Dickens insisted on taking both Mr. Sweeney and Flora home.

"I enjoy nothing more than driving around London after midnight. There is a sinister part of this old city which only comes alive then."

Mr. Sweeney was dropped off at his boarding house. He told Flora he meant to keep in touch with her and said good night to Dickens.

As they drove on Dickens said, "He's a remarkable old fellow. His determination amazes me."

"I would never have managed to get to you if he had not helped," Flora said.

Dickens laughed. "I don't know whether I should thank him or not. Now I find myself involved in another grave social injustice. I seem to be forever finding causes or having them thrust upon me."

They reached 9 Knox Street and Dickens got out of the carriage with her. He eyed the red-brick hospital, which had no lights showing at its windows.

He said, "It is a macabre-looking place. Are you afraid to go in alone?"

"No," she said. "My room is not far from the entrance. I can go straight to it without entering the hospital."

Dickens stood facing her. "I dislike sending you in there but perhaps it is wise. You'll be on hand as a witness to report to Inspector Field when he arrives here tomorrow."

"Yes," she said. "And I may have a chance to tell Mrs. Miller that he is coming."

"Be sure you don't put them on their guard," Dickens warned her. "We must take them by surprise to expose the worst of their perfidy."

"I understand."

The author bade her good night and waited until she was inside the hospital. From the vestibule she watched him drive off into the darkness. Only then did the first stirrings of fear shoot through her. Suddenly she felt alone and in danger.

She continued on to the corridor which passed the doctor's offices and led to her own room. From the cellar she heard a sharp, melancholy cry of some patient. Then the silence settled heavily again. It seemed she had never known it to be so silent.

She reached her own room, lit a candle, and took off her cloak. The rooms occupied by Kitty and Dr. Storch were nearby and she felt she could call on Kitty at least if she continued to be so afraid. She tried to tell herself that her fear was childish, but it didn't help.

She was about to start undressing for bed when she thought she heard a creak in the corridor outside her door. She stood motionless and listening for a moment, terrified that some would-be intruder was lurking out there. But who? Again she regretted her decision to return to the hospital.

In the next second the door of her room was thrown open to reveal a sneering Oates. As the short, red-faced man came into the room towards her, she saw that he was drunk and in a nasty temper.

Chapter Thirty

"How DARE you burst into my room?" Flora cried.

Oates stood there swaying drunkenly. He ignored her angry reprimand. "So you're back!"

"Get out of here!" she told him. "I'll call the doctor!"

The bow-legged man laughed harshly. "The doctor is deep in a drugged sleep. He can't help you."

"Kitty then."

"She's gone."

"Gone?"

"She's gone. She and the doc had a fight early tonight and she packed her bags and left. Good riddance, I say! So you just have me to deal with, my girl. Where were you today and all night?"

She backed over by the fireplace, terrified that she would have to deal with the drunken Oates alone. "The doctor told me I could have the day off to see friends."

"Did he?" Oates enquired sarcastically. "Real toffs I suppose, those friends of yours. Brought you back in a carriage, didn't they?"

"What difference does it make?"

He lurched forward a step. "I'll tell you what difference it makes. I don't want any toffs' leavings. I'm going to teach you a lesson so you won't go running off to be a rich man's fancy again!"

"You're mad!" she cried.

"What you need, my girl, is a good flogging. And Oates is going to give it to you." As he finished saying this he hurled himself at her.

She'd been crouching in fear by the fireplace. As he sprang to attack her she automatically caught up the heavy poker and used it as a weapon. She struck him on the head with all her strength. He was caught by surprise and felled like a slaughtered ox. He lay still on the floor with his hands sprawled out, blood flowing from his temple.

The full horror of what had happened struck her. She was certain she had killed him. She moved quickly around him, found her cape, and ran out of the room, heading for the front entrance of the hospital. She knew she could not remain there any longer.

Frantically she ran along the walk through the lawn to the gates. Just as she reached the sidewalk beyond she heard the clatter of horses' hooves approaching. She looked down the street to see a carriage emerging from the fog-ridden darkness. In the next moment she recognized the carriage as the one hired by Charles Dickens.

It came to a halt by her and Dickens and the other two men jumped down from the vehicle. Dickens said, "Is something wrong?"

She nodded tearfully. "I was attacked by the warder and hit him with a poker. I think I may have killed him."

Dickens gave the men with him a worried look. "What do you say, gentlemen?"

"We'll go in and find out," the older man said. And he quickly asked her where he would find Oates. Then he and the younger man hurried off towards the hospital entrance.

"I had misgivings about leaving you," Dickens told her.

"I asked the driver to turn around and come back here to make sure you were all right."

Still trembling, she said, "It was dreadful!"

"You say this Oates attacked you?"

"Yes. He was drunk. He said the doctor was in a drugged sleep and Kitty, his assistant, had left. I knew I was alone and at his mercy. When he came at me I used the poker."

Charles Dickens said grimly, "He deserved it."

"But if I killed him?"

"Then it was done in self-defense."

The younger man came running out of the hospital and joined them on the sidewalk. "He's not dead. He's coming around now."

The older man appeared. "I stayed long enough to make sure he's not too badly hurt. We'd better get on our way. He could come out here after us and raise a lot of trouble."

"You're right," Dickens said. "Let us board the carriage at once."

When they were all seated in the carriage, returning to the central part of the city, Charles Dickens told Flora, "You'll have to manage without your belongings until Inspector Field takes over that place tomorrow. He'll get them for you then. I'm taking you to my hotel. You can remain there overnight, until the Inspector talks to you. Then we can decide about your future."

By the time they reached the hotel in Shaftesbury Road she was less hysterical. Charles Dickens had her assigned a room and saw her safely to her door. That night she slept soundly and the next day she remained at the hotel until Inspector Field and Charles Dickens came to question her late in the afternoon.

Inspector Field was a bluff, stout man with a keen mind. He brought Flora her bag filled with her clothing and personal possessions. And he informed her, "We are closing the hospital and sending the genuine patients elsewhere. Mrs. Miller and the others who appear to have been mere prisoners will be released."

Dickens smiled at her, "So you need not worry any more."

She asked, "What about the doctor and Oates?"

"The doctor is in a bad way," Inspector Field said. "I have sent him to hospital for treatment. Oates tried to attack one of my men and he is now in jail. By the time we complete your testimony and that of the others he is liable to remain in jail for a long while."

Flora gladly recited all she had seen and heard at the private hospital. She could feel little sympathy for the doctor or Oates but she was glad Kitty had left before the raid. She learned that when the police had searched the second floor they had discovered the doctor's wife dead in her bed, a victim of her alcoholism.

Charles Dickens found Flora a job as a sales clerk in a book-shop in the Strand. He also found her lodgings above the book-shop in the same building with a Scottish family named Burr.

Malcolm Burr and his wife, Dorothy, were a pleasant childless couple. Mr. Burr also worked in the bookstore where Flora was employed thanks to Charles Dickens. It seemed that she had at last found an interesting position and a good home.

Dickens had to leave on a reading tour, but he stopped by the bookshop to bid her goodbye before going. "You are perfectly safe here," he told her. "Now you must begin to see some more of what this great city has to offer. You must visit the theaters, the symphony concerts and the art galleries."

She promised she'd take his advice and she did. The Burrs were fond of theater so she often went with them. She kept promising herself to arrange to go out to Armitage House and see Enid, but she never did seem to get around to it in her busy new life.

Malcolm Burr came down with pneumonia and was rushed to the hospital. He had to remain in the hospital some weeks. Dorothy and Flora visited him regularly.

One evening when Flora had gone alone to bring him a treat of homemade custard, she left the hospital ward where he was a patient earlier than usual. As she walked down the wide corridor she met one of the maids who worked along with the nurses in the hospital. It took only a second for her to realize that it was Dolly.

"Dolly Wales!" she cried.

The girl came limping quickly to her crying, "Flora!"

It was a joyous reunion but Flora at once noticed that Dolly looked much thinner than in the old days. She asked her if she had been ill.

Dolly smiled wryly. "I was run down by a dray. They brought me here and didn't expect me to live. But I did. I've still got a limp but I'm gaining strength all the time."

"But the work must be very hard here."

"It's the stairs I mind most," Dolly said. "But I need work and they offered me a job."

"You need something less strenuous. Why don't you go back to Armitage House? At least you wouldn't have to work so hard there."

"I don't think they'd have me back."

"Let me see Henry Armitage and ask him," she suggested.

"Why did you leave? I expected you'd still be there after you came back from China."

"A number of reasons," she said. "Among them, Henry Armitage married when he was in China. I felt with a wife he didn't need me. His wife has plenty of time to tutor Enid."

"Mr. Henry married! Imagine that!"

"There have been many changes," she said.

"I'll bet that Jessica is still around! And Mrs. Brant! I won't go back if Mrs. Brant is still there. She made my life miserable," Dolly complained. "I meant to stay until you came back but I couldn't."

Flora said, "At any rate I can talk to Henry Armitage and see what he has to say. And you must keep in touch with me." She gave Dolly her address.

The meeting with Dolly had an interesting result. She made up her mind to seek out Henry Armitage at once. The next day she asked the owner of the bookshop for an extra hour at lunch. She went upstairs and changed into her best bonnet and dress. Then she hired a carriage to take her to Henry's London office.

Considering the long while she'd put off this excursion it proved to be a very short trip. She paid the cabby and went inside. A male clerk greeted her. She told him she wished to speak with Henry Armitage. Within a few minutes she was ushered into the inner office where he sat.

He rose with a smile to greet her. "Flora! What a nice surprise!" he said. He looked as handsome as ever.

"I've been meaning to come see you for a long while," she said.

"Do sit down. You've let a lot of time go by before returning to see me."

She smiled. "I've been terribly busy. How is Enid?"

"Well. She still complains of missing you."

"And Han Li?"

His face shadowed slightly. "Her health has not been the best. I fear our English climate is not good for her."

"I'm sorry to hear that."

"I hope she'll improve as she becomes more used to our cold and fog."

"I hope so. And your father?"

"He is about the same. I don't think there has been any decline in his condition since you were with us." He paused. "And Jessica is well and busy. She has taken up riding lately. I hope you have come here today to say you'll return to Armitage House and resume as governess to Enid. She often speaks of you."

"No," she said. "I'm sorry. Mr. Charles Dickens, the writer, found me a post in the Grossmith Book Shop and I am thoroughly enjoying working there."

"You have acquired some eminent friends."

"We met by accident," she said, without going into the details. Then she told him about her meeting with Dolly and how the girl had suffered a severe injury and needed lighter work than she was engaged in at the hospital. She wound up by asking, "Is Mrs. Brant still acting as your housekeeper?"

"It's strange you should ask me that. She and her husband have gone to live with their only daughter in the country. We have a new housekeeper, a pleasant and competent young woman."

Delighted by this news, she said, "I asked you to hire Dolly once, some time ago. Now I'm asking again. I think she would regain her health much more quickly in the suburbs. And the work would be lighter."

"Of course we'll take her back. Have her come to the office here when she is ready and I'll see she gets transportation to Armitage House."

"That is most kind of you. No doubt she will be able to leave the hospital at the end of the week. I'll see her and tell her a job is waiting for her." She stood up. "Now I must leave. I had to ask for an extra hour off to get here. I don't want to be late returning to the shop."

The handsome young man came around the desk. His blue eyes regarded her seriously. "You are sure you won't change your mind about returning with Dolly? It would make us all very happy."

Flora could not help but think it would annoy at least one person, Jessica, but she did not say this. Instead, she told him, "If I should decide to leave the bookshop I will come and talk to you about returning. That is the best I can promise at the moment."

He studied her with fond eyes. "You helped make Armitage House less of a bleak place. I will not give up hoping you'll be with us again one day. In the meantime why don't you visit us and see Enid? She'd be so pleased."

"I will," she said. "Just as soon as I get a day free."

"Don't forget!"

"I won't," she promised as she bade him goodbye.

She hired a carriage to take her back to the shop and as she sat back to think about the meeting during the return journey she decided that she still cared far too much for Henry Armitage. And in spite of being married he continued to seem fond of her. Because of the strong mutual attraction they had for each other she did not trust herself to go back to Armitage House for visits.

She saw Dolly at the hospital during one of her visits to Nelson Burr. She told her that Mrs. Brant had left Armitage House and her old job was open for her. Dolly arranged to leave the hospital at the end of the week and spend Sunday with Flora at the Burrs' before reporting to work on Monday.

Sunday afternoon Flora took Dolly out to tea at one of the busy entertainment gardens which dotted the West End. They found a table not far from the Viennese String Orchestra, which was playing a selection of lovely waltzes. The place was full of young people and Dolly was very taken with it.

Over tea and cakes Dolly confided, "I have a young man now, Flora. And he has promised to come and take me out on my days off at Armitage House!"

"A young man? You didn't tell me!"

The younger girl blushed. "I've been keeping it for a surprise. You see, it's someone you know."

"Someone I know?" Flora said, even more astonished. "Who?"

Dolly laughed. "You'd never guess. Shanks."

"Shanks!"

"Yes. You see, you've even forgotten him. He was the gawky lad who worked at William Booth's mission and had been a pickpocket before he reformed."

At once she recalled the tall, young man who looked like a scarecrow in his ill-fitting clothes. "You laughed at him and thought he was awkward at your first meeting."

"I know," Dolly admitted with a twinkle in her eyes. "But I grew to like him."

"He was amusing and really very nice."

"And he's ever so much improved now," Dolly assured her. "You know that William Booth has formed his Salvation Army and Shanks is an officer in it. You should see him in his blue uniform and red cap. He's almost good looking."

"So he did stay with William Booth. I'm glad."

"He's doing very well and has charge of a small mission in the East End. When I was run over by the dray, he came to visit me in the hospital. That's part of his duties, visiting the sick and injured in hospitals. When he recognized me he came every day until I was better."

"That was kind of him."

Dolly sighed. "I was thinking I'd never get myself a young man now that I have this awful limp, but Shanks said he didn't mind that at all. And he asked me if we could start keeping company and I said yes. So we have been ever since."

She smiled at her friend across the table. "I'm truly happy for you, Dolly. Have you any marriage plans?"

"Not for a while. But we do plan to be married. Shanks wants me to join the Salvation Army and then we can work together."

"I think that would be exciting," Flora said.

"I haven't made up my mind yet, but I think maybe I will join." She gave her a searching glance. "What about you? Have you found yourself a beau?"

Flora shook her head. "No one."

"But you must have met dozens of young men in that bookshop," Dolly insisted.

"Never the right one," she said.

Dolly gave her a knowing glance. "I think I know why," she said.

"Why?"

Dolly said, "I believe you're in love with Henry Armitage. I always thought so."

She blushed in confusion and said, "That's ridiculous!"

"No, it isn't," the other girl persisted. "I've seen the way you look at him and the way he looks at you. I've never seen two people more in love. Why did he have to marry that Chinese girl and spoil it all?"

"She's only part Chinese," Flora protested. "And in any case he married her because he loved her. What better reason? Anyway, it's not important since he's married now."

"It is important if it spoils your life," Dolly argued. "You must find someone else. You can't be a spinster all your days pining for him."

"I live my life as I like to," she said. "I have no need of romance. The Burrs are wonderful company for me and take me everywhere. I have other good friends like old Mr. Sweeney with whom I have an evening meal once a week. Afterwards he often takes me to a music hall. I have a very good time."

"That's all right now," Dolly said. "But you'll want a home of your own one day and by that time old Mr. Sweeney will be long dead and buried."

"Please don't talk that way about him, he's a nice old man," she protested. At the same time she felt a twinge of melancholy because she knew it was true.

Dolly went on, "And that's why you won't return to Armitage House. Because it would torture you to be in the same house with Henry and his wife."

"There are other reasons."

"Name them."

She shrugged. "Jessica, for one. I'm sure she's still as jealous of Henry as ever. She's continuing to live there and she apparently has no plans for marriage."

"Why should she?" Dolly said with distaste. "We both know she's in love with Henry!"

Flora sighed. "If you don't mind I'd rather not discuss the matter any further."

"Just as you say," Dolly told her. "But I know what I know."

In the weeks following Flora thought of this conversation many times and she had to admit to herself that her friend had been right. She was in love with Henry Armitage and because of that she never entertained serious thoughts of any other young man.

Mr. Grossmith, the owner of the large bookshop where she worked, was a funny little man who looked like a frightened, gray rabbit with heavy sidewhiskers. He was short and often only his bald head would show over a stack of books. But he was a staunch friend of Charles Dickens, a successful businessman, and very protective of all his employees.

Flora worked in the section devoted to new books, which was one of the busiest areas of the store. She had little time to rest during the hours the store was open.

Mr. Grossmith liked to refer to her as his Charles Dickens girl since it had been the famous writer who'd brought her to the store. One day the bald little proprietor came to her and said, "I saw your friend yesterday."

She had been dusting some books with a feather whisk and she stopped in her work to smile and ask him, "Who?"

"Charles Dickens. And I'm sorry to say he's not looking at all well. Very drawn and haggard."

"He works too hard."

"Without a doubt. And then he is having marital troubles. All London has heard the rumors regarding his separation from his wife. There is said to be a young actress involved. You know how fond Mr. Dickens is of the theater and theater people."

"I do," she said. "Probably the rumors are false. People in the public eye are always the subject of scandalous attacks."

"Perhaps. I don't know. I only wish that Charles did not look so ill. We cannot afford to lose a novelist of his talent."

She said, "Surely it isn't that serious. He is likely just weary and troubled."

She discussed this with old Mr. Sweeney when they met for a fish-and-chips dinner at the Fox and Hounds a few nights later. "Have you seen Charles Dickens lately? They say he looks very ill."

"I read something of that sort in one of the weekly papers," the elderly clerk agreed. "But he seemed very well when he came to your aid at the mental hospital."

"That was many months ago," she pointed out. "And he did complain of being weary at the time."

"His new novel *Great Expectations* is his very best," Mr. Sweeney said with enthusiasm. "If you see him tell him that I said so."

It was about ten days later that she did see Charles Dickens briefly. He came into the shop to speak with Mr. Grossmith about buying copies of some play. When he'd finished with the little man he came across to greet her. He looked as distinguished as usual in his overcoat with a cape, but he was carrying a cane and leaning on it heavily as he walked with a distinct limp. It was his face that worried her most and haunted her afterward. His handsome bearded face was gaunt and lined. The hollows in his cheeks were noticeable.

When he smiled and spoke to her he made her forget his altered appearance with his air of charm. "Well, Miss Bain, how is your life progressing now?" he asked. "No wild adventures?"

"Only the ones I read in books," she said, with a smile for him. "I like it that way."

"Most people do," he said. "That is why novels remain popular. You are still living above with the Burrs?"

"Yes."

"I shall be leaving for America in a few days," he said. "When I return you must come and visit me. We can reminisce about that night when you apprehended me after my readings."

"I'd like that very much."

He put on his black top hat. "I have a young lady friend of about your age, an actress named Ellen Ternan. I'd like to have you two meet. I'm sure you'd get along famously."

With that he left the store. But he had said enough to let her know that the whispers going the rounds were based on fact. She'd heard Ellen Ternan named as the girl with whom the famous novelist was having an affair and now he had confirmed it.

Shortly after Mr. Dickens' visit to the bookstore she received a letter from Dolly with some pointed mentions of what was happening at Armitage House. Word had been received from China of the death of Yenn Li, father of the lovely Han Li. She had not been well and this sad news had sent her into collapse. She'd been bed-ridden for nearly a month. Jessica was becoming more and more the sole mistress of the old mansion. Enid and her possessive aunt did not get along. Dolly said that Henry Armitage looked wan and troubled and that the hauntings at the mansion were continuing. Several of the other servants swore they had seen Lily's shrouded figure standing by the pool.

Flora at once sent a letter of condolence to Han Li and

in return received a polite, beautifully written note with a plea that she visit Armitage House soon. Flora could not bring herself to do this.

The warm days of summer came. She heard that Charles Dickens had returned from his American tour and was now living in the country. It was common gossip that the actress Ellen Ternan was living with him. But it was agreed that his marraige had been less than perfect and he did not lose the public sympathy. Flora hoped that she might one day see her distinguished friend again, but he did not present himself at the bookshop.

It was near closing time on an August evening and she had planned to attend a concert in the park with the Burrs. She was about to leave the shop to go upstairs when a man in a top hat entered. He stood for a few seconds staring at her in amazement before he came hurrying over to take her hands in his. It was Chen Li, Han Li's Chinese cousin, looking very Western in his smartly tailored, man-about-town clothes.

"My dear Flora," he said with a happy smile. "How good to see you again!"

Flora could scarcely believe it was Chen Li. She'd almost forgotten the pleasant, Oxford-educated Chinese who was standing facing her. "Chen Li!" she said with deep emotion.

"It has been two years," he told her. "But I promised you I would one day be coming back to England and here I am."

"You did promise," she remembered.

"You have heard about Yenn Li?"

"Yes. I'm so sorry. His death must have been a rude shock to Han Li."

"It was," he agreed. "I have just come from a few days at Armitage House. She is not well. She resembles a faded flower. I learned from her and Henry where to find you."

"I'm so glad you took the trouble," she said.

"I would not dream of visiting England without seeing you," the young Chinese said earnestly.

"What about you, Chen?" she asked. "Have you married?"

He smiled sadly. "No, I think you are aware why. I told you when you were in China."

"You loved Han Li."

His eyes met hers. "Just as you loved Henry Armitage."

Flora smiled.

"I have taken over in the business," he said. "And I have also moved into the house of Yenn Li. It is large for a bachelor but surely one day I shall marry and there will be a wife and children."

"And many concubines?"

"Never," he said. "I have embraced the Western conception of single love. I think that enough for any man, more than a great many are capable of."

She studied him with affection. "It is so good to see you, Chen."

"I trust that we shall see much of each other," he said. "I will be in England at least another month before I return to Canton. There is so much theater, ballet, and opera to catch up on. I shall depend on you to be my escort and make sure I see all the important things."

"I'll do my best," she promised.

So quite abruptly everything changed for her. Life took on a brighter hue. Chen Li wanted to make the most of his relatively short time in London, so their evenings were a continuous round of outings. She found it necessary to dig into her meager savings and purchase two new gowns to dress properly for him.

Chen also liked to do outdoor things so they went boating on the Thames, played croquet in the park, and even tried the new sport of bicycling. Chen invariably won their games of croquet and she blamed this on her voluminous crinoline skirts.

"My dress gives you an unfair advantage," she teased him.

There was a twinkle in his eyes. "Then we shall look for a game in which your skirts will be no hindrance."

He took her to the Ladies' Archery Club at Kensington Gardens. They were the guests of an older woman friend of one of Chen's Oxford dons. Chen was an expert at the sport, Flora a novice.

"I've hardly had a bow in my hand," she lamented.

"You may have a natural talent for archery," Chen suggested.

It turned out that she did. As they were driving back to her lodgings Lady Madge Waring came to mind. She recalled the frightening moment when the young mistress of the adjoining estate had wantonly fired an arrow at a tree and almost sent it through her. She could never decide if it had been an accident or not. But she did know that Lady Madge had been very fond of Henry.

She turned to Chen. "Lady Waring, who lives next to Armitage House, is skilled at archery."

"Is she? I've met her," Chen said. "Did you know she is now a widow?"

This came as a surprise. "I hadn't heard. So old Sir Thomas finally died?"

"Yes," Chen said. "But she has decided to remain on the estate. At least for a year or two. Many people felt she would sell."

"Oh," she said casually. But she was thinking that Lady Madge was not apt to sell as long as Henry Armitage lived next door.

The time went by at a hectic pace and soon it was only ten days before Chen's ship was due to sail. They were at a large restaurant which featured dancing and Chen brought her back to their table breathless and happy. He smiled at her across the table. "You see I am adept at your British dances!"

"Indeed you are. You dance very well."

He sighed. "But soon I will be far away and I shall have no dancing partner."

"I know," she agreed. "I'm beginning to think of that. I shall miss you greatly. I'm trying to lie to myself and not admit the loneliness I'll know after you've gone."

Chen reached out and took her hand in his. "We have a proverb in China which goes something like this: 'When a wise man traps a partridge and he expected a pheasant he tells himself that the partridge is the superior bird.' I think you and I have wasted enough time lamenting pheasants. Why don't we be wise and settle for partridges?"

She stared at him. "Are you saying what I think?"

"I'm asking you to marry me," Chen Li said simply. "I know now that I love you. I hope you might learn to love me in the same manner."

"I have always liked you, Chen," she said. "In fact you're closer to me than anyone I know, and except—" she halted, unable to say Henry's name.

"I understand," he said evenly. "And I shall also have a sense of loss deep in my heart. But all that is past. The love we are fortunate to have now is of this moment. Wouldn't we be foolish not to grasp it?"

"We would, indeed," she said, her eyes filling with happy tears.

There wasn't any time for elaborate plans. Henry and Han Li wanted the wedding to take place at Armitage House. But Chen refused, explaining to Flora that Han Li was still in mourning for her father. So it was arranged that a quiet ceremony would be held in a London chapel with Henry and Han Li present as attendants. Enid was also to be there as flower girl. They invited Jessica, Lady Madge Waring, and old Bradford Armitage as well.

Neither Jessica nor Bradford Armitage attended. The old man offered his declining health as an excuse and Jessica sent a cold rejection without an explanation. Lady Madge was on a visit to Paris and that eliminated her.

The afternoon of the wedding and the reception in the Trafalgar Restaurant's private suite afterward was a pleasant one. The ceremony, performed by an Anglican clergyman friend of Chen's, was dignified and lovely. Flora made a dainty bride in white satin and lace. Chen was handsome in cutaway coat and striped trousers. Henry and Han Li stood up for them.

In the restaurant a small group of friends gathered to celebrate the affair with a feast and champagne.

Old Mr. Sweeney was there dancing a lively mazurka to the violin music that added to the merriment. He vowed,

"I shall save every farthing and arrive in China to be god-parent to your first son!"

Chen laughingly accepted the offer. "We could not be more honored."

Enid was full of childish happiness at being reunited with Flora. She hugged her over and over again and spoke of her love for her. "I had always hoped you'd return to me and now that will never be," she said.

"I shall come for a visit," she promised.

The Burrs were there, and so was old Mr. Grossmith who whispered to her, "Did you invite Charles Dickens?"

"No. I thought it would be an imposition."

"Nonsense," the bookshop proprietor told her. "You should have. I'm positive he would have come."

Shanks came, remarkably neat and serious in his uniform as an officer in Mr. Booth's new Christian Army. And Dolly caught the bride's bouquet.

It was Henry who solemnly took Flora's hands in his and told her, "I know you're going to have the happiness you've always deserved."

"Thank you," she said, looking up at him with a small smile.

Later, Han Li, who had become more frail-looking over the years, drew her aside and whispered to her, "You are so fortunate. You were wise not to return to Armitage House. It is a house cursed with evil spirits."

Chapter Thirty-one

FLORA HAD never expected to return to China, much less return as the wife of Chen Li. But Canton seemed very familiar and good to her. The great house on the hill with its three courtyards and elegant furnishings was exactly as it was when Yenn Li had been the master. In a way it was a real homecoming.

Chen was a model husband. He combined the sensitivity and seriousness of his own race with the knowledge and social polish of the Western world. Their home quickly became the gathering place for the many European expatriates living there and Flora soon became the most popular hostess in Canton.

She loved the color and the clamor of the city with its beggars and bazaars, temples and pagodas. She also enjoyed the beauty of the countryside. There was a difference in the tone from England. Here she was overwhelmed by green—pine green, rice green, moss green, and the green of sea water. She admired the wisteria, the wild grape, and the white incense lilies bowing in the wind like polite white-frocked nuns.

Among the guests who often came to the house on the hill was David Forest. He was a tall, rugged, handsome man with a thick head of sandy hair. He wore clothes well and was one of the most eligible bachelors in the European community. He was in Canton as a representative of the United States government and so was given a good deal of deference.

He had been an officer of the Union Army in the Civil War that was still ravaging his home country and had been invalided out of the service only a few months before being sent to China as a government agent. Half-blind in his left eye (though there was nothing to indicate this) he suffered from severe headaches at times as a result of his injuries. David Forest was a close friend of Chen Li's, so he soon became a good friend of Flora's. Because he had no special business hours to keep he often dropped by in the afternoon for a gin and tonic and conversation.

It was during one of these afternoon visits that he began to ask her about her past. He said, "Chen tells me you have had an extremely interesting life. I'd like to hear about it."

They were seated in wicker chairs in the first courtyard, which she had come to use chiefly for entertaining because she admired the fountain there. She gave the tall young American an amused look. "Not interesting by your standards. I have never been in a battle."

"War is not interesting," David Forest said. "It is like being in a charnel house with the bodies being piled up by a mad butcher."

She raised her eyebrows. "I thought men liked the excitement, challenge, and chance to show bravery offered by war."

"Those who expect those things are soon disillusioned. War is a rotten business and I pray that my country will soon be done with it."

"I hope so, too," she said.

He stared at her. "But you didn't answer my question. What about your interesting life?"

"It hasn't been all that exciting, though I have met Charles Dickens."

"Dickens!" he exclaimed. "A favorite author of mine. Tell me how you met him."

She told him how she'd taken the position at the mental hospital with Dr. Storch, eventually learning of the horrors that existed there. She explained how she'd gotten Dickens interested in the scandalous situation and the events that had followed.

"Oates went to prison for a long term," she said. "Dr. Storch died a few months later."

"I call that a most thrilling experience," David Forest said enthusiastically.

"I have had others, but now I'm content to settle down in the calm atmosphere of China."

"It isn't all that calm," the young American warned her.

"No?"

"No," he said. "There are gambling dens in the city, which can be dangerous to enter, and outside the city there are wandering groups of bandits in the hills."

"Bandits?"

"Definitely. There have been a number of robberies and murders. You have not heard about it because you've been away."

"This must be a fairly recent development. Is there nothing to be done?"

"Most of the merchants take guards with them when they have to make journeys into the interior."

"Chen has not mentioned this to me."

David Forest smiled. "He is a considerate husband. He does not want to worry you."

"I must discuss it with him," she said.

"The risk for him is small since he seldom leaves Canton," David said. "I didn't mean to upset you."

"I'm grateful to you for telling me," she said. "I do not want to be a protected wife who knows nothing of what is going on in the world outside."

"A good deal is going on," David said soberly. "I'm having a difficult time getting the supplies I'm able to round up through the Rebel blockade safely."

"Is there no end to the war in sight?"

"Not yet. But one continues to hope." Changing the subject, he said, "I understand that when Yenn Li was alive his daughter lived here with him. She was a great beauty, they say."

"She still is," Flora said. "She married Henry Armitage and lives in England, but her health has suffered in the British climate."

"I'm from Boston," David Forest said. "Have you heard of it?"

"Certainly. It is the center of culture in your country," she said. "Charles Dickens has often lectured there."

"That is so. I saw him once, from a distance. I was coming down Beacon Street and rounded the corner of Tremont in time to see him leaving the Parker House. He was stepping into his carriage. A man on the street near me tapped my shoulder and said, 'There goes the finest writer of this century, Charles Dickens.' I watched with more interest then and caught a good look at him as the carriage went by. He had a thoughtful, rather noble, face."

"I know of no other living author I more admire," she said. "And I like him as a person."

"He surely was kind to you." Then with a twinkle in his eyes, he added, "But that would not be hard for him. You are a charming person."

She shook her head. "Not really."

"I disagree," he said. "You are the toast of Canton. And if I weren't a one-eyed Jack I'd be wishing that I had met you before Chen. I never thought much of English women but you have won me over."

"You must have met many English girls here. You are very popular. You can have your pick."

"None of them are like you."

She laughed. "You say that because you know I'm safely married and not a threat to your bachelorhood."

"Not at all," he told her. "I'd gladly sacrifice my single state for you."

"I will be on the lookout to find you a suitable young woman," she promised.

"Matchmaking!" he groaned. "It never does work out." He drained his glass and got up. "I must get back to the city. Thank you for another pleasant interlude."

She rose to see him out. "You are always welcome in the house of Chen Li."

He nodded. "I know that. But it is you who make my visits worthwhile."

When Chen Li and Flora finished the evening meal they often lingered over their teacups. They had much to discuss and were always glad to be reunited after the separation of the day. On this particular evening after her discussion with David she brought up the subject of the bandits.

"David Forest tells me there are bandits in the hills outside Canton," she said.

Chen made a mild gesture with his left hand. "But there have always been bandits out there."

"He says it has been more dangerous lately."

"Perhaps," Chen said. "I would not know. I pay little attention to such things."

"You should. If you travel I shall worry about you."

Chen Li smiled. "That bolsters my feeling of importance, but at the same time it makes me unhappy that you should worry about me. I believe that our futures are predestined. Our lives will take the appointed turns, so to worry about what will happen is futile."

"I wish I could trust myself that completely to fate," she said.

Her husband told her, "My dear, you have nothing to say about it if my theory is correct. My life will follow its pattern in the great plan of things and so will yours. No amount of concern will change either of our paths."

Flora gave him a gentle reproving look. "You always manage to use your native philosophy to prove me wrong. It isn't fair. I'm not one of your placid countrymen, I'm a neurotic English-woman!"

"And I wouldn't wish you a hair different," he said across the table.

"Are you truly happy in our marriage?" she asked plaintively.

He chuckled. "When I am not you will know soon enough. I will stock the second courtyard with concubines!" he said teasingly, knowing she had a horror of the practice.

In August, on the seventh day of the seventh moon, they held a great party to celebrate the Spinning Maid Day. Everyone in the European colony attended, as well as many of Chen's Chinese friends. The tables groaned with golden needles and shrimp cushions, red stewed rabbit, partridge, and moon cakes among numerous delicacies.

A Chinese orchestra provided native music during the meal and afterward a German orchestra provided music for waltzing, mazurkas, and other dances. It was a subtle blending of the East and West. David Forest in dinner jacket was one of the stars of the occasion.

Towards the end of the evening Flora and her husband were able to relax a little and spend some time with the tall American. Most of their guests had left and the few who remained to dance or listen to the music while they had final drinks were close friends.

Seated in the star-lit first courtyard David asked Chen, "Just what is this Celebration of the Spinning Maid all about? We've been celebrating all evening and I don't know why."

Chen Li smiled. "It deals with a figure familiar in your own American folklore, the cowboy."

"I didn't know you had cowboys in China," David said.

"Well, a slightly different sort of cowboy," Chen said. "The legend concerns a boy who lived long ago in China and had a water cow as a pet. When the animal finished pulling his plow he would lead her to the greenest pastures where there was also plenty of water. He always talked to the animal and one day the cow replied, 'Lead me to the river, master. There you will find a cure for loneliness.' And he did."

David laughed. "There were plenty of cows on my grandfather's farm but none of them talked to me."

Chen continued, "They went to the river and found

seven dazzling beauties there swimming in the moonlight. The cow said, 'These are heavenly princesses. The six bathing in a group are all lovely, but the one bathing by herself is the most wonderful of all. She has the gift of spinning fleecy clouds to hide heavenly secrets from earth.' "

Flora gave David a delighted glance. "Now you begin to see how it all fits in."

He nodded. "The spinning maid. Go on, Chen."

"The cow told the youth, 'If you want to wed this princess and be lonely no more, hide the pink robe on yonder rock. Hide it and then she cannot ride back to heaven on her crane.' The cowboy quickly hid the robe and when the other six beauties rode back to heaven, the loveliest princess was left searching for her robe. She was very sad but not for long. The cowboy joined her and she fell in love with him. She consented to stay on earth and marry him."

"Is that the end of the story?" David asked.

Chen shook his head. "No. They lived happily for seven years. But trouble was brewing. No clouds floated in the sky to hide the heavenly doings from man. The Empress of Heaven sent a message demanding the princess return to her duties. When the cowboy came home that evening the princess was gone. Of course he turned to his pet cow and told her his troubles.

"The cow told the youth not to grieve. She said, 'I shall die very soon. When I do, wrap yourself in my hide and together we shall join the Spinning Maid in heaven.' And several days later the cow did die. The youth did as he'd been told. In his beloved cow's hide he journeyed up to the Spinning Maid's palace. She was delighted to see him and they sang and danced and feasted. But as they made merry the spinning wheel lay idle once again. The Sky Empress was enraged. In a flash she drew a line across the sky, which became the Milky Way, and cut the heavens in two. On one side she placed the spinning maid who became the star Vega and on the other the cowboy, the star Altar. Since the spinning maid could not do her duty when the cowboy was around they had to be separated."

Flora protested. "That is a sad ending."

Chen smiled at his wife. "Not the end," he said. "The

399

cruel separation of the two brought criticism from all corners of the sky. And the Emperor of Heaven asked his Empress to be merciful. 'Let the two sweethearts meet at least once a year,' he suggested. After a little the Empress agreed. But there had to be a bridge for the Spinning Maid to cross the Milky Way and meet her cowboy. The magpies heard about the need and flew to heaven where each magpie grasped the feathers of another in its firm bill and made a bridge for the Spinning Maid to run across to her cowboy every Seventh Day of the Seventh Moon!"

"You see," David Forest told Flora, "Chen gave you your happy ending after all. As he always will." He rose to leave. "Thank you both for your gracious hospitality and forgive me for envying the fine marriage you have just a little."

"Your presence always honors my house, good friend," Chen told him.

Flora smiled at the tall American. "I'm still searching for the right English girl for you."

When the last of the guests had gone and Chen had kissed her good night she tried to sleep. But she couldn't. She blamed the excitement of the party but deep in her heart she knew it was more than that. This night had in a way been an expression of their great happiness together. She had found a placid harbor in the love of Chen Li which she had never hoped for.

Chen knew that Henry Armitage had been first in her heart for a long while, just as Chen had thought of no one except the lovely Han Li. But in his wisdom he had surmounted all that and they had worked out an almost perfect marriage. So perfect in contrast to the loneliness she'd known in London she feared that it could not last. Something would have to spoil it.

But why? Chen believed in the vagaries of fate. Nature ordains and man complains was a theory which made any worries on his part seem pointless to him. He'd tried to make her embrace the same philosophy but she was not sure that she could manage it. There were times when she became terribly frightened.

This fear brought back memories of Armitage House.

And that in turn made her wonder about those who still lived there. She had not had a letter from Dolly in a long while and so was out of touch with the happenings at the house. The mails had been slow of late, which left her without news for months. So much could happen in only a day. What about Henry and Han Li? She knew they dearly loved each other but was the house, the house that Han Li had whispered about in fear, destroying their love?

Usually when morning came she scoffed at the fears of the night. But on the morning following the party she still felt deeply distressed. Distressed without knowing the reason why. She had taken the old amah who'd helped with Enid in her employ and now she turned to her for help.

"Do you know of a reliable soothsayer?" she asked.

"In the street of the Gray Rat there lives an ancient master. He can see all the future."

"Would you take me to him?"

The amah shrugged. "Do you wish to know what lies ahead, mistress?"

"Yes."

"Most people would prefer it otherwise. But if it is your wish I can take you to the old man this afternoon."

So it came about that Englishwoman, Flora Bain, who ought to have been completely without superstition, found herself following the old woman through the slums of Canton. Beggars spied Flora and came up and pulled at her clothing begging alms. She tossed some coins to them and when they kept following her had to plead with the amah to shout out that she had no more coins.

The soothsayer lived in the rear of a hovel owned by his daughter, a sour-looking woman of middle age. Flora was shown into the dark cavelike room smelling of pungent spices. She discovered a very old man with a long white beard and black mandarin hat sitting cross-legged at a crystal ball. He motioned for her to sit on the floor opposite him.

She passed over a number of silver coins to him as the amah had suggested. He took the coins, placing them somewhere in the depths of his robe. Then he gazed into the crystal with his watery blue eyes and concentrated for a long moment.

"You are the wife of Chen Li?" he said at last.

"Yes."

"You have come to learn the future."

"I have."

He passed a thin hand over the crystal ball. "I see signs of much happiness in the crystal."

She nodded. "We are very happy."

"Your happiness will soon be more complete."

"What do you mean?"

The old soothsayer eyed her gravely. "I see the birth of a son."

"Are you certain?"

"I always know," the old man said.

It was not what she'd expected to hear but it filled her with joy. The thought of presenting Chen Li with a son was very satisfying. She recalled old Mr. Sweeney's promise that he would come to China to be godfather for their first son. If the prediction became a fact she would ask Chen to send the old man money for passage. She missed him as she missed other of her friends in England.

She asked, "What else do you see in the crystal?"

The bearded ancient stared at the glass ball again. Then he said, "I see a dragon."

This puzzled her. "A dragon? What can that mean?"

The old man shrugged. "The dragon is a threat and a destroyer. I cannot tell you more."

"But you must!" she pleaded.

"The crystal has clouded."

It was impossible to get more information from him. So she left the old man and the small cavelike room to rejoin the amah. It had been a strangely upsetting experience. She'd been both pleased and frightened by the seer's prediction. Worst of all, she had a feeling he'd seen more in the crystal than he'd wanted to tell her. He had deliberately held back something from her.

Later, on an afternoon when she and David were seated in the courtyard again, she told him all about the incident.

"You mustn't tell Chen I consulted a fortune teller. He would be angry."

"You may depend on me."

"I gained nothing," she said. "The fortune only upset me."

"Aren't you happy at the prospect of having a son?"

She smiled. "I will be if it comes true."

"Make me a promise."

"What?"

"Call him David."

She stared at him. "Are you serious?"

"Yes," he said. "I never expect to have a son, or a daughter for that matter. Most of my life is probably used up now."

"You're not thirty yet!" she chided him.

"I still say that most of my life is gone. I'm a soldier of fortune. Few of us live to be old men. None of us want to."

She smiled. "You're the most attractive man in Canton. You are bound to marry."

"The most attractive one-eyed man," he corrected her.

"I still say the girls here won't allow you to be a bachelor long," she joked.

"And I say, if you have a boy call him David."

"Why not? But it must be with the approval of Chen Li."

"Of course," David Forest said, taking another sip of his drink. "That is most important."

She sighed. "The thing which worried me was the old man's reference to a dragon as a destroyer. He made me afraid that either Chen or I might be going to succumb to some dread fever or the like. Or perhaps the boy if we have him."

"You mustn't pay too much attention to those old soothsayers," David told her. "They have to say something to mystify you and perhaps bring you back."

His words eased her worrying a little. "You could be right," she agreed. "He may have said that to bait my return." She gave a deep sigh of relief. "I'm so glad I confided in you. You have no idea how dependent I have become on you and your advice."

His eyes met hers. "If only you were completely dependent on me," he said. "But that is a dream."

One evening at dusk a few weeks later when she knew she was going to have a child she told Chen Li part of the conversation she'd had with David. She was careful to omit the part about her seeing the fortune teller but she did tell him of David's request.

Chen was standing with his arm around her. In a delighted voice, he said, "David wants our child named after him if it should be a son?"

"Yes. But only if you agree. You may want to name our son after yourself."

"No. I do not want your son and mine to have a Chinese name, at least not for his Christian name. I can think of none better than David."

"We must tell him," she smiled. "And then I'll probably disappoint you both by having a girl."

"Your girl baby would be like the most priceless jade to me," Chen assured her.

"I have one request," she said.

"You need but name it!"

"At times I'm lonesome for England. I would like to have one of my English friends here when the baby is born. He expressed himself as wishing to act as godfather to our child. But he is a poor man and does not have the money for the journey here and back."

"I'm a man rich in so many things, including you," Chen Li said. "I shall send your friend the passage money by the next mail. As I remember it was old Mr. Sweeney who expressed the wish."

"Yes," she said. "He was so good to me when I was lonely. And it was he who saw that I met Charles Dickens. It all seems so long ago," she said dreamily.

"In a way it is," he agreed.

"I wish there would be some word from England," she worried. "I have not heard from Dolly in an age."

"There is a ship due from Southampton before the

week is out," Chen Li said. "There should be a quantity of mail aboard, and undoubtedly the letters you are expecting."

"I hope so."

Chen Li, as he so often did, proved to be right. She did receive letters from both Dolly and Han Li in the mail. She read extracts from them to Chen Li as they sat together in the courtyard.

"Dolly is married. She has left Armitage House and married Shanks. She's also joined the Salvation Army and is working with him in a new mission."

"It is what she wanted," Chen said.

"Now what does Han Li have to tell us?"

"She still complains of poor health and I can read between the lines. I'm certain Jessica is treating her as cruelly as she dares."

Chen lost his usual calm. "I trust not."

"I know Jessica," she said. "She's in love with Henry. Anyone married to her brother she automatically hates in a mad kind of way."

"Han Li would be no match for that sort of hatred," he worried.

"That is what terrifies me," she sighed. "And there is something else?"

"What?"

"The ghosts. You know I've told you how the ghost of Lily is said to haunt that old house. No one really knows for sure how she came to her death. Many doubt she was a suicide as was reported. So the story goes that her spirit still returns. I know. I have seen the ghost."

Chen frowned. "You must not dwell on such things."

"I do not think Han Li will ever be happy in that house. Henry's first wife wasn't and her life ended when she died in childbirth."

He said, "Han Li has had no children."

"Luckily she has Enid to take care of."

"That's true," he agreed.

She put down the letter. "When our child is old enough we must return to England and see if there is not something we can do for Han Li. You could talk to Henry and so will I. Make him understand that Han Li needs more than average protection in that house."

Chen smiled at her. "In a year or possibly a year and a half we can sail back to England."

It was something to dream about during the months of her pregnancy. For some reason she could not understand as her time drew near she became less happy in her surroundings. The foreign atmosphere seemed to press in on her, becoming almost a threat. There were no parties now and David Forest was away on business, so she was very much left with the Chinese for company.

She learned that old Mr. Sweeney had already left England. Now she counted the days until he would arrive. Having him there would be a link with home. It wasn't that her love for Chen had declined in any way but merely that he didn't understand her feelings. China was his home despite his British education. He was able to easily adapt to either civilization. She had thought she could also, but now she wasn't so certain.

At last the great day arrived. The ship bearing Mr. Sweeney docked in Canton. Chen made a special trip to bring him to the house on the hill. She watched from an upper window as the old man sprang jauntily out of the rickshaw with his bag in hand. It seemed he would go on forever and that he could adapt to anything.

She went down to greet him in the doorway and he threw his arms around her. "I've come in time for the important event," he said happily. "And I've brought Charles Dickens' latest book with me."

"So good!" she exlaimed amid happy tears.

Chen stood smiling at them in the background. "Now," he said, "we can proceed with the birth of my son."

She smiled at him wanly. "It will be a week or two yet."

"We can be patient," Chen Li said, "now that Mr. Sweeney is here."

The old man chuckled and nodded. "I'll while the days away for you Flora by reading aloud Charles Dickens *Our Mutual Friend*. It may be the best yet!"

Chapter Thirty-two

FLORA KNEW her time was near. Mr. Sweeney had been sitting with her in the first courtyard reading from *Our Mutual Friend* when the thunderstorm drove them inside. She sat in the living room with the old man, watching the angry lightning flash against suddenly dark clouds, and hearing the rumble of thunder ominously close. Then the raindrops came down like furies!

Mr. Sweeney stood by the window. "A bad storm," he said.

"They can be bad here," she agreed.

"When will Chen return?"

"He should be home tonight. But the storm could keep him late. Perhaps it won't last long since it's so intense," she said hopefully.

"It's very black out," the old man said. The lightning and thunder were coming at regular intervals. The rain would fall in a deluge, stop, and then begin over again. Then he came back and sat near her. "We haven't seen Mr. Forest too often since his return."

"No. I think he hesitates to intrude on me. He feels I'm not well."

"And you're not."

"I wish the baby would come," she said with a small moan, "and get it over with."

"My mother had nine of us. And she outlived all but three. I'm the oldest living."

The thunder came again with a smaller flash of lightning accompanying it. When it ended Mr. Sweeney said, "Chen has asked me to consider taking a clerking job here with him. Wants me to help with the English accounts."

"Why don't you? It's so good to have you here."

"I think I'll try it. If I can manage, he can keep me on. I don't want him just making a job for me."

"Chen is very wealthy," she told him. "Even though he is in partnership with the Armitage family I think he has much more money from his own family. He can afford to do what he wants."

"I still will have to be useful if I stay on. You understand?"

"Of course I do."

He smiled at her. "It was a lucky night you came to Mrs. Lingley's boarding house and we met."

"I wonder if she still uses that ear trumpet?" Flora asked, laughing at the memory. They talked some more about the experiences they'd had in London. Gradually the storm eased and the sky lightened. Flora sat up until late hoping that Chen Li would get home that evening as he'd planned. The trip from the nearby city shouldn't have taken more than two days so it had to be the storm which had held him up.

At last she rose. "I guess I'd better go to bed. I don't think Chen will return tonight. It's far too late now."

"I was thinking the same thing," Mr. Sweeney said. "He'll likely arrive first thing in the morning."

She had great difficulty in sleeping that night. The storm should have cleared the air but somehow it hadn't. She tossed restlessly and dreamt of Chen. Then she had a fantastic nightmare in which a huge, crimson dragon came up the hill to the house and crashed down the surrounding walls as it advanced. It came crawling across the lawn, a monstrous, loathsome reptile. Next it began to push down the house with its sheer weight. She retreated to the court-yard and the dragon's head appeared above her, its red forked tongue flashing.

She awoke from her dream with a tortured scream which brought the ancient amah running into the room to see if she were needed.

Flora waved her away. "It is all right," she said. "Only a dream." But the memory of it had left her trembling.

Before dawn she managed to get a little sleep. Later she was awakened by the sound of excited Chinese voices down below. She got up quickly, put on her dressing gown, and smoothed back her hair. Then she went down-stairs to see what the commotion was about.

Old Mr. Sweeney was standing by helplessly. He gave her a despairing wave. "They won't say a word to me in English."

Flora saw that one of the men who'd arrived and was causing much of the commotion was a senior assistant in her husband's office who spoke English. She went directly over to him. "What is the matter, Mr. Wong?"

The several others who had been jabbering around him fell back in silence. Stoical Mr. Wong gazed at her with no hint of expression on his broad face. "I am the bearer of bad news, Mrs. Li."

She swallowed nervously. "What sort of bad news?" And all the while she was telling herself not to believe that this was anything really important. It couldn't be!

Mr. Sweeney had come up beside her with a frown on his round face. He addressed himself to Mr. Wong. "What have you come to tell us?" he asked.

Mr. Wong rubbed his hands together uneasily. "It is a great tragedy," he said. "A great tragedy for us all. I have to inform you, Mrs. Li, that your husband is dead."

She gasped. "Chen dead? No! I don't believe it!" She stood there wide-eyed and stunned, swaying a trifle from shock.

Mr. Sweeney had a protective arm around her. "Easy now." And he asked Mr. Wong to tell what happened.

"The bandits!" Mr. Wong said. "We have been warned but now it is worse. They were waiting for the caravan of goods. Chen Li was one of the first to fall in the ambush."

She was staring at the messenger of bad tidings. "When?" she asked in a low voice which she didn't think of as belonging to her.

"Early yesterday," Mr. Wong said. "One of the bearers managed to escape and brought us the news this morning. He did not dare begin to find his way back until nightfall. He came all the way in the storm."

She touched the back of her hand to her forehead, trying to keep her emotions under control, desperately wanting not to shame Chen in any way. She closed her eyes and moaned, "Get me David Forest."

Mr. Sweeney shouted in nervous anger. "You heard her! Get the American!"

Mr. Wong stared at him. "You do not understand."

She opened her eyes and looked into the stolid, yellow face. "What do I not understand?"

"The American. David Forest. He was with your husband."

"David was with Chen?"

"Yes. He knew the danger presented by the trip and insisted on accompanying him for protection."

"Then where is David now?" she demanded, thinking she was being tortured endlessly.

"I am sorry," the man said. "Mr. Forest is also dead. None of them escaped except the bearer."

The double tragedy was more than even her sternest efforts could cope with. She felt the darkness press in around her as she collapsed in Mr. Sweeney's arms.

From then on it was all darkness and pain. She screamed and tossed in a long agony that went on without cessation. She was vaguely conscious of voices directed at her and people moving about her bed but she really didn't take in anything. She had a dreadful fever and there were the pains. Pains such as she'd never experienced before.

Then she began to have a series of weird dreams. Dreams in which she was back in England fighting to free herself from the house of Mrs. Fernald. At another moment she would be back in the garden of the mental hospital with the blond Martin attempting to throttle her. And there was the pond! The pond with the ghost of Lily standing silently by it.

She opened her eyes, staring dully at the ceiling. It was daylight and she was in her bed. Moreover she was drenched with perspiration, almost too weak to move. She thought she heard a door open and looked to see Mr. Sweeney and the European doctor who lived in the other part of the city enter the room. She thought the big dark-haired man was a German. He had arrived in one of the great sailing ships and had decided to remain and set up a practice among the many Europeans living in Canton.

She gave a deep sigh as she looked up into the inquiring faces of the two men bending over her. She wanted to speak but she didn't know what she wanted to say.

Mr. Sweeney's face was bright with hope. "She's awake. Her eyes are open. She's going to live."

"Maybe," the doctor said in his halting English. "But first we must be sure the fever has run its course."

She made a great effort to say, "Sweeney!"

"That's me!" the bald man said happily and took one of her perspiring hands in his. "Just you keep trying and you'll be all right."

She sank back into unconsciousness once again. Next time when she awoke the wrinkled amah was sitting at her bedside keeping watch. It was after dark, as there were candles burning on her bedside table. She felt strangely remote to the room around her. It was almost as if she were floating in space. Greatly relaxed and floating easily through a limitless area.

The old woman saw her stir in the bed and open her eyes. At once she hurried out of the room. A few minutes later she returned with Mr. Sweeney.

"Flora! So you've finally come out of it!"

She stared up at him. His voice seemed strangely distant. "How long?"

"Weeks."

Her next question was, "My child?"

He shook his head. "I'm sorry," he said.

She closed her eyes. So even that small hope of keeping a part of Chen had been taken from her. China had seemed to give her everything, then in the end she had instead been stripped of all she'd loved.

The night marked the beginning of her recovery. It also marked a strange change in her way of thinking. She wanted to turn her back on everything Chinese. As soon as she was well enough she called in Mr. Wong and asked him to offer her share of the export business to whatever individual or syndicate wished to buy it. She also put up her house for sale.

Mr. Sweeney argued with her. "Are you certain you want to sell this house? There may be a time you'll want to return to it. You and Chen Li were happy here."

"When I leave Canton I never wish to see it again," she said in a bitter voice.

"Time often changes our feelings."

"Never in this case. I want to get away and not remember any of it."

"Whatever you think best."

During those days of her convalescence he was a pillar of support. She often thought it must have been providence that had made her send for him to join her in China. And that set her thinking about Chen's theories that fate decided it all and the individual was really powerless to change anything.

Her love for Chen had not dimmed. Her hatred was reserved for the China which had taken him from her. She hurried ahead with the sale of the business and the house. Then she booked passage for herself and Mr. Sweeney on the next sailing to Southampton.

She had written Henry and Han Li about Chen's death. Now she sent a second letter telling them that she would be returning to England on the *Prince George* and the approximate date of her arrival. She did not know what her plans would be but she hoped that she would be able

412

to make a short visit to Armitage House and talk with Henry and Han Li.

The voyage back to England was uneventful except for a single bad storm as they neared the Cape of Good Hope. But the staunch ship weathered it all and by the time they left the Canary Islands on the last lap of their trip the sea was calm and pleasant.

She and Mr. Sweeney often sat out in deck chairs when the weather was mild. On one of these afternoons as they neared England she began to discuss her future plans.

"Chen has left me a very wealthy woman," she told him. "I can scarcely go back to working in Mr. Grossmith's bookshop and living with the Burrs. Yet I want to do something useful with my life and money."

"You are young, Flora. I predict you will marry again. There has to be a great deal of happiness still ahead for you."

"Just now I don't think so."

"Give yourself some time," he urged her.

She suddenly brightened. "There is one thing I can do! Help Mr. Booth with his new Salvation Army. When I was in need he helped me. I shall have no trouble getting advice. Dolly and Shanks are working with the new army. They will tell me where money is needed most to promote it."

"Very good," Mr. Sweeney said. "And at the same time it will offer you an interest."

She smiled at him. "What about you?"

He shrugged. "I shall make out. I don't know whether my post at the drygoods shop will be open to me but if not I'll find something else."

"Do you think I'll have you looking for employment and perhaps winding up in the workhouse ward? You are no longer young, Mr. Sweeney."

"I can still look after myself," he said with assurance.

Flora glanced across at the old man bundled in blankets in his deck chair. "You don't think I'm going to let a valuable person like you get away. I want you to work for me."

"For you? In what capacity?"

"Call it companion and advisor. I shall have to have someone to assist me in my charity work and in setting up a home for myself in London. I need you, Mr. Sweeney. Don't desert me."

His round face lit up. "I have never been one to desert a lady in distress. You can count on me, Flora, as long as you need me."

"That could be a very long while," she warned him.

The *Prince George* docked in the very early morning. An hour later Flora and Mr. Sweeney left the ship, their luggage to follow soon. As they walked up the wharf a familiar figure came down to greet them. It was Henry Armitage in top hat, dark coat, and suit.

He took Flora in his arms. "My dear Flora," he said. "You have my deepest sympathy."

"I know," she said. "How did you manage to be here so soon?"

"I took lodgings here for the night," Henry said. "I had heard the ship was to dock this morning."

"It is so good of you," she said.

"The very least I could do." He turned and shook hands with Mr. Sweeney who had been standing discreetly a step or two behind them.

"I'm sure Chen's death proved a dreadful shock for Han Li," Flora said.

"It did," he said quietly. "There is a small inn just up the hill. Why don't we go there for tea and a bit of food while your luggage is being landed."

They reached the inn and took a table in the nearly empty dining room. As Henry ordered for them she had a chance to study him more closely. She saw that his face was lined much more deeply than it had been and he looked pale.

She asked him, "Have you been ill? You don't look well."

"I have been rather unwell lately," he admitted. "But I must say that you have recovered nicely from your own illness. The long sea voyage certainly must have done you good."

"Nothing like it," old Mr. Sweeney said. "I feel like a new man."

Flora nodded. "It *was* good for us. And how is Han Li's health?"

Henry's face was solemn. He took a deep breath. "I've been saving this until we reached here," he confessed. "I'm sorry to have to tell you that Han Li is dead."

"Dead!" she gasped.

"Yes. It happened not too long after I received your letter telling me of Chen's murder by bandits."

"What happened to her?"

"She took her own life."

"Took her own life!"

"Yes. She had been in a deep depression. The news of Chen's murder seemed to be the last straw. It was less than a week after she received the news that she killed herself."

Flora sat back in her chair weakly. "I feel guilty."

"Not at all!" Henry protested.

"How can you blame yourself?" Mr. Sweeney said. "You could not keep the news from her. She would never have forgiven you if you'd tried."

Flora listened to them and realized that they were right. No matter how badly she felt she could not reasonably blame herself for the suicide. The seeds of self-destruction had already been in the girl before she'd learned of Chen's death.

"How did she take her life?"

His eyes met hers. "The pond."

"The pond!"

"Yes."

"Han Li drowned herself in the same way that Lily did."

"Yes. I fear she must have gotten the idea from hearing the story of Lily's tragic death. It was an easy way for her."

"Horrible!" Flora said. "Horrible!"

"It was a bad time for all of us," Henry said. "Especially for Enid. She is fourteen now, you know. Old enough to be aware of everything. She had become very close to Han Li."

"I know that," Flora said.

"Enid is still not herself. I'm worried about her," Henry went on. "She is very much alone now. I can't give her the time I should."

"And Jessica?"

He grimaced. "You know Jessica. She has never been fond of Enid."

"I know," she said unhappily.

"Enid talks of no one but you."

She smiled sadly. "Poor dear!"

"In a way that is why I am here today," he went on. "I'd have come in any case. But I was determined to meet you for a selfish reason of my own. Enid needs you badly. I want you to visit with us at Armitage House for a little and see if you can bring her out of her depression."

Flora hesitated. "I don't mind calling by but I had no plan to stay with you. Mr. Sweeney is now my companion and advisor and I was planning to take rooms in some London hotel until I had time to find a house."

"You and Mr. Sweeney are both welcome at Armitage House," Henry said. "There is plenty of room for you. I have a carriage here at the livery stable near the wharf. We can load on your things as soon as they're on the dock."

She turned to Mr. Sweeney. "What do you think?"

"It is up to you, Flora. I imagine the child does need you."

She sighed. "Very well," she told Henry. "I'll be your guest along with Mr. Sweeney, but we can only stay with you a few days. Just so I have a chance to brighten Enid some."

"That is all I ask."

After they finished their lunch, Henry had the carriage sent around. They drove back to the docks to pick up their baggage and began the drive to Armitage House.

Along the way as she sat close to Henry in the carriage she asked him some of the questions which were troubling her. "About Han Li's suicide, had she talked of taking her life?"

"No."

"I can't think of Han Li as a suicide. She wasn't that sort of person."

"She had been very unhappy."

"Because of Jessica?"

"That and many other things," he said with difficulty. "As an example she'd taken a strong dislike to the house."

"I can understand that."

"I think it was knowing about Lily's suicide and the fact that Lily's ghost had been said to haunt the house that upset her."

"It upset me."

"But you must allow for servants' talk. The illiterate love to talk of ghosts and the like. That doesn't mean the story is true."

She said quietly, "I saw the ghost."

"You did?"

"Yes."

"Probably, because like Han Li, you heard the ghost story, you mistook the first shadow you saw afterward for the phantom."

"I'm not that easily impressed," she said.

"Han Li became very nervous. She insisted on sleeping with a lamp on in her room. She was very insistent about it."

"What about the bolts for inside the doors? Did you install them?"

"No," he said, with a look of guilt on his face.

"I suggested it before I left," she reminded him. "That was years ago."

"I discussed it with Jessica and she was against bolts on the doors."

"Brave Jessica!" she said sarcastically. "Why did you allow her to rule you?"

"She was in charge of the house. Han Li never felt equal to taking over management of the household affairs. So Jessica has been the one with responsibility."

Flora couldn't resist asking, "Do you suppose she had any responsibility in Han Li's suicide?"

"What?" He demanded incredulously.

"I'm serious."

"You're asking me if my sister might not have been responsible for Han Li's death? That's ridiculous. Han Li did exactly what Lily did. She threw herself in the pond and drowned."

"Some people questioned that Lily took her own life."

"Well, it didn't reach my ears," he replied.

"You must have closed your mind to it. Just as you closed your mind to the suggestion of bolts on the doors. I fear you were negligent in protecting your lovely wife. Han Li may have died because of your failure to protect her."

She did not mention her other fear—that he might have been responsible for Han Li's death. The lovely Chinese wife he'd brought to Armitage House had died in exactly the same fashion as Lily. There were people who still avoided Henry because they felt he'd been Lily's killer.

Flora did not believe this nor did she ever want to believe it. Motives? To be rid of a sick wife could always be a motive to a man of violence.

In a carefully controlled voice she asked, "Does Lady Madge Waring still live in the adjoining house?"

He looked faintly surprised by her question. "Yes. She is still staying on there."

"Do you see her often?"

"Quite often. After all, we are neighbors."

"Of course."

"You make it sound a crime."

"Sorry. I didn't mean to."

"Lady Madge and I have been friends since childhood. She has been very lonely since her husband's death."

"I would expect so. Do she and Jessica get along any better?"

Henry said bitterly. "Jessica does not get on well with anyone. Not even with my father."

"How is your father?" she said. "I intended to ask you about him earlier."

"He is older and somewhat more feeble, but he still gets around fairly well. His mind is as clear as ever. He has also been asking to see you."

She glanced across at the other seat in the dark interior of the carriage. Mr. Sweeney was sound asleep there. The motion of the vehicle and the near darkness had lulled him off.

She said, "Poor Mr. Sweeney!"

Henry said, "He has come to mean a great deal to you."

"Like an uncle or a grandfather. He is a good man."

"How fortunate that he was in China when you lost Chen."

"Yes. He came to be godfather to my child," she said in a small, sad voice.

"You lost the child as well," Henry said. "I am sorry."

"Chen would have liked it to have lived."

"Of course," Henry said. "Have you kept any links with Canton? I know you've sold the business. What about your home there?"

"I sold it as well."

"Then you're not planning to return."

She shook her head. "No. All that I loved in China is lost to me. There is nothing to return for."

"I'm sorry it ended as it did."

Flora smiled. "If Chen were here he would tell you that it was what was meant to be." She glanced out the side window. "We're at the gates of Armitage House already!"

"Yes," Henry said. "We have arrived."

The carriage rolled in the gravel roadway to the ancient mansion and she saw its familiar stone walls once again. They passed the pond with its placid green surface. Fear shot through her as she recalled the last whispered words of Han Li about the evil spirits which inhabited the old house.

Chapter Thirty-three

A SHARP cry came eerily out of the darkness somewhere and woke her. She sat up in bed, waiting to see if it would come again. It had been as mad and terrifying as any she'd heard in the past. In fact it had been exactly like those phantom cries she'd heard when she'd first arrived at Armitage House as governess.

All was silence now. At her own request she had been installed in the same room she'd used before. Mr. Sweeney had been given a less impressive room down the corridor not too far from her. She wondered if he'd heard the cry. She must check with him in the morning.

Her greeting at Armitage House had been a warm one, except for Jessica. She had not appeared until it was time to be seated at the dinner table, and when she had shown herself her manner had been cool and formal. Flora thought the years had taken their toll too heavily from the auburn-haired beauty. She looked much older and more irritable.

In contrast, Bradford Armitage had not seemed to

change at all. And he had been very kindly in his reception of her. But it was Enid who had undergone the most striking transformation. She was much taller now, and more the young lady.

But Enid was not in as happy a state mentally as she seemed to be physically. As soon as she'd greeted Flora she'd begun to cry and lament the death of Han Li. Flora saw that the girl had been badly shaken by this second suicide at the house within a few years. She'd attempted to offer her some sort of comfort.

And now there were weird screams echoing through the great stone house once again. They probably had never ceased. Han Li had spoken bitterly of the evil spirits that she felt were destroying her happiness. What had she seen and heard that had so depressed her?

Flora knew that she could not remain long at Armitage House since she could not bear its baleful atmosphere. She did not want to be caught up in any more tragedies here, and she felt unless there was a change the pattern of tragedy was due to be repeated.

Staring into the shadows she watched for any hint of the ghost. The phantom usually revealed itself after the cries were heard. She recalled seeing the handle of her door turn, creaking slowly open, then the ghost had appeared. She prayed that nothing of that sort would happen on her first night of her return visit.

Why had she allowed herself to be talked into returning? It was chiefly because of Enid. She had learned of the girl's upset state and had wanted to help her. And also she had felt some sympathy for Henry. Whether she had any affection for him she no longer knew. Her emotions had been dulled by the tragedy of the death of her beloved husband.

It was evident that Henry had been shattered by the loss of Han Li even though the marriage had not seemed to bring the happiness it had promised. Yet Flora blamed him some for the tragedy.

She remained sitting up in bed, her mind filled with this strange mixture of thoughts. Now she would remain a few days to insure that Enid was set on the right path. Once the girl was adjusted to the tragedy of her stepmother's death Flora intended to return to London. Then she would have Mr. Sweeney look up Dolly and Shanks while she tried to find a suitable property to purchase. She also wanted to see some of her old friends, but that could wait. She began to feel sleepy again and sank back on her pillow. There had been no more screams and no more hint of a ghostly intruder.

When she awoke again it was a foggy day with a touch of drizzle, the sort of weather she'd never known in Canton and had probably missed. At least she didn't find herself so resentful of it now.

Mr. Sweeney was at the breakfast table with Enid when she joined them. The two seemed to be getting on very well together. "This young lady has an excellent mind, Flora."

"I know," she smiled. "I helped train it."

Enid looked delighted. "Mr. Sweeney has been telling me all about his being in China. He knew my amah and he's been a lot of places I remember."

"Then you two will have a lot to discuss," she said, feeling this would be good for Enid.

"Yes, I have a lot to catch up on," the girl agreed.

Mr. Sweeney paused over his toast and jam to ask Flora, "Did you rest well last night?"

"For the most part." She did not want to bring up the matter of the eerie cries in front of Enid.

"I wondered. I was wakened a little after midnight by a most terrifying scream."

"I know," she said with a warning glance for him. "We can talk about it later."

"Very well," Mr. Sweeney said, catching on.

Unfortunately it was too late as Enid spoke up with a troubled look on her face. "I heard it too! I guess maybe everyone hears those cries. It's the ghost. Han Li's ghost they say now, though they used to claim it was Lily's."

"Do the calls come every night?" Flora asked.

"Almost every night," Enid claimed. "It's strange, but no one wants to talk about it here. They just say it's Han

Li's unhappy spirit. But I don't know. I heard the cries before Han Li drowned herself."

"I don't think we should discuss it," Flora said.

Enid spoke up. "But if no one talks about it how are we ever going to find out the truth?"

It was a good question, but Flora considered the subject a morbid one and did not want to talk about it at length in Enid's presence.

"We can talk about it another time."

"That's what father always says," Enid complained.

"He's saying that for your own good," Flora told her.

Enid looked forlorn. "And Jessica won't even let Han Li be mentioned."

"You mustn't allow Jessica to worry you," she said.

The youngster regarded her with sad eyes. "I have missed you so!"

She smiled. "Well, now I'm back and I have brought Mr. Sweeney as well."

"It's wonderful," Enid agreed. "But you won't stay, will you?"

"I'll stay long enough."

"Jessica says you won't. She says you're only going to be here a day or two."

"How can she know?" Flora asked, annoyed that Jessica should tell all this to the youngster.

"Jessica says you're richer than we are now and that you don't want to be bothered about me any longer."

"Jessica is wrong. It doesn't matter whether one has money or not, one is faithful to friends. And you are my friend."

Enid brightened. "You mean that?"

"I do," she said firmly.

"May I tell that to Jessica? She's always so hateful to me!"

"I wouldn't say anything. Let it be our secret. That's often the better way."

The idea of a secret seemed to appeal to Enid. "Very well," she said rising from the table. "Will you go over my lessons with me like you used to when I was a little girl after you've had breakfast?"

"We'll see," she said. "And you're not all that grown-up; you're only four years older, you know."

"I feel a lot older," Enid said. And she gave Mr. Sweeney a smiling glance before she left. "I want to talk to you about China again later."

After Enid left the dining room Flora told Mr. Sweeney, "I'd say you've made a friend."

"So it seems," he agreed.

She took a sip of her tea. "Now we can talk freely about the cry in the night. I didn't want to when the child was here. What did you make of it?"

The old clerk shuddered. "It chilled my flesh."

"Where did it seem to come from?"

"I don't know. It could have been from anywhere, but it sounded fairly near."

She sat back in her chair. "When I was here before I heard it. Just as Enid says. Then they said it was the spirit of Lily the girl who died in the pond first. Now that Han Li followed her they say the ghost must be hers."

"It's a strange house," the old man said, glancing around the dark-paneled dining room with its several still life paintings of fruit and flowers.

"A sinister house," she said. "Haunted by tragedy for years. First, Bradford Armitage's wife jumped over the side of a ship bringing her back from China because she was very ill and in pain. Later Enid's mother died in childbirth. Then Henry hired a series of governesses to look after the girl. Jessica made life miserable for all of them because she wanted Enid placed in a school. Lily, my predecessor, was silly enough to fall in love with Henry and her body was found in the pond. It was decided that it was a suicide."

"And then after Henry married Han Li she also found a reason to drown herself in the same pond. I find that odd," said Mr. Sweeney.

"So do I," she agreed. "I can believe that news of Chen's death was a blow to her. But she had never been in love with him. He was her cousin and she only thought of him as that. I think her death was timed at that moment to make it seem a suicide."

"You're suggesting it was murder?"

"I can't help but think it might be."

"And Lily was murdered as well?"

"Why not? If murder should be involved I'm convinced they were both killed, by the same person and for the same reason."

"Ah!" he said, astounded. "Then how do you account for the ghosts?"

"I can't account for them. I'm asking myself who most likely murdered Lily and Han Li."

"You mean who had the most motive?"

"Yes. And I think of several people, not excluding Henry."

Mr. Sweeney stared at her. "You'd even suspect him?"

"One must consider all the possibilities. There is an attractive woman living near here whom you do not know. A titled woman. At the time I came here first her husband was still alive, but there was gossip that she and Henry were having an affair. I wondered if Lily hadn't found out and threatened to expose them. That she tried to get Henry for herself by blackmailing him about his romance with Lady Madge Waring."

"And you think he would kill her for that?"

"Maybe. The blackmail could have ruined Lady Madge at the time. If her late husband had found out he would have turned his back on her."

"That does make a motive," Mr. Sweeney agreed. "But what about after his marriage? Henry loved Han Li. Why should he kill her in the same monstrous fashion?"

"Lady Madge became free to marry him in the meantime. But Han Li was in their way."

"Well, it does fit so nicely it terrifies me!" the old man said worriedly.

"I feel the same way," she said. "But I don't want the child to guess."

"All your theories center around this Lady Madge Waring it seems."

"Not all of them. Jessica is possessive and a possible murderess. She is insanely in love with Henry and resents any other female being near him."

"I realized that at dinner last night. She was listening to every word that passed between you two, looking at you with daggers in her eyes."

"Exactly. So I do not rule her out. Nor Bradford Armitage, either. He is old, perhaps insane, and definitely eccentric. I once found him at work on his own coffin in the attic.

"I agree with Enid. The only way to learn the truth is to face this. I would hate to always feel suspicious of Henry and I shall unless the mystery is cleared."

"Perhaps the ghosts are trying to reach someone with a message," Mr. Sweeney said. "That may be why this phantom prowls at night and fills the air with a chilling cry."

She rose from the table. "I want you to keep Enid occupied and happy. It will give me a chance to look around and investigate a few things for myself."

Mr. Sweeney was also on his feet. "You must be cautious. If there should be a murderer in the house you do not want to be the next target."

"I have the feeling I have already been a target. But no matter."

They left the dining room and she joined Enid. They spent an hour reviewing the work she'd done with her stepmother in the past few years.

At the finish Flora said, "I think Han Li did very well. You are as far advanced in your studies as you would have been with me."

Enid sighed. "She was very beautiful and kind to me. But always so sad."

"Did she ever suggest that she was thinking of taking her life?" Flora asked.

"Not to me. But I did notice that she used to stand by the pond for long periods. Just stand there staring into it.

"I asked her about it once. I went up to her and she seemed to be lost somewhere in her thoughts. She turned to me, startled. And I asked her why she was always going to the pond and gazing into it."

"What did she say?"

"She said it reminded her of China and a pond she used

426

to sit by. I said, I didn't remember any such ponds near the house of Yenn Li."

"And what did she answer to that?"

"She said the pond was somewhere else. And I told her that I hated the pond because Lily had drowned herself in it and I saw them dragging the body out."

"We've talked enough about such things,'" Flora said. "You'd better go play with the coachman's children."

"I don't play with them anymore," Enid quickly told her.

"Why?"

"They're too old to play with now," she said. "The oldest girl is sixteen and married, and the fifteen-year-old has gone to work for a family in the next village. The boys are doing stable work."

Flora smiled sadly. "How quickly you all grow up. And what are you going to do with your free time?"

"I read and I sew. Han Li taught me how to do fine embroidery. Just now I'm going to visit Lady Madge Waring. She gives me an archery lesson every morning when the weather permits. She is a pretty lady, but very lonely since her husband died. Father invited her over here a few times, but Jessica complained and she was never invited again. But I still go over there for my archery lessons though Jessica doesn't like it."

"I see," Flora said. "Well, you'd better get along and not keep Lady Madge waiting."

"I'll tell her you're here," Enid said.

"If you do," Flora said, "you might also tell her I'll try to visit her for tea if she's at home. I'd like to see her again."

"I'm sure she'd be gald to see you," Enid said. "Let Mr. Sweeney know I want to talk with him this afternoon."

"I will," she promised.

When Enid left Flora remained seated on the sofa in the living room sorting out the various lesson books. She was still at this task when Jessica came into the room with her usual arrogant air.

"Oh, this is where you are!" she said.

Flora looked up from the books. "I was just going over Enid's lessons with her."

Jessica smiled coldly. "It's not likely you'll assume the role of governess again with all your wealth."

"I'm not planning to. But I was interested to see how Enid had progressed."

"Far enough to enter a boarding school I hope. For years now her father has been offering her tender age as an excuse not to send her away. Considering that many poor youngsters marry at the age of fourteen or fifteen I see no reason for coddling her further."

"But her father must make the decision."

"I hope you will not try to influence him."

"I'm not sure I understand you," she said.

Jessica eyed her angrily. "I'm saying you have no right to come here interfering after all this while."

"I came at the invitation of your family. Or so I thought."

"Certainly not by any wish of mine," Jessica said candidly. "You're being here will only mix Enid up, and she's confused badly enough as it is."

"You may be sure I do not intend to harm the child," she said rising. "I only wish I could be as certain about everyone else here."

And having said that Flora left Jessica standing alone in the living room. She moved down the hall until she reached the area of the library. There she heard the voices of Mr. Sweeney and Bradford Armitage emanating from the room.

Upon entering the library she found them seated across from each other in leather chairs arguing the merits of Thackeray and Dickens. It seemed that Bradford Armitage had great admiration for Thackeray, while Mr. Sweeney couldn't see that he compared to Dickens as an author.

She smiled as she joined them. "I can tell you two have found a subject to discuss."

Bradford Armitage rapped his cane on the floor. "The trouble is, my girl, that this fellow has a one-track mind. All he can think of is Dickens, Dickens, Dickens!"

"And a very good subject to think about," Mr. Sweeney told him.

"I'll not argue anymore. Read some more Thackeray before you make so rash a decision about quality." He gave his attention to Flora. "It makes this sad house a little brigher to have you back."

"Han Li's suicide must have been a frightful shock, following after Lily's as it did."

The old man nodded. "It was. Who would expect her to do a thing like that! She became very neurotic after she was ill with pneumonia. None of us expected her to survive but she did."

"She wrote me of her illness after she'd recovered," Flora said. "I thought the tone of her letter sad."

"I'm sure Henry did his best to make her happy. Perhaps it was a mistake to bring her here from her native land."

"She wanted to come. She had been raised to speak English and revere English customs. Her father planned it that way because her mother had been English."

"I realize that," Bradford Armitage said. "Yet I'm certain it was very difficult for her here in this house."

Flora looked at him directly. "She was frightened. I know that."

"Did she tell you that?"

"Yes. At my wedding."

"Frightened of what?"

"I don't know," Flora admitted. "But she did say something about evil spirits."

"The ghost!" he said. "The ghost again!"

"She seemed to believe in it and be afraid of it."

"I know. I'm sure it was very real to her."

"Did she ever mention it to you?" Flora asked him.

"No. She moved about the house like a gentle wraith, saying very little."

That afternoon the weather cleared and Mr. Sweeney and Enid went for a walk. This gave Flora the chance she'd wanted to go over to the adjoining estate and renew her acquaintance with Lady Madge Waring. She put on a smart green dress and bonnet and carried a matching parasol.

Taking the path through the woods she avoided asking for a carriage and drawing attention to her visit to the neighboring estate. Within a relatively few minutes she emerged from the section of tall trees and began crossing the wide, rolling lawn of the Waring property.

As she neared the house she saw Madge Waring with someone out on the rear lawn playing croquet. She went directly to her rather than going to the house. Lady Waring was youthful-looking in a neat white dress suitable for outdoor activity. On seeing Flora she put down the mallet and came across to greet her.

"Enid said you might call on me," she began.

"I hope you don't mind," Flora said.

"I'm delighted to see you. Please accept my sympathy. I know of the great loss you have suffered."

"And you had a similar one."

"Sir Thomas was old and could not have clung to life much longer," Lady Madge said. She was wearing a small straw hat to protect her from the sun. "Your loss was more tragic since your husband was young."

"Chen was very young to die," she agreed.

"Let us go inside. My housekeeper has tea ready and waiting for us."

The white and pale blue living room of the Waring house was a great contrast to the grim and somber atmosphere of Armitage House. The room was furnished in elegant period style to further heighten the mood of lightness. They sat down at the tea table and Flora studied the woman across from her. Madge Waring had not changed at all in the four years since she'd seen her.

Madge passed her tea and said casually, "Do you plan to remain at Armitage House long?"

"That depends."

"I see," the other woman said taking up her own cup.

"I'm worried about Enid. She seems to have been badly upset by her stepmother's suicide."

"Yes, I know."

"What do you think about it?"

"You are asking me what do I think about Enid's condition or what do I think about Han Li's suicide?"

"Let us begin with the suicide first," she said quietly.

Madge bit her lower lip. "I think there is a curse on the people in that house."

"That has been whispered for years."

"It makes it none the less real," Madge said urgently. "I don't know what really may have happened to Han Li anymore than I know what happened to Lily. But I do know her spirit is returning to haunt the house."

"Why are you so certain of that?"

"I have seen her."

"The ghost of Han Li?"

"Yes."

"Where?"

"By the pond."

"Tell me about it," she urged.

The terror in Lady Madge Waring's eyes was too real to be simulated. In a taut voice, she said, "I do not sleep well lately. Often I go for strolls outdoors. One night—it was a moonlit night, almost as light as day—I decided to walk farther than my usual distance. I took the path through the woods to the pond.

"I didn't feel afraid at all until I reached the bank of the pond. Then all at once I knew that I was in danger. That I wasn't alone. I could almost feel unseen eyes fixed on me. I looked around but there was no one in sight.

"I was almost frozen with fear. I didn't dare walk back through the woods and I didn't want to bother the Armitages. Jessica has behaved very unfriendly towards me though I get along well enough with her father and Henry. I stood there by the pond trembling and hating myself for exposing myself to such an experience. The feeling that I was not alone continued. As I looked across the pond I saw a figure standing on the other side. I knew it was Han Li."

"How did you know?"

"I know because she began walking around the edge of the pond towards me. I wanted to run, to escape. But I couldn't. And each minute she was coming nearer to me! I saw her dripping clothes, and her face. I shall never forget her face. The black hair drawn back, the slanting eyes, the yellow of her skin. It was Han Li back from the dead! She'd been drowned weeks before."

Chapter Thirty-four

FLORA CLOSELY watched the near-hysterical young woman as she gave account of that night and knew that she was either telling the truth or she was a most accomplished actress. Madge had communicated the horror of that moment for her with great impact. Flora asked her what happened next.

"Her hand reached out to touch me. I screamed and somehow managed to turn and flee to the path through the woods. I didn't stop running until I reached the safety of this house. And nothing would ever make me go over there again at night!"

Flora said to her, "I can believe that you were badly upset. Is it possible you were so frightened you imagined you saw Han Li when it was someone else. When I was here before, the servants all insisted they were seeing Lily's ghost."

"I'm sure I saw the ghost of Han Li," Lady Madge said. "But why should you concern yourself about it? What difference can it make to you now?"

"Han Li was my friend, and my husband's cousin. She stood up for me at our wedding. Enid is very dear to me, and she is suffering from what is going on over there."

Lady Madge had recovered her calm. "My advice to you is to leave Armitage House as soon as you can and never return."

When she reached Armitage House after having had tea with Lady Madge the first person she met was Mr. Sweeney. He greeted her with an inquiring look.

"Was your afternoon a profitable one?" he asked.

"I may have learned a little, I'm not sure."

"I spent a long while with Enid. She talked continually about China. I'd say the stay she had there made a great impression on her. I then searched the house for the old man."

"Bradford Armitage?"

"Yes. The housekeeper said he'd gone upstairs. I went up there but everything was under lock and key. I have never seen such a large attic space locked away from a house. Not only that but I saw no sign of him. I don't think he was up there. All the doors I saw were padlocked on the outside."

"I wonder where he went," she said.

"Probably hiding from me," Mr. Sweeney said with disgust. "He'll never prove to me that Thackeray writes better books than Dickens."

"I'm sure of that," she smiled. "You know I think I shall ask Henry for the use of a carriage tomorrow. You and I are going up to London to see if we can locate Mr. Dickens and also to try and get in touch with Dolly and Shanks."

That evening she approached Henry Armitage about the use of a carriage for a day's expedition to London. She did not go into the details of her planned trip.

"Of course you can have a carriage. It will be ready for you right after breakfast. Will you return in time for dinner?"

"I would hope so," she said.

"Fine. How did you make out with Enid today?"

"Very well," she said. "Her studies are remarkably advanced. I'd say Han Li was an excellent teacher. Enid is exceptionally bright. You have a right to be proud of your daughter."

"I am," he said. "If we could somehow put an end to the dark tragedies that have been afflicting us here life might go on more smoothly."

"That is true," she said.

"You know, Flora, you have changed a good deal."

"Have I?"

"I noticed it almost the moment you came off the ship. You have matured. You are a much more level-headed woman than you were when you acted as governess here."

"I have experienced a lot since then. But surely all of us have. I lost Chen and you lost Han Li. I thought you two would be happily married forever."

"We were happy until she came here. I should have left this accursed place long ago."

"But you haven't," she observed quietly, thinking this might be just a pretense for her benefit.

"Chiefly because of my father and Jessica," he said. "I have sacrificed my marriage and my happiness to them."

"Well, at least you fully realize what you've done and why. I think the question is now, are you willing to sacrifice your daughter as well?"

"Enid will be safe here. I only ask that she get over the shock of Han Li's death."

"And I'm going to try to help her." But she didn't tell him that going to London was part of that. She didn't fully trust him as yet.

That night before she went to bed she spent some time in the adjoining room where Enid slept. The youngster was full of questions, and when it came time to sleep she begged Enid to leave the door between their rooms open as she had done in the old days. Flora consented and in the manner of her term as governess left a single candle burning on her bedside table as a precaution against any unexpected happenings in the night.

She slept soundly, content with the knowledge that she

would be going to London the following morning. Once again she was awakened by a macabre scream, to be repeated several times before there was silence. She automatically glanced through the door to Enid's room and to her horror saw the figure of the phantom standing at the foot of the youngster's bed!

"Enid!" she cried out. And she threw back the bedclothes to go rescue the sleeping girl. But by the time she reached the doorway the phantom had vanished into the shadows. She went on into the room, wide-eyed and heart pounding as she stared into the dark corners for some sign of the ghost.

Enid was half awake and sitting up. "What is it?"

Not wanting to alarm her she said, "I heard some weird screams and then I thought there was someone in here."

Enid gave her a strange look. "The ghost."

Flora stared at the girl. "Why do you say that?"

"Because I have seen her before."

"You have?"

"Yes. She always stands at the foot of my bed," the child said with an accuracy that sent a chill down Flora's spine.

Now there were voices outside the door. Flora knew that others must have heard the screams. When she opened the door there was an assembled company of Henry, Jessica, and Mr. Sweeney in dressing robes.

Henry asked her, "What is wrong?"

"I was wakened by screams."

He looked at her oddly. "I heard screams as well. But they came from in here."

Flora hestitated, then admitted, "I did cry out when I heard the other screams. I was wakened out of a sound sleep."

Jessica was plainly annoyed. "Of course the caterwauling came from in here. The question is, was it you or Enid?"

"I was the one who screamed."

"I thought so," Jessica said with a sneer. "I seem to remember something of your nightmares before."

"Will you be all right, now?" Henry asked.

"Yes," she said.

Mr. Sweeney gave her an encouraging nod before Henry closed the door and they all went back to their rooms. Flora turned to Enid, who was still sitting up in her bed.

"I didn't come out of that very well, did I?"

"It wasn't your fault," the child defended her. "And Jessica is always trying to hurt people."

"So it seems," she said wearily. "I think the best thing for us all now is to get back to sleep. I have to go to London early in the morning."

Enid looked at her worriedly. "But you are coming back?"

"Yes. I'll be back," she promised.

Nothing more happened in the night. By ten the following morning she and Mr. Sweeney were on their way to London. She had no set plan in mind but she decided she would first call at Mr. Grossmith's bookshop.

The day was fine and the streets of London were again crowded with vehicles. Hackney cabs, drays, and omnibuses vied with one another for space in streets which never seemed wide enough. She read the advertisements on the back of the buses shouting the praises of Zebra Grate Polish, Pears Soap, and Horlick's Malted Milk. The further they advanced into the city the more difficult progress became. Their driver cursed loudly at times.

Flora directed him to a side street near the bookshop where he could wait while they walked the rest of the distance. As they opened the door and entered it seemed nothing had changed.

Little Mr. Grossmith saw them almost immediately and came hurrying to greet Flora. "My dear Flora, how good to see you again. I heard about your sad loss from the Burrs. Have you decided to return to the shop?"

"I don't think so," she said with a smile. "Not that I wasn't treated well here. But I have other things I must do. I have come to ask you about Charles Dickens."

Mr. Grossmith looked sad. "Poor Dickens! How he has aged!"

"Is he in London?" she wanted to know.

"Yes. He has been for several weeks. You know that his son Walter died in India last year?"

"I had not heard about it."

"A great shock for him," Mr. Grossmith said. "And I also hear the young man was rather deeply in debt to his regiment at the time of his death. Poor Dickens has not had very good luck with his children."

"Do you know where I might reach him?" she asked.

"I believe he lives partly in rented accommodations here in London and partly in Gad's Hill. But I have not sent books to him for some time so I can't tell you his address."

"I'm very anxious to talk to him."

"You could try his publishers," the bookshop owner said.

Mr. Sweeney bobbed his head. "That seems like a sound idea."

So they left the bookshop and made their way through several short, crowded streets to the publisher's offices. A young man there greeted Flora with a saucy smile and asked what he could do for her. She told him.

He scratched his head. "I'm not supposed to give his home address to anyone."

Mr. Sweeney appealed to the youth, "But we are old friends!"

The young man pulled at his celluloid cuffs as he considered. "I tell you what," he said at last. "I can't give you his address but I can mention where he's lunching today. It's a favorite spot of his, the Trafalgar Restaurant."

"I know it," she exclaimed. "I've been there several times."

"He should be arriving there about now," the youth said. "He's having lunch with our Mr. Kent."

"Thank you," she said, as she and Mr. Sweeney already were making their way out.

They hurried back to the carriage and she gave the surly driver instructions on how to reach their new destination. Once again they had to fight traffic and now it was noontime traffic. After a long, trying ride they did reach the Trafalgar Restaurant. Bearded, top-hatted men were entering the popular eating place in a line and she and Mr. Sweeney joined them.

Inside it was loud talk, tobacco smoke, and the aroma of fine food. A busy headwaiter came to greet them. "Do you have a table reserved?" he asked brusquely, ready to send them away if they hadn't.

She spoke up quickly. "We are joining Mr. Dickens."

"Oh?" he said. "Then you should take the stairs on the right and go to private Salon C. I believe Mr. Dickens and a companion have already gone up there."

She thanked him and she and Mr. Sweeney started up the stairs. As they neared the top he said breathlessly, "I trust that he remembers us."

"I'm sure he will," she said, but she was a little nervous. They reached the landing and began a search of the salon doors.

They finally reached the door just as a shirt-sleeved waiter was coming out. He held the door open for them and she was the first to enter with old Mr. Sweeney close on her heels. Charles Dickens was sitting at a table with a thin man of middle age. Dickens had his eyes fastened on some sort of business paper and was not aware of her entrance.

She had a good opportunity to study him before he noticed her and she was shocked by the transformation in him since she had last seen him. His hair and beard had gone gray and his face was more gaunt. He didn't seem the energetic, dashing Charles Dickens she had known.

He looked up before she had an opportunity to announce her presence. He smiled and said, "My dear Miss Bain, it has been years since I've seen you!"

"Mr. Dickens!" she said warmly and stepped forward to him.

He rose with difficulty and as he winced made a joke of it, saying, "I have a touch of gout. The rich man's disease I'm told, so I really can't afford it." He took her hand and pressed it. Then he turned to his friend who had also risen, "Mr. Kent, my publisher's bookkeeper, who reminds me of my abject dependence on him. This is Flora Bain, a young woman whom I rescued from a fearful situation one night."

"How do you do, Miss Bain," Mr. Kent said with a bow.

She turned to bring Mr. Sweeney into the group, "You remember Mr. Sweeney who wanted only your autograph."

Dickens shook hands with the old man. "Of course. But how strange that you two should still be together. Sit down and tell me all about it."

It was a long story she had to tell. She began with her wedding to Chen Li and brought it up to date with her experience with the ghost at Armitage House the night before. Charles Dickens listened to her with avid interest. He ordered dinners and wine for them all and it became a festive occasion.

As the meal progressed he told her, "I do not like what you have told me at all. I fear you are now in more danger than when I rescued you from that mental hospital."

"I need your advice badly," she said.

The famous man considered. "The question, as I see it, is whether or not there is a real ghost in that house."

"Why do you say that?" she asked.

Charles Dickens said, "Simple. If it is a ghost you are dealing with, and I firmly believe in the existence of supernatural creatures, it probably accounts for all that has happened. But if you are dealing with a murderer or a murderess pretending to be a phantom, it is an entirely different matter. A matter to be handled in a much different way.

"I'm presently working on a mystery yarn myself," Dickens said, "The main character is one Edwin Drood." He smiled across the table for Mr. Sweeney's benefit. "Mind that you are on the lookout for it when it is published."

"Count me as a reader, sir," Mr. Sweeney said happily.

"I would like to visit Armitage House and see it all first hand," Dickens said. "But I am not well. It would not be wise for me to attempt it. I have barely the energy to meet my present commitments."

"If you will just advise me," she said.

"I can do better than that," Charles Dickens told her. "I shall contact one of London's leading spiritualists and send him out there. If he cannot make contact with your phantom then you can be certain the ghost is a spurious one and you are dealing with a criminal."

"When can you arrange it?" she asked.

"I will send a message this afternoon. I think I can have him get in touch with you in a few days. He will be able to hold a seance as soon as you give him permission."

"Thank you, Mr. Dickens," she said. "I'm sure this is just the help I need. What is the man's name?"

"The medium's name is Daniel Douglas Home. He is famous for his work in contacting spirits on the other side. I think he is a singularly gifted man."

So it was settled. She and Mr. Sweeney left the company of Charles Dickens and his friend full of hope. The novelist saw her to the door of the salon. He held her hand for a long moment before they said goodbye. "You have had a strange life, my dear. I hope that soon it will become more tranquil and you will have your full share of happiness."

Touched by his words she thanked him and gave him a farewell smile. It was to be the last meeting they would ever have. The next time she would see Charles Dickens would be when she attended his funeral. But she did not know that then.

Returning to the carriage she instructed the driver to take them back to Armitage House. She and Mr. Sweeney relaxed on the return drive to the old mansion. She felt she had managed the situation in the best way possible.

But that evening she was to discover that others might not agree with her. She made it a point to take Henry aside and tell him the details of her excursion to the city and her motive in going there. He listened with what seemed growing amazement. Soon she became concerned that she had decided to be perfectly frank with him.

"Don't you see how cleverly Mr. Dickens worked this out? If his friend finds no ghost we know someone is playing phantom. And that someone probably murdered both Lily and Han Li."

Henry asked her, "Who did you say was being sent here to hold a seance?"

"Daniel Douglas Home," she said. "Charles Dickens says he is famous."

"Of course he is!" Henry declared angrily. "But do you know what that means? It means that this house and my family will be subjected to merciless publicity. Whether a ghost is uncovered here or not there will be stories about what has been going on here in all the papers. We'll be disgraced!"

She stared at him in consternation. "I can't believe you feel that way!"

"I do. And when your Daniel Douglas Home gets in touch with us I shall refuse to allow him to have a seance here."

"After all the trouble I've gone to?"

"Yes," he said, curtly. "I regret your trouble but I must protect my family."

"I see," she said. "In that case I feel Mr. Sweeney and I should leave tomorrow."

"Enid will not want to see you go."

But Flora knew that she must leave. She did not want to remain here in the sinister atmosphere any longer. More and more she feared that Henry and Madge were partners in the murders of Lily and Han Li.

She informed Mr. Sweeney they would be leaving in the morning. Then she went into Enid's room to say good night and tell her. As she'd expected Enid protested loudly. But she told the girl there could be no changing her mind.

Flora then added, "I'm going to have a house in London soon. And I intend asking your father if you can come and live with me just as you would in a boarding school. I could act as your tutor and we would have wonderful times together in London."

"Do you mean it?" Enid asked happily.

She hugged the youngster to her. "I do. Just because I'm leaving tomorrow, doesn't mean I'm deserting you."

After she tucked Enid in bed she went on to her own room. The door between the two rooms was open as usual. She changed into her nightgown and slid between the cool sheets. It would be her last night at Armitage House. When she reached London she would get word to Charles Dickens about what had happened and have him cancel any arrangements he'd made to send the medium out to the estate.

She fell asleep with all this running through her mind. And she slept until she was awakened by the touch of a wet hand on her face. She roused from her sleep with a scream, staring wild-eyed at the shrouded apparition standing at the side of her bed. In the dull glow of the candle-light she could not make out the features hidden by a dark cowl.

Then the wet clawlike hands of the phantom intruder reached for her throat. She tried to dodge to one side to escape the threatening hands but she didn't manage it. As the fingers closed around her throat she managed a frightened, half-strangled scream. Then she clawed wildly to free herself from the mad throttling grip.

In the next room Enid had wakened and seen the attack on her. Enid was screaming loudly for help as Flora tumbled to the hard floor with the phantom, gasping and astride of her. For a few seconds Flora fought free of the ghost but then those hands got a death grip on her throat once more. She felt her breath cut off and knew it was near the end.

Vaguely in the distance she was aware of a door bursting open and other voices. But she was too faint to care much. Then she saw Henry drag the mad creature off her.

Henry tore the cowl from the phantom to reveal a thin, parchment face with yellowed skin, and dark hair pulled back. An almost Oriental face, but not the face of Han Li. It was the face of an older woman, a much older woman. In the arms of Henry she struggled and literally frothed at the mouth.

Old Mr. Sweeney came to Henry's assistance and between them they dragged the struggling madwoman from the room. Bradford Armitage came into Flora's room leaning heavily on his walking stick and gazed down at her with tears brimming from his eyes.

"Forgive me," he said. "The charade is over. I've tried to protect her all these years. But it is over now. She would have killed you as she did Lily and Han Li."

"Who?" she asked dully, still in a sitting position on the floor.

"My wife," Bradford Armitage said. "Mad since those long years ago in China. I have looked after her and cared for her myself. Her quarters were in the attic. But she found a way to escape from them and after that it was only a matter of time."

Flora struggled to her feet and a frightened Enid came to press against her. "That madwoman I saw just now is the same woman in the painting in the landing although she is horribly changed. She didn't throw herself overboard from that ship as you told everyone."

"No," the old man said. "That cursed Chinese fever she suffered from not only ravaged her looks and darkened her skin and hair but ravaged and darkened her mind as well. I wanted to spare the children seeing their mother like that. I brought her here. I thought it would be all right. She had grown to be hostile and violent toward all but her immediate family but I didn't know she would actually kill."

"Did the others know?"

"Yes," Bradford Armitage said. "But I swore them to silence. She was their mother. Each time she killed we hoped it would be the last."

"Did Han Li know about her?"

"We didn't warn her," the old man said. "And that was wrong. I shall always feel guilty. And now my wife will end her days in a madhouse. There can be no other choice." He turned and limped out of the room.

Enid gazed up at Flora plaintively. "My grandmother."

"You mustn't think about it," she said. "The woman is ill. You cannot blame sick people for what they do."

So the mystery of the phantom of Armitage House was at last a mystery no more. The following morning a carriage took Henry's mother to a private mental hospital which the local doctor had recommended. It was a grim morning for all of them but perhaps beyond the grimness lay hope.

Jessica kept out of the way and had her breakfast served in her room. It was evident that she did not want to face Flora. Henry spoke a few quiet words of apology to her before he left with his father to deliver the madwoman to the hospital.

"You will likely have gone before I return."

"Yes, I expect so."

"I hope I will see you one day again when you are settled."

"I imagine so," she said quietly.

After he left she finished packing. Then she said goodbye to Enid and the other carriage took her and Mr. Sweeney to a London hotel. They lived in the hotel for several weeks until she found an airy, elegant house with a lovely garden and they moved in.

It was a time of great activity for her. She and Mr. Sweeney were kept busy directing a host of workers, who were painting, papering and repairing the house. At last all was in order and she invited her first guests, Dolly and Shanks.

They came to dinner and made an attractive couple in their uniforms. Before they left she broached the subject of helping them with their mission and they promised to discuss the matter with William Booth for advice.

As Dolly kissed her good night, she said, "I knew good would come of our friendship but never anything as important as this!"

Shanks, very grand in his officer's uniform, winked at her. "The next thing, Miss Flora, is to get yourself a good husband."

She smiled and shook her head. "I fear that is a long way off."

And so it seemed. But she did remember her promise to Enid, so she wrote Henry and asked him if he might be willing to have his daughter live with her for at least a few months of the year. In return she offered a fine home and her talents as a tutor. She ended the letter by wishing his father and him well.

The answer to her letter came a few days later when Henry arrived with Enid and her bags.

"It was a fine offer you made, Flora," he said. "I couldn't turn it down."

"I'm glad," she said. "I was afraid Jessica might interfere again."

"Oh, no!" Enid exclaimed. "Jessica ran off with that awful Colonel Noel Tarrant. She's not at Armitage House anymore."

Henry nodded. "That's true. It seems she had been in secret contact with him all these years. She has a little money of her own and he knew it. She's going to marry him, she says. I say they deserve each other!"

Flora shook her head and smiled gently. "Life is so full of the most unexpected things. You will come back and see Enid occasionally?"

Henry's handsome face was happier than she'd seen it in some time. "I hope to come by regularly," he said. "If I'll be welcome."

"You're always welcome," she said, taking his hand in hers for a long moment. Later they would plan other things. The bond would grow.

THE BIG BESTSELLERS
ARE AVON BOOKS!

ROSEMARY ROGERS

Author of the tumultuous epic bestseller
SWEET SAVAGE LOVE

A rapturous tale that spans three continents,
following beautiful young Lady Rowena Dan-
gerfield from the shimmering palaces of exotic
India, to the rich splendor of the Royal Court
of London, to the savage New Mexico frontier,
where Lady Rowena finally meets a man with a
will as strong as her own . . . and their powerful,
all-consuming love towers to the limits of human
passion!

20529/$1.75